John Yeardly

**Memoir and Diary**

John Yeardly

**Memoir and Diary**

ISBN/EAN: 9783337119270

Printed in Europe, USA, Canada, Australia, Japan

Cover: Foto ©Raphael Reischuk / pixelio.de

More available books at **www.hansebooks.com**

# MEMOIR and DIARY

OF

# JOH ARDLEY,

Gospel.

LES TYLOR.

ce with my God, and in that love
our nation, and every man our

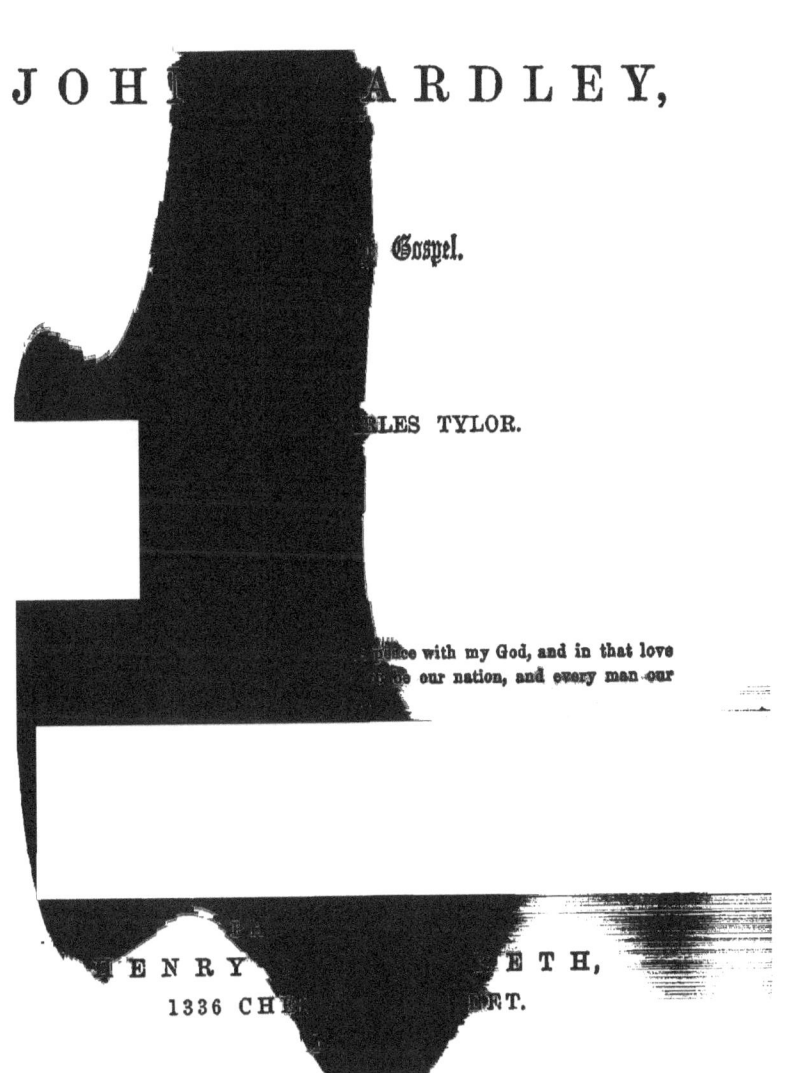

ENRY ETH,

1336 CHE ET.

# CONTENTS.

## CHAPTER I.

## CHAPTER II.

## CHAPTER III.

## CHAPTER IV.

## CHAPTER V.

## CHAPTER VI.

## CHAPTER VII.

# CHAPTER VIII.

## THE SECOND CONTINENTAL JOURNEY, 1827–28.

### PART I.—GERMANY.

# CHAPTER IX.

## THE SECOND CONTINENTAL JOURNEY, 1827–28.

### PART II.—SWITZERLAND.

# CHAPTER X.

## HOME OCCUPATIONS AND TRAVELS IN ENGLAND AND WALES, 1828–33

# CHAPTER XI.

## THE THIRD CONTINENTAL JOURNEY, OR THE JOURNEY TO GREECE, 1833–34.

### PART I.—THE JOURNEY TO ANCONA.

# CHAPTER XVI.

REMOVAL TO STAMFORD-HILL, AND COMMENCEMENT OF THE FIFTH
CONTINENTAL JOURNEY, 1843-48.

# CHAPTER XVII.

COMPLETION OF THE FIFTH CONTINENTAL JOURNEY, 1849-50.

# CHAPTER XVIII.

DEATH OF MARTHA YEARDLEY, AND JOHN YEARDLEY'S JOURNEY TO
NORWAY, 1851-52.

# CHAPTER XIX.

HIS JOURNEY TO SOUTH RUSSIA, 1853.

# CHAPTER XX.

### FROM HIS RETURN FROM RUSSIA TO HIS LAST JOURNEY, 1853-58.

# CHAPTER XXI.

### LAST JOURNEY AND DEATH, 1858.   CONCLUDING REMARKS.

# MEMOIR

OF

# JOHN YEARDLEY.

## CHAPTER I.

FROM JOHN YEARDLEY'S CONVERSION TO THE COMMENCEMENT
OF HIS PUBLIC MINISTRY.

### 1803—1815.

JOHN YEARDLEY was born on the 3rd of the First
Month, 1786, at a small farm-house beside Orgreave
Hall, in the valley of the Rother, four miles south of
Rotherham. His parents, Joel and Frances Yeardley,
farmed some land, chiefly pasture, and his mother is
said to have been famous for her cream-cheeses, which
she carried herself to Sheffield market. She was a
pious and industrious woman; but, through the miscon-
duct of her husband, was sometimes reduced to such
straits as scarcely to have enough food for her children.

Before they left Orgreave they were attracted towards
the worship of Friends, and several of the family, including two of Joel Yeardley's sisters, embraced the
truth as held by the Society. In the year 1802 they
removed to a farm at Blacker, three miles south of
Barnsley, and attended the meeting at Monk Bretton,

(1)

or Burton, near that town, where the meeting-house then stood. At Blacker it was John's business to ride into Barnsley daily on a pony, with two barrels of milk to distribute to the customers of his mother's dairy. His elder brother Thomas worked on the farm.

Their attendance at Burton meeting brought the family under the notice of Joseph Wood, a minister of the Society, residing at Newhouse, near Highflatts, four miles from Penistone. Joseph Wood had been a Yorkshire clothier, but relinquished business in the prime of life, and spent the rest of his days in assiduous pastoral labor of a kind of which we have few examples. To attend a Monthly Meeting he would leave home on foot the Seventh-day before, with John Bottomley, also a Friend and preacher, and at one time his servant, for some neighboring meeting. He would occupy the evening with social calls, dropping at every house the word of exhortation or comfort. The meeting next day would witness his fervent ministry. In the afternoon they would proceed to the place where the Monthly Meeting was to be held the following day, which they would attend, filling up the time before and after with social and religious visits. In the intervals of the Monthly Meetings, when not engaged on more distant service, it was his practice to appoint meetings for worship in the villages around Highflatts, and very frequently to visit those places where individuals were "under convincement," particularly Barnsley and Dewsbury, where at that time many were added to the Society. On his return home from these services he would spend the day in an upper room, without a fire, even in the severest weather, writing a minute account of all that had happened.

It was in 1803 that Joseph Wood first had intercourse with Joel Yeardley's family. Under date of the 19th of the Fourth Month, he says, speaking of himself and some other concerned Friends:—

We felt an inclination to visit Joel Yeardley's family, who are under convincement, and who have lately removed from near Handsworth Woodhouse. We went to breakfast. He and Frances his wife, with Thomas and John their sons, the former about nineteen, the latter seventeen years of age, received us in a very kind and affectionate manner, expressing their satisfaction at our coming to see them. They appeared quite open, and gave us a particular account of the manner of their convincement and beginning to attend Friends' meetings, which was about four years ago. I believe there is a good degree of sincerity in the man and his wife, and the two sons appear to be tender and hopeful.

The next month Joseph Wood repeated his visit, and gives an account of the interview in the following words:—

5 mo., 1803.—Having ever since I was at Joel Yeardley's the last month, felt my mind drawn to sit with the family, and this appearing to me to be the right time, I set out from home the 14th of the Fifth Month, in company with John Bottomley. Got to Joel Yeardley's betwixt four and five o'clock. After tea, Thomas Dixon Walton and Samuel Coward of Barnsley came to meet us there. In the evening we had a precious opportunity together, in which caution, counsel, advice, and encouragement flowed plentifully, suited to the varied states of the family. I had a long time therein first, from 1 Cor. xv. 58; John Bottomley next. Afterwards I had a pretty long time, after which J. B. was concerned in prayer. At the breaking up of the opportunity I had something very encouraging to communicate to their son Thomas, who, I believe, is an exercised youth, to whom my spirit felt very nearly united.

Joel Yeardley unhappily did not long remain faithful to his convictions. He not only himself drew back from intercourse with Friends, but was unwilling his sons should leave their work to attend week-day meetings, and did all in his power to prevent them. This is shown by the following narrative from Joseph Wood's memoranda:—

As William Wass and I were going to attend a Committee at Highflatts, on our Monthly Meeting day, in the morning, we met with Thomas Yeardley of Blacker, near Worsbro', a young man who is under convincement. I was a little surprised to see him having on a green singlet and smock frock. He burst out into tears; I inquired the matter, and if something was amiss at home; he only replied, "Not much;" and we not having time to stop, proceeded, and he went forward to my house. This was on the 19th of the Ninth Month, 1803.

After the Monthly Meeting was over, I had an opportunity to inquire into the cause of his appearance and trouble, and found that he was religiously concerned to attend week-day meetings, which his father was much averse to; and in order to procure his liberty he had worked almost beyond his ability; but all would not do, his father plainly telling him that he should quit the house. The evening before, he applied to him for leave to come to the meeting at Highflatts to-day; but he refused, and treated him with very rough language. However, as the concern remained with him, he rose early in the morning and got himself ready; but his father came and violently pulled the clothes off his back, and his shirt also, and took all his other clothes from him but those we met him in, telling him to get a place immediately, for he should not stop in his house. Being thus stripped, he went to his work in the stable; but, not feeling easy without coming to meeting, he set out as he was, not minding his dress, so that he might but be favored to get to the meeting.

This evening we had an opportunity with him in my parlor, much to our satisfaction. The language of encouragement and consolation flowed freely and plentifully towards him through William Wass, John Bottomley, and myself; and afterwards, in conference with him, we found liberty to advise him to return home (he having before thought of procuring a place), believing if he was preserved faithful, way would in time be made for him, and that it might perhaps be a means of his father's restoration; as at times, he said, he appeared a little different, not having wholly lost his love to Friends, and always behaved kindly to them. He took our advice kindly, and complied therewith. After stopping two nights at my house, he returned home.

Joseph Wood did not suffer much time to elapse before he paid another visit to Blacker, to comfort the afflicted family. It was from this visit, as we apprehend, that John Yeardley dated his change of heart. " I was convinced," he said on one occasion, " at a meeting which Joseph Wood had with our family."

7 *mo.* 17, 1803.—Thomas Walker Haigh and William Gant accompanied us to Joel Yeardley's, where we tarried all night; but the two young men from Barnsley returned home after supper. Joel was from home, but after tea we had a religious opportunity with the rest of the family, in which I had a very long consolatory and encouraging testimony to bear to the deeply-suffering exercised minds from John xvi. 33. Afterwards I had a pretty long time, principally to their son John, who I believe was under a precious visitation from on high. He was much broken and tendered, and I hope this season of remarkable favor will not soon be forgotten by him.

On his return home Joseph Wood wrote him the following letter :—

Newhouse, 10 mo. 24, 1803.

BELOVED FRIEND, JOHN YEARDLEY,

Thou hast often been in my remembrance since I last saw thee, accompanied with an earnest desire that the seed sown may prosper and bring forth fruit in its season, to the praise and glory of the Great Husbandman, who, I believe, is calling thee to glory, honor, immortality, and eternal life. And O mayest thou be willing in this the day of his power to leave all and follow him who hath declared, "Every one who hath forsaken houses, or brethren, or sisters, or father, or mother, or wife, or children, or lands, for my name's sake, shall receive an hundred-fold, and shall inherit everlasting life."

Not that we should be found wanting in our duty to our near connexions, for true religion does not destroy natural affection, but brings and preserves it in its proper place. When our earthly parents command one thing, and the Almighty another, it is better for us to obey God than man, and herein is our love manifested unto him by our obedience to his commands though it may sometimes clash against our parents' minds. At the same time it is our duty to endeavor to convince them, that we are willing to obey all their lawful commands, where they do not interfere with our duty to Him who hath given us life, breath, and being, and mercifully visited us by his grace. I thought a remark of this kind appeared to be required of me, apprehending if thou art faithful unto the Lord, thou wilt find it to be thy duty at times to leave thy worldly concerns to attend religious meetings, which may cause thee deep and heavy trials; but remember for thy encouragement, the promise of the hundred-fold in this world, and in that which is to come, eternal life.

Thou art favored with a pious though afflicted mother, and a religiously-exercised elder brother, who, I doubt not, will rejoice to see thee grow in the truth. May you all be blessed with the blessing of preservation, and strengthened to keep your ranks in righteousness, and may you be a strength and comfort to each other, and hold up a standard

of truth and righteousness in the neighborhood where your
lot is cast.  Do not flinch, my beloved friend; be not
ashamed to become a true follower of Christ.  When little •
things are required of thee, be faithful; thus shalt thou be
made ruler over more; when greater things are manifested
to be thy duty, remember the Lord is able to support, who
declared by the mouth of his prophet formerly, "Mine
heritage is unto me as a speckled bird, the birds round about
are against her."  But if the Lord be on our side, it matters
little who may be permitted to arise against us, for his power
is above all the combined powers of the wicked one, and he
will bless and preserve those who above all things are concerned to serve him faithfully, which that thou mayest be
is the sincere desire of thy truly loving and affectionate
friend,

JOSEPH WOOD.

The word which had been so fitly spoken took deep
root in John Yeardley's heart, and on the following
New-year's day he went up to Newhouse to converse
with his experienced and sympathizing friend.

On the 1st of the First Month, 1804, (writes Joseph Wood,)
John Yeardley came to my house, on purpose to see me.  He
got here betwixt ten and eleven o'clock in the forenoon,
attended our meeting and tarried with us until after tea,
and then returned home.  He is a hopeful youth, tender in
spirit, and of a sweet natural disposition; was convinced of
the truth in an opportunity I had at his father's house, and,
I hope, is likely to do well.  I love him much, and much
desire his preservation, growth, and establishment upon the
everlasting foundation, against which the gates of Hell are
not able to prevail.

Shortly after this, we obtain from John Yeardley's
own hand an insight into the depth of those religious
convictions which had so mercifully been vouchsafed to

him. The manner in which this interesting memo-randum concludes is quaint, but it expresses a resolution to which he was enabled to adhere in a remarkable degree throughout the course of his long life ; for of him it may be said that, beyond many, his pursuits, his aims, and his conversation were not of the world, but were bounded by the line of the Gospel, and animated by its self-denying spirit.

*Blacker, 2 mo.* 9, 1804. — As I pursued these earthly enjoyments, it pleased the Lord, in the riches of his mercy to turn me back in the blooming of my youth, and favor me with the overshadowing of his love, to see the splendid pleasures that so easily detained my precious time. He was graciously pleased to call me to the exercise of that important work which must be done in all our hearts, which appears to me no small cross to my own will, and attended with many discouragements ; yet I am made to believe it is the way wherein I ought to go ; and I trust Thou, O Lord, who hast called, will enable me to give up, and come forward in perfect obedience to the manifestations of thy divine light, so as a thorough change may be wrought, that I may be fitted and prepared for a place in thy everlasting kingdom. Though at times I am led into great discouragement, and almost ready to faint by the way, fearing I shall never be made conqueror over those potent enemies who so much oppose my happiness, O be Thou near in these needful times, and underneath to bear me up in all the difficulties which it is necessary I should pass through for my further refinement, whilst I have a being in this earthly pilgrimage. Strong are the ties that seem to attach me to the earth ; but O! I have cause to believe, from a known sense, stronger are the ties of thy overshadowing Spirit than all the ties of natural affection. Great and frequent are the trials and temptations, and narrow is the way wherein we ought to walk ; alas! too narrow for many. O may I ever be preserved, faithfully pressing forward to the eternal land of rest!

Dear Lord, who knowest the secret of all hearts, thou knowest I am at times under a sense of great weakness; but thou, who art always waiting to gather the tender youth into thy flock and family, hast mercifully reached over me with thy gathering arm. Mayst thou ever be near to strengthen me in every weakness; and make me willing to leave all, take up my daily cross, and follow thee in the denial of self, not fearing to confess thee before men. Always give me strength to perform whatsoever thou mayest require at my hands; wean my affections more and more; attract me nearer to thyself; and lead me through this world as a stranger, never to be known to it more but by the name of JOHN YEARDLEY.

In the Third Month Joseph Wood again addressed his young friend by letter, encouraging him to be steadfast in trial, and to beware of the gilded baits of the enemy; and promising him, that if he followed the Lord faithfully, his works should appear marvellous in his eyes, his wonders be disclosed to him in the deeps, and he on his part would be made willing to serve him with a perfect heart.

In the Sixth Month, again visiting Blacker, he had a "precious, heart-tendering religious opportunity with all the family."

About this time Joel Yeardley was so much reduced in his circumstances as to be obliged to give up farming, which compelled his sons to seek their own means of livelihood. Thomas and John went into Barnsley, where they applied themselves to the linen manufacture, and were taken into the warehouse of Thomas Dixon Walton, a Friend, who afterwards married a daughter of Thomas Shillitoe.

In the First Month, 1806, Joseph Wood records another interesting interview with his young friend:—

1 mo. 7.—I called on Thomas Dixon Walton and John

2

Yeardley, with whom I had a religious opportunity in which the language of encouragement flowed freely; I being opened unto them from Luke xii. 32; "Fear not, little flock, for it is your Father's good pleasure to give you the kingdom."

In the Third Month of this year John Yeardley made application for membership in the Society of Friends, and was admitted in the Fifth Month following, being then twenty years of age. His brother Thomas had joined the Society some time before. The brothers are thus described by one who knew them intimately:—Thomas, as a man of homely manners, of hearty and genial character, and greatly beloved; John, as possessing a native refinement which made it easy for him in after-life to rise in social position, but whose reserved habits caused him to be less generally appreciated.

The call which John Yeardley received, and which he so happily obeyed, to leave the world and enter by the strait gate into the kingdom of heaven, was accompanied, as we shall afterwards see more fully, by a secret conviction that he would one day have publicly to preach to others the Gospel of salvation. A sense that such was the case seems to have taken hold of Joseph Wood's mind, in a visit which he made him some time after his admission into the Society.

1 *mo.* 29, 1808.—Sat with T. D. Walton and his wife, and his man John Yeardley. I had two pretty long testimonies to bear from Colossians iv. 17. I had to show the necessity there was for those who had received a gift in the ministry to be faithful, and, as Satan was as busy about these as any others, to be careful to withstand his temptations, that nothing might hinder our fulfilment of this gift,

nor anything be suffered to prevail over us that might hinder its proper effect upon others.

After Thomas was gone to breakfast, my mind was unexpectedly opened in a pretty long encouraging testimony to John, from John xxi. 22—"What is that to thee? follow thou me;" having gently to caution him not to look at others to his hurt, but faithfully follow his Master, Jesus Christ, in the way of his leadings.

In 1809 John Yeardley married Elizabeth Dunn. She was much older than himself, "plain in person," but "full of simplicity and goodness," and of a "most lovable" character. Like her husband she had come into the Society by convincement; and like him she had partaken in a large degree of the paternal sympathy and oversight of Joseph Wood. She had been a Methodist, and was one of the first who joined with Friends at Barnsley in the awakening which took place there in the beginning of the century.

John Yeardley and his wife inhabited, on their marriage, a small house at the southern extremity of the town, whither very soon afterwards was transferred the afternoon meeting which it was customary to hold at some Friend's house in Barnsley. The morning meeting continued to be held at Burton until 1816, when a new meeting-house was built in the town.

They had only one child, a son, who died in infancy.

John Yeardley commenced his Diary in 1811; and this valuable record of his religious experience, and of his travels in the service of the Gospel, was maintained with more or less regularity to the end of his life. The motive which induced him to adopt this practice is given in the following lines, with which the manuscript commences :—

It may seem a little strange that I should, in my present

situation, attempt to keep any memorandums of the following
kind; but feeling desirous simply to pen down a few broken
remarks as they may at times occur to my mind, I apprehend
no great harm can arise; and if, by causing a closer scrutiny
into my future stepping along, they should in any degree
exercise my mind to spiritual improvement, the intended
purpose will be fully answered.

The first entry is dated the 6th of the Tenth Month,
1811:—

*First-day.*—Have been sweetly refreshed at our little meeting this morning. I have long felt assured that Time calls
for greater diligence in me than has hitherto been rendered.
And when I consider the innumerable favors and privileges
which I enjoy at the hands of Divine Providence, beyond
many of my fellow-creatures, and the few returns of gratitude
I am making, it raises in me an inexpressible desire that my
few remaining days may be dedicated, in humble obedience,
to Him whose great and noble cause I am professing to
promote.

How unstable is human nature! On sitting down in
meeting this evening I got into a state of unwatchfulness,
which continued so long as to deprive me of the refreshment
my poor mind so often stands in need of.

In the entries which follow, the progress of the inward
work and the preparation for future service are very
evident:—

13*th.*—Went to our morning gathering in a low frame of
mind, and was made afresh to believe that were we more
concerned to dwell nearer the pure principle of Truth when
out of meetings, we should not find such difficult access
when thus collected, but each one would be encouraged to
come under the precious influence of that baptizing power
which would cement and refresh our spirits together. O
then, I firmly believe, our Heavenly Father would in an

eminent manner condescend to crown our assemblies with
the overshadowing of his love, and enable us not only to roll
away the stone, but to draw living water as out of the wells
of salvation.

17*th.*—"Create in me a clean heart, O God, and renew a
right spirit within me," was a language which secretly passed
my mind in meeting this morning; and though inwardly poor
as I am, yet I dare not but acknowledge it a privilege to be
favored even with a good desire.

24*th.*—Was a little refreshed at our morning gathering,
my spirit being exercised under a concern that I might not
rest satisfied with anything short of living experience; and I
felt comforted with a lively hope that He whom my soul
loveth will not fail to manifest his divine regard to one who
is sincerely desirous to become acquainted with his ways. O,
how shall I render sufficient thankfulness for such a favor,
thus to be made once more sweetly to partake of the brook
by the way.

Thought the evening sitting rather dull, though the
ministry of T. S. was lively, which is a confirming proof that
however favored we may be at certain seasons, yet if at any
time we suffer our attention to be diverted from the real
object, it frustrates the design of Him who I believe intends
that we should wait together to renew our strength.

In the Eleventh Month Henry Hull, from the United
States, accompanied by John Hull of Uxbridge, visited
Burton, and had good service their, both amongst Friends
and with the public. They lodged at John Yeardley's,
and, in describing their labors and the pleasure he derived from their society, he records his thankfulness at
being placed in a situation in life such as afforded him
the opportunity of entertaining the Lord's servants.

His disposition was lively and strongly inclined to
humor, and he early felt the necessity of having this
natural trait of character subjected to the rule of hea-

venly wisdom.  Under date 27th of the Eleventh Month he says:—

I feel a little compunction for having these few days past given way too much to the lightness of my disposition, and not being sufficiently concerned to seek after that stability and serious reflection which never fails to improve the mind.

On the 26th of the Twelfth Month he records a state of spiritual poverty.

Such, he says, has been the instability of my mind, that my "Beloved is unto me as a fountain sealed." But, he adds, I feel a little tendered this evening, on reading over a few comfortable expressions in a letter from my friend Joseph Wood.

This condition of mind continued for some months, when he thus breaks forth:—

3 mo. 8, 1812.—How pleasant it is once more to be favored with a few drops of living water from the springs of that well which my soul has had for many weeks past to languish after, and which I trust has been wisely withheld in order to show me that, although it is our indispensable duty to persevere in digging for it, yet it is only in His own time that we are permitted to drink thereof.

His just appreciation of the nature of meetings held for the discipline of the Church, and of the spirit in which they are to be conducted, is shown in an early part of the Diary.

3 mo. 15.—Was at our Preparative Meeting. The queries having to be answered, I was led into deep thoughtfulness respecting the same, and inwardly solicited that the Father of mercies would lend his divine aid, in the performance of such important duties; which I have reason to believe was in some measure answered, for they were gone

through with a degree of ease and comfort to my own mind. May I ever keep in remembrance the testimonies of his love which are so often manifested!

8 *mo.* 17.—Meeting for discipline at Burton. The fore-part was conducted, I think, to edification; but in the latter, one subject occupied much time unnecessarily, and did not conclude to general satisfaction. When some whose spirits are not well seasoned, speak to circumstances which they may not have sufficiently considered, it sometimes does more harm than they may at first apprehend.

The entries in the Diary at this time shew many alternations of discouragement and comfort, and of that deep searching of his own heart from which he seldom shrank, and which is the only way to the liberty and peace of the soul.

4 *mo.* 12.—In contemplating the gracious dealings of the Almighty with me from time to time, I have been led to query, Is it not that I might, by patiently submitting to the turnings and overturnings of his most holy hand, become fashioned to show forth his praise? But alas! where are the fruits? Is not the work rather marring as on the wheel; can I, in sincerity say, I am the clay, Thou art the potter? I feel weary of my own negligence; for it seems as if the day with me was advancing faster than the work. I fear lest I should be cast off for want of giving greater diligence to make my calling sure. O may he who is perfect in wisdom strengthen the feeble desire which remains, and melt my stubborn will into perfect obedience by the operation of his pure spirit.

In the next memoranda which we shall transcribe we see when and how his mind was imbued with the love of Scriptural inquiry and illustration. Two or three good books well read and digested in younger life often form the thinking habits of the man, and supply no small part of the substance, or at any rate the

nucleus, of his knowledge. This shows the vast importance of a wise choice of authors, at the time when the
mind is the most susceptible of impressions, and the
most capable of appropriating the food which is presented to it. Those who knew John Yeardley will
recognise the intimate connexion between these early
studies and the character of his future life and ministry.
If any should think his language on this or kindred
subjects marked by excessive caution, they must bear in
mind the comparative by unintellectual circle in which
he moved.

I trust, he writes, under date of 4 mo. 28, a few of my
leisure hours for two or three weeks past have been spent
profitably in perusing some of A. Clarke's Notes on the
Book of Genesis; and although I am fully aware that the
greatest caution is necessary, when these learned men undertake to exercise their skill on the sacred text, yet I am of
opinion, if used with prudence and a right spirit attended to,
it may tend considerably to illustrate particular passages. I
think this pious man has not only shown his profound knowledge of the learned languages, but some of his observations
are so pertinent and so judiciously made, as may have a
tendency to produce spiritual reflection in the mind of the
reader.

5 mo. 24.—Having read with some attention Fleury's
" Manners of the Israelites," by A. Clarke, I am convinced
that even a slight knowledge of those ancient customs tends
to facilitate the proper study of the sacred writings; for
many of the metaphors so beautifully made use of by the
prophets and apostles, and even our dear Redeemer himself, to convey a spiritual meaning, seem to have had an
evident allusion to the antique manners and customs which
I find explained in this little volume.

The commotions referred to in the reflections which
follow, were no doubt the great European war which

was then raging.  Buonaparte, it may be remembered, was at that time making preparation for his Russian campaign, and a universal alarm prevailed as to the final result of his insatiable lust of conquest.

5 *mo.* 7.—In viewing the commotions of the times, it has induced me seriously to consider the great importance of procuring, as far as ability may be afforded, a free access to the never-failing source of our help; and in a little contemplating this subject I have been comforted in a hope that, if we only abide stedfast and immovable, He whom the waves of the sea obeyed will in his own time speak peace to the minds of his tossed ones, and a calm will ensue.

The perusal of Elizabeth Smith's "Fragments" occasions him to remark how profitable it is to read the writings of others; but he wisely adds:—

I am often desirous not to rest satisfied with a bare perusal of these, believing they are only advantageous to us so far as they stimulate to a closer attention to that inward gift, which alone can enable us to witness the same experience.  It is often a query with me, how am I spending this precious time, which passes so swiftly away never to return? and, in order to answer this query aright, how desirable it is to dwell with thee, sweet solitude! to turn inward, to examine and correct the defects of our own disordered minds; how delightful it is to walk alone and contemplate the beautiful scenes of nature. Yet in these retired moments, when viewing the works of a divine hand springing up to answer the great end for which they were created, I am often deeply perplexed with a distressing fear lest I should not be found coming forward faithfully to answer the end of Him who has created man for the purpose of his own glory.

The meetings for the discipline of the Society were often times of spiritual refreshment to him.

6 *mo.* 23.—I left home to attend our Quarterly Meeting at York. The meetings for business were generally satisfactory; on re-examining the answers to the queries, divers very weighty remarks were made. I thought the two meetings for worship favored seasons; and, although I left home with reluctance, I cannot but rejoice at having given up a little time to be made a partaker of the overflowing of that precious influence which, I trust, made glad the hearts of many present.

The extracts which follow develope still further the progress of his inner life, and the secret preparation of the future preacher of the Gospel and overseer of the flock of Christ.

6 *mo.* 29.—A deep-searching time at meeting yesterday, wherein I was given to see a little of my own unworthiness The secret breathings of my spirit were to the Father and fountain of life, that he might be pleased more and more to redeem me from this corrupted state of human nature, and draw me by the powerful cords of his love into a nearer union with the pure spirit of the Gospel.

7 *mo.* 6.—Thought an awful solemnity was the covering of our small gathering yesterday morning, under which I felt truly thankful to the Dispenser of every gift; and was enabled to crave his assistance to maintain the watch with greater diligence, and pursue the ways of peace with alacrity of soul.

29*th and* 30*th.*—The General Meeting at Ackworth was large, and I thought very satisfactory through all its different sittings. The meeting for worship was a remarkable time; the pure spring of gospel ministry seemed to flow, as from vessel to vessel, until it rose into such dominion as to declare the gracious presence of Him who is ever worthy to be honored and adored for thus condescending to own us on such important occasions. Iron is said to sharpen iron; and I thought it was a little the case with me at this season, feeling very desirous to enjoy that within myself which I so much admire in others.

8 *mo.* 13.—Many days have I gone mourning on my way, for what cause I know not; but if I can only abide in patience till the day break and the shadows flee away, then I trust the King of righteousness will again appear.

25*th.*—In contemplating a little the character of that good man, Nehemiah, I cannot but think it worthy our strictest imitation, when we consider the heartfelt concern he manifested for the welfare of his people, in saying, " Come and let us build up the wall of Jerusalem, that we be no more a reproach." This proved him to be a man of a noble spirit and a disinterested mind, and, I say, worthy our strictest imitation ; for to what nobler purpose can we dedicate our time than in endeavoring to build up the broken places which are made in the walls of our Zion ?

In the following entry is shown a just insight into the nature of man, and a discernment of the uses and limits of human knowledge. Although John Yeardley's talents were not brilliant, and his opportunities were scanty, he possessed that intellectual thirst which cannot be slaked but at the fountain of knowledge. At the same time he was sensitively alive to the necessity of having all his pursuits, of whatever kind, kept within the golden measure of the Spirit of Truth.

11 *mo.* 11.—In taking a view of some of the temporal objects to which my attention has of late been more particularly turned, with a desire to enlarge my ideas and improve my understanding in some of the more useful and extended branches of literature, it has excited in me a considerable degree of caution, lest thereby I should, in this my infant state of mind, too much exclude the operation of that pure in-speaking word which has undoubtedly a prior right to govern all my actions. But I have long been convinced that the active mind of man must have some object in pursuit to engage its attention when unemployed in the lawful concerns of life, otherwise it is apt to range at large in a boundless

field of unprofitable thoughts and imaginations. I am aware that we may be seasonably employed in suitable conversation to mutual advantage, and I trust I am not altogether a stranger to the value of *sweet retirement;* but there is a certain something in every mind which renders a change in the exercise of our natural faculties indispensable, in order to make us happy in ourselves and useful members of society; and it is under these considerations that I am induced to apply a few of my leisure hours towards some degree of intellectual attainment, in the humble hope that I may be preserved in that path which will procure at the hands of a wise Director that approbation which I greatly desire should mark all my steps.

The next extract from the diary will find a response in the hearts of many who read these pages.

1813. 2 *mo.* 17.—Never, surely, was any poor creature so weary of his weakness! Almost in everything spiritual, and even useful, I have not only been as one forsaken, but it has seemed as though I was to be utterly cast off. When I have desired to feel after good, evil has never failed to present itself. O, when will He whose countenance has often made all within me glad, see meet to return and say, "It is enough!"

6 *mo.* 27.—The thoughts which he put into writing under this date seem to have been occasioned by entering into business on his own account.

Am now about to enter the busy scenes of life, which sinks me into the very depth of humility and fear, lest the concerns of an earthly nature should deprive me of my heavenly crown, which I have so often desired to prefer even to life itself. But O, should there remain any regard in the breast of the Father of mercies, for one who feels so unable to cope with the world, may he still be pleased to preserve me in his fear, and not only to take me under the shadow of his heavenly wing, but make me willing to abide under the guidance of his divine direction!

7 *mo.* 15.—"Cause me not to return to the house of Jonathan the scribe, lest I die there." These words of our weeping prophet have sensibly affected my heart this morning, under a prevailing desire that my gracious Father may not permit me to remain as in the prison-house of worldly affairs, lest I die my spiritual death there.

We shall see that he was not successful in business; and it may be that the disappointments he experienced in this way were in some sort an answer to these ardent prayers to be kept from the spirit of the world.

Under date 21st of the First Month, 1814, he writes:

I trust the few temporal disappointments I have met with of late have been conducive to my best interest, having had a tendency to turn my views from a too anxious pursuit after the things of time to a serious consideration of the very great importance of a more strict reliance on the never-failing arm of divine support, for the want of which I believe I have suffered unspeakable loss.

About this time he had frequently to mourn over the difficulty of fixing his mind in meetings for worship. He often complains of "wandering in the unprofitable fields of vain imagination;" but sometimes also he bears a joyful testimony to the Lord's power in enabling him to unite in spirit with the living worshippers.

The fear of man is one of the most universal of the besetments which try the faith of the Christian; and it may be encouraging to some to see on this point the confession of one whose natural character was that of a strong and independent mind.

2 *mo.* 6.—I am too apt to let in that slavish fear about men and things which renders me unable to cope with the

world, and even unfits me for properly seeking after the assistance of my Maker. O, may He who sees my weakness enable me to overcome it!

During the summer of this year, several parties of Friends travelling in the work of the ministry came to Burton; Sarah Lamley of Tredington, with Ann Fairbank of Sheffield; Ann Burgess (afterwards Ann Jones); Elizabeth Coggeshall from New York, with Mary Jefferys of Melksham; and John Kirkham of Earl's Colne. The labors of these Friends are recorded by John Yeardley with delight and thankfulness. He accompanied John Kirkham to Sheffield, where they found Stephen Grellett.

How sweet it is, he remarks, to enjoy the company of these dedicated servants, whom their great Master seems to be sending to and fro to spread righteousness in the earth! I often think it has a tendency to help one a little on the way towards the Land of Promise. When I consider these favors, I am led to covet that a double portion of the spirit of the Elijahs may so rest on the Elishas that others may also be raised to fill up the honorable situations of those worthies, when they shall be removed from works to rewards.

But of all the above-named, the visit of Sarah Lamley and Ann Fairbank was for him by far the most memorable, and was the means of developing that precious gift of ministry to which he had been called from his youth. The extracts from his Diary which are given below speak of this visit, and most instructively describe the time and manner in which he first received his gift, as well as the weight which the approaching exercise of it brought upon his mind.

5 mo. 27.—Sarah Lamley and Ann Fairbank lodged six nights with us, and I accompanied them to Dirtcar and

Wakefield. I can acknowledge their innocent and agreeable company has been truly profitable to me, and has united me very closely to their spirits in tender sympathy.

7 *mo.* 30.—Such a load of exercise prevails over my spirit, that it requires some extra exertion to support it with my usual cheerfulness of countenance. If I go into company, I find no satisfaction; for I cannot appear pleasant in the society of my friends, feeling it irksome to discourse even on matters of common conversation. From the feelings which have attended my mind, it is evident that the cloud is at present resting on the tabernacle, and I never saw more need for me to abide in my tent. And O that patience may have its perfect work! for there is much to be done in the vineyard of my own heart, before I can come to that state of usefulness which I believe the Great [Husbandman] designs for me. The secret language of my heart is, May his hand not spare nor his eye pity until he has subdued all in me which obstructs the progress of his divine work!

31*st.*—I trust I was once more favored, in meeting this morning, to put up my secret petition in humble sincerity to the Shepherd of Israel, that he would be graciously pleased to help my infirmities. In the afternoon meeting I thought the petition was measurably answered; for towards the conclusion the rays of divine light so overshadowed my mind as to induce a belief that I should be assisted to overcome that spirit of opposition which has too long existed to the detriment of my best interests, if there was only a willingness to abide under the forming hand.

8 *mo.* 1.—I now feel freedom to give a short account how it was with me under this concern from its commencement down to the present time.

I remember well, about the year 1804, when in my father's house at Blacker, once being in my chamber, in a very serious, thoughtful frame of mind, receiving an impression that if ever I came to receive the truth which I was then convinced of, to my everlasting benefit, I should have publicly to declare of the gracious dealings of Divine Goodness to my soul. The impression passed away with this remark deeply imprinted in my mind, that if ever a like concern should come to be matured, I should date the first intimation of it from this time. I was apt to view it for a long time as the mere workings of the enemy on my mind, and when it has come before my view, I have often secretly said, "Get thee behind me, I will not be tempted with such a thing." By these means I put it from me, as it were, by force, not thinking it worthy of notice and often praying to be delivered from such a gross delusion. At other times it would come with such weight on my spirit, that I could not avoid shedding tears, and acknowledging the power which accompanied the revival of so important a matter; and was led to query, If there is no real intention of a heavenly nature, why am I thus harassed? and O the fervent sincerity in which I desired that the right thing might have place, and if it was wrong, that I might be enabled to find a release in His time who had appointed the conflict! And I do believe, could I then have come at a perfect resignation to the divine will, I might have been brought forward in a way which would have afforded permanent relief to my own mind; but such was my dislike to the work, that I suffered myself to be lulled into a state of unbelief as to the rectitude of the concern.

Thus many outward circumstances transpired, and some years passed over, with my only viewing the matter at a distance, until He who first laid the concern upon me was pleased to bring it more clearly home to me, and seemed at times to engage his servants, both in public and private, to speak very clearly to my condition. And although I had a concurring testimony in my own mind to their declarations, yet I had always an excuse to flee unto by secretly saying, It may be intended for some one else; until the Most High was graciously pleased, by the services of his sincere handmaids, Sarah Lamley and Ann Fairbank, in their family visits to Friends of Barnsley, as mentioned last Fifth Month, to speak so clearly to my situation in their private opportunity with us, as to leave no room for excuse; but I was forced to acknowledge, Thou art the man. Indeed, Sarah Lamley was led in such an extraordinary manner, that I had no doubt at all but that she was favored with a clear and full sense of my state. She began by enumerating the many fears which attended the apostles in their various situations; how that Satan had desired to have some of them that he might sift them as wheat in a sieve; "but," added she, "I have prayed for thee, Peter, that thy faith fail not, and when thou art converted strengthen thy brethren." And how it was with Moses when the Almighty appeared to him in a flame of fire in the bush, and that it was not until the Most High had condescended to answer all Moses' excuses that he was angry with him, and even then he condescended to let him have Aaron, his brother, to go with him for a spokesman. Also how it was with Peter when the threefold charge was given him to feed the lambs and the sheep. "It is not enough," said she, "to acknowledge that we love the Lord, but there must be a manifesting of our love by doing whatsoever he may command." Methinks I still hear her voice, saying, "And O that there may not be a pleading of excuses, Moses-like!" Thus was this valuable servant enabled to speak to my comfort and encouragement, which I trust I shall ever remember to advantage; but O that I may be resigned to wait the appointed time in watchful humility, patience, and fear! for I find there is a danger of seeking too much after outward confirmations, and not having the attention sufficiently fixed on the great Minister of ministers, who alone is both able and willing to direct the poor mind in this most important concern, and in his own time to say, "Arise, shine; for thy light is come."

12 *mo.* 22.—My poor mind has been so much enveloped in clouds of thick darkness for months past, that I have sometimes been ready to conclude I shall never live to see brighter days. Should even this be the case I humbly hope ever to be preserved from accusing the just Judge of the earth of having dealt hardly with me, but acknowledge to the last that he has in mercy favored me abundantly with a portion of that light which is said to shine brighter and brighter unto the perfect day.

3

We shall leave for the next chapter the relation of his first offerings in the ministry, and conclude this with a striking passage which we find in the Diary for this year.

John Yeardley was all his life very fond of the occupations of the garden. A small piece of ground was attached to his house at Barnsley, which he cultivated, and from which he was sometimes able to gather spiritual as well as natural fruit.

Under date of the 22nd of the Seventh Month, he writes:—

A very sublime idea came suddenly over my mind when in the garden this evening. It was introduced as I plucked a strawberry from a border on which I had bestowed much cultivation before it would produce anything; but now, thought I, this is a little like reaping the fruit of my labor. As I thus ruminated on the produce of the strawberry-bank, I was struck with the thought of endless *felicity*, and the sweet reward it would produce for all our toils here below. My mind was instantly opened to such a glorious scene of divine good that I felt a resignation of heart to give up all for the enjoyment of [such a foretaste] of *endless felicity*.

# CHAPTER II.

1815.—AFTER the long season of depression through
which John Yeardley passed, as described in the last
chapter, the new year of 1815 dawned with brightness
upon his mind. He now at length saw his spiritual
bonds loosed; and the extracts which follow describe his
first offerings in the ministry in a simple and affecting
manner.

1 *mo.* 5.—The subject of the prophet's going down to the
potter's house opened so clearly on my mind in meeting this
morning that I thought I could almost have publicly declared
it; but not feeling that weight and certainty which I had
apprehended should accompany the performance of such an
important act, I was afraid of imparting that to others which
might be intended only for my own instruction; and so it has
ended for the present. But I am thankful in hoping that I
am come a little nearer to that state of resignation which was
so beautifully exemplified by our great Pattern of all good,
who when He desired the bitter cup might pass from Him,
nevertheless added, "Not my will, but thine be done." And
if I am at all acquainted with my inward feelings, I trust I
can in some degree of sincerity say that my heart desires to
rejoice more in the progress of this state of happy resignation,
than at the increase of corn, wine, or oil.

He first opened his mouth in religious testimony in
the First Month of this year. The occurrence seems to
have taken place in his own family; it yielded him a
"precious sense of the Divine Presence." He began to

(27)

preach in public a few months later, but not without another struggle against the heavenly impulse.

The friendship which Joseph Wood entertained for John Yeardley strengthened with revolving years. When he visited Barnsley, he was accustomed to lodge at his house; and writing to him in the year 1811, about a public meeting which he felt concerned to hold, he says, "I can with freedom write to thee, feeling that unity with thy spirit which preserves us near and dear to each other, and in which freedom runs."

In the Fourth Month of this year, when Joseph Wood received a certificate to visit some of the midland counties, J. Y. felt desirous "of setting him a little on his way."

On the 14th, he says, we went to Woodhouse, where we had a meeting, and my friend was enabled to speak very closely to the states of many present. When in the meeting, I felt a very weighty exercise to attend my mind with an intimation publicly to express it. But this exposure I dared not yield to, under an apprehension that it might be wrong in me, considering the occasion on which I had come out; but truly I left the place under a burden which I was scarcely able to bear.

It was on the 20th of the Fourth Month that he began to speak in public as a minister of the Gospel. He thus records the event:—

I felt myself in such a resigned frame of mind in our little week-day meeting, that I could not doubt the time was fully come for me to be relieved from that state of unspeakable oppression which my poor mind had been held in for so many years past. Soon after I took my seat, my mind became unusually calm, and the presence of the Most High seemed so to abound in my heart and spread over the meeting, that after some inward conflict I was unavoidably constrained publicly to express it, in nearly the following words: " I think I have so sensibly felt the precious influence of divine love to overshadow our little gathering, that I have been ready to say, It is good for us to be here; or I might rather say, It is good for us to feel ourselves under the precious influence of that protecting power which can alone preserve us from the snares of death." This first [public] act of sub-mission to the divine will was done with as much stability of mind and body as I was capable of; and I thought the Friends present seemed sensible of my situation and sympa-thized with me under the exercise. I trust the sweet peace which I afterwards felt was a seal to my belief that I had been favored with divine compassion and approbation in the needful time.

In the Fifth Month John Yeardley attended for the first time the Yearly Meeting in London. He describes the business as very various and instructive, but bewails his own condition as that of " one starving in the midst of every good thing."

It seemed at times, he says, as though Satan himself was let loose upon me, and permitted to try my faith and patience to the utmost; but I hope the conflict had its use in teaching me to know that it is not by might, nor by power, but by the Lord's Spirit, that we are enabled to prevail.

This was the commencement of another season of spiritual poverty. In reading a few of his memoranda during this time, many a Christian traveller may see his own mourning countenance reflected as in a glass.

11 *mo.* 8.—I have for a long time felt so depressed in spirit, and so inwardly stripped of every appearance of good, that I have often secretly had to say with tried Job, " O that I were as in months past, as in the days when God preserved me!"

16*th.*—Death and darkness are still the covering of my poor mind, and I am ashamed to acknowledge that I have for

months past sat meeting after meeting a victim to the bane-
ful consequences of wandering thoughts, scarcely being able
to recollect myself so much as to ask excuse of Him who sees
in secret.   In these times of deepest desertion I am selfish
enough to feel a longing desire for a ray of light or a smile
from the countenance of Him, under whose banner I have
many times sat with the greatest delight in days that are
past.

O, how hard it is to regain divine favor when once sacri-
ficed through the sorrowful act of disobedience!   O may I
sit as in dust and ashes, and, with the noble resignation
and spirit of a true, dedicated follower, say, I will patiently
bear the indignation of the Lord, because I have sinned
against him!

Nevertheless, even in his times of deepest humiliation,
moments of heavenly comfort were interspersed.

11 *mo.* 23.—A more improved meeting than I had reason
to hope from cross occurrences, which are too apt to ruffle
the unstable mind.   During our silent sitting together, I was
comforted in contemplating the many encouraging passages
we have left on sacred record; two of which, spoken by one
of large experience, were particularly solacing to my exercised feelings: "Many are the afflictions of the righteous,
but the Lord delivereth him out of them all;" and "The
young lions do lack and suffer hunger, but they that seek
the Lord shall not want any good thing."   O, thought I, if
we could only procure Him on our side who has the thoughts
of all men in his keeping, what should we have to fear!   We
should then be brought to acknowledge that it behooves a
Christian traveller to crave the assistance of Him who can
enable us to suffer with becoming fortitude and resignation
all the afflicting dispensations of life, rather than desire to be
preserved from meeting them.

The hard matter which is the subject of the next
extract embodies a difficulty that has perplexed many.

It is always encouraging to find companionship in doubts and trials, and perhaps the consideration which pacified the mind of John Yeardley may be helpful to some who are tried in the same way. The passage, no doubt, has reference to his own want of better success in business.

11 *mo.* 30.—When any circumstance in the common course of life, which has appeared to turn up in the direction of Divine Providence, has not answered my expectation, or on deliberate consideration it has not seemed prudent for me to step into it, I have sometimes felt greatly discouraged, and been ready to conclude, How could this thing be ordered under the direction of best wisdom! But let me ever remember, He who has his way in the whirlwind knows what is best for us; and were it not for these incitements to an exercise of feeling, the mind would be apt to lie dormant, and not be preserved alive in a proper state to prove all things and hold fast that which is best.

About the end of the year he was obliged to spend several days in London on business. The course of his affairs seems to have been uneven, and the great city was probably uncongenial to his retired habits. He says:—

12 *mo.* 15.—I do not remember that my feelings were ever more discouraging, both inwardly and outwardly. When the mind is ruffled about the things of time, it is hard work to make any progress towards the land of peace. I try to get to the well of water; but truly it may be said I have nothing to draw with.

Yet even under these circumstances his daily religious practices—those which no competitor for the meed of peace and the crown of glory can dispense with—were not without avail.

16*th*.—In reading and retirement before I left my room, I received a little hope that I should be preserved in a good degree of patience through the cross occurrences of the day, which was measurably the case.

The life of a Christian is very much the history of outward and inward trials. How happy it is when these serve only to deepen his experience! The nature of John Yeardley's spiritual trials has been fully shown: his temporal crosses have also been glanced at; they consisted mainly of want of success in business, in which, indeed, he was little fitted to excel, under the keen competition of modern times.

1816. 1 *mo.* 4.—A new year has commenced, but the old afflictions are still continued, both inwardly and outwardly; for even in temporal affairs disappointments rage high. But O what a privilege to sink down to the anchor-hope of divine support! This is what I can feelingly acknowledge this evening to be as a brook by the way to refresh my poor and long-distressed mind. O, how ardently do I desire that this season of adversity may be sanctified to me for everlasting good, and prove the means of slaying that will in me, which has too long been opposed to the will of Him who paid the ransom for my soul with nothing less than the price of his own precious blood.

The difficulty of making his way in the commercial world increased until the risk of "failure began to stare him in the face." The fear of such a result sank him exceedingly low; but through all he was permitted to keep his footing upon the rock, and to behold a spiritual blessing under the guise of temporal adversity.

7*th*.—Surely it is a mark of divine favor to feel the supporting hand of my heavenly Father underneath, to bear up my drooping spirits in this time of adversity. I think I was never more sensible of his powerful arm being made bare for my deliverance; and yet, unaccountable to tell, I am almost afraid to trust in him. O, my soul, wherefore dost thou doubt, when thou feelest the glorious presence of thy Redeemer's countenance to shine upon thee?

In the meeting this morning, he continues, my mind was profitably exercised in contemplating the following subject. When our dear Lord was about to perform the miracle of feeding the multitude, he commanded them to sit down upon the grass. They were undoubtedly hungry, and this might create in them too great an anxiety to be satisfied in their own time; but that all things might be done in order, and without interruption, they were commanded to sit down and wait the disposal of their food from the bountiful hand of their great Master. In looking at the subject, I thought it a lively representation of the state of mind we ought to labor after, when favored to feel hunger and thirst after righteousness; not frustrating the design of the Most High by being too anxious to be filled in our own will and way, but patiently waiting the time of Him who giveth to all their meat in due season, and that which is most convenient for them. And what greater privilege could we desire than to be fed at the Lord's table?

*9th.*—As my precious wife and I were consoling each other this evening, she remarked that the dispensation we were now suffering under was probably in answer to our prayers. This brought strikingly to my remembrance a secret petition which I have frequently put up in the most fervent manner I have been capable of, when deeply lamenting my unsubjected will; I have even cried out aloud, "O make me willing; do, Lord, make me willing, make me willing!"

O then may I submit to the means, if for this end they are appointed, and resign my all, body, soul and spirit, into the hands of Him who gave them; and may I patiently endure the swelling of Jordan in a manner that will enable me to bring from the bottom, stones of everlasting memorial.

After this he was led for a while by the Good Shepherd into the green pastures and beside the still waters.

*1st mo.* 15.—Our Monthly Meeting at Wakefield, and a heavenly meeting it was.

*29th.*—I left home for a journey into the north on business. I had many precious seasons of retirement as I rode along, and I humbly trust my soul has been enabled to cultivate a more intimate acquaintance with her Beloved, in such a way as will not easily be erased from my remembrance.

Notwithstanding the deep and varied experience he had passed through, his unwillingness to expose himself as a preacher of the gospel was still strong, and sometimes obstructed the performance of his duty.

*8 mo.* 20.—Joseph Wood had a public meeting at Pilley. I felt something on my spirit to communicate to the people in the early part, but thinking the meeting was not sufficiently settled to receive it, I reasoned away the right time; another did not offer during the whole meeting for me to relieve my poor mind, so I brought my burden home with me, which indeed proved such as I really thought I should have sunk under.

The "severe stripes," as he terms it, which he received on this occasion at length produced a willing mind.

*9 mo.* 10.—I went with my dear wife to attend the burial of my cousin Joseph Watts at Woodhouse, and was at the meeting there on Fourth-day the 11th. It was largely attended by relations and friends. I felt so sensibly the danger that some present were in of trifling away the reproofs of conviction, that I could not forbear reviving the language which was proclaimed to the Prophet Jonah, when he had fled from the presence of the Lord and was fallen asleep in the ship, "What meanest thou, O sleeper, arise, call upon thy God." After commenting a little on the subject, I sat down under great solemnity which seemed to cover the meeting, and I can thankfully say the fruit of obedience was sweet to my taste.

12 *mo.* 1.—Went to meeting this morning with a fearful apprehension lest I should have to expose myself in that which is so contrary to my natural inclination. And so it proved; for I had not sat long, before I was made willing to express what rested weightily on my mind, and that was the case of Gideon, when the angel appeared to him under the oak as he threshed wheat. I commented a little on the subject, which afforded me great satisfaction and joy.

In the following entry, notwithstanding the tardy obedience which it records, we find his commission as one of the Lord's watchmen sealed upon his mind.

1817. 4 *mo.* 7. In meeting yesterday morning I was enabled publicly to relieve myself of a little matter which had been a burden on my mind for two or three meetings past, in which I had felt pretty smartly the rod which is held over the head of the disobedient. In this instance, human nature seemed stubborn in a double degree, but after it was over I felt my peace flow as a river. Methinks I now hear this language proclaimed in the secret of my heart: I have made thee a watchman unto the house of Israel; therefore hear the word at my mouth, and give them warning from me. O what an important charge! May I duly consider the weight of it, and so watch over my own conduct, in thought, word and action, that I may not be pulling down with one hand that which I may be endeavoring to build up with the other. If I am to be an instrument in the hand of the Almighty, may he graciously condescend to prepare and sharpen the arrows he may see meet to shoot through the medium of his poor servant, so that they may sink deep, wound the hypocrite, and comfort the pure divine life in the hearts of his children.

A few weeks after this, John Yeardley attended a remarkable meeting held by Joseph Wood, in which they were made to sit in heavenly places in Christ Jesus.

4 *mo.* 29.—I attended another public meeting appointed by J. W. at Middletown, about ten miles from here. When I entered the town I felt very flat, and was ready to say, The fear of the Lord is not in this place; but after the meeting was gathered, I soon found what poor creatures we are, to judge of these things without waiting for best direction; for I think it was the most extraordinary time I ever knew. My friend bore a long and powerful testimony, to the tendering of many present. If I ever forget it while in my natural senses, I fear I shall be near losing my habitation in the truth; for it was as if heaven opened, and the Most High poured down his blessed Spirit in an unbounded degree.

All this time his business affairs went on more and more adversely; and although he never failed punctually to meet all his money engagements, his want of success led in this year to a change of residence to Bentham.

Three months before he left Barnsley he writes:—

"Surely there is a vein for the silver, and a place for gold where they fine it." Pecuniary difficulties seem as if they would eat up every green thing; but I hope and trust that He who has often said, Peace, be still, will so regulate the heat of the furnace that I may be able to bear it with becoming patience, until there be nothing left in me but what resembles the pure gold fit for the Master's use. When I reflect on what my poor mind has passed through for more than two years past, I am convinced nothing short of that Arm which brought the Israelites through the Red Sea could have supported me. And O, should he ever loose my bands, that I may serve Him freely, may I never forget the many covenants made with Him who has so often heard and answered my prayer when in deep distress!

Through the assistance of some of his Barnsley friends, an offer was made to him of a situation in a flax-spinning mill at Bentham, which was then or had lately been the

property of Charles Parker, a minister in the Society of
Friends. He accepted the offer; and an extract from
a letter to his wife, when on a journey, will show the
motives under which he acted in this important step.

Hawkshead, 6 mo. 28, 1817.

MY VERY PRECIOUS DEAR,

When I wrote thee last, my time and feelings would not
permit me to say much on our impending prospect of leaving
Barnsley; but since then this very important subject has
obtained my most serious and weighty consideration, and I
am now free to communicate to thee my feelings, in order
that thou mayest weigh them duly and compare them with
thy own while we are separated. In the first place, in taking
such a step, we must be reconciled to sacrifice our present
comfortable home, our relations and friends—in short, all
that may seem near and dear to us as to the outward. With
respect to our spiritual prospect, I must confess, if any service
is designed for me in the Church militant, I have sometimes
apprehended it might be within the compass of our present
Particular and Monthly Meetings; but should this be ordered
otherwise in best wisdom, I trust I shall be relieved from the
oppressive feeling, and in a short time see my way clear. On
the other hand, if this change takes place, we have a probability of a comfortable living, and of being relieved from the
extreme anxiety attendant on trade, when the whole responsibility rests on our own shoulders.

H. R. [one of the firm who had offered to employ him]
seemed rather desirous for me to come. If we should agree,
he wants me to go over directly to lay down plans for a few
weavers' houses, and to make other arrangements to save
time until we could remove.

I don't much like the situation of the house in the town,
but I think another might be had if required. They have
a nice one in Low Bentham, with a good garden attached,
which would be at liberty in next Fifth Month; this would
be a pleasant walk from the mill by the water-side all the

way, which might be useful to my health after being confined
in the warehouse, and much nearer to the meeting. It is a
very small meeting indeed; there are only about two female
Friends; but, should we be in the right place, the smallness
of the number would not preclude our access to the divine
spring.

I don't know how we shall come on with the thread trade,
but it seems as if we were to be done out with both thread
and linens, for there is scarcely any thing selling with me on
this journey.

John Yeardley and his wife removed to Bentham in
the Eighth Month, 1817. Bentham is a considerable
village on the north-west border of Yorkshire, a few
miles from the foot of Ingleborough; and it was at that
time, according to the division of the county adopted
by the Society of Friends, comprised in the Monthly
Meeting of Settle.

After a season of deep spiritual poverty, during
which he found no place for the exercise of his gift,
John Yeardley began to speak in ministry in the little
meeting to which he now belonged. On recording the
circumstance he remarks :—

Thus does a gracious Father lead on his children step by
step, baptizing them first into one state and then into another, in order to qualify them to drop a word in season for
the comfort of others. Little did I think under the recent
buffetings of the Enemy, that I should ever have had to open
my mouth again in the way of declaring the everlasting goodness of a gracious Redeemer.

This memorandum was made a few days after the
occurrence to which it refers, on his return from Settle
Monthly Meeting, and is accompanied by the record of
a fresh unfolding to his mental eye of the need of gospel
laborers, and of his own vocation to the work.

In my return I had rather an unusual opening into the state of society, and the great want of laborers therein ; and querying with myself, By whom shall the Lord send? I thought I felt the weight and power of the everlasting gospel upon me to preach, so that I was willing to say, Here am I; send me. O the importance of this language! May the same Spirit which I trust raised it in my heart preserve me in every state to the end of time! Amen.

The extract which follows treats of the same subject, —the calling and exercise of the ministry. From this, and from the whole tenor of what has been extracted from the Diary, will be seen in what his ministry consisted, and what was the call and the power which was required in every successive exercise of it. May it serve as a word of caution and instruction to such as are disposed to reduce this heavenly gift to a mere effort of Christian good-will, or to consider the exercise of it as placed, whether in regard to time or subject, at the disposal of the minister. It will be observed how John Yeardley, in after life so abundant in word and doctrine, and so catholic in his ideas and sympathies, received his vocation as a divine gift immediately from above, and served in it an apprenticeship altogether spiritual, and apart from human learning or instruction.

10 *mo.* 26.—I have been very much instructed to-day in reading and reflecting on the 37th chapter of Ezekiel. When the prophet was asked if the dry bones could live, he was wise enough cautiously to answer, "O Lord God, thou knowest;" but when he was commanded to prophesy unto them, and say, "O ye dry bones, hear the word of the Lord," this was hard work, yet there was no conferring with flesh and blood. No reasoning from probabilities, nothing but an implicit faith and dependence on the divine power which was then upon him, could have enabled him to

do it. O what an instructive lesson! When the poor instruments may feel so weak and the state of things so low,
that there may not be the least probability of good arising, it
is enough if they can only do the will of their great Master,
and be enabled to say with the holy prophet, "I prophesied
as the Lord commanded."

John Yeardley did not take his actual farewell of
Barnsley until the end of the year. The reflections
which he has recorded on leaving his home of so many
years are very characteristic of the man:—

1818. 1 *mo.*—The Twelfth Month was spent at Barnsley
in settling my affairs. Just before I left Bentham for that
purpose, I was exceedingly unhappy at the idea of leaving
my home, friends, &c. at Barnsley, and thought the parting
feeling would be almost more than I could support. I was
enabled to pray fervently to the Father of spirits, that he
would be pleased to afford me strength to bear the change
with Christian fortitude, and resign all to the disposal of his
divine will; and thankful I am to relate, he so answered my
request that I could leave the place to which I had been so
long attached without a sigh. I have no doubt my removal,
without consulting more of my friends, will appear strange
to many. This I could never feel liberty to do; nor could I
make any person living acquainted with my entire motive,
but my precious wife. Whatever may be the opinion of
others, this is a matter which rests between me and my God;
and I often think it a favor that we are not accountable to
man, who views too much the outside appearance, while He
with whom we have to do looks at the heart.

After I had left Barnsley I went to Pontefract, to spend a
few days with my friends there, where my poor lass had been
for a week. I don't know that this time was unprofitably
spent; but this I know—it never requires more care and
watchfulness to be preserved in a seasonable frame of spirit
than when the mind is set at ease to enjoy the company of a

few intimate friends. We are too apt to get our thoughts dissipated, and thus our conversation becomes less seasoned with grace than it would be if the girdle of truth were kept tightly bound.

The next entry notices a remarkable interview which he had with a woman Friend from America:—

15*th.*—This day a meeting has been held at the desire of Hannah Field from North America. I stepped down to see her at J. Stordy's; and in the few minutes we were together, before she took leave, she addressed herself to me in a very feeling manner. Although she was an entire stranger, she spoke so pointedly to my state of mind, and expressed the reward of faithfulness in such encouraging terms, that my feelings were in nowise able to resist the power which attended, but I was forced to acknowledge it as a nail fastened in a sure place.

Amongst some letters addressed by Elizabeth Yeardley to Susanna Harvey of Barnsley, is one in which mention is made of the visit of Hannah Field to Bentham; and, although the passage does not relate to the private interview described above, it is interesting as the reminiscence of a remarkable woman.

Bentham, 2 mo. 2, 1818.

We have been favored lately with a visit, unexpected but highly acceptable, from that great minister, Hannah Field, from America. She very much resembles Sarah Lamley; and when she began, it seemed as if one had been informing her of the state of the meeting. Her discourse began with the parable of the Ten Virgins, which was very beautiful but awful. Addressing herself again, she was very consolatory and affecting. She is tall and inclined to *embonpoint;* her age fifty-three.

In the Third Month of this year, the Monthly Meet-
4

ing from which he had recently removed, that of Pontefract, recorded its approval of his ministry. It is not
usual for meetings to do this in the case of one who
has gone to reside elsewhere. The practice at that
time was, in Yorkshire at least, in issuing a certificate
of removal for a Friend who had begun to exercise the
ministry and was still under probation, to notice the fact
of his preaching, without pronouncing a judgment upon
it. But when the usual document of removal was asked
for at the Monthly Meeting, on behalf of John Yeardley,
the meeting paused upon the words which noticed his
offerings in the ministry, and solemnly resolved then and
there to give him a full certificate as a minister in unity,
and to "recommend him as such to the Quarterly
Meeting." It happened that men and women Friends
were together, the latter remaining whilst Joseph Wood
laid a concern for some religious service before the joint
meeting.

John Yeardley remarks on this act of his late Monthly
Meeting :—

The concurrence of my friends with my small offerings
cannot but feel comfortable and encouraging to a poor timor-
ous creature like me; but the awful consideration of ranking
among the servants who speak in the Lord's name humbles
me to the dust. Surely those who are designed to minister
before the Lord in his holy temple ought to bear the inscription of holiness upon them. The means by which this
inscription is obtained is so painful to flesh and blood that
we are always ready to shrink from the operation. When we
have borne the furnace heated to a certain degree, we are
ready to fancy nothing but pure gold remains; until the
refining hand sees meet to administer fresh [trials], then we
are ready again to cry out, If it be thy will, let this cup
pass by.

In the Sixth Month he joined Joseph Wood and William Midgley of Rochdale, in visiting some neighboring meetings. Of Kendal, which was one, he says it appeared to him " as if a remarkable revival was taking place in those parts;" and he concludes his short account of the journey with an acknowledgment of the satisfaction he felt in having given up to this little service.

Joseph Wood in his diary relates the same visit more at large. We have extracted the account of that portion of it in which John Yeardley was engaged, and believe the reader will find it interesting in several respects.

1818. 6 *mo.* 10.—Reached my beloved friend John Yeardley's house, in Bentham, about half-past eight o'clock, where we took up our quarters, and where we were favored with a renewed feeling of that love which had many times nearly united our spirits together.

On the 11th we spent this day very comfortably with these long-beloved and truly valuable friends, and in the evening had a public meeting appointed for Friends and people of other societies in their meeting-house in Bentham, about a mile and a half from their house. We walked thither, it being very pleasant through the fields. The meeting began at half-past six, and held two hours and a quarter. A pretty many who usually attend meetings, and a great concourse of people of other societies, attended, so that the meeting-house, both above and below stairs, was well filled, and several were in the passage and in an adjoining room. A precious solemnity mercifully overshadowed us, whereby the minds of many were prepared to receive what the Lord was pleased instrumentally to communicate to the many different states; and O that they may individually profit thereby! for sure it was a time of favor unto many. I had a very long testimony to bear therein, first from Isaiah lviii. 1, 2. John Yeardley held a pretty long time next, from John ii. 4. I next, from 1 Cor. xiv. 19.

On the 12th we set out for Wray in Lancashire, five miles, John Yeardley being our guide, taking his wife and Ann Stordy along with him in a taxed cart. We had a very pleasant ride thither, down a beautiful valley, through which the river Wenning runs; had on our right hand a fine view of Hornby Castle, now in part gone to decay. Got to Wray about half-past ten, and went to the meeting, which began at eleven o'clock. Twenty-three persons attended, one of whom appeared to be of another society. I sat therein for a considerable time in a very low state, and feeling a concern to stand up, I gave up, although in great weakness: different states opened and were spoken to in the authority of the gospel; and I had a long testimony to bear from Luke xv. 8. John Yeardley had a pretty long time next, from Lam. iii. 26; afterwards I was concerned in prayer, and felt truly thankful for the renewed mark of divine favor, and secretly rejoiced that my lot was cast here.

On the 13th John Yeardley accompanied Joseph Wood to Kendal.

It was with difficulty, says J. W., we got into the town for the crowd of people; the Parliament being dissolved, and a new election of members about to take place; and there being an oppostion in this county; Henry Brougham, the favorite candidate of the people, against the Lonsdales. They were waiting his arrival in the town to canvass for votes. After tea I went to Thomas Wilson's; his house was nearly opposite the inn where Henry Brougham put up. When he arrived the populace took his horses from the carriage, and hurried him into the town, and to the inn, four flags flying and a band of music went before him. After he alighted he went into an upper room, and addressed the largest multitude of people that I ever saw collected, from the window, for about an hour, in a very impressive manner; and so great was the crowd in the street that many fainted. All was quiet, and, after he had done, they separated in a becoming manner.

On the 14th we attended their meetings in Kendal. The

forenoon meeting began at ten o'clock. It is large, and was
pretty open and satisfactory. I had a long testimony to bear
therein, first, from John xv. 14. John Yeardley had a pretty
long time next. He opened from these words: "O thou, the
God of Abraham, Isaac, and Jacob, manifest thyself that
thou yet reignest in Israel." I next, from Proverbs ix. 12.

After visiting several other meetings, Joseph Wood
came to Lancaster, where he was again met by John
Yeardley.

On the 21st we attended both their meetings in Lancaster.
The forenoon meeting began at ten o'clock. When we got
there we were agreeably surprised to find dear John Yeardley,
who had walked this morning fifteen miles to meet us. The
meeting was large of Friends, and it proved a time of renewed
visitation unto many who were afar off, and of encouragement
to those who were nigh. I had a very long testimony to
bear therein, from Matt. xxii. 12. John Yeardley had a
short but very acceptable time next, from Esther iv. 14. Afterwards I was concerned in prayer.

Elizabeth Yeardley speaks of this visit in one of her
letters:—

J. Y. went to Lancaster, though the day was unfavorable.
He trudged on foot to meet Joseph Wood, and got in good
time for the meeting, fifteen miles distant, and returned home
the same evening. J. W. was very much favored all the
time he was in those parts; he really appears endowed with
astonishing powers.

The same letter affords a glimpse of the social position which John and Elizabeth Yeardley occupied at
Bentham:—

We are very quiet, have kind neighbors, a very pleasant
habitation, and little society, plenty of books both of the
religious and amusing kind, and leisure to meditate on the

one thing needful, which is to fit us for that place to which
we are fast hastening :—

> ' For who the longest lease enjoy
> Have told us with a sigh,
> That to be born seems little more
> Than to begin to die.''

(13th of Seventh Month, 1818.)

John Yeardley, no less than his wife, found in
Bentham a seasonable retreat from the harassing cares
of the world. A memorandum made in the autumn of
this year shows that the doubts with which he was
perplexed on the subject of his removal from Barnsley,
were entirely dispelled, and that the change in his abode
and position had been the happy means of relieving him
from the load of anxiety which once seemed ready to
crush him.

1819. 9 *mo.* 15.—The tender, merciful Father who shelters
our heads in battle has covered mine when many things were
hot upon me. He has provided a retreat for me until the
fury of the oppressor be overpast. I have often wondered at
the cause which drove me from my former residence, but I
now begin to see pointedly the hand of Providence bringing
me to this place of quiet retreat. Should He who has brought
me thus far see it to be for my good to set me on the banks
of deliverance, may I have no desire to live for anything but
to sing his praise!

After being recognised by the Church as a minister,
he was again tried with a season of spiritual desertion;
and this phase in his religious history, with his reflections upon it, and the holy resolution and hope with
which he concludes, may be useful in strengthening the
faith of others under similar circumstances.

10 *mo.* 4.—O what a stripping time have I had since I
wrote last! My pen would fail to set forth the inward deser-

tion I have experienced for months past, so that my poor
mind is almost worn out with waiting and watching in the
absence of the Bridegroom of souls.  My enemy seems to
have set up his throne in me, and leads my wandering
thoughts captive at his pleasure.  I have no weapons of my
own to fight him with, and it seems as if Infinite Goodness
had refused me the grant of that armor which I have before
experienced the means of putting my adversary to flight.
For what end this may be I know not, but the suffering time
is hard to the natural part.  If I am left to perish, O may it
be in praying, trusting and believing in my Redeemer's love!
and if I am not suffered to behold again the brightness of his
glorious countenance here on earth, may I be favored with
it shining on me in heaven!

At the commencement of this year, 1819, apprehending himself required to pay a religious visit to the families of Friends in Barnsley, he consulted Joseph Wood
on the subject, who encouraged him "not to be afraid
to pursue" the path which had been opened before him.
In relation to this prospect of service, J. Y. has the following pertinent remarks on the ministry:—

2 mo. 19.—If I am suffered to go, may the humble spirit
of Jesus go with me, and put a word in my heart that may
prove as a sword in my hand, with which I may fight his
battles!  This is the only way in which his servants can
minister so as to reach the witness in the hearts of his children.  We might speak on subjects which might seem right
and fit in themselves, but it is as our hearts come to be acted
upon immediately by the Spirit of truth, the same principle
which prepares us to utter sound words, prepares also a coun-
terpart in the minds of others to receive them.  Thus it may
be said we become *one* in spirit and truly edified together in
the love of the Gospel.

In order to perform the visit, J. Y. had, in the good

order in use amongst Friends, to receive the concurrence of his Monthly Meeting.

3 *mo.* 10.—Was at the Monthly Meeting, where I mentioned to my friends my prospect of visiting Barnsley, and obtained their sympathetic concurrence, with a copy of a minute expressing their full unity and approbation.

My feelings on the occasion were very different from what I had anticipated. A divine solemnity appeared so to cover the minds of all present, that the enemy was trodden under foot, and not a fear was suffered to approach. What condescending goodness of a tender Father to his weak children!

Some interesting notice of this service, and of the journey which he made to perform it, is contained in his Diary.

13*th.*—The evening before I set off, I was earnestly engaged in supplicating for divine protection both inward and outward; and an assurance was given me that it should be granted, and in a manner so clear as I had no right to expect. These words were as if spoken distinctly in my outward ears: "A hair of thy head shall not be hurt." In the confidence of this promise I went forth, and found it mercifully made good; for though I was overturned in the mail on the road, a hair of my head was not hurt, and not so much as a fear was suffered to come near.

On the 18th, after visiting all the families, he attended the Week-day Meeting, where he had to review his labors, and to address the assembled Friends "nearly in these words:—In the course of my little proceedings among my friends in this place, I have sometimes been baptized for the dead, while at other times I have been made to rejoice in the resurrection of life: I hope this is a language my friends will understand." After this he preached to them on the case of Nicodemus,

saying that there may be a time when our Heavenly
Father, in his tender compassion for our infant state,
permits us to come to Jesus by night or in secret; yet
when he is pleased to say, " Arise, shine, for thy light is
come, and the glory of the Lord is risen upon thee,"
danger will betide us if we then flinch from an
open confession. Some time after he had finished, a
woman Friend rose and uttered a few words. She had
never before been able to overcome the force of her
natural fears.

In noticing this circumstance, J. Y. says he does so
because, before he went to Barnsley, he asked that if his
small services were acceptable, the Most High would
give him a sign, by owning his labors with his sensible
approbation, and making him an instrument to help
forward his work in the hearts of his children.

On another occasion, in allusion to a similar occurrence, he has the following reflections:—

" The Jews require a sign, and the Greeks seek after
wisdom ; but we preach Christ crucified." I am like the two
former, because I dare even to ask a sign and to seek after
wisdom ; but to be like the latter is what I covet most
sincerely—to preach Christ crucified, not only in words, but
in life and conversation. If I err in sometimes asking a sign,
I trust it will be forgiven, because it is done in the simplicity
of my heart, to know my Father's will, and we have examples
of this having been granted to the worthies in times of old.
—(12 mo. 8.)

In the Twelfth Month of 1819, John Yeardley
attended the Quarterly Meeting at York, and had some
religious service on the way. His account of this little
journey is preceded by some instructive reflections on
his own infirmities and lack of ready obedience.

9 *mo.* 15.—I feel exceedingly discouraged at my own obstinacy in not keeping more humble, watchful, and attentive to the inward monitor. I am sensible loss is sustained in a religious sense by giving way too much to an airy disposition.

12 *mo.* 12.—When I consider the many years which have elapsed since I first enlisted under the Lord's banner, I find cause deeply to reproach myself for want of a more early and implicit obedience to the *divine will;* the want of which, I fully believe, has been the means of plunging me into seas of trouble and years of perplexity. I fear the time lost will never be redeemed. O, should I ever have to warn others to beware of the rock on which I have split, surely it may be done through heartfelt experience indeed! And as the glorious light of the sun begins mercifully to verge from under the cloud, O, may I never, never forget the sacred covenant made in the days of my deep distress, that if the Lord would loosen my bonds, then would I serve him freely.

25*th.*—I went to Thornton to R. W.'s, and next day to Lothersdale Meeting, accompanied by D. W. and some other part of R. W.'s family. The forepart of that meeting was very trying, at which I did not wonder, if we might judge from a previous feeling; for ever since the prospect of this little visit presented to my view, I felt a load on my spirit which I could not by any means cast off. On entering the place, I thought, when our dear Lord sent forth his disciples, he commanded them to take neither purse nor scrip; and that if this state of poverty of spirit was any badge of discipleship, some of us might claim to wear it. The language of the weeping prophet came also before me—"O that my head were waters, and mine eyes a fountain of tears, that I might weep day and night for the slain of the daughter of my people." It was hard work for me, a poor stripling, to have to intimate such close things; but the conclusion was easier to the natural part, I having to address a few to whom the language seemed to go forth, of " Mary, the Master is come, and calleth for thee."

I went from thence to the Quarterly Meeting at York,

which was thinly attended. The meeting for worship seemed a cloudy season; however a little matter impressed my mind which I was thankful in being enabled to get rid of, though hard to flesh and blood, it being the first time my voice has been heard in this Quarterly Meeting in ministry. The meeting for business was long and tedious, being protracted four and a half days by an appeal. It was disagreeable in its nature, but was conducted in a way to afford information and instruction to the minute observer of men, manners and things.

1820.—Our first extract from this year's diary contains a short but beautiful reflection:—

2 *mo.* 18.—I am convinced it would be better for us to live more in the inward spirit of prayer; we should live in nearer union with the Father of love; receive more of his heavenly embraces; the heart would be prepared to know more of his holy will, and receive power to perform it.

When John Yeardley left Barnsley he commenced a correspondence with his brother Thomas, which lasted until the death of the latter. J. Y.'s letters have been preserved, and supply us with much that is valuable in his character and Christian experience. The following extract shows the power of sympathy which he possessed towards those with whom he was entirely intimate:—

4 mo. 24, 1820.

Thy affectionate letter I received with pleasure, though some parts of its contents penetrated the deepest recesses of my heart, and excited in me every tender sympathetic feeling of a brother and a friend.

I rejoice that thou hast found freedom to speak so candidly the undisguised language of thy heart; to me it seems like a voice from the dead, because I conceive it to be the voice of that awakened principle in thee which, as in many others, may have been held too long in captivity through the predomi-

nance of the surfeiting cares of the world. Whenever thou
inclinest to unbosom to me thou mayest do it with freedom
and in confidence, for, be assured, if thy complaints cannot
meet with relief, they will at least meet with a welcome
reception and a heartfelt condolence; for I could have no
claim to the least of the Christian virtues, if I were destitute
of a feeling regard for the sufferings of a friend, and especially a brother.

A few months afterwards he was again called upon
deeply to sympathise with his brother. The occasion
this time was the perplexity in matters of business in
which Thomas Yeardley was involved. He expressed
his feelings in a letter in which he not only gives the
soundest Christian counsel, but also shows how he
was himself indebted to the same maxims for the preservation of his honor and of his spiritual life and usefulness. The firm and practical manner in which the
subject is treated render his remarks of permanent
value.

Bentham, 8 mo. 7, 1820.

MY DEAR BROTHER,

Thy affectionate letter of the 24th I have received, and
need not tell thee how sensibly I am concerned for thy present situation.

I do hope thou wilt not lose sight of the object thou hast
now in view, to get relieved in some way from the excessive
load of business which presses upon thee, for we can none of
us carry fire in our bosoms too long without being burnt.
We shall not be justified in the sight of Him with whom we
have to do, if we do not endeavor to place ourselves in such
a situation as will best answer the end for which he has designed us. It would convict us of a very weak and erroneous
idea of a Supreme Being, to suppose that he could not or
would not prosper our endeavors with equal success in a
more restricted way of trade, when our motives are purely to

serve him faithfully. Surely, He who cares for the sparrows will not suffer *us* to fall to the ground without his notice.

Thou wilt be ready to say it is an easy matter to speak of these things on paper; but believe me, my dear brother, I know a little of what I say. There was a time when I was as extensively engaged in business, *according to my means,* as you are now. I have had large sums of acceptances to provide for, with nothing towards them but what was in the uncertainty of the drapers' hands. When I have set out on a journey I have had to take the distressing fear along with me, that if I failed of getting in almost every shilling that was due to me, I failed in paying my acceptances. Add to this, the painful prospect of losing my property until I could not pay my just debts, and then mention a situation which would place an honest mind in a greater degree of perplexity. O! had it not been for the preserving hand of my gracious Redeemer, I had never lifted up my head above the waters which were ready to overwhelm me. In the midst of all this I received a firm conviction, that if I wound up as speedily as circumstances would admit, I should measurably be safe; but if I suffered the impression to pass away disregarded, I might be hurled along with the stream and never more be able to recover myself. It seemed as if my eye was fixed on a star which shone quite on the other side of the [waters]; and I was thus enabled to wade through, without knowing what course to take when I got to the other side. I do not mention this as being in the whole applicable to thy case; but as a fellow Christian traveller towards the celestial city, I earnestly intreat thee, in the love of the gospel, never to consider thyself on a level, or at liberty to act in full scope, with the man of business, who thinks himself created to pursue the things of time without being responsible to his Creator for endeavoring to reach a situation in life which would enable him to prepare for eternity. Thou wilt not be long at a loss what to do if thou dost not overlook the secret motive in thy own breast. Do not grieve at losing a little of what thou hast; it will come again, if for the best, and may bring the double reward of peace. If thou attendest to that directing Hand which has hitherto preserved thee as a monument of thy Heavenly Father's mercy, thy victory is already sure, though thou mayst not know it. It is not for the best, consequently not permitted, that we should always see our way. Were this the case there would be no exercise of faith. The servant of the prophet was blind as to the power which preserved them, when he saw a host of the enemy encamped against them: he cried out, "Alas, my master, how shall we do!" But his master answered, "Fear not; for they that be with us are more than they that be with them;" and the prophet prayed that the young man might be made to see. And when his eyes were opened, what did he see? Why, he saw the mountain full of horses and chariots of fire round about them. The Lord's chosen people are continually encircled with these chariots of fire, otherwise it would not be possible to be so mercifully preserved from harm. Should it be insinuated to thee that thou art not of this chosen race, let me tell thee, we become children of the Most High as soon as he has raised in us a desire to serve him, and we become willing to abide under his protecting wing whatever changes may take place in our own feelings during the operation of his holy hand upon us.

Nothing is more important in the life of a Christian than the manner in which he turns to account the opportunities for serving his Lord which continually spring up before him.

6 *mo.* 23.—Going last evening to Wenington, to repeat my French lesson, my friends there asked me to call with them on a sick person; feeling quite free to do so, I went with them. On sitting quietly by the bedside, a little matter came before me, which was communicated from these words: "Affliction cometh not forth of the dust."

On my return home, I could not but reflect on the necessity of having our bow strung, and being always alive to the interest of souls, and endeavoring to imitate the example of our great Master, whose whole life was employed in continually going up and down doing good.

# CHAPTER III.

In 1822 John Yeardley went to reside in Germany. As his residence abroad constituted one of the most remarkable turns in his life, and exercised a powerful influence on the rest of his career, we shall develop as fully as we are able the motives by which he was induced to leave his native country. By means of his Diary we can trace the early appearance and growth, if not the origin, of the strong Christian sympathy he ever afterwards manifested with seeking souls in the nations on the continent of Europe, and especially amongst the German people.

The first hint concerning his desire to go abroad is contained in the account of a dream, under date of the 2nd of the Ninth Month, 1818, regarding which he felt much disappointed, because he could not recollect the names of the places in Germany about which he had in his dream been interested. The next year (the 19th of the Fifth Month) he had a second dream on the same subject, in which he supposed his friend Joseph Wood was about to go on a religious mission to the Continent, and he brought out his Atlas to find the places for him. On being asked if he meant to accompany him, he said he "was not prepared to answer at present." In the relation of a third dream, which he had the next year (the 25th of the Eighth Month, 1820), the locality to which his mind was attracted is first indicated.

(55)

"Pyrmont and Minden," he says, "rested very closely with me, and to them I felt bound."

It might not have been worth while to have made allusion to these dreams, which ought perhaps to be regarded rather as the continuation or echo of his waking thoughts than as their original source, but for the deep importance which John Yeardley himself attached to them. He considered that by them was first made known to him the divine will respecting his future course; and that his longing desire to recover the name of the forgotten locality of the first dream was answered in the last. It can admit of little doubt that the same conviction of their more than common significance, which led him to cherish as sacred the remembrance of these night-visions, helped to form and sustain his resolution in carrying out the project with which he connected them.

Just before the occurrence of the last dream, his faith in the heavenly source of the invitation which, whether waking or sleeping, he had received, to go over and help his Christian brethren on the Continent, was confirmed by a prophetic message from John Kirkham, who, in the course of his religious travels, again visited Yorkshire.

8 *mo.*—Our dear friend, John Kirkham, from Earl's Colne, Essex, slept at our house on Second-day, the 7th, and had a meeting with our few on Third-day. How wonderfully was he enlarged; and I could not but admire how he was favored to speak to the states of some present. I could set my seal to every word he uttered, and say, This is the very truth. Before he left us he had a select opportunity in our family, and said a great deal about being faithful to our own vision. He seemed to answer a question in my mind as fully as I had any right to expect; for I had almost asked it as a sign that

if I were not deceived in my vision he should be led to speak
on the subject. He said emphatically, " We cannot be faithful to the vision of another man, we do not know it except it
be revealed to us; but we must be FAITHFUL TO OUR OWN
VISION."

On the 9th I accompanied him to the Monthly Meeting at
Settle, and I once more desired that, if my feeling in former
times had not deceived me, this servant of the Lord might be
led to speak on the same subject; and indeed he scarcely said
anything else but what had the strongest bearing on my request. What encouraging favors do I receive at the hands
of so good a Master!

A few months later we find the charge to foreign
labor renewed, with an intimation of the wide field in
which he would have to work ; an intimation which was
amply verified in his future travels.

11 *mo.* 26.—At meeting something involuntarily entered
my mind like this, I will make thee a preacher of righteousness to many nations. I felt not only a desire to be made
willing to be sent, but also a desire to be prepared.

A few days after noting this impression he thus com-
munes with himself on this topic, which now began to
absorb the greater portion of his thoughts.

12 *mo.* 3, *First-day.*—As I walked alone to the meeting
this morning, I thought within myself, What can be the
cause that I so often feel drawn in spirit towards the land of
——? My thoughts have now for a long time past so frequently and so involuntarily revolved on the subject that I
begin to be very jealous over them, and to query whether it is
the workings of self-imaginations. If this is the case, O that
I may be relieved from them. But however unaccountable
my feelings may be, a secret love towards some unknown
souls in —— is so strong at times, that if I had wings I
should for my own inward peace visit them in body as I now

5

do in spirit. It seems as if my spiritual eye saw in those
parts what we may call a seed (the seed of the kingdom sown
in the heart) that wants to take root downwards and spring
upwards, but which is almost choked with the tares of superstition. Are there not scattered up and down in ——, many
whose souls are verging from under the clouds of thick darkness, and from under the bonds of idolatrous superstition,
towards that glorious liberty which is brought to light by the
gospel? Something in me secretly craves an opportunity to
tell those precious creatures that the time appears near at
hand when this glorious gospel light will shine so clearly that
they will discover a Saviour in the secret of their own hearts;
and it is to him (I could tell them) that they must look for
the perfection of their salvation. Should there be anything
of the right savor in my heart concerning this matter, I
humbly hope that in due time it will be brought to maturity,
and my way made plain and easy—*plain*, so that I cannot
possibly mistake the pointing hand of divine wisdom, and
*easy*, so that when I hear the command I may be enabled to
obey.

A very instructive time at meeting. The subject above-
mentioned glanced in my view, and with it the never-failing
objection, If I am at all "apt to teach," can it or will it be
required of me to leave those here and others in this land
who have need of instruction? This objection was immediately answered in a way which I never before experienced.
They have, besides many teachers, the unerring light of Jesus
in their own hearts unto which they know they ought alone
to look for direction. And if they neglect or overlook the
means in themselves, it is not in my power, a poor instrument,
to do them any good. So it may be said of others to whom
I may apprehend myself called. It all revolves on this single
and important point,—What is the *divine will* concerning me?
If I can only know this and am enabled to do it, all will
be well.

In the Autumn he attended Liverpool Quarterly
Meeting, an occasion which was one of the most memo-

rable seasons of his life.  His narrative of it is very characteristic:—

9 *mo.* 19. — My dear wife and I left home to attend Liverpool Quarterly Meeting.  Through mercy we arrived safe there, but I, as usual when from home, felt very low and poor in spirit, and was ready to call in question my coming to the place.  For although I received, as I thought, a proper signal before I left home, yet one or two circumstances occurred to discourage me from going, which I pressed through with some firmness ; however, such was my uneasiness the first night in Liverpool, that I was very desirous, if my being there was in right wisdom, something might turn up to convince me that I had not done wrong in leaving home.  And blessed be the name of Jesus, I had not been long in the first meeting (their Monthly Meeting the day before the Quarterly,) before I was perfectly satisfied. There were present Willett Hicks and Huldah Sears from America, and Mary Watson from Ireland.  In the early part of the meeting my mind was engaged in meditating on— "God will enlarge Japhet and dwell in the tents of Shem," and so it proved.  The silence was broken by W. Hicks with these words: "Great men are not always wise, neither do the ancients understand wisdom."  Others present were much favored, and the meeting ended in heavenly harmony.

After it was over I found to my surprise and joy, my brother and sister from Barnsley, whom I had expected to come to Bentham to accompany us to Liverpool, and their not coming to Bentham first was one of the causes which had discouraged me in leaving home; for I once had concluded, in my wavering, to leave my going for their determination, thinking if they came it would be the means of getting me off, if not, I should give it up ; but it so fell out that they took the nearest way to meet us there, without writing us word, and it would have been a great disappointment had I not been there.  I should not have written so much about a seeming trifle but to show the necessity of firmness in doing what is pointed out, unless some reasonable cause prevents.

Now to the opening of the Quarterly Meeting for worship, which was like the day of Pentecost, when the place was filled with a rushing mighty wind from heaven. The first stream of ministry flowed again through W. H., who appeared from these words: "In the last day, that great day of the feast, Jesus stood and cried, saying, If any man thirst, let him come unto me and drink." It was indeed applicable; for all seemed athirst, and were invited and admitted to drink of the waters of life freely; those who were afar off drew nigh, and those who were near were enabled to acknowledge the might of Him who had called them to his footstool, and crowned them with his presence. Huldah Sears and Mary Watson were also much favored in testimony. What opened on my mind to express was this: "God speaketh once, yea, twice; yet man perceiveth it not." I thought we were bound to acknowledge that our God still reigned in Israel, and was condescending to speak to his people. Immediately afterwards M. R. appeared a long time in supplication, and then H. S. both very powerfully; so that goodness seemed to rise higher and higher, until we swam in divine life. This blessed, heavenly meeting will be remembered by some to the latest period of time.

After this event John Yeardley speaks of being favored with more enlargement of love towards the members of his small meeting; and also of having, when attending a public meeting at Wray with Joseph Wood, to kneel down in prayer for the congregation.

10 *mo.* 20.—To my humbling admiration, he writes, I had in the conclusion to kneel down and call on the name of the holy and high God of the whole earth, that he would be pleased to continue the blessing which he had already condescended to pour down on our heads. This is a most awful act of worship: I trust the intimation to it was attended with proper weightiness of spirit.

This meeting was a remarkable season, and is thus described in Joseph Wood's journal:—

*Bentham*, 10 *mo.* 20.—We [J. W. and James Harrison] set out for Wray, our beloved friend John Yeardley being our guide. We called by the way at Thomas Barrow's, of Wenington Hall, and drank tea; then proceeded to Wray. There were but few Friends here, but they have a very large ancient meeting-house, and my concern being principally towards the inhabitants, and proper information thereof being given, abundance attended; the meeting-house both above and below stairs was pretty well filled; and their behavior was deserving of commendation. The Lord's presence eminently crowned the assembly, and the truths of the gospel were largely and livingly declared amongst them, and it was a time of extraordinary favor to many. I had first a long testimony to bear therein, from Luke iv. 41. A pretty long time of silence then ensued, and great was the solemnity which appeared to cover the assembly. After which John Yeardley stood up and said, Some were ready to say there was no worship without words, but from the precious solemnity which he believed had covered many minds since the former communication, he was ready to conclude many were feelingly convinced to the contrary. He was then pretty largely led forth in opening the advantage of silently waiting upon God. I a pretty long time next, from Isaiah liv. 11, 13. James Harrison next, from Matt. xiii. 44. John Yeardley was next concerned in prayer. The meeting held about two hours and a half.

*21st.*—About the middle of the day my companion (J. H.) called upon me, and betwixt twelve and one o'clock we left here for Lancaster, Thomas Barrow being our guide, and his wife, Charlotte Russell, and Emma Hodgson, accompanying us. Emma Hodgson is the daughter of a clergyman of Rochdale: she had been some time on a visit at Thomas Barrow's and went with the family to the meeting at Bentham when we were there, and was much reached and tendered therein; and attending the meeting at Wray last evening she de-

clared after her return that she was fully convinced of the
truth.

Returning to John Yeardley's diary for this year, we
find some passages from which profitable instruction
may be gathered.

11 *mo.* 8 was the Monthly Meeting at Settle; my dear love
and I both attended. To me it was a poor low season; if
there were any good, I was too much like the heath in the
desert,—I knew not when it came. In addition to this, it felt
as if I had to mourn over the barren state of some others. O,
how I dread the state of a lukewarm Quaker! May I ever be
preserved from this sorrowful state of a lukewarm Quaker!
I believe it is often the means of bringing a damp over our
solemn assemblies.

12 *mo.* 7.—*Query.* What is the most likely means for me to
adopt to approach nearer to holiness? *Answer.* To spend
more time in retirement silently to wait upon God. The more
conversant I am with him, the more I shall know of his will
and receive power to do the same. To do the will of the
Almighty is the way to perfect holiness. The nearer acquaintance we cultivate with him, the stronger will become the ties
of his affection. The more devoted we are to him, the more
confidence will he repose in us.

Catching then a glimpse of the glorious calling of
the Gospel minister, he breaks forth in the following
strain:—

If I am ambitious in anything on earth, it is to be eminently useful in His cause. I can say with the wise man, I
ask neither riches nor honor, except the honor which cometh
from doing the will of God; but I do ask for "an understanding heart." I trust I can say in the deepest sincerity that
I could renounce, if they were in my power, the riches and
honor of ten thousand earthly worlds in purchase of a double
portion of that holy unction which rested on Elisha's spirit.

These are bold sayings, but my Saviour tells me that as there is no limitation to his goodness to grant, so there is no limitation in asking of him for the gift of his Holy Spirit. But then what manner of man ought this to be on whom shall be conferred such great honor! Surely it must be left to Himself to prepare the vessel before he pours in the oil.

We have already made an extract from the diary of the 3rd of the Twelfth Month in connection with John Yeardley's call to visit Germany. The same diary supplies us with the description of a spiritual opening for the benefit of others with which he was favored in the same meeting.

In my minute for First-day last I mentioned its being an instructive meeting to me. Towards the conclusion a simile of this kind arose and spread before my view: As wax when melted by the fire or the candle is then only capable of receiving the impression of the stamp put upon it, so also are our minds only capable of receiving impressions of divine good when our spirits are melted and contrited before the Lord. As these seasons are not at our command, it appeared to me to be of the highest importance for us to endeavor to preserve and improve them as the best means of testifying our gratitude to the great Donor. The impression which the above contemplation made on my spirit proved like a morsel of bread to my soul, which I found I could not conceal, though I struggled hard to eat it alone, it seeming so insignificant to hand to others; but at length I gave up, and felt it to be a time wherein some among the few present were melted as wax before the fire, and had a portion of divine goodness afresh imprinted on their minds; and my spirit craved that they might not prove as "the morning cloud and as the early dew that goeth away."

On the 7th of the Twelfth Month Elizabeth Yeardley was suddenly prostrated by an alarming attack of illness,

from which, however, she soon rallied, though she never
entirely regained her previous state of health.   Possibly
her husband alludes to this afflictive occurrence in the
following memorandum:—

12 *mo.* 10.—How varied is our passing along in this vale
of tears!   First-day last was a day of brightness, and this
day has been one of comparative death and darkness.   I
have been made to know something of the saying recorded
by the prophet,—"Who is among you that feareth the
Lord," &c., "that walketh in darkness and hath no light."
This has appeared to be my portion this day, and I find it
hard work to "trust in the name of the Lord and stay upon
my God."

Some further remarks in his diary for this day turn
upon the subject of the ministry, and the passage he
quotes shows how deep and heart-searching is the work
of preparation for an enlarged and effectual gospel ministry, whatever be the denomination among men to which
the preacher belongs:—

In the course of reading the life of Mary Fletcher I find
much deep instruction and encouragement.   Many of her remarks have proved like a goad to spur me on in the way of
holiness.   An extract made by her from Dr. Doddridge's life
aptly speaks the language of my heart, when in my silent
breathing to the Almighty I am led to crave an enlargement
of my gift in spiritual things:—
   "There must be an enlargement of soul before any remarkable success on others; and a great diligence in prayer and
strict watchfulness over my own soul previous to any remarkable and habitual enlargement in my ministry; and
deep humiliation must precede both."

1821.—The first entry in the diary of this year turns
upon the ever-present subject of his going abroad, and

is penned under feelings of the deepest solemnity. It is followed the next day by another on the great duty of self-examination.

1 *mo.* 2. This day I have felt singularly impressed with a desire to be more devoted to my Maker. I believe it is his will that I should be more given up to serve him; and if spared with life and strength, my few remaining days must be spent in his cause. A presentiment of this kind has for some time past prevailed with me; and from the calm, awful, and weighty manner in which it is at times brought over my spirit, I am induced to think it cannot be the mere phantom of the imagination. The prospect of a temporary residence on the ——— seems rather to increase than otherwise. How it may terminate, or the time when to move, is yet uncertain to me. O, how the prospect humbles me! I trust I can, in some degree say, with the good old patriarch, that his God shall be my God, and if He will only give me bread to eat and raiment to put on, I desire to serve him.

1 *mo.* 3.—This day I am thirty-five years old. Whether I may be spared as many more, or whether I may only survive as many months, weeks, days or hours, as I have now lived years, is altogether in the breast of Him who has hitherto preserved me as a monument of his mercy. How awful the consideration! To think that we may be called to give an account at any hour of the day, and not frequently to examine the state of affairs between us and our God, is complete infatuation. Strange as it may seem, as it regards myself I stand condemned. I am sensible sufficient attention is not paid to the important work of self-examination. O that this fresh year may produce fresh vigilance!

In the Second Month, Ann Jones, accompanied by her husband and Isabel Richardson, visited Bentham on a religious mission. Ann Jones had much service, both in public and private. What she had to declare to John Yeardley in particular was very remarkable, and reminded him of the discourse of Sarah Lamley in 1814. He says:—

> She said a good deal which so struck home to my feelings, that I have not been so deeply reached in the same manner since dear Sarah Lamley visited families at Barnsley. (*Letter to his brother.*)

In the Third Month he found it to be his duty to attend some meetings of Friends in going and returning from the Quarterly Meeting at Leeds. In his diary of the 14th of the Third Month he speaks of making the necessary application to the Monthly Meeting for its sanction, and, in that and some succeeding entries, records his feelings on the occasion, and the help which he received by the way.

> This was new work to me; how I was humbled before I could be made willing to mention my concern to my friends! which was done in such a faltering manner that I believe many sympathized with me. When I had received the meeting's approbation, I was thoughtful how I should get most conveniently on my way. After our meeting I received a letter from dear S. S., saying that he had felt a prayer raised in his heart, that I might be helped in my undertaking by Him from whom best help comes, and that he was most easy to propose accompanying me on my way in his gig. A very agreeable companion he proved to be, and for this little act of dedication he shall not lose his reward.
>
> I left home on First day, the 25th, for Newton, over the Fells. There fell much rain the day before, which swelled the waters so that my wife and I became very thoughtful how I should get over the river to Newton, over which there is no bridge. I thought that should I be favored to get over safe and dry I would take it as a sign for good in the journey; and so it was in mercy granted; for when I came to the water-side, I met a man on horseback who let me ride his horse over. This was in a wild part of the country, with

not a house near. Simple as this may appear to some, I could not but acknowledge in it a providence for which I was thankful.

At Newton, where I expected to meet only three or four, more assembled than the larger end of the house would hold. I was met by dear D. W. from Stockton; I could not but think we looked like two poor striplings before a great army. I should have sunk under my fears, had I not been enabled to get down to that Power which can bear up above the fear of man.

In the afternoon I went to Thornton, and sat down with the family. This was a precious season, and it felt doubly so from our having been on the barren mountains, both literally and spiritually.

I went next morning, accompanied by D. W., to Lothersdale. This was also a good meeting: I had reason to believe the God whom I was endeavoring to serve had answered my prayer in sending his angel before to prepare the way; I seemed almost borne off my feet by the power of Divine love.

We dined at S. S.'s; and after dinner I could not quit the room without expressing what I felt towards him, which melted us all into tears. S. S. joined me, and we went to Skipton to be at the meeting at five o'clock. Before we came there I felt such a sense of poverty that it seemed as if my spiritual life was going to be taken from me; and even when I got to meeting, the same feeling remained, which introduced my spirit into a state of suffering not easily to be conceived. On our sitting down I felt there was something on the mind of S. S., and I feared lest, by suffering the reasoner to prevail, he should be unfaithful; but he expressed a few words which seemed as the key to the treasury.

I went that evening to Addingham, and had a meeting next morning, where I sensibly found a little strength: we seemed to sit under our own vine and fig-tree, where none could make us afraid. We lodged and dined at our kind friend J. Smith's, in whose family I had something given to me to minister.

From Addingham they went to the Quarterly Meeting at Leeds, where John Yeardley received intelligence of the sudden decease of his beloved friend Joseph Wood. J. W. had been engaged in testimony and supplication in the meeting at Highflatts on First-day morning, and was taken unwell during the evening, and died in a few hours. After the Quarterly Meeting John Yeardley went to attend the interment, and on his way had a meeting with the Friends at Barnsley.

It was, he says, a favored time, and we were humbled and instructed together. We went to Highflatts to tea; when I got to the place where the remains of my dear friend were laid, I stood silently by the coffin in tears, saying in spirit, If it be thy mantle I am designed to wear, may I receive it with humility, reverence and fear! This feeling awfully impressed my mind, because my dear friend had said more than once to me, If I have any place in the body, I bequeath it to thee. The meeting was very large and was a precious season; the occasion on which we were met seemed to give wings to our spirits to fly upwards.

This spring Elizabeth Yeardley's disorder began to assume a serious form. A short memorandum from her hand discloses in a touching manner her state, both physical and spiritual.

3 mo. 29.—" Regard not distant events: this uneasiness about the future is in opposition to the grace received." This sentence from my old favorite, Fenelon, was much blest to my spirit this evening, when I had foolishly been thinking about future sufferings. O, sufficient for the day is the evil thereof. Perhaps a few rolling suns may, through the merits and mercies of my Lord, see this poor worm translated to his Paradise.

The first direct allusion to anxiety on her account

which appears in her husband's diary bears date the 5th of the Fifth Month. Her debilitated state seems to have been the cause of their deferring to a future day their contemplated removal to Germany, which was otherwise to have taken place about this time.

In the summer of this year he was himself laid for some weeks upon a bed of sickness, with a complaint of the stomach. He viewed this time of suffering as profitable in assisting his resolution to undertake the religious mission to which his mind was still continually directed. In a letter to Thomas Yeardley, of the 1st of the Ninth Month, he says, "Such is my stubborn will that I am not to be effectually pleaded with, until I am brought down into the valley of Jehoshaphat, or judgment." His wife, who was too ill to leave her chamber, has a memorandum respecting her husband's illness, under date of the 29th of the Eighth Month. It seems to have been the last which her pen ever traced.

Since I wrote, my dear husband has had an awful attack; but the Lord has again been merciful in restoring him to ease once more. Yesterday (may the Lord enable us to keep covenant) we laid our *Isaac* on the altar. O, to be wholly our kind, our Heavenly Master's, who cares to provide for us, for soul and body; who takes nothing from us but what he knows would harm us, and gives us a hundred-fold of that which is good in lieu.

Prior to this time John Yeardley had not confided to his brother the thought which so long had occupied his mind. In the letter just referred to he speaks of it as "an important concern which had long been the companion of his secret thoughts by day and his visions by night," and says:—

It now seems to be approaching so near a state of maturity that I feel freedom to communicate it to thee.

For about three years past I have had an increasing apprehension that it would be required of me to take up a *temporary residence* among those who profess with Friends on the other side of the water, particularly with the few in the neighborhood of Minden and Pyrmont, and probably at some time with those in the South of France. But my visit is likely to be paid in a way different from any that have been made before. I have never seen that the nature of my concern would require any document from the Quarterly or Yearly Meetings; neither do I think it would answer my present views; because the secret language of my heart has been for many months past, "Go dwell among them, go dwell with them."

I should be in want of some employment, and the first thing that presents to my view is to offer my services to a few of my friends in the yarn and flax trade; articles which are largely imported into Yorkshire, and which seem to be the natural production of the country, within the circle where I should be likely to reside.

His brother's answer to this letter was most consoling and encouraging: in reference to it he says, it seemed with him as it was with Peter in the prison, when the angel smote him and the irons fell off.

And O, he adds, that I may be willing, now that a little light begins to shine, to gird myself, bind on my sandals, cast my garment about me, and follow my Lord, thinking no hardship too much to endure for so good a Master. (*Diary,* 9 *mo.* 21.)

Although in reality not far from her end, his wife's state had not as yet excited immediate alarm. On the 23rd of the Ninth Month J. Y. writes:—

My precious E. Y. is yet so weak that there is a probability of its being an obstacle in the way of our removal; but there is this consolation,—if the work be of the Lord he will not frustrate his own design; if it be not his doing we must submit to have the whole overturned.

In a few days he became aware of her critical state.

9 mo. 29.—The indisposition of my dear wife has taken such an alarming turn that I yesterday began to have serious apprehensions as to the issue. I have watched with her night and day, and my prayers have been unceasing for her restoration, I trust not without a due reverence to the divine will. But I did not feel as though nature could give her up until yesterday, when as I stood retired by the bed-side of my dear lamb, endeavoring to feel after resignation, I gave her up as fully as human nature, through divine aid, was capable of. Then it sprang in my heart, Where is the man that can offer up an Isaac? He shall go for me, and I will send him. There seems a spark of hope that even now, when the knife is lifted up, the voice may yet be heard,—" Lay not thy hand upon the lad, for now I know that thou fearest me."

My precious dear has been to me in my late exercise a never-failing instrument of strength, comfort, and encouragement: in general her faith has been much stronger than my own. Should it please Heaven to restore her, O that there may be an increased desire that it may be for no other cause, but that her heart, her hands and her feet, may unite with mine in sounding forth our Redeemer's praise, if required, even to the ends of the earth.

The following entries record the last hours of the dying Christian wife, and the feelings of her bereaved husband:—

10 mo. 25.—Last night we expected my dear lamb would have sunk away. How the awful event is to terminate is known only to Him on whose bosom I trust she has always rested; for in no other place could she be preserved in the state of peace which she appears to possess.

29*th.*—A most awful morning; my dear lamb is no more! She sweetly fell asleep in the bosom of her Saviour, at one o'clock this morning. The closing scene was perfect ease and peace. From the first of her illness she seemed aware how it would terminate, and was perfectly resigned. During our being at Bentham she has often said it was a place provided by Providence to afford her that religious retirement she had long desired, and which she took the most scrupulous care to improve. When in health she would tell me of late that perhaps she might be taken away in order to set me more fully at liberty to do the Lord's work.

11 *mo.* 18.—This day two weeks was the solemn ceremony of committing to the silent dust the remains of my very precious and dearly beloved Elizabeth. I had dreaded the day very much; but through prayer, mixed with a degree of faith, which was mercifully granted, I was wonderfully supported. In the meeting I felt the divine influence so near, and so to prevail over my spirit, that I was constrained publicly to thank the Father of mercies for his goodness.

This day I visited, perhaps for the last time, the place which encloses the cold relics of one so dearly beloved; and as I stood weeping over the grave, it sprang in my heart, She is not here but (she) is risen. What an unspeakable consolation to be enabled to leave the dust behind, and hold sweet communion and converse with the spirit. Ever since her departure it feels as though her spirit had never left me, but was hovering and fluttering around me to administer comfort on every afflicting occasion; and O, saith my spirit, that this precious feeling may remain with me for ever.

12 *mo.* 20.—I feel to lament the loss of my dear lamb more than ever, at least so far as I dare. No one but myself knows the comfort which the late awful event has deprived me of; but I no sooner remember the hand which administered it than all complaining is hushed into silence, and I am made to rejoice that she is so safely deposited where trouble cannot reach.

From this moment John Yeardley felt himself quite

free to pursue the path of duty which had been opened before him, viz., to go and reside in Germany.

In the Eleventh Month he left Bentham to sojourn awhile with his brother, and on the 9th of the First Month, 1822, he received a certificate of removal from Settle Monthly Meeting, addressed to the Friends of Pyrmont and Minden, which certified that he was a member of the Society of Friends, and a minister well approved by the church.

Before we pursue further the sequence of events, two passages from the diary may be here transcribed, which could not have been inserted in the order of time without interrupting the narrative. The first of these conveys a lesson of practical wisdom, and exhibits the method by which the writer was able to succeed and to excel in what he undertook. It is the true comprehension and resolute acting upon maxims such as these, which makes so much of the difference between one man and another.

1821. 7 *mo.* 2.—No man can excel in everything; therefore it is highly important for each mind to consider attentively for what it is calculated, and what end it is designed to answer by him who created it. As secular affairs are often more expedited by a judicious arrangement, than by hard doing indiscriminately at the mass; so will undertakings of superior importance be more advantageously attained by keeping a single eye, and looking for best direction to make a proper selection of what ought to be done and what ought not to be done. I was long too much wavering on this head, to my great loss; but I now hope it is become a settled point, and I have clearly seen for what service I am designed in the church militant here on earth; therefore, through the assistance of divine grace, I hope to pursue nothing but in subordination to this main design. For a little mind to aim at great things would be to thwart the whole; but to

6

endeavor to be faithful in small things, seems to be the way to attain the end.

From the other entry we shall extract only a few words, but they are words fraught with deep instruction :—

9 *mo.* 7.—" Without holiness no man shall see the Lord." Without purity of heart we cannot see the pointing of the Divine Finger.

On the 18th of the Second Month, John Yeardley attended Pontefract Monthly Meeting, held at Wakefield.

It was, he says, a precious season; I felt my friends very near to me in spirit, and expressed to them in tenderness and love what lay on my mind; and in the conclusion the power and goodness of the Most High were so awfully felt that I could not forbear kneeling down to offer him thanks, and to supplicate that he would be pleased once more to bind up the breaches in the walls of our Zion, and grant that when we were separated one from another we might never be separated from his presence.

I now begin, he continues, to feel very anxious to set forward for my destination on the other side of the water. What an awful situation mine appears to be! O that faith and patience may be granted equal to the occasion!

1822. 2 *mo.* 26.—I never read in my dear lamb's diary but it feels to season my heart with good. It is as though her writings were impregnated with a degree of sincerity and resignation which were so eminently the characteristics of her innocent spirit. O, I repeat it, that my precious Saviour may be pleased to appoint her angel spirit to be my guardian through life, until I shall be joined with her in heaven and we both unite in singing his praise.

About this time his brother, Thomas Yeardley, began to exercise the ministerial office.

3 *mo.* 3.—Attended Woodhouse Meeting, which was to me a very trying one. My brother Thomas spoke the feeling of my heart in something like these words:—" They come unto thee as the people cometh, and they sit before thee as my people, and they hear thy words, but they will not do them."

3 *mo.* 18.—This day was held the Monthly Meeting at Barnsley. The Testimony concerning our much-esteemed friend Joseph Wood was read and signed by the meetings at large. When I consider the legacy, so to speak, which this dear friend used to say he should bequeath to me, this language seems to prevail in my heart:—"Moses my servant is dead; now therefore arise. As I was with Moses, so I will be with thee; I will not fail thee, nor forsake thee."—Joshua i. 2, 5. This is an awful consideration; but why should any despair? May not the faithful mind say, "This God is our God; he will be our guide, even unto death." I desire most sincerely to be kept in humility, whatever the probations may be which are necessary to fit me for the design of Him who hath given me life, breath and being.

On the 2d of the Fourth Month he quitted Barnsley, accompanied by his brother Thomas.

I think it a favor indeed, he says, to be relieved from a doubting mind as to whether I should go or stay; for I can truly say that, let the result prove what it may, I go with an undivided heart.

Elizabeth Dell had a meeting at Pontefract this day, where I met her; it was a very satisfactory meeting, and it was pleasant to meet with several Friends here whom I did not expect to have seen again. The parting opportunity with E. D. has left a savor on my mind which I hope will not soon be forgotten.

Before he left England he opened negotiations with several mercantile houses, who gave him orders for linen yarn from Germany. At Hull he writes:

4 *mo.* 12.—My detention here, waiting for a fair wind

to Hamburg, has not been unpleasant; my friends are exceedingly kind, but my feelings in a religious sense have been rather depressing.

His heart was full of serious thoughts in anticipation of the voyage, which was then more formidable than it is now; but the joyful hope of a glorious immortality, if death should be suffered to overtake him, bore him up above his fears.

14th.—May I be preserved in a holy reliance on the Arm of strong Power for help. "O Lord God, who is a strong Lord like unto Thee, or to thy faithfulness round about Thee? Thou rulest the raging of the sea: when the waves thereof arise, Thou stillest them." O may it please him to carry me in his bosom, and protect me from the dangers of the sea. But should it please him to permit that I go down to the bottom, may I be fully resigned in humble confidence that I shall again arise to shine brighter with him in everlasting glory. Amen.

We shall conclude this chapter with a few extracts from Elizabeth Yeardley's letters, which well depict her character and experience; and with a copy of the weighty and pertinent testimony regarding Joseph Wood which was issued by Pontefract Monthly Meeting.

---

7 mo. 13, 1818.—The broad way seems more and more crowded, while the road to Zion is thinly scattered with poor wayworn travellers; each, or nearly so, of the former living as if there were to be no hereafter, and earth was to be their eternal home. I have thought that as our Blessed Redeemer's arms were extended wide on the cross to embrace perishing sinners, so do these short-sighted mortals extend their arms and their wishes in grasping unsubstantial vanities, and that craving one of *Mammon*, the most fascinating of all, as it increases with age.

9 *mo.* 24, 1819.—I hope by what I have felt of the keen arrow of adversity piercing the heart, it will teach me, when I see it wounding any of my fellow-mortals, to endeavor to soothe, if I have nothing else in my power towards healing the wound. Let thee and me be determined, in the name of the holy Jesus, to follow him and not look on others. He is leading us into the pure green, ever green, pasture of humiliation, where the sheep of his pasture love to lie. I own the road is not very pleasant; the descent is rugged, and many times the poor traveller is ashamed of being seen hobbling down by his former acquaintance; but when once within the sacred enclosure, the sweet air that breathes humility hushes all stormy passions to rest. I read and read again of all those holy folks being divested of self, and anxiously do I desire to be so too, but by the marks they lay down I am very far from that attainment. However, He who said, Let there be light, and there was light, can add this to the rest of his inestimable blessings showered on my unworthy head.

4 *mo.* 14, 1820.—We are sometimes led to expect pity from people where we think we have a sort of claim, and here we often feel disappointed. Persons at ease cannot feel for the sensations of pain in others, any more than prosperity can feel the seasons of adversity. Couldst thou have a look into the houses and bosoms of the inmates of most in B. or other places, thou wouldst find a something sorrowful, a burden the possessor would be glad to be quit of. Let us, then, go forward with hope, and endeavor to be truly thankful for the many mercies showered on our heads, who have not rendered . as we ought that gratitude so greatly His due. O look at the bulk of the population in England, whose children are looking up to them for a meal, and they have it not for them; and then let the tear of thankfulness fall. To be thankful is to feel a spark of heavenly flame; to be thankful is to increase the blessing already poured forth. O that I possessed more of this blessed spirit; for truly it is angelic!

*A Testimony of Pontefract Monthly Meeting concerning*
JOSEPH WOOD, *deceased.*

This our esteemed friend was born at Newhouse, near
Highflatts, within the compass of this Monthly Meeting, on
the 26th of the Fourth Month, 1750.  His parents, Samuel
and Susanna Wood, members of our Society, were concerned
for the best interest of their children.  In his youth he gave
way to some of the vanities incident to that period of life,
but when approaching manhood he was happily brought under
the restraining power of Truth, and often humbled in deep
inward exercise.  Once being in the fields in the night season,
he exclaimed, Lord what shall I do, or whither shall I go?
The answer in the secret of his own heart was as intelligible
as if spoken to his outward ear,—Whither wilt thou go,
Have not I the words of eternal life?  Soon after this he
attended a neighboring meeting, when a ministering Friend,
who was a stranger, stood up with the words which he had
received as an answer to his inquiry, and enlarged upon the
subject in a manner suited to his tried state of mind.

In the year 1779, in the twenty-ninth year of his age, was
his first appearance in the ministry, in great fear and brokenness of spirit: but being obedient to the manifestations of
truth, he experienced an advancement therein, and was a good
example, adorning his profession by a circumspect life.  His
testimony was not with the enticing words of man's wisdom,
but in demonstration of the Spirit and of power.  Neither
was he forward to offer his gift, patiently abiding in the deep
till he felt the holy fire burn.  He was at times led in a plain
close manner to the unfaithful professors of truth, but had
the word of consolation to the rightly exercised, unto whom
he was indeed a nursing father.  He was especially useful to
such as the Lord was gathering from the barren mountains
of an empty profession to the knowledge of the truth, and
he was frequent in solemn supplication for these, and for the
awakening of those who were at ease in Zion.  His heart
being enlarged in gospel love, he was anxious for the salva-

tion of all, and was frequently engaged to appoint meetings amongst those not in profession with us. For this service he was eminently gifted, and his ministry on these occasions was often attended with the powerful baptizing influence of the Spirit, to the convincement of many. He was concerned to impress on the minds of his friends the necessity of a due attendance of week-day meetings, believing that such as were negligent in this duty never experienced an attainment to the state of strong men in the truth. That our dear friend was zealous for the proper support of discipline in our religious body was sufficiently evident from the part he took in the exercise of it in his own Monthly Meeting; for active service in this important branch of church government he was eminently gifted.

In the course of his religious labors, he visited the meetings of Friends generally in most of the Quarterly Meetings in England, and many meetings within the principality of Wales; and divers of them repeatedly.

During the latter period of his life, feeling his bodily strength decline, he was anxiously desirous that no service required of him should be omitted. His zeal increased with his years, and he became more abundant in labor for the promotion of the Christian cause. In a memorandum made about a year before his death, he writes, "This day I attained the seventieth year of my age. May the remainder of my days be so devoted to the Lord's service, as, when the solemn message of death is sent, I may have nothing to do but to render up my accounts with joy!" In the last Monthly Meeting he attended, he expressed amongst us that he had seen in the vision of life that day, that there were of the youth there present those who, if they were faithful and kept in their innocency, would become instruments of good, and finally would shine as the stars, for ever and ever.

The day before his death, the first day of the week, he appeared in his own meeting at Highflatts, in a powerful testimony, beginning with these words of Moses to Hobab: "We are journeying unto the place of which the Lord said, I will give it you. Come thou with us, and we will do thee good; for the Lord hath spoken good concerning Israel." In the course of his testimony he had in strong terms to urge the necessity of a preparation for an awful eternity. In the afternoon of the same day he complained of a pain in his breast and arms, but was not considered in danger. He retired to bed at his usual hour; but he slept little, and quietly departed about five o'clock the following morning, the 26th of the Third Month, 1821; and was buried at Highflatts the 31st of the same; (many Friends and others attended the meeting on this solemn occasion, which was eminently owned by the presence of the Great Shepherd of Israel;) aged seventy-one years, a minister about forty-two years.

# CHAPTER IV.

## 1822-24.

JOHN YEARDLEY left Hull on the 14th of the Fourth Month, and arrived at Hamburg on the 21st. For the purpose of attending the Exchange, and of becoming acquainted with the language, he hired a lodging in the neighborhood of the city, where he remained for some weeks. Writing to his brother, under date of the 23rd of the Fourth Month, he says,—

In the neighborhood of Hamburg, lodgings are not easily obtained for so short a time as a month. We succeeded in procuring a room three miles from the town, at Eppendorf, in the house of three young women, sisters. It is a charming walk, mostly over the fields. It is quite a cross for me to go on 'Change; but as it is the only place for information, I must submit to it, my visit to this place being for instruction in the language and mode of conducting business: but, from what I have yet seen, it will be quite the best for me to proceed into the interior of the country in a few weeks.

What his reflections were when he found himself actually an inhabitant of the land where for so long a time he had mentally dwelt, will be seen by the following entry in his Diary. The maxim with which it concludes may be said to be the motto which he inscribed on his shield for the remainder of his life.

This morning I am thankful to feel something of a peaceful serenity to cover my mind, and am well contented in being placed on this side of the German Ocean. I consider it an unspeakable blessing that I do not feel so much as a wish to return, until the time may come that I can see clearly that it is right for me so to do. Should I not be favored with health and strength to do what I have sometimes thought designed for me before I set my foot in this land, or should my Heavenly Father see meet to cut short the work in righteousness and not permit that I ever see my native country again, his gracious *will be done*. I leave this as a testimony that none need to fear his rightly sending forth those who ask and rightly wait for his counsel. I do not know why I should thus write: I trust it proceeds from a resigned heart; and I will add, for fear I should never have another opportunity, that I should wish all to know who have known me, that I have no reason to doubt the rectitude of my crossing the water with a prospect of a residence in this country, and that should time with me now close, I die in peace with my God, and in that love for mankind which believes "every nation to be our nation, and every man our brother."—(6 *mo.* 8.)

The next day's diary consists of a short but earnest prayer.

*First-day morning.*—O, gracious and most merciful Father, be pleased to strengthen my hands for the work that is before me; be pleased to give me the power of speech; be pleased to give me thy word, with power to publish it to those whose hearts thou shalt be pleased to prepare for the reception of it.

The family with whom he lodged at Eppendorf strongly engaged his religious sympathy.

I spent, he says in his diary of the 8th of the Seventh Month, about nine weeks at E. in a very agreeable manner with the family of three young women. The one who is the mistress of the house is very seriously inclined. She told me she had read a play-book giving a description of our Society in the character of one of its members, and ever since she had had a particular desire to see one of us, and that she could not but admire with thankfulness that she had been gratified in having one to reside under her roof. She had heard of Thomas Shillitoe's being in Hamburg; and when I told her he was now in Norway, she asked me his business there. I told her that our Friends had sometimes a desire to visit their brethren and other religiously-disposed people in foreign lands, and that such was his errand. She replied, "Yes, and I believe it is also yours: this is Gospel love indeed; while so many here will not think for themselves, you come so far to visit and help them." In saying this she was overcome with tears.

John Yeardley left Hamburg on the 2d of the Seventh Month, and arrived at Pyrmont on the 5th. Writing to his brother, he says:

I have now had a specimen of German travelling. Thou wilt be sure I was very bold to set off quite alone except the driver, but it proved far easier than I had anticipated. Instead of having a conveyance to seek when I got over to Harburg, there was a man on the steam-packet who offered to take me in his carriage, and the whole of my packages, to Pyrmont.

A great part of the country between Harburg and Hanover is very dreary and barren, much resembling Bentham Moor; but the road is much worse, being in many places not less than eighteen inches or two feet deep in sand. When we came near Celle and Hanover, the country became quite different, being very fruitful, and the prospect charming. Nearly all the way from Hanover to Pyrmont it is beautiful travelling, and the road mostly good. Pyrmont and the scenery in the surrounding neighborhood is beautiful beyond description.

At Eppendorf he had been cheered by a visit from Benjamin Seebohm and John Snowdon, from Bradford, who informed him that a committee from the Yearly

Meeting were on their way to Pyrmont. This was to
him most welcome news, and the Friends reached
Pyrmont almost as soon as he did; but though their
company was so cordial to his mind, their presence did
not relieve him from the burden of religious exercise
which he began to feel on behalf of the members of the
Society in that place, as soon as he took up his residence
amongst them.

*Diary.*—7 *mo.* 16.—The Committee from the Yearly Meeting—viz., Josiah Forster, Joseph Marriage, and Peter Bedford
—have visited the families of Friends here, and attended the
Preparative Meeting which was held on First-day last. Things
here appear to be very low every way among those who profess with us; yet there are a few sincere-hearted to whom I
already begin to feel closely united in spirit.

From the time of my arrival until First-day last, I do not
remember ever to have been more oppressed in mind. I
could, if I dared, almost have wished myself in England
again, for I feared I should not be able to obtain any relief.
I went to meeting on First-day in fear and trembling; but,
as is sometimes the case, it proved better than I had expected.
When we are stripped of all help but what comes from the
Lord alone, it is then that he delights most to help us.
Through the acceptable assistance of my friend B. Seebohm,
I was enabled to communicate what came before me, and the
great dread which I had always had of speaking through an
interpreter was mercifully removed, for which I was truly
thankful. The three Friends were favored most instructively to labor in the meeting for business. They are now
gone to Minden; I feel tenderly united to their spirits in
much love.

John Yeardley's residence was at Friedensthal, a
hamlet about a mile from the town of Pyrmont. In a
letter to his brother he thus describes the situation of
the place, and his own comfortable accommodation:—

My mother inquires as to my mode of living, and if I have
comfortable accommodations. Please to tell her that I am
provided for in a way which is exceedingly agreeable to me.
I have a large airy sitting-room with three windows, and a
bed-room adjoining, situated, on one side, under the shelter
of a wood, and the other opens to a beautiful and romantic
dale. The mode of cooking is just as I would wish it; I am
only anxious sometimes that my very kind friends of the
house are too much concerned for my help and comfort. It
seems scarcely possible to find an outward situation more
suited to my wishes. When I have studied in the house, I
take my books in suitable weather into the wood, and there
walk and read and think. It is true I am sometimes very flat
for want of company; but if I incline to go to Pyrmont,
they are always pleased to see me, and would willingly have
me always with them.—(2 *mo.* 17, 1823.)

Very soon after his arrival at Pyrmont, John Yeardley
entered into active service in behalf of the gospel. In
what religious state he found the people towards whom
he had so long been attracted in spirit, and how he was
enabled to preach to them the word of life, is exhibited
in several entries in his Diary.

7 *mo.* 21.—The Two-months' Meeting was held at Minden;
I went, along with several of my friends from here. The first
sitting was very large, many coming in who do not usually
attend. It was a very solid meeting; I thought there was
the good savor of an honest-hearted few to be felt among a
mixed multitude. Such was the sweet, peaceful satisfaction
I felt after this meeting, that I almost said in my heart, This
is enough to repay me for setting my feet in Germany.
These are precious seasons, yet I always recur to such in
fear, and rejoice with trembling; for in the midst of the
Lord's goodness to his children one seems to be falling on
one hand, and another on another; so that the language
seems to be, "Will ye also go away?" and truly we shall

never be able to stand if we look not for help to Him who has the words of eternal life.

About this time Thomas Shillitoe arrived in Germany, in the course of his religious visit on the Continent; and John Yeardley, on his return to Pyrmont, united with him in a visit to the families of Friends belonging to that meeting.

8 *mo.* 13.—My feelings are this morning deeply discouraged. I am entering on a visit to the families here with my dear friend T. S., whose company I have had since the 23rd ult. This service is to me a very important one. It is an easy matter to say to a brother or a sister, Be comforted, be strengthened; but it is no light matter to dip so feelingly into the state of our fellow-mortals, as to feel as though we could place *our* soul in their soul's stead, in order that they might be strengthened and comforted.

8 *mo.* 20.—The visit has been got over to our great satisfaction. In some sittings, deep exercise and mourning; in others, cause of rejoicing over the precious seed of the kingdom, which is alive in the hearts of some. There seems to be a remarkable visitation once more extended, especially to the youth.

In conjunction with Thomas Shillitoe he proposed to the Friends, as only one meeting was held on First-days, to have one in the evening for religious reading, holding it at Friedensthal in the summer, and at Pyrmont in the winter. The proposal was immediately complied with, and the institution proved a valuable auxiliary to the edification of the members.

8 *mo.* 25.—The reading meeting this evening has been a precious season; O, how all spirits were melted together! May the blessing of the Lord rest upon this humble endeavor as a means of bringing us nearer to himself.

28*th*.—Our English Friends [Benjamin Seebohm and John Snowdon] have taken their departure.  I feel a little solitary, but I think it a great favor to be preserved from a wish to go with them; nothing will do for me but entire resignation to the Lord's will and work.  Little did I think when I left my home in England, that a work of this sort awaited me in Germany; indeed, I came blind in the gospel; I knew nothing; but now I see such a field of labor if I am faithful: how shall it ever be accomplished?  O, prepare me, dearest Lord, for without thy heavenly hand to assist me I must faint.  O, may I ever seek thy counsel, and be thou pleased to lead me step by step, and give strength according to the day.

29*th*.—To-day I have for the first time expressed a few sentences in broken German in our little meeting.  I do not know whether they might be very clearly understood, but I hope the attempt to do what I conceived to be the Lord's will, will be accepted by him.  O, that he may be pleased to give me the power of speech!

In the Ninth Month he went to Hanover with Thomas Shillitoe, who had a concern to see the authorities regarding the observance of the First-day.  They did not meet with much success in their object; but they made the acquaintance of Pastors Gundel and Hagemann, the latter "nearly blind and very grey, but truly green in the feeling sense of religion," and who rejoiced in his heart to find a brother concerned to reform those things which had long laid heavy on his mind.

The two friends travelled together to Minden, where they parted, and John Yeardley returned to Pyrmont by Bielefeld.

The neighborhood of this town, he says, is remarkably fine.  There is a very high hill, partly formed by nature, and partly by art, from which we can see quite round, without any interruption, even into Holland.  Here, from the ap-

pearance of the bleach-grounds, I could fancy myself in
Barnsley. But, as Sarah Grubb says, I can have no pleasure
in fine prospects; my mind in these journeys is always too
much exercised with matters of a more serious nature.

In the latter part of the month John Yeardley went
again to Minden, to unite with Thomas Shillitoe in a
visit to the families of Friends. They commenced their
visit at Bückeburg, where they had a remarkable interview with the family of the Kammer-rath Wind, which
is related at length in T. S.'s journal (vol. i., p. 388).

The place which seems in these visits to have engaged
J. Y.'s sympathies the most strongly was the village of
Eidinghausen.

We had, he says, a very favored meeting in the room
where their meeting is usually held. In the sitting in the
evening, with the family where we lodged, many of the neighbors came in, who seemed to have no wish to leave us. I
thought of the words of the dear Saviour, when seeing the
multitudes he had compassion on them, because they were
as sheep having no shepherd. Truly these have no outward
shepherd who cares much for their spiritual interests. I felt
my heart much warmed in gospel love towards them, and we
invited them to give us their company again next day, which
most of them did. In this meeting there was something
expressed so remarkably suited to the states of some present,
that after it was over a woman confessed it had been as was
declared, that she herself was one to whom it belonged; and
she gave us a short relation how it had been with her in
former days.

The love which these simple, honest-hearted creatures
manifest towards us does away with all distinctions and the
difference of language. O, that He who teaches as never
man taught may be pleased to guide them and bring them to
himself that there may be one shepherd and one sheep-fold.
All our toils in this weary land will not be too much if we

can be made the instruments of helping only one poor soul on its way Zionwards.

10 *mo.* 8.—I returned yesterday evening from Minden, with a thankful heart, to come again to my quiet and romantic habitation in Peacedale. The strong fortifications which are made, and now making, around Minden, give it an appearance of gloom and oppression which is scarcely to be borne. O, how uncomfortable do I feel when within its walls; but in its neighborhood there are a few friends to whom I am tenderly united in spirit.

He concludes this entry with an allusion to the homely and even hard manner of life to which many of these were accustomed.

To some of our Friends in England who are dissatisfied with their outward situation, I would say, Come and see how these live on the Continent.

The 29th of the Tenth Month was the anniversary of his wife's death. His diary for this day is an affecting transcript of his feelings on the occasion.

The shock which my earthly happiness received this day twelvemonths has been, this evening, piercingly renewed in the recollection of almost every minute transaction which accompanied the awful event of the closing moments of my precious lamb. For truly like a lamb she lived, and was well prepared to become an angel-spirit. O, happy spirit, thou art at rest; then why should I mourn thy loss? Surely He who knows the weakness of our frame will forgive, for he himself gave us the example in weeping over those he loved. The Almighty has been very good to me; he has put it in the hearts of those with whom I reside to care for me with an affectionate interest. O, for greater diligence, that the day's work may keep pace with the day. What shall I do, but pray for more strength to be made able to do all that

7

may be required of me. I never saw the advice of our dear Saviour more necessary for myself than at the present time, " Be ye wise as serpents and harmless as doves."

Soon after this he had a return of his complaint in the stomach, which caused him to exclaim—

We are indeed but dust and ashes; how quickly the slender thread may be cut, and reduce this frail tabernacle to that state of earthly composition from which it was formed. But the spiritual part in us must have an abiding somewhere *for ever;* this is the awful consideration which ought continually to affect our hearts. Is it not a strange infatuation to rank the moments of affliction among the evil events of our lives, when these may prove the very means of bringing back our wandering feet to the path which leads to everlasting life?

He then reviews his own situation, his calling and his work.

It is often the consideration of my heart, What has brought me into this country? what have I done? what am I doing? and what have I to do? The enemy is not wanting to distress my poor mind on the point of these four important queries. But to the first I can answer, An humble submission to what I believe to be the leadings of Divine Wisdom. To the second, through the assistance of never-failing love, I have done what I could and have found peace. To the third, I am desirous through divine aid to do what I can; and to the fourth, which refers to the future, I must commit it into the hands of the Judge of the whole earth, who alone is able to guide my feet in the sure path. I feel in the present moment desirous to keep eternity continually before my view, and to let outward things hang more fully on the dependence of Him who suffers not a sparrow to fall to the ground without his notice. (11 *mo.* 30.)

12 *mo.* 1.—The reading meeting this evening has been a precious time. Our spirits have been much tendered in

reading some account of the lives and deaths of our worthy Friends recorded in Sewel's History. Tears so overpowered the reader and the hearers, that the reading was at times obliged to be suspended until we had given relief to our feelings.

In addition to this meeting, John Yeardley established another for the young, to be held on Fourth-day evening, "in which they might improve themselves in reading, and acquire a knowledge of the principles of the Society, with other branches of useful information." The young women were to bring their work; and it was his delight to interrupt the reading with religious instruction, and such remarks as a father makes for the improvement and gratification of his children. We see him here for the first time in a character in which he was well known to the present generation in various parts of England, viz., as an instructor and guide of the youth. In noticing in his Diary the formation of the Youths' Meeting at Pyrmont, he comments with pleasure on the innocent cheerful manners of his audience, and on the advantages which might be looked for from this kind of social intercourse.

The last entry in this year records an occasion of near approach to the throne of grace in prayer in the little congregation at Pyrmont.

12 *mo.* 29, *First-day.*—A most remarkable season of divine favor in our evening assembly. The awe which I had felt over my spirit the whole of the day, and not feeling freedom to break my mind in the meeting in the morning, induced me to look to the evening opportunity with fear and trembling, which indeed is always the case when I feel the Master's hand upon me. The most solemn act of worship, that of public supplication, so powerfully impressed my mind, that I believed it right to yield to the motion, which I humbly trust was

done in due reverence and humility of soul. Our spirits were so humbled under feelings of good that it seemed as if the secrets of all hearts were presented before the throne of grace, to ask forgiveness for former transgressions, strength to serve the Most High with more acceptance, and to be finally prepared to reign with him in glory. O how these seasons of refreshing will rise up against us in the great day of account, if we are not concerned to improve by them! Grant, dearest Father, that I may experience a nearer and stronger tie to do thy will more perfectly ; and let it please thee to remember those in this place and this land for whom my spirit so often secretly mourns and prays.

The Diary of 1823 opens with a profound and solemn reflection.

1823. 1 *mo.* 4.—For want of faith we are too much inclined to serve ourselves before we are willing to serve the Great Master, thinking we may be able to do much for him afterwards, when it will more accord with our situation in life. But, alas! this time may never come; if we thus put by the *acceptable season,* our lives may close with our only having performed very imperfectly the part which had been designed for us in the Church militant. Painful would be the sting when appealing to the Judge of the earth, in a moment when we no longer possessed the capability of serving him, should the declaration be, Thou hadst a desire to serve me when in health and strength, but thou wished *first* to *serve thyself.* My time was not then thy time, therefore *thy time* is not now *my time.*

A letter to his brother, written in the summer of this year (6 mo. 9), gives a description of the mode of bleaching in use in Germany, which will, we believe, be interesting to the English reader. John Yeardley says :

Wilt thou not be surprised when I tell thee that I am about to commence yarn-bleaching ? Thou mayst be sure there is a pretty certain prospect of considerable advantages, with not much risk, to induce me to make the attempt. The advantages are threefold—safety, expedition and cheapness. The first consists in the simplicity of treatment and safety of the ingredients, no chemical process being made use of; the second arises from the heat of the climate; the last is easily accounted for from the low price of labor and the cheapness of the raw material, which is produced in abundance in the neighborhood. In the country around, for a very considerable distance, almost every family make their own linen; they grow or buy the flax, spin the yarn and get it woven, and either bleach it themselves or send it to others who have better conveniences in water, &c. As the spring commenced, I noticed these little bleaching-plots wherever I went, and often wondered that the color was so good. Knowing that such people could not possibly be at any great expense or risk in the operation, I concluded it must be done by dint of time and labor, supposing that the yarn and cloth must lie at least a few months on the grass; but, on inquiry, I was surprised to find it was made quite white in three weeks or a month. To make a further proof, I sent two bundles of yarn to two different places to bleach; it is now returned of a very good color and perfectly strong, though it has been in bleaching only a month and two or three days, and although the greater part of the Fifth Month has been unfavorable for bleaching. As to any risk of the yarn being tendered, it is quite out of the question; it seems to be done by the operation that nature points out. I have found a very convenient place for the purpose of making trial; there is plenty of good clear water. There is a prospect of having honest workpeople, and at very reasonable wages—not more than 6d. or 8d. a day; there are many honest creatures to be had at these wages who have nothing in the world to do.

From the first of my leaving England, I had no expectation of being liberated from this country before the expiration of about four years, and I have always been desirous that something should turn up that would afford me support by suitable employment; so that what I have now in view does not

seem to clash with my former prospects. It is (he adds with
affectionate feeling) a source of great consolation that I can
always unbosom my mind so freely to thee; and I consider
it among the greatest blessings I enjoy, that thou hast never
yet failed of being made an instrument of support to me, and
my prayer is that thou mayst never lose thy reward.

Pyrmont is one of the oldest watering-places north of
the Alps. The inhabitants are very much dependent on
the visitors who resort thither during the three summer
months, and amongst whom may frequently be reckoned
some of the first families in Europe. This year, 1823,
the Prince and Princess of Prussia (the present Regent
of Prussia and his consort) were there, and one Fourth-
day morning attended the Friends' Meeting. The meeting-house stands in one of the *allées*, and although its
position is not central, it is sufficiently public to be an
object of attraction to the curiosity of strangers. A
memorandum under date of the 18th of the Sixth Month
records the royal visit, and John Yeardley's spiritual
exercise on the occasion.

6 *mo.* 18.—To-day the young prince and Princess of
Prussia, with the Princess their mother, and the Hofmeister,
have been at our Fourth-day meeting. They entered with
such seriousness on their countenances that I felt my spirit
suddenly drawn towards them in love, and a secret prayer
was raised in my heart for their everlasting good. Feeling
the influence of divine love to increase, I believed it right to
kneel down, and in brokenness of spirit I expressed what had
opened on my mind, which afforded me peace; and I hope
good to others was imparted, although I may say through
the unworthiest of instruments. For truly I have for some
time been as in a state of death and darkness, owing to my
unwatchfulness. O what would I give for more circumspec-
tion, that I might be more prepared to receive the *word*, and
when command is given, publish the same. But, unworthy

creature, I often deprive myself and others of seasons of good
through my negligence and barrenness. When will the time
come when I can say, all earthly things are under my feet,
and the cause of religion and virtue rules predominant in my
heart! Lord, hasten the day; and preserve my feet in thy
path in the midst of many snares; and rather let me die than
be suffered to do anything which would dishonor thy gracious
and holy Name, and the profession I am making of thee
before the world. Loose my bands, and enable me to say in
sincerity of heart, I am willing to serve thee freely.

With the cause for self-condemnation which is alluded
to in this entry was no doubt connected the neglect to
keep up his Diary; no entry occurs for more than five
months previous. It was probably much more difficult
in the position which he occupied in Germany to maintain a spirit of watchfulness and self-recollection than
among his more experienced Friends in Yorkshire. There
is an allusion to this in an entry of a little later date.

7 mo. 8.—My mind feels a little more gathered than it has
been for some time past; but the little outward difficulties
which are continually arising have a great tendency to disperse the best feelings. I think it is almost the greatest
lesson that we have to learn, to stand so fast in times of
trouble as not to suffer loss. If we would so conduct ourselves that the change of times and seasons should not have
such an unfavorable influence on our minds, this would be
one great point gained; it would enable us to meet the difficulties of the day in a better state to combat with them.

But if daily trials abounded of a nature the most
likely to retard his spiritual progress, we shall see that
He who had appointed his lot, provided in his faithfulness the needful corrective, and by the discipline of filial
fear in the ministry of the word, kept him safe in his
sanctuary.

The attendance of visitors at the meeting-house was often numerous, althogh it was seldom that they re- mained during the whole time of worship. Meetings of this kind were very trying to John Yeardley's faith and feelings; but sometimes they were seasons of heavenly blessing such as abundantly to make amends for past humiliation.

7 mo. 6.—To-day the small meeting-house and passage were quite filled with strangers, and I was told many went away who could not get in, and some remained under the windows. No creature on earth knows what my poor mind suffers when I go to meeting under such circumstances. Many whom curiosity brings in the expectation to hear words may some. times be disappointed, but I hope there are some whose intentions are sincere, and who are desirous to be informed the way to Zion. I hope strength was afforded me to preach Christ crucified. O that the Lord may support me in these very trying seasons, and take from me the fear of man, and fill my heart with a holy fear of offending Him whom I humbly trust I am desirous of choosing to be my Lord and Master.

7 mo. 27.—"Bless the Lord, O my soul, and all that is within me bless his holy name." Notwithstanding my many seasons of poverty and inward distress, the foregoing language is sometimes put into my heart on my return from our meetings, which are, in the bathing season, almost always crowded with strangers. Their manner of coming in and going out during the time of worship is exceedingly disturbing, and yet I cannot but admire the stillness which prevails when anything is delivered. The help which I at times experience in these trying seasons is wonderful in my eyes. When I am concerned to stand up in His dread and fear, what have I else to fear? This fear would always cast out the fear of man which ever brings death; and yet so weak am I, that after all these precious helps and comforting times, I tremble when the meeting-day comes again lest I should fail

in doing the Lord's will. Such is my fear before I can rise
to my feet in meetings that I say with Samson, Be with me
this once more that I may bear testimony to thy name; then,
if it be thy will let me die for thee, and I will not think it
too much to suffer. O that He would be pleased to enlarge
his gift in my heart, and be unto me mouth and wisdom, and
give me tongue and utterance to declare his name unto the
nations.

7 *mo.* 30.—Our Fourth-day meeting to-day has been a precious heavenly season. Much more weightiness of spirit
appeared to exist in the strangers who attended, and consequently more stillness. I had not long taken my seat before
I believed it right to stand up with the words of the apostle,
"Awake to righteousness and sin not, for some have not the
knowledge of God; I speak this to your shame." The
women's side was nearly full of richly-clad females; they
bore the marks of worldly distinction, and were indeed as fine
as hands and pins could make them. But the tenderings of
divine love reached the hearts of some among them in a particular degree. I felt such a nearness of spirit towards them
that I had great openness in speaking of the things which
came before me. After meeting they very willingly accepted
of some books. One of them was much reached, and went
into the little plantation to weep. Another went to her to
comfort her; but she replied, Go from me and leave me alone.
We may truly say with the apostle that God is no respecter
of persons, but those who fear him and work righteousness
will be accepted of him, to whatever nation, kindred, tongue
or people they may belong. All distinctions of religious
sects and party spirit are laid aside when our hearts become
prepared to embrace each other in true Christian love. I do
believe the Lord's work is begun in the hearts of many in this
land; and the fervent prayer of my spirit is that he may be
pleased to carry it on to perfection, and that we may live to
see the glorious day when righteousness shall cover the earth
as the waters cover the channels of the sea. O Germany,
Germany, what does my heart feel on account of thy inhabitants! It seems as if I could tread thy soil for the remainder

of my days if I could only be made the instrument of helping
on their way those scattered ones who are athirst for the sincere milk of the word of life.

One of the females who visited our meetings came to the
school room on Seventh-day, and requested the favor of
having a few books to peruse and circulate. She said she
was from Osnabrück, and that there were a number of people
in that place who had a great love to the Friends of our
Society. Such opportunities afford the means of circulating
a knowledge of the truth to those whose hearts may be preparing to receive it; and if such are only awakened to seek
after the ways of holiness, although they may never come to
be of our number on earth, they will be found among the
number of the saints in heaven. The bathing-list this season
already amounts to 2500 persons, in which number there
are many who are desirous to inquire the way to Zion. It
is much to be desired that the peculiar advantages which
Pyrmont affords for spreading in the different parts of the
Continent books illustrative of our religious principles should
be judiciously embraced, particularly as there appears such an
openness to receive them. I can truly say I have been
thankful that my lot has been here this summer, and I trust
I have not flinched from doing what I believed to be required
of me.

In his letters to his brother, John Yeardley makes
frequent mention of his mother. In the Ninth Month
he heard of her being seriously ill, and he thus writes
in reference to her state, in a letter dated the 29th of
the Ninth Month:—

The state of my dear mother's health is truly alarming;
but as I have received no further account from thee, I am
flattering my poor panting heart with a comfortable hope
that she may have taken a turn for the better, and will yet
live to see the hour when we shall once more embrace each
other in my native land. If she should be taken away without my being permitted to see her again, it would be a cup

which I could not tell how to drink. This brings poignantly to my remembrance one of the most trying hours of my life, and yet the support then received was wonderful.

As I rode along the road in the course of this summer on a journey of business, my dear mother was brought to my remembrance in such a very remarkable manner, that I seemed to have a spiritual interview with her; and she was brought so near to my feelings, that I thought it probable I should never see her again until we met in eternity. I scarcely know how I felt, but it was as if my spirit accompanied hers into the regions above. I noted down the circumstance when I got home; for it had made such an impression on my mind, that I should not then have been surprised to have heard of her departure.*

The following instructive remarks occur in the Diary about this time :—

10 *mo.* 27.—My retirement and reading this morning has been more tendering to my spirit than for a long time past. I read and considered the institution of the Passover, when the Israelites were led out of Egypt; and it appears clear to me that the sprinkling the door-posts with the blood of the lambs, as commanded, was a type of our Saviour's blood which was shed for our transgressions, and that we must be saved by his becoming our paschal lamb. As the destroying angel only passed over the doors and preserved those who had received the mark, so can we only be saved by being willing to apply the blood of our dear Saviour to wash and cleanse us from our sins. What a beauty there is in the connection of Scripture truths when we read them with a simple heart prepared to receive the right impression which may be opened!

The Friends of Minden and the little company of awakened people at Eidinghausen, who on his first

---

* The memorandum here referred to is in the Diary, under date of the 18th of the Sixth Month.

coming to Germany had taken so firm a hold of John Yeardley's mind, continued to excite his religious sympathy, and he again visited them in the latter part of this year.

(*Minden.*)—On Seventh-day last, the 1st of the Eleventh Month, I left home in company with some of my dear Pyrmont friends to attend the Two-months' Meeting, and to spend a few days with my dear friends of this place. I lodge with Frederick Schmidt, and feel myself perfectly at home. It is a most orderly and agreeable family, consisting of himself, daughter, and housekeeper; and the time passes pleasantly away when I am only enough concerned to improve the opportunities afforded by this good man's company. He was one of the first in this place who was convinced of the religious principles of Friends, and his beginning was small both in temporals and spirituals. I cannot but admire how his endeavors have been prospered. He remarked the other evening in conversation, that it was of great advantage to the Friends to persevere in their outward callings, and not to jump (as he expressed it) out of one thing into another. This would be the means of establishing their credit as men of business.

11 *mo.* 7.—Sarah Grubb mentions* that when she visited Minden, she met with great kindness and attention from a councillor of the place, who on their leaving accompanied them a little way out of the town to an inn, where he had provided coffee, and had invited a few of his friends to take leave of them. This was at the house of my worthy host [Frederick Schmidt], who then kept the inn at Kuckuk, and had for some time been under deep [religious] impressions. He related to me that her discourse in the meeting she had had in the town had affected him, and yet he could not give her his hand, but went into the garden to weep; but after she had got into the carriage and driven from the door, she suddenly made a stop, came again into the house, and asked

---

* Life of S. Grubb, 2nd ed., p. 219.

for him. He being called, she had a remarkable opportunity with him; she told him she believed the Lord had a work for him to do in this place, and that he would have to stand foremost in the rank, and when the time came he must not flinch from doing what his Master would require. This has in a remarkable manner been fulfilled to the present day, and affords an encouraging example to the poor tried servants of the Lord to be faithful to apprehended duty. Although they may not live to see the effect of their labors, yet their Lord and Master will not leave himself without a witness in the hearts of his people; praised be his name.

14*th.* Since Thomas Shillitoe and I visited Eidinghausen, there has been a remarkable revival to a sense of religion; a number come together in a sort of society every First-day afternoon, to read, sing, and pray for the edification one of another. As all things have a beginning, this may perhaps prove a step to a more perfect way of worship. I had long felt inclined to visit the meeting in Eidinghausen, and had looked towards accomplishing it from Minden.

I went there on the 9th inst., and my intention to be there being known a few days before caused many of these awakened people to attend the meeting so that the little school-room was quite full, and many stood in the passage. I was truly thankful to be amongst them, for it proved a most satisfactory season. They are a rustic set of folks, but have each a soul to save or to lose, and all souls are of equal value in the sight of the Judge of the whole earth. Lewis Seebohm kindly gave up his time to attend me as interpreter, for I still prefer help of this sort when it can be done through one who is so feelingly capable. I often feel as a poor wandering stranger in a strange land, and yet I dare not complain. The goodness of the Lord is great towards me; he opens the hearts of those whom I am concerned to visit, to receive me into their hearts and houses, so that it affords me great freedom in speaking to them on serious subjects relating to their best interests, both spiritual and temporal. I am convinced if we mean to be useful to a people of a strange land, all must be done in a spirit of love and humility; with the weak we must be willing to become weak; only we must be on our guard and not flinch from our well-known testimonies.

The reflection contained in the passage which follows is of deep significance, and the lesson it conveys is one which the Church has as much need to learn now as at any former period.

15th.—We find recorded in the writings of our ancient Friends that occasionally a few words spoken in the course of common conversation made a deep impression on the minds of those to whom they were addressed. The cause must have been that they lived in a more retired state of mind, and were consequently better prepared to feel the smallest of good impressions in themselves, and were also more attentive to embrace every opportunity of improving the minds of others. I fail in this respect; I do not live enough in what may be truly called a spirit of prayer. I must be more watchful over my thoughts, words and actions, and improve my seasons of retirement; for there is no other way of preservation than by waiting and praying for a renewal of spiritual strength.

John Yeardley then reverts, as he so often does, to the love of souls in Germany, which was the means of causing him to leave his native land, and which he says had not diminished during his eighteen months' residence among them. To these thoughts he adds some considerations regarding the temporal condition of the Society of Friends there, on account of which he was often very solicitous.

The situation and welfare of the Society here have long occupied the warmest feelings of my heart. I am of the mind, with other Friends who have visited these parts, that there is a precious hidden work begun in the hearts of many in Germany, who suffer under oppression, on account of the many discouraging circumstances which have existed among them, and which yet prevail, to the great hindrance of the Lord's work. There are causes for which no human remedy can be prescribed. I have often said in my heart, If the Lord help them not, vain is the help of man. Much has been done for them by our dear Friends in England, and much still remains to be done, in order that they may be preserved together and not become dispersed as though they had never been a people.

The effectual means of help seems yet to fail,—that of putting the families in the way of helping themselves by suitable employment. The families who live in the neighborhood of Minden, mostly on small parcels of land, have until now got on with a tolerable degree of comfort, by cultivating their land in summer and spinning yarn in winter; but now the depression is so great that if they could be put into the way of earning threepence a day, they would embrace it with thankfulness. I have been very diffident in proposing any plan for their assistance, knowing that some former proposals have failed of accomplishing the end. But I have consulted with those who are best acquainted with their situation, and we think it safest for them to continue their own employment of spinning yarn, and endeavor to mend their trade by placing it on this footing. They must spin such an article as I can make use of in sending it, with what I buy from other people, to my friends in the linen business in England. I am to give them a little higher price than they can elsewhere obtain, and those who have no flax of their own must have a little money advanced to purchase some, which they must repay in yarn. When the yarn is disposed of in England, and a profit on the same can be obtained, it must be distributed among them as a premium to encourage industry and good management in producing a good article. If this does not answer, I cannot see any thing at present that will.

How far this scheme was put in practice we are unable to say, but we believe it was not accompanied by any successful result.

In the next entry he speaks of the advantage which he derived from keeping a diary.

11 *mo.* 17.—I was this evening accidentally induced to read over a few of my former memorandums; and it humbled my spirit to retrace the dealings of my merciful Father with me. I am glad that I have from time to time penned down a few remarks by way of diary, although it has been done interruptedly and very imperfectly. It proves a means of enabling me to see a wonderful concurrence in the ways of Divine Wisdom which has led me in a way that I knew not, and hitherto preserved me through the mercies of his love: praise be to his Name now and for ever. Amen.

After his return from Minden he accompanied John and William Seebohm, who were going on a journey of business to Leipzig. They went by way of Brunswick and Halberstadt, and returned by Nordhausen and Eimbeck. In this tour through the heart of Germany, John Yeardley made many observations on the state of agriculture, the cities, and the character of the people. Of the last they met with several curious traits, some of them sufficiently annoying.

On many great roads, says J. Y., there is a summer and a winter way, running parallel to each other, with a rail across, on which is a notice that the way is forbidden by a fine of 6*d.* or 8*d.* for each horse, that the traveller may know when to take the summer or the winter road. We stopped on the way [they were not far from Wolfenbüttel] to give our horses a little bread, and our coachman drove to the side of the road to make way for carriages to pass. But he had inadvertently gone over the setting on of the road; and the roadmaster came to us, and told us we must not feed our horses there, as it was not allowed to drive over the stones on the side, under a penalty of three shillings per horse. The evening of

the same day we fed our horses at an inn, and walked before,
leaving the man to follow us. I and my young friend W. S.
sought the cleanest part of the way by walking in the course
made for the water, which was green and clean; but so soon
as we came by the inspectors, who are mostly employed on
the road, one of them told us we must mind for the future
and keep the right footpath, or pay 6d. each. This I considered as an infringement of English liberty, and was ready
to reason with him on the subject; but I reflected that I was
a stranger, and that it is always better and more polite to
submit quietly to the regulations of the country in which we
live, than bring ourselves into difficulty through incivility or
contention.

In returning from Leipzig, J. Y. and his friends committed a more serious offence against the pragmatical
regulations of the German States.

On our journey homewards we had much perplexity with
some cloth, &c. which J. S. had bought in Leipzig to bring
to Pyrmont. This arose from want of better information
respecting the laws of the Prussian territory. They are exceedingly strict as to duties. All kinds of wares are allowed
to pass through the country at what may be called a reasonable excise; but those travellers who have excise goods with
them must preserve a certain road, called the Zoll-strasse.
It was our lot to miss this road; for apprehending ourselves
at liberty to pursue what road we pleased, we took another
way. But we found our mistake when we came to the place
where the duty is paid; for we were informed we had taken
the wrong road, and that transit duty could not be received;
we must either pay the full excise as when goods remain in
the Prussian territory, or return back until we came again
into the Zoll-strasse. It took some time to consider which
was best to be done. To be sent about we knew not whither,
and on roads scarcely passable, would prove a serious incon-
venience; and on the other hand it was exceedingly mortify-
ing to pay for such a trifle so enormous an excise. The
officer was very civil, but told us it was not in his power to

do otherwise. We concluded it would be best and cheapest
to pay dearly for our error rather than be retarded on our
journey. We had a regular receipt for what we paid, but
inadvertently departing again from the appointed way, we
were in danger of paying the full duty a second time, or having the goods taken from us. So much for travelling with
excise goods.

Early in 1824, John Yeardley returned for a few
months to England. He had ingratiated himself so
thoroughly into the esteem and love of his Pyrmont
friends, that his departure even for a short time was the
signal of lamentation through the whole meeting. On
the 11th of the First Month he had a farewell meeting
at Friedensthal, which was attended by almost all his
friends. With his parting blessing he had some counsel
to impart.

I have so much place, he says, in their minds, that whatever I say, either in counsel or reproof, is always received in
love. Such a scene I never witnessed; the dear lambs all
wept aloud; we were indeed all melted together. May the
Shepherd of Israel never leave them nor forsake them, and
may they become willing to follow his leading. I can truly
say that on their behalf my pillow has been often wet with
my tears.

On the 3rd of the Second Month, he left Friedensthal,
accompanied by a young Friend whom he was to conduct
to a temporary residence in England, and in whose religious welfare he was deeply interested. While waiting
in Hamburg for a vessel, he felt keenly his solitary
situation in the world.

2 *mo.* 9.—I think I never felt poorer in spirit and more
discouraged than at present. It seems as if visiting my native
land had no cheering prospect for me. If it were right in

the divine sight I could almost wish to spend the whole of
my life in solitude; but I must be willing patiently to suffer,
and endeavor to fill the place appointed for me on this stage
of action.

A vessel sailed for England the day before their arrival at Hamburg, a circumstance which at first made him
regret he had not used more expedition on the way.   But
he immediately recollected it might be for the best that
he was left behind.   This proved to be the case; for the
vessel with which he would have sailed, meeting with
contrary winds and dark weather, ran aground, and was
obliged to put back, and when J. Y. left the Elbe she
was lying in Cuxhaven harbor.

They landed at Hull on the 19th.

# CHAPTER V.

FROM HIS RETURN TO ENGLAND IN 1824, TO THE COMMENCE-
MENT OF HIS FIRST CONTINENTAL JOURNEY IN 1825.

On setting foot again in England, the dejected state of mind which had accompanied him on the journey returned with renewed force.

2 *mo.* 19.—I do not know how to describe my feelings in landing on my native shore: I feel a poor discouraged creature. May He who knows the sincerity of my heart be pleased to strengthen my poor mind, for I feel almost overwhelmed with fears and difficulties.

Still deeper was his emotion on visiting again the home of former days.

2 *mo.* 20.—Left Hull, and came by way of Selby and Wakefield to Barnsley. I felt my heart exceedingly burdened before I reached the place: it seemed as if all the bitter cups I had drunk in former times were going to be handed to me afresh. This may not be, perhaps, altogether on my own account. There is at times a fellow-feeling with others; and on my reaching this place, I soon felt my spirit dipped into sympathy with some of my dear connexions, who are not without their trials.

A few days afterwards, in allusion to the religious service of Elizabeth H. Walker of West Chester, U. S., in a public meeting for worship at Barnsley, he says :—

I do not really know what is the matter, but I fear I am going backwards from all that is good. When I look at the usefulness of others, O what an insignificant, useless being I appear!

(108)

This lowly opinion of himself, however, was not to serve as an excuse for idleness, and it was proposed to him to bear Elizabeth Walker company in a religious circuit in some of the midland counties, previous to the occurrence of the Yearly Meeting.   He accepted the proposal; and they travelled together through part of Staffordshire, Warwick, Worcester, and Oxfordshire, visiting the meetings of Friends, and sometimes inviting the attendance of the public.

The dispirited state of mind which John Yeardley had brought with him from Germany accompanied him on this journey, and on the 30th of the Fourth Month he writes :—

I walked last evening in the fields, in a solitary frame of mind, being very low in spirits on many accounts.   My own unfaithfulness deprives me of strength to cast off my burden as I go along; consequently I grow weaker and weaker, which is indeed diametrically opposite to growing stronger and stronger in the Lord.   Lamentable case!   O for a speedy alteration for the better!

*Fifth-day, the 6th of Fifth Month, at Sibford.*—This is a pretty large meeting, and there are a good many sweet-looking young folks.   The lovely countenances of such are always refreshing to me, and it is not much wonder if I have a little more openness for labor, which was the case in this place.   But in general I sit and bemoan my own uselessness. I have been a burden to myself in this little journey, in fearing I might be so to my friends; but I ought to be very thankful that they do not seem to think me so, but are desirous to encourage me.   I think if it was otherwise, it would be more than I could bear.

In the Fifth Month, he attended the Yearly Meeting in London.   At the Meeting of Ministers and Elders, an unusual number of certificates were granted for reli-

gious service abroad.    These various concerns drew from
him the following reflections:—

As I sat under the weighty consideration and disposal of
these subjects, I felt a degree of rejoicing to spring in my
heart, that there are still members who hold the promotion
of the cause of righteousness in the earth dear to the best
feelings of their hearts.    It is indeed cause of heartfelt gratitude that the Divine Master is directing the feet of his
messengers not only to the borders of this isle, but also into
distant parts of the earth.

During the Yearly Meeting John Yeardley lodged at
William Allen's, at Plough-court and Stoke Newington,
and was introduced to several Friends with whom he
had not before been acquainted.

The acquaintance which I have made with many dear and
valued Friends in the neighborhood of London has, I hope,
been a little strength to me in the best things.    It is truly
pleasant to be treated with such genuine kindness; but it is
nothing for the soul to build upon,—we must look for a more
sure foundation than the favor of the great and good.

Elizabeth H. Walker had a meeting with the younger
part of the Society in London and the neighborhood.    In noticing this meeting J. Y. has some dis-
criminating remarks on the exercise of the ministry.

During this as well as many other meetings for worship,
I sat under religious exercise, but could seldom believe it
required of me to take part in the public ministry.    I often
think, when many exercised brethren and sisters are present,
there would be a danger of interrupting the true gospel
order, if all were not careful to wait on the Great Minister
of the Sanctuary.    If we patiently abide under the rightly
baptizing power, what we may apprehend preparing in our

hearts for utterance may often be delivered by others, and
we only have to say, as it were, Amen. We may also be
brought into a right willingness to speak in the Lord's name,
and still be excused ; this may be, perhaps, a preparation of
an offering which may be called for at another place. O the
importance of knowing the word rightly to be divided, and
when and where the offering is required !

A part of Elizabeth Walker's errand in coming to
Europe was to visit the Friends in Germany; and it
was proposed that John Yeardley should take charge
of her and her companion, Christiana A. Price of Neath,
on his return to Pyrmont. They went together through
Essex and Suffolk, having meetings on their way; but
at Ipswich it appeared that C. A. Price's health was
unequal to the journey, and Elizabeth Walker proceeded to Hull to cross the water from thence with
another company of Friends who were bound for the
Continent. J. Y. was thus left to proceed alone to
Pyrmont, and he sailed from Harwich on the 19th of
the Sixth Month. When in Suffolk he went to Need-
ham to see " dear ancient Samuel Alexander."

I had, he says, long known this fatherly man by name and
person, but had had no acquaintance with him until now:
his company and conversation were exceedingly pleasant and
instructive to me. In the evening I took a walk in a large
plantation which he had himself planted when young, and
had now lived to see afford him a comfortable retreat.

John Yeardley was taken ill when in Suffolk, and on
settling down again in his quiet home at Friedensthal he
writes:

7 mo. 15.—I am drinking salt-spring-water, and my health
is mercifully restored. The air of this country seems to suit

my constitution better than that of England. Time is very precious. I think, to keep a more correct journal of what I do each day might be very useful, by inducing a more narrow scrutiny how each hour is spent; for I know not how many more may be allowed me to prepare for eternity.

To this resolution he did not adhere. With the exception of two short entries in the same month, he wrote nothing in his diary for the remainder of the year. The difficulties of his position, perhaps a lack of sufficient employment, and the want of that instant watchfulness without which the disciple is ever prone to stray from his Master's side, seem to have again produced, as they did twelve months before, a season of spiritual famine.

His own gloomy condition did not, however, altogether disable him from sympathizing with others. In a letter to his brother of the 4th of the Eleventh Month he says:—

I have of late been in such a low tried state of mind, that I have been discouraged from writing thee, under an apprehension I should say nothing that would afford thee any satisfaction in reading. But though I may not have it in my power to relieve thee, I hope it will not be unpleasant to thee to know that thou art still more dear and near to me than ever thou wast in the times of more apparent outward prosperity. It is a high attainment to know how to set a right value on perishable things, and it requires no small degree of fortitude to bear the depression of apparent temporary adversity, in that disposition of mind which becomes the character of a true Christian. Although, according to our apprehensions, the storm may last long, yet it most assuredly will blow over, and then greater will be our peace than if we had never known a tempest.

On resuming his Diary, which he did in the

First Month of 1825, John Yeardley gives an account of the events which happened to him during the previous few months.

In the Seventh Month 1824, Thomas Shillitoe and Elizabeth H. Walker came to Pyrmont, and to the latter J. Y. gave his assistance in various religious engagements. After her departure he again visited Minden, with the neighboring villages of Eidinghausen and Hille. His visit to the last-named place (1 mo. 13, 1825) was marked by a singular circumstance.

Finding a sudden draft [in my mind] to be at the reading meeting in Hille, to begin at two o'clock, there seemed but little time; however, proposing it to my dear friend John Rasche, he was quite willing to accompany me, and driving quickly we came in due time. When the [meeting] was over, the Friends told me they thought it very remarkable that we should come unexpectedly on that day, and that what was communicated after the reading was particularly suited to the state of a woman Friend present, who was laboring under the temptation that she had committed the unpardonable sin, and could find no rest day or night. I could not prevent them from expressing their thankfulness for such a mark of Providential interference, in this way to afford the poor woman a little relief and encouragement.

Four days afterwards, having then returned to Friedensthal, J. Y. adds:—"Since our visit to Hille, the person above-mentioned is dead!"

The depression under which John Yeardley labored, from the loss of that comfortable presence of his Lord which had been almost from his youth as a lamp shining continually upon his head, seems to have reached its lowest point in the early part of this year. Under date of the 24th of the Second Month he says:—

I have this morning once more been enabled to pour out

my sorrowful spirit before the Father of mercies in a way
that has afforded me some relief and encouragement. In
bitterness, and, I may almost say, in agony of soul have I
spread before him some of those circumstances which have
been a cause of unspeakable distress to me for many months
past, and rendered me unfit for almost every service, temporal
or spiritual.

Thou knowest, O gracious Father, I long to have my ways
and steps regulated by thy holy will.  Therefore I beseech
thee, have mercy on my faults, and blot out from thy remembrance all my sins, and everything wherein I have in weakness offended thee ; and be pleased to give me strength to
become more perfectly and lastingly thine.  O how sensibly
do I feel my own weakness, and that without thee I can do
nothing, not for a moment preserve my own steps.

In the midst of his discouragement his mind was
directed towards the accomplishment of another part of
the commission which had been entrusted to him before
he left England,—viz., to sojourn for a time amongst
the Friends in the South of France.  Accordingly,
early in the Third Month he went to Minden, and laid
before the Two-months' Meeting, his intention of going
to Congenies for this purpose, and also of seeking a
religious interview with some serious people in the
neighborhood of Cologne.

This information, he says, was received by my friends with
much sympathy and, I trust, weightiness of spirit, and I felt
a little strengthened by the expression of their feelings and
unity with me in this concern.  A certificate of their approbation was ordered to be drawn up.  No creature on earth
knows how this prospect humbles me.  I always think I
am dealt with in a remarkable manner,—somewhat different
perhaps from others.  Notwithstanding all the seemingly
insurmountable difficulties which stand in the way, and which
are far too numerous to particularize, my peace is connected

with my obedience. What will be the result I know not; the way appears not yet quite clear as to the time of departure. O Lord, favor me to wait on thee for the spirit of discernment not to step forth in the wrong time.

The obedience which he practised in committing himself in simple faith to this religious prospect prepared the way for a temporal blessing, as well as for the return of inward joy. He little knew, when persecuted by the Accuser of the brethren, and mourning over the weakness of his own corrupt nature, that his Lord was about to provide for him a congenial and helpful companion, in the room of her whose loss had left him solitary in the world. Without this timely sacrifice of his own will, it could not have been so easy for him to make the journey to France in the way in which it was done, and which was the means of bringing about the union which shed so much comfort on the remainder of his life.

Between two and three months after the meeting at Minden, he received the information that Martha Savory, accompanied by Martha Towell, was about to pay a religious visit to the Friends at Pyrmont and Minden. He had been introduced in London to Martha Savory as a minister of the gospel, and one who had been abroad in its service, but his acquaintance with her seems to have been slight.* On receiving this intelligence he writes:—

The prospect of seeing a few dear Friends from my native land would be cheering, but I am really so cast down that I

---

* The introduction was made by Thomas Shillitoe, at the time of the Yearly Meeting. He said to M. S., "Let me introduce thy brother to thee." "Brother!" she exclaimed, with surprise. "Yes," answered the good old man; "all who have been on the Continent are brothers and sisters."

seem as if I could not, and almost dare not, rejoice in anything. May this low proving season answer the end for
which it is permitted!

As he apprehended the Friends who were coming
from England might require a guide, John Yeardley
went to meet them at Rotterdam. His journey, and
the singular coincidence of Martha Savory's concern
with his own, are described in a letter to his brother,
written after his return from Holland.

Friedensthal, Pyrmont, 7 mo. 14, 1825.

MY DEAR BROTHER,

On my return from Holland I received thy long and
very interesting letter. Martha Savory and her companion
Martha Towell are now acceptably with us. They expect to
spend two or three months with us, and then we have some
prospect of going in company to the South of France. As
this has fallen out in a rather remarkakle manner, it may not
be amiss just to explain it to thee. We were entire strangers
to each other's concern; but as soon as my friends in London
heard of my prospect from the copy of the minutes of our
Two-months' Meeting and of my certificate, dear William
Allen wrote to me desiring a more particular description of
my views, time of departure, &c., and mentioned at the same
time M. S.'s concern, which had already passed the Quarterly
Meeting, and it was fully expected she would be liberated
[by the Meeting of Ministers and Elders] to visit Pyrmont
and Minden, and afterwards, if *suitable company offered*,
proceed to some parts of the banks of the Rhine, Switzerland, and Congenies, in the south of France. I wrote to
W. A., and explained to him my prospect, which was to visit
a few individuals in the neighborhood of Cologne and pass
through Switzerland to Congenies. I then received a letter
from our dear friend M. Savory, stating that she and W. A.
had been much struck with the remarkable coincidence in
our views; our prospects being to the same places and in the

same way; and that it seemed in the pointing of Truth for us to join in company.

Fifth mo. 26th, I left Friedensthal to visit my friends in Minden and its neighborhood; and after spending about two weeks there, I felt very much inclined to give our friends the meeting at Rotterdam. I set off, accordingly, the 7th of the Sixth Month, and travelled seven days through a desert country to Amsterdam. I went almost one half of the way by water, across the Zuider Zee from Zwolle to Amsterdam. After spending a few days in Amsterdam, I went, with J. S. Mollet, who is the only Friend in that city, to Rotterdam, where we met with M. S. and M. T. Thomas Christy, junior, had accompanied them from London. M. S. had letters of recommendation to many persons in Amsterdam, whom we visited; and though some of them were first-rate characters in the place, it is surprising with what affection and kindness they received us. J. S. Mollet accompanied us to Pyrmont.

An account of his journey, both going and returning, is also contained in J. Y.'s diary: it presents some additional notices which claim a place here.

Before leaving Minden for Rotterdam, he twice visited Eidinghausen, and saw some young men who were under suffering because of their refusal to serve in the militia.

One in particular (he says, in writing up the diary), a sweet young man, at this moment may be in torture. O, how I feel for him! My soul breathes to the Almighty Father of mercies on his account, that he may be strengthened to endure all with patience for the sake of his Lord, who has given him a testimony to bear against the spirit of war and fighting.

At the conclusion of the second meeting at Eidinghausen, he says:—

The meeting was fully attended, and I afterwards dined

alone in the schoolroom with a light heart.   I thought I could
say, After the work is done, food tastes sweet.

At Rotterdam, John Yeardley and his companions
made the acquaintance of a "very interesting missionary student, who believes he has a call to go on a
mission to the Greeks, and is waiting for an opening:
his name is Gützlaff."   At Amsterdam, a letter from
Gützlaff introduced them to the priest of the Greek
church in that city, Helanios Paschalides, a man of
child-like spirit, and long schooled in affliction, who had
become awakened to his own religious wants, and who
believed himself called to return to Greece and instruct
his countrymen.   These two interviews are memorable,
as being, probably, the commencement of the strong
interest which J. and M. Y. evinced in the Greek
people, and which issued, years afterwards, in a religious
tour in that country.   At Zeist, where there is a settlement of Moravians, the ministers, finding the Friends
desired to convene their members in a meeting for
worship, readily consented.

The meeting, writes J. Y., was more fully attended than
we had expected.   There is much sweetness of spirit to be
felt about these people, but a want of stillness.   I thought
some of the hearers were prepared to see further than their
teachers, and the time may yet come when some may be
drawn into a more spiritual worship.   We left them a few
tracts, and they kindly gave us a few little books of theirs.
It is remarkable in what a spirit of love they received us.

The Friends reached Pyrmont on the 1st of the
Seventh Month, and shortly afterwards made a visit
amongst the members from house to house in that place,
and at Minden.   On the 28th they visited a number of
seriously awakened persons at Lenzinghausen, who felt

the necessity of spiritual worship, and to whom their hearts were much enlarged in gospel love.

Walking in the garden, writes John Yeardley, in a very solemn and solitary frame of mind before the meeting, I had such a feeling as I scarcely ever remember to have had before. I thought I saw, as in the vision of light, as if a people would be gathered in that neighborhood to the knowledge of the truth. It appeared to me to be in the divine appointment that our dear M. S. was come to visit Germany, and a large field of labor seems to be appointed for her in this land if she is faithful.

The next two months were occupied with various religious services, public and private, not omitting meetings at Eidinghausen and Hille, where, as on former occasions, J. Y. found his heart to go out towards the people with strong emotions of Christian love. About 150 attended at the former, and 300 at the latter place.

# CHAPTER VI.

## 1825-6.

THE time was now come for John Yeardley and Martha Savory to pursue their journey to the Rhine, Switzerland and France. They left Pyrmont on the 11th of the Tenth Month, 1825, and beside Martha Towell, were accompanied as far as Basle by William Seebohm as interpreter. Every member of the party wrote in one way or other an account of the journey, and we have availed ourselves of these various sources in the following narrative.

Passing through Paderborn, they arrived at Herdecke on the 13th. Regarding his feelings in this place John Yeardley writes :—

This morning I was greatly dejected, and fearful we might find none of the people whom we were seeking. As I was walking pensively outside the town, I recollected what 1 once read in " Cecil's Remains,"—that a way may suddenly open before us when we the least expect it. This was now to be verified ; for after we had entered the carriage with the intention of going to Elberfeld, and while we were waiting for a road-ticket, I accidentally fell into conversation with our hostess, and making inquiry for people of religious character, learnt that there were a number of such in the neighborhood.

The Friends alighted, and sent for a member of this little society who resided in the town. He informed them that a meeting was held at Hageney, about six miles distant, at the house of a pastor named Hücker. Being disposed to visit this pastor, they took their informant with them as guide, turned their horses in the direction opposite to Elberfeld, and drove along a very bad road to his house. They found him occupied in teaching some poor children. He told them that their visit was opportune and remarkable, for that he had been denounced as a delinquent before the Synod of Berlin, which had sent him a string of questions on doctrine and church-government. He had returned a reply to the questions, and was then waiting the determination of the synod, whether he was to be displaced from his cure or not. The Friends examined his answers, and were well satisfied with them: the worship which he and his little flock (about thirty in number) practised was of a more spiritual character than that of the national church. Martha Savory expressed her deep sympathy with him in his difficult and painful situation, and John Yeardley also addressed him in words of consolation and encouragement.

At Elberfeld, where they arrived on the 15th, they met with several interesting persons. One of these, a young pastor named Ball, became greatly endeared to them. He informed them that when he had been severely tempted, he had found support and deliverance in silent waiting on the Lord. Another was Pastor Lindel, who resided at some distance from the city, in the Wupperthal; he had been brought up a Roman Catholic, had seen many changes, and suffered not a little persecution. He took them to see a neighbor, an aged man, weak in body, but strong and lively in spirit. This man told them he was present at a meeting at

9

Mühlheim held by Sarah Grubb, about thirty years before; and that, although ninety years old, he recollected the words with which she concluded her discourse: " By this shall all men know that ye are my disciples, if ye have love one to another." This love, say the narrators of the occurrence, was felt amongst us on this occasion, and at parting the good old man gave us his blessing.

They quitted Elberfeld on the 19th, and proceeded to Düsseldorf, where the reception they met with was equally open and gratifying. They spent an evening at Kaiserswerth with Pastor Fliedner, who was occupied in vigilantly guarding a little flock of Protestants surrounded by unscrupulous Romanists. He evinced much interest in the management of prisons, and was endeavoring to introduce improvements in that of Düsseldorf: he had met with Martha Savory in one of her visits at Newgate.*

The next day they went to Düsselthal, and inspected the institution there. The Count Von-der-Recke conducted them himself through every department.

His countenance, says John Yeardley, evinces the magnanimity and kindness of his heart; it is remarkable and precious that so young a man should dedicate his whole time and fortune for the benefit of the orphan and the destitute.

At Creveldt, the next town where they stopped, Pastor Molinaar and his wife, who were Mennonists

---

* Pastor Fliedner has since become more extensively known by the institution for Deaconesses which he has founded at Kaiserswerth, where, with many other useful and exemplary women, Florence Nightingale was trained. Kaiserswerth has become the parent of several other kindred institutions.

received them in a very cordial manner: the latter had seen Thomas Shillitoe at Amsterdam. J. Y. relates several visits which these worthy persons and some of their Christian friends paid to them at the inn.

*22nd.*—In the evening Pastor Molinaar came, with his wife and some friends, to tea. They inquired very narrowly respecting our principles. Pastor M. turned the conversation on women's preaching, and, after some explanation, appeared to be pretty well satisfied with our views on this subject. The Mennonists hold strongly to the use of Water Baptism, and the pastor and his wife defended this practice, the latter with much earnestness. But when we had unfolded our sentiments, and William Seebohm had read a passage from Tuke's "Principles," the pastor, seeing that we aimed only at the spiritual sense, acknowledged that he had often queried with himself whether the usage could not properly be dispensed with, and said that he intended still further to examine the question. Our certificates were then read; and after we had conversed on our church discipline, the company separated in mutual love.

The Friends inquired of the Mennonists whether any of their Society would incline to sit with them on the First-day evening.

Our friend, Martha Savory, told them we could not promise that anything should be uttered, seeing this could only take place through the immediate operation of the Holy Spirit. At the appointed time there assembled about fifty persons. After a short conversation they seated themselves, and when we had sat awhile in silence, M. S. found herself moved to address them in a feeling manner, W. S. interpreting; and I relieved my mind in German as well as I was able. Before we separated, Pastor Molinaar rose, and in the name of the rest expressed his heartfelt satisfaction, adding that he hoped we should remember them for good, as they should not fail to pray for our preservation.

*24th.*—We told Pastor M. that it would be agreeable if he
and any others of his friends who wished to take leave of us
would come to the hotel.   At seven o'clock, instead of a few
as we expected, there came about thirty.   The ladies seated
themselves quite sociably, and took out their work, but were
evidently prepared to lay it aside in the hope of having another religious sitting.   But as we believed there were those
present who had come from too great a desire to hear words,
we were on the guard not to satisfy this excited inclination;
and the evening was spent in agreeable conversation.   Before
we separated, however, we thought it well to read our Yearly
Meeting's Epistle, which was acceptable to all.   Pastor M.
especially was pleased with the part about church-discipline,
and said he considered it of real advantage that the epistle
had been read in that company, as there were several young
women present who might receive benefit from it.

Feeling attracted towards the inhabitants of Mühlheim
on the Ruhr, the Friends again turned out of the direct
road and crossing the Rhine a little beyond Duisburg,
arrived in the evening at Mühlheim.   They found a
company of Separatists in the neighborhood of the
town, some of whom they visited; and the next day
they passed over the Ruhr, and, with the assistance of a
school-master, convened a meeting for worship.   At the
time appointed nearly three hundred persons assembled,
mostly of the poorer class.   They were seated in a large
school-room, the men on one side and the women on the
other, waiting in silence.   They had a good meeting,
and at the conclusion the auditory expressed their unwillingness to part, and their desire that those who had
ministered to them should visit them again.

On the 27th, after calling upon some descendants of
Gerhard Tersteegen, our Friends proceeded through
Düsseldorf to Cologne.   They were disappointed of

finding in the neighborhood of this city, that company
of religious people on whose account they had felt much
interested, and of whom they had heard •that " they
held principles like the Quakers, and were as obstinate
in them as they are." They did no more here than call
upon a few serious persons in the city, and then went
forwards to Neuwied, hoping there to hear of them.

At Neuwied, besides becoming acquainted with the
Moravian preachers and others, they were called upon
by some of the *Inspirirten*, who invited them to their
meetings. They attended one of these; but, being dissatisfied with the manner of the service, and not finding
relief for their spiritual exercise, though the opportunity
of speaking was offered without reserve, they in turn
invited the company to meet with them the next morning
after the manner of Friends. The meeting was held to
mutual satisfaction, and one of the leading men amongst
the *Inspirirten* expressed the hope that it would be
blessed to them; for he was, he said, sensible of the want
of less activity and more of silent waiting in their religious assemblies.

The society to which these people belonged divided
in 1818 into two branches, after an awakening which
took place that year; those who separated believing it
to be incumbent upon them to lead more self-denying
lives, and dwell more closely under the influence of the
Holy Spirit. This new connection was the people of
whom our Friends had heard; and they learnt that they
had retired to a place called Schwartzenau, near Berlenburg, a small town at the eastern end of the barren hilly
region known as the Sauerland. The distance of this
place from Neuwied is considerable, and the roads
amongst the worst in Germany; but John Yeardley

and Martha Savory apprehended they could not peacefully pursue their journey without attempting to visit
them.

Accordingly they left Neuwied on the 1st of the
Eleventh Month, and proceeded to Montabauer. The
road led them at first amongst some of the choicest
scenery of the Rhine; but after a while they left the
river and struck into the interior of the country, in a
north-easterly direction. The next day they passed
through a place where, a few months before, a Diligence
had been robbed. The robbers, who had been taken a
fortnight after the offence, were then, as they were informed, in Limburg gaol, and were to be hanged the next
day. They were ten in number, all members of one
family. At Burbach they met with an English landlord,
thirty-five years resident in Germany; he was delighted
to see his fellow-countrymen, and exerted himself to
give them the best entertainment his house afforded.
The country they passed through was very hilly, and
overgrown with forest; now and then a solitary dwelling was seen in the bottom of the deep valleys.

On the 3rd they came to Siegen, an ancient and
antique town on the side of a high hill, looking, as one
of the party observed, as though they had reached the
end of the world. And, indeed, it seemed almost like
the end of the civilised world; for they were informed
that the road from thence to Berlenburg was in such a
miserable condition that they could take their carriage
no farther. They resolved, however, to make the attempt, and providing themselves with a tandem horse
(*vorspann*) and a guide, and sending on their luggage,
they set forth on the way to Letze, a village where they
proposed to lodge; but the waters were abroad from the

overflow of the rivers, and the road being extremely
narrow, and the ruts deep, they made very slow
progress. Sometimes the way was so impracticable
that they had to take the carriage through the woods
which skirted the road. Darkness and rain coming on
obliged them to halt for the night at Netphen, and seek
shelter in the humble dwelling of a woman, who at first
took alarm at the unexpected appearance of so many
strangers. The account which the guide gave respecting
the travellers dispelled her fears, and she did what she
could by hospitality to make up for the scantiness of
her accommodation. She gave them also some information respecting the *Inspirirten*, whom they were
on the way to visit, speaking favorably of them. The
next morning, before they started, they were able to
offer her spiritual good in return for her temporal kindness, John Yeardley ministering to her condition under
religious exercise; and they trusted his words found
entrance into her soul.

On the 4th they pursued their way, up hill and down,
the carriage sometimes becoming so firmly fixed in the
narrow deep ruts, that it was necessary to take out the
horses, and for the men of the party, with the assistance
of passers-by, to lift it over to more even ground.

At length they arrived at Erndebrück, and drove to
an inn; but not finding their luggage, they went to
another, and while they were preparing to start for
Berlenburg, William Seebohm went to the Custom-office
to show the ticket of clearance they had received on
entering the Prussian territory at Burbach. This ticket
should have obviated all delay attendant on the examination of the luggage; but it happened, most unfor-
tunately, that the custom officer was the landlord of the

inn they first came to. Their leaving his house without
taking refreshment was, in his eyes, an unpardonable
offence, and on William Seebohm presenting to him the
ticket, his countenance and language betrayed the pas-
sion which raged in his breast. He declared their
trunks should be examined in the strictest manner;
and when they represented the necessity they were
under of speedily pursuing their journey, and desired
him to despatch the business as quickly as possible, he
replied by detaining them until they were obliged to
send back the horse and guide, and consent to pass the
night under his roof. He then demanded their passports, and finding they had not been *visé'd* at all the
towns through which they had passed, and that the
travellers had departed from the route described in
them, he sent for a gendarme, and placed them under
arrest. They were not allowed to take anything from
their trunks without being watched by the gendarme;
and when they took out a letter of recommendation,
written by Dr. Steinkopf to the clergyman of the place,
whom they had requested to call upon them, the gendarme insisted on first reading it. On their expostu-
lating with the landlord at being treated in this manner,
instead of making a direct reply, he strutted up and
down the room, repeating continually, "Ja, ja, ja, ja!
they shall know what they went away from my house
for, and that there is a custom-office here." The Friends
took their evening meal, as is usual in Germany, in one
of the sleeping-rooms—that which had been allotted to
Martha Savory and Martha Towell. Into this chamber,
when they had eaten, the landlord brought a party of
eight or nine men to take their supper. After supper
the men smoked, and some of them did not even refrain

from showing their ill-breeding in a more disagreeable way. William Seebohm overheard the landlord and the gendarme say to each other, " These people are travelling this way to visit the Separatists, and strengthen them in their religious opinions; but we will disappoint them."

The next morning they were favored with a short season of solemn communion, in which they were given to believe that the Name of the Lord would be their strong tower. Their liberation, in fact, was near; for their envious jailor, finding probably no excuse for longer detaining them, suffered them to depart, but sent the gendarme to guard them as far as Berlenburg. The man proved to be an excellent guide, and being eager to bring them to the magistrate of that town, where they could be more effectually checked in their schismatical object, he was very useful in shouldering the carriage when they came to a stand in the miserable roads.

The town of Berlenburg presented a dismal spectacle, the greater part having recently been burnt down; so that they had some difficulty in making their way through the ruins. They were subjected to no delay at the Custom-house, but, before being allowed to go to an inn, were conducted by the gendarme to the Castle, to be examined by the *Landrath*, or magistrate. While John Yeardley and William Seebohm were taken into the justice-chamber, Martha Savory and Martha Towell remained in the carriage, where they were presently surrounded by a crowd, who gazed with astonishment at their equipage, no such vehicle having been seen in the town for many years, aud probably never any persons in such attire. Being weary of waiting, and anxious to know the result of the examination, they left

the carriage and ascended to the magistrate's room.
They were politely received, and arrived just as he
had concluded the examination and was declaring the
Friends entirely free from the requisitions of the law.
The letters of recommendation which they presented
were very helpful in procuring this result. At the
Landrath's request, they stated the object of their journey, and the reasons which had induced them to deviate
from the route described in the passports, of all which
he caused a note to be taken. At the conclusion he
politely dismissed them with the salutation, " Go where
you will, in God's name ;" and the abashed and disappointed gendarme was obliged to imitate his superior
and make them a parting bow. The magistrate referred
them to two of the citizens, for information regarding
the Separatists, but remarked that he considered a visit
to Schwartzenau at that critical moment would not be
without danger.

One of the persons on whom the Landrath recommended the Friends to call was the Inspector of the
Lutheran or State Church of the country; and on the
6th, which was First-day, after a time of worship in
their own apartment, they received a visit from this
personage. Wishing to act with entire openness, they
informed him of their desire to see the Separatists, and
invited him to accompany them. He gave them the
names of several with whom they might freely have
intercourse. As the interview proceeded mutual confidence increased, particularly after reading their certificates; and the Inspector expressed himself gratified
with the liberality entertained by Friends towards people of other religious persuasions.

It snowed all the next day, and the roads were deep

in water, so that M. S. and M. T. remained in-doors;
but J. Y. and W. S. walked to Homburgshausen, a
village about a mile and a-half from Berlenburg, to call
upon an aged man, a Separatist of the old connection.
He had heard of their arrival, and was overjoyed to see
them; he looked upon it as a providential occurrence
that they should have been sent there at that juncture.
His forefathers, he said, had been settled there many
years, and had hitherto enjoyed liberty of conscience;
but now he feared they were about to be deprived of
that privilege. Before the Friends left Berlenburg, he
called at their inn with several more of his society; he
appeared to be a truly pious man, and looked, they say,
exactly like *a good old Friend*. He declared himself to
be fully convinced of the value of silent worship, but
said that their people in general were not prepared to
adopt it; however they rejected outward baptism, and
the use of the bread and wine, and refused to bear
arms. He had been many times summoned before the
magistrates to be examined upon his religious belief.
On one of these occasions the Landrath asked why he
did not take the bread and wine, and why he did not
have his children baptised. He answered that if he
was to conform to these ceremonies it would be as
though he had received a sealed letter in which nothing
was written. He and his people were solicitous with
the Friends to have a meeting with them; but the minds
of John Yeardley and his companions were pre-occupied
with a desire first to see the New Separatists, who were
then under persecution, and they did not think it proper
to accede to the request.

In reply to a message which they sent to some of the
new society, they received, through a young woman

(for the men were afraid to come to the inn), a pressing invitation to visit some of them who lived in a retired spot called Schellershammer, not far distant. They immediately accepted the invitation. The road, which was impassable for a carriage, was covered with mud and water. They were received into a very humble dwelling by a pious young man and his family, with whom also they found some of the New Separatists from Schwartzenau. On sitting down with this company the restraining presence of the Lord was felt, under which they remained for some time in silence. Then the poor people opened to them their situation with humility and freedom. The young man above-mentioned had just drawn up a statement of their religious principles, which had been sent to the authorities. This statement he showed to the Friends, as also a letter to the King of Prussia, which had been prepared by one of their ministers, but which, from its lofty assumption of prophetic authority, they could not approve. These people called their ministers, *Instruments;* and they had fallen into the specious error of attributing to their effusions, whether spoken or written, equal authority with the Holy Scriptures. On other points their principles resembled those of Friends; as the disuse of outward ceremonies and of oaths, and their testimony against war. It was on these accounts that they were persecuted. They appeared to dwell under the cross of Christ, and to live in much quietness of spirit. Under the existing circumstances the Friends did not feel bound to appoint a general religious meeting with these people. They contented themselves, therefore, with unfolding their sentiments in conversation, giving them books, and before they left Berlenburg, addressing them by letter, in which they enlarged particularly on the subject of the ministry. They also left some copies of their Friends' books with the old society; and both parties declared their belief that the visit they had received was in the order of Divine Providence, and took leave of them in love and confidence.

The friends quitted Berlenburg on the 9th of the Eleventh Month, and proceeded towards Frankfort. After a day's journey over bad roads, they were glad to find themselves once more on the *chaussée.* They arrived on the 11th at Frankfort, where they called on a few pious individuals, but stayed a very short time in the city, being desirous of visiting some Old and New Separatists at Lieblose, near Gelnhausen, about twenty-four miles from Frankfort.

The next morning they accordingly went to Gelnhausen, and had social interviews with members of both associations, but failed to make use of the opportunity they had of holding a meeting for worship with the Old Separatists, which they afterwards regretted.

They then went forward to Raneberg, about six miles distant, to see the *Instrument* who wrote the letter to the King of Prussia which was shown to them at Schellershammer. They found him a young man, inhabiting an apartment in a lonely castle, romantically situated on a high hill. The access to the spot was through a forest, and by a very bad road. Whatever prejudice in regard to him they might have imbibed from the style of his letter was at once dispelled by his appearance; his look was so humble, so devoted, and with such "extreme sweetness of countenance." John Yeardley and Martha Savory conversed with him a long time; he did not rightly comprehend the nature of the Christian

ministry, but he listened calmly and patiently to all
they had to say. They left some books with him, and
received some in return, descriptive of the awakening
which gave rise to the division in the society of *Inspirirten*. He was then about to set out on foot to pay
a religious visit to the members of his own profession in
various parts of the country; when at home he worked
at his trade, which was that of a carpenter.

The party retraced their steps to Hanau, and the next
day pursued their way southwards. They passed through
Darmstadt and Heidelberg to Pforzheim. Here they
called on Henry Kienlin, whom they found a *Friend* in
principle and practice, and who had given many proofs
of his fidelity to his principles by the persecution he had
endured from his relations, and the pecuniary loss he
had suffered for refusing to comply with ecclesiastical
and military demands. He was a man of station and
influence in the town. He had not previously had personal acquaintance with any members of the Society
of Friends, but had read many of their writings. He
accompanied the travellers five miles out of the town to
a little flock of Separatists, who had not yet obtained
religious liberty, and to whom it was forbidden under
a severe penalty to attend meetings held by strangers.
On the visiters entering the house of one of them, a
number presently collected; and as they stood together,
a solemn feeling pervaded the assembly, and John
Yeardley was moved to address them in gospel testimony. Henry Kienlin followed, explaining the principles of Friends clearly, and giving them some suitable
advice. They were laboring under the want of discipline and organization, and of some one properly to
represent their case to the government. Some of them

called the next day at Pforzheim, to see the Friends again before they left.

The next place where they halted was Stuttgardt, to which city H. Kienlin gave them his company. Here they visited Queen Catharine's Institution, a school for the training of girls in reduced circumstances, as teachers, &c., where 170 young persons were being educated. They were also introduced to a number of pious individuals, and among them to Pastor Hoffmann of Kornthal, whose excellent institution they were unable at this time to visit. An appointment had been made for them to meet at Basle Louis A. Majolier of Congenies, who was to serve as their guide and French interpreter through Switzerland and France, and they felt obliged on being informed of this appointment to pursue their journey more quickly than they otherwise would have done.

Returning to Pforzheim, they stopped at Mühlhausen, where they called on Müller, minister of a congregation, consisting of 170 persons, who had separated a few years before from the Catholics. This young man received them with openness and affection, and before they parted, John Yeardley had something to say to him under religious exercise, which he received in the love in which it was spoken. From Pforzheim they went direct to Basle, through Freiburg. On their arrival they were much disappointed to find that Louis Majolier had waited for them many days, and hearing no tidings of them, had returned to Geneva, supposing they had gone on to that city by another route.

At Basle they were introduced to many pious persons, conspicuous among whom was Blumhardt, inspector of the Mission-house, who behaved towards them "as a

loving and kind father in Christ." He encouraged them
in their concern to have a religious meeting with the
students.   The meeting took place in the evening when
the young men were collected for supper and devotion;
they received the word which was preached to them in
gospel love, and manifested towards our friends no small
degree of tenderness and affection.   John Yeardley
says:—

We had reason to believe there are among them many
precious young men who are preparing for usefulness.  The
grounds on which this place is conducted are different from
most of the kind.  None are sent out but those who can
really say they feel it to be their religious duty to go to any
certain people or country.  A sweet young man, who was
extremely attentive to us, Charles Haensel, is since gone to
Sierra Leone to teach the poor negroes, from a conviction of
duty.

One day during their sojourn, C. Haensel took them
to a meeting for worship, held in the house of C. F.
Spittler.

J. Y. says, we sat until they had performed part of their
worship, and then the leader signified to the company that a
few Friends from England were present, and told us that if we
had anything to offer we had full liberty to do so.  Silence
ensuing, dear M. S. found herself constrained to address them
in a way suited to the occasion; I was also enabled to express
what came before me.  They afterwards expressed their
thankfulness for the opportunity.

From Basle William Seebohm returned to Pyrmont,
and the English Friends, hoping that they might meet
Louis Majolier at Berne, went forward to that city, but
were again disappointed.

Although they were anxious to reach Geneva as quickly as possible, the attraction of gospel love towards Zurich was so strong that they could not continue their journey until they had visited that city. They arrived there on the 2nd of the Twelfth Month. The state of their own feelings and the refreshing Christian intercourse which awaited them are thus described in the Diary:—

First-day, we sat down to hold our little meeting. It was to me a low time, but I still thought the hand of divine help was near to comfort us, and before the close dear M. S. was drawn into supplication in a way which expressed the feelings of all our hearts. After this season of spiritual refreshment, we called on Professor Gessner, who, with his wife and family, was truly glad to see us. Being near dinner-time, we could not stay long; but their daughter offered to accompany us to her aunt's this afternoon, and accordingly came to our inn, and went with us to "Miss" Lavater, who, with Gessner's wife, is a daughter of the pious author Lavater. She received us with open arms, but spoke only German, or at least but very little French, so that M. S. conversed with her in German. She spoke of Stephen Grellet with much interest and affection: he lives in the remembrance of all in this country who have seen and known him, as well as William Allen. How pleasant it is to find that such devoted instruments have left such a good savor behind them! Wherever we follow dear Stephen, his presence has made a sufficient introduction to us; but I regret exceedingly my own incapability of being sufficiently useful in these precious opportunities which we meet with: but, as we often say in our little company, This is like a voyage of discovery; and our humble endeavors, however weak, may have a tendency to open the way for others who may be made more extensively useful, should such ever be led to visit the solitary parts where we have been.

We were invited to drink tea this afternoon by our friend

10

Gessner, and on a nearer acquaintance found this a precious
family; his wife is a sweet-spirited person, and their daughters pious young women. One of them, in particular, I
thought not only bore the mark of having been with her
Saviour, but a desire was also expressed in her countenance
to abide with him: may He who has visited her mind draw
her more and more by the cords of his love and preserve her
from the evil which is in the world! When tea was ended,
we dropped into silence, and Pastor Gessner offered up a
prayer from the sincerity of his heart, and it was evidently
attended by the spirit of divine grace and life. Afterwards
dear M. S. and I expressed what was on our minds; I interpreted for her as well as I could, and I hope they understood
it. We were all much tendered in sympathy together, and
I think the visit to this family will not soon be forgotten:
we took leave of them in the most affectionate manner, they
expressing sincere desires for our preservation.          ˌ

On their return to Berne they met with some pious
ladies:

One of whom, says John Yeardley, spoke German with
me, and entered pretty suddenly on the subject of the bread
and wine supper, or sacrament. She seemed to have lost
sight that there is a spiritual communion which the soul can
hold with its Saviour, and which needs not the help of outward shadows; but it is remarkable when our reasons for the
disuse of such things are given in simplicity and love, how
the feelings of others become changed towards us; they then
see we do not refuse the administration of them out of obstinacy, but from a tender conscience.

On the 8th they drove to Lausanne, and the next
day to Geneva. John Yeardley has preserved, in his
diary of this part of the journey, a little anecdote of
French character which naturally struck him the more
forcibly from his having hitherto been conversant only

with the phlegmatic temperament of the Germans.   The coachman, it should be said, was of that nation.

On the road between Nyon and Geneva a little incident occurred which showed us the liveliness of the French temperament.   A man got up behind our carriage, and our coachman very naturally whipped him down.   The man followed us quietly for a while, but at length his wounded dignity overcame his patience, and he came up to our coachman and began to speak furiously on the impropriety of his having whipped him.   Finding he could make nothing of one who understood not what he said, he addressed himself to our friend Martha Towell, and said he knew he had done wrong; but the coachman should have told him to get down, which was customary in their country, and not to have whipped him.   M. T. was prepared to appease his wrath by a mild reply, which eased the poor·man very much; otherwise I think we should have had more trouble with him; but he seemed to be quieted, and said, Teach your coachman to say, in French, "descendez."

They reached Geneva just in time to prevent the departure of Louis Majolier:

Who, says Martha Savory, was indeed rejoiced to see us after all his anxiety.   But, she continues, great as was our mutual satisfaction at meeting, I am inclined to think it would have been better if this plan had never been proposed, as it was a means of preventing some movements which might have tended much to our relief; and his mind was in such an anxious state about home that he could not give himself to anything that might have opened at Geneva or Lausanne (to which I expected to return), but begged us, very earnestly, to return with him to Congenies, as soon as possible.— · (*Letter to E. Dudley.*)

They found the religious world at Geneva in a state of convulsion.

The secret poison of infidelity, says J. Y., has a good deal sapped the principle of real religion; and the clergy of the Established Church have preached a doctrine tending to Socinianism. A few young ministers have boldly come forth and separated themselves, and are determined, in the midst of persecution, to preach Christ and him crucified. Some of these seem to have gone to the opposite extreme, for they hold too strongly the principles of predestination. It is a remarkable time in this neighborhood, as well as at Lausanne, where many are awakened to seek more after the substance of religion.

At Geneva they formed a friendship with several persons, among whom were Pastors Moulinier and L'Huillier, and Captain Owen, an Englishman. With the last-named they were united in close bonds of religious affection; they were enabled to administer to his spiritual wants, and he was forward to render them assistance in every possible way.

The journey from Geneva to Nismes was tedious, occupying more than a week.

On approaching Nismes, John Yeardley says, the beautiful olives and vineyards, together with the wild rocky aspect around, form a pleasing sight; and to see them pruning, digging, and dunging about the trees, reminds one of the relations of Scripture history.

At Nismes they went to see the amphitheatre :—

From the top of which, says J. Y., we had a view of the city and the surrounding neighborhood, which is indeed beautiful. The great number of olives, vines, fig-trees, &c., excite a train of ideas pleasing and indescribable.

In travelling through Switzerland John Yeardley had been often brought into a low state of mind, and on approaching Congenies, the final object of the journey,

his heart was stirred to its depths.  It is very instructive
to observe what were his feelings in reaching a place to
which his mind had been so long directed.

The road, he says, was better, and the outward prospect a
little enlivening; but it is not easy to describe the feelings
my mind was under in approaching a place which has so long
occupied my thoughtfulness to visit.  The prospect is discouraging, but I must be content and sink down to the spring
of life, which can alone make known the objects of duty and
qualify for their fulfilment.  In the midst of all my spiritual
poverty a stream of gratitude flows in my heart to the Father
of mercies, that he has been pleased to preserve us in many
dangers, and bring us safe to this part of his heritage; and if
it should be his will that I should have nothing to do but to
suffer for his name's sake, may he grant me patience to
bear it.

Martha Savory's feelings on the same occasion were
also those of deep gratitude for the preservation experienced during their journey, united, she says, with an
humbling sense of many omissions and great unworthiness, yet of help having been mercifully administered
in the time of need.—(*Letter of* 2 *mo.* 10, 1826.)

Edward Brady was spending the winter at Congenies
for the sake of his health, and his society was a source of
no little comfort to John Yeardley; who, however, still
frequently labored under spiritual depression.

Before dinner, he writes under date of the 23rd of the
Twelfth Month, we took a walk to M. S.'s windmill, from
whence we had a fair view of Congenies and the neighborhood, which is of a wild description.  On reflecting on the
place and circumstances connected with it, my mind was
filled with various ideas, but none of them of an encouraging
nature.

His discouragement was increased by ignorance of the language, and, with his accustomed diligence, on the morrow after his arrival he commenced learning French. On the recurrence of his birth-day, which was nearly coincident with the beginning of the year, he says:—

I am once more entered on a new year of my life, I fear without the last having been much improved; and to form resolutions of amendment in my own strength can avail me nothing. May He who knows my infirmities assist me to overcome them and to become more useful in his cause. My discouragement still continues; I don't feel those refreshing seasons which I have often experienced in times past; the pure life is often low in meeting, and I am not so watchful and diligent to improve my time and talent as I ought to be. I often feel as one already laid by useless, and the language of my heart is, "O that I were as in days past!"

Soon after their arrival at Congenies, Martha Savory met with a serious accident. Thinking a ride would be beneficial to her health, when the rest of the party drove one afternoon to Sommières, she accompanied them on horseback. She had not a proper saddle, and her horse being eager to keep up with the carriage set off down-hill at so rapid a rate as to throw her to the ground. The cap of one knee was displaced by the fall, and, although she soon recovered so as to be able to walk, the limb continued to be subject to weakness for some years.

As soon as M. S. was sufficiently recovered, she and her companions visited the Friends at Congenies and the neighboring villages from house to house, and also assembled on one occasion the heads of families, and on another the young people of the Society. In reviewing a part of this service John Yeardley says:—

3 *mo*. 6.—It has been a deeply exercising time, but has tended much more to the relief of our minds, at least as regards myself, than I had anticipated. From the discouraged state of mind I passed through for the first few weeks at this place, I expected to leave it burdened and distressed, but am thankful to acknowledge that holy help has been near to afford relief to my poor tossed spirit, and I have cause to believe it is in divine wisdom that I am here.

On the 13th of the Third Month they took leave of their friends at Congenies to return to England, being accompanied by Edward Brady, and during part of the journey by Louis Majolier. By the way they had some religious intercourse with Protestant dissenters at a few places; but at St. Etienne, where they had expected to remain a fortnight, they found the door nearly closed to their entrance; a company of pious persons in this town were at that time so nearly united with Friends as to bear their name.

These, says John Yeardley, in a letter, are now reduced to about twenty in number. They have suffered and still suffer much persecution from the Roman Catholics. They are forbidden by heavy fines to meet together, except in very small companies. We met them several times in their small meetings to much comfort; there are a few among them who have stood firm through the heat of trial, and these are precious individuals. The priests are exceedingly jealous. On our arrival in the town we held our little meeting with these pious people on First-day morning; the priest came to the house of the woman Friend where we had been to demand who we were and where we lodged, and said it was we who had caused them to err, and he would convince us in their presence that we were not only in error ourselves, but had led them into error also. But we saw nothing of him, and left the place in safety, which we considered a great favor; for such has been their rage that they have dared to shoot at some missionaries who have been in the neighborhood (*Letter to Thomas Yeardley,* 4 mo. 19.)

The rest of the journey through France was in general dreary, the external accommodation being bad, and the consolation of spiritual intercourse very scanty. At Arras, however, they were refreshed by the company of a Protestant minister, a liberal and worthy man, who had "to stand alone in a large district of weak-handed Protestants among strong-headed Catholics." ·

Arriving at Calais, Martha Savory and Martha Towell, with Edward Brady, crossed over to England, leaving John Yeardley to follow at a later period. On the 14th of the Fourth Month he writes:—

My dear companions left for England. I watched them from the pier until I could bear to stay no longer, and then returned sorrowfully to my quarters, and soon repaired to the little retired lodging we had engaged for me in the country, where I spent a few days in learning French, &c. In taking a retrospect of our long journey I feel a large degree of peaceful satisfaction in having been desirous to fulfil (though very imperfectly) a religious duty; and these feelings of gratitude excited a wish that the remainder of my few days might be more faithfully devoted to the service of my great Lord and Master.

The little lodging of which he speaks was "a retired chamber on the garden-wall;" and having left it for a few days to go to Antwerp with the carriage and horses which they had used on the journey, on his return it had already acquired, in his view, something of the character of home.

The beautiful green branches, says he, modestly looking in at the window, give me a silent welcome; and the little birds chirruping in the garden, which is my drawing-room and study. I cannot but acknowledge how grateful I feel in being permitted to rest in so quiet a retreat, shut up from many of those anxious cares which have perplexed the former part of my life.—(*Diary*, 4 mo. 27.)

The last few words 'of this memorandum may seem at first sight to refer to his temporary seclusion from the world in his little hermitage at Calais; but there is little doubt that they have a wider significance, and contain also an allusion to his anticipated union with Martha Savory. The prospect of this union seems to have sprung up during the journey, and to have become matured before they separated at Calais; and the effect of it was, amongst other things, to set him free from the necessity of pursuing business any longer as a means of livelihood, and to ensure to him a provision sufficient for his moderate wants.

On the 12th of the Fifth Month, John Yeardley left Calais for London. At the inn in Calais, a little incident occurred, the relation of which may be useful to others.

A serious Frenchman, who was going on board the same packet, was struck with my not paying for the music after dinner, and was much inclined to know my reason, believing my refusal was from a religious motive. At a suitable opportunity he asked me, and confessed he had felt a scruple of the same kind, and regretted he had not been faithful. This slight incident was the means of making me acquainted with an honest and religious man, as I afterwards found him to be.

How important it is to be faithful in very little things, not knowing what effect they may have on others!

# CHAPTER VII.

## 1826–27.

During his stay in London, John Yeardley attended the Yearly Meeting, and the Annual Meetings of the School, Anti-slavery, and other Societies, with which he was much gratified. Soon after the termination of the Yearly Meeting, he went into Yorkshire to see his mother.

6 *mo.* 13.—I left London in the mail for Sheffield, and on the 14th slept at my dear brother Thomas's at Ecclesfield, who took me on the 15th, to Barnsley. I was truly thankful to be favored to see my precious mother once more. On the 19th, I attended the Monthly Meeting at Highflatts. It is not easy to describe the various thoughts which rushed into my mind on seeing so many Friends whom I had known and loved in former days. The meeting was a much-favored time, although we felt the want of some of the fathers and mothers who are removed.

In the next entry there is an allusion to the disastrous commercial panic by which this year was distinguished.

7 *mo.* 24.—Have been very low and deserted in mind for a long time past. It is a time for the trial of my patience, and yet I have many favors for which I ought to be truly thankful. It is a precious privilege to be relieved from the commercial difficulties which at present abound in the trading world. May it be my lot ever to keep so, if consistent with the divine will.

8 *mo.* 21.—Monthly Meeting at Wooldale. The meeting

was exceedingly crowded with strangers; there was not room in the house to hold all who came. I had been very low all the morning, and to see such a number of people at the meeting sunk me low indeed. I was enabled to turn inward to Him from whom help alone comes; and blessed be his holy Name, he did not forsake me in the needful time, but was pleased once more to give strength and utterance to communicate what came before me. My certificates from Germany and Congenies were read and accepted, and many Friends expressed much unity and sympathy with me on my return to them, which was a comfort and strength to me.

On the 1st of the Ninth Month, he again went to London. During his stay in the city, he took the opportunity of visiting the Industrial Schools at Lindfield, founded by William Allen; a kind of institution which always engaged his warmest sympathy and approbation.

With the new turn which was given to the course of his life by his betrothal to Martha Savory, it is not surprising that he should have considered his residence abroad to be brought, in the order of Divine Providence, to a natural termination, and that he now turned his attention to taking up his abode again in his native land. In selecting a place of residence, he seems to have had no hesitation in making choice of the neighborhood of Barnsley; the spot, as the reader may remember, which seemed to him, when he was obliged to remove to Bentham, as that which had the first claim upon his gospel services. The state of his mind, whilst preparing his intended residence at Burton, the same village where he used to attend meeting in his early days, may be seen by the following memorandum:—

9 mo. 26. *At York.*—It was a large Quarterly Meeting. Living ministry flowed freely, and I thought even poor me

was a little refreshed: but I have been for a long time in a deplorable state, in a spiritual sense.

Since the Quarterly Meeting, my time and thoughts have been much occupied in fitting up our intended residence at the cottage at Burton; and I may truly say, I have been cumbered about "many things," which, I think, has kept my mind in a poor, barren state. O the many weeks that I have had to sit with my mouth in the dust to bemoan my own inward misery! My conflict of mind has been increased by the trying state of my precious mother's health. My attendance on her in this poorly state, and at this season of the year, when I lost my poor dearest Bessie, reminded me strongly of my dear departed lamb.

Before his marriage with Martha Savory was accomplished, he was called upon to attend the deathbed of his mother, and to follow the remains of his father to the grave.

11 *mo*. 16.—On the 3rd I left the cottage, and took my luggage to go from Barnsley by the coach to London. Stepped down to take leave of my dear mother, but found her so weak that I could not at all think of leaving her; and was indeed glad that I did not go, for the dear creature continued to grow weaker and weaker till a quarter past three o'clock on Seventh-day morning, 4th of Eleventh Month, when she peacefully breathed her last. She was fully sensible to the close, and also fully sensible that her end was near.

Her precious remains were interred at Burton on the 7th, after a meeting appointed for the occasion at Barnsley. In her room, before we left Redbrook [where she had resided], I was enabled to petition the throne of mercy for a little help and strength through the remainder of the solemn scene, which, I think, was in a remarkable manner granted. After having paid the last tribute of affection and duty to our endeared parent, fourteen of our dear friends and relations

dined with me at the cottage. It is remarkable that the
opening of our residence should be in this awful manner;
but we were much comforted in feeling in the midst of all
our sorrow, the greatest degree of peace and quietude on the
solemn occasion.

On Fourth-day, being the day after we had taken leave of
our precious mother's remains, I went with my brother and
sister to see our poor dear father, who had been ill in bed
about two weeks. We arrived about seven o'clock; but, to
our great surprise, about an hour before we reached the
place, our beloved father had fallen asleep, never to wake
more in this world. This was indeed awful, but the Judge
of the earth must do right. We attended the interment on
First-day, the 12th. The meeting-house at Woodhouse was
pretty full, and a good and tendering meeting it was. It felt
hard work to labor among a number of worldly-minded
people; but I have learned to consider it one of the greatest
of privileges to be appointed to service, even though attended
with suffering. Since this time my poor mind has felt more
tender and more susceptible of good. O that it may continue, and that I may remain humble and watchful for the
time to come, and live prepared for that awful change which
I know not how soon may be sent to my dwelling!—
(11 *mo.* 16.)

On the 18th he pursued his journey to London, and
on the 21st, at Gracechurch-street Monthly Meeting,
he presented his intention of marriage with Martha
Savory. " In a private interview at Elizabeth Dudley's,"
he writes, " Richard Barrett and E. Dudley expressed
their full unity with our intended union, in terms of
much interest and encouragement." On the 13th of
the Twelfth Month the marriage took place at Gracechurch-street Meeting-house.

The time in silence, says the Diary, was very solemn, and
acceptable testimonies were borne by William Allen and

Elizabeth Dudley. After meeting we adjourned to the Library to take leave, where a stream of encouragement flowed to us from several of our dear friends, which felt truly strengthening. About twenty of our friends and relations dined at A. B. Savory's at Stoke Newington. The day was spent, I trust, profitably, and on parting, about seven o'clock, we had a comfortable time, and something was expressed by my M. and self, and dear W. Allen. After taking a very affectionate leave, we posted on to Barnet. My brother Thomas and J. A. Wilson took us up the next morning; and we four came down in the coach to Sheffield, and [the next day] to Ecclesfield to dinner, and arrived at our humble cottage the 15th of the Twelfth Month, I trust with thankful hearts.

---

It is appropriate to give in this place some account of Martha Savory's character and Christian experience. That our notice is brief and incomplete, is owing to the loss of most of her own memoranda, and of the letters she addressed to those with whom she was on intimate terms. She possessed, it will be seen, an intellectual character and disposition, as well as an experience, very different from those of her husband. It does not follow, however, that this dissimilarity was a hindrance to their joint service in the gospel, any more than to their social harmony and love. It may be, on the contrary, that Martha Savory's quickness of understanding and of feeling, the readiness with which she apprehended the sentiments and condition of others, her conversancy with the allurements of city life, and the perils of unbelief from which she had been rescued, fitted her in a peculiar degree to be her husband's helper in the ministry, especially in their travels on the Continent.

She was born in London in 1781, and was the daughter of Joseph and Anna Savory. To an active and vigorous understanding she united a strength of will which would brook little control, together with much energy and fearlessness; and the propensity to follow the vain inclinations of the unregenerate heart displayed itself in an indulgence in much that was inimical to the restraints of Christian principle. Her disposition was generous; all her emotions were ardent, and were seldom subjected to the discipline of a corrected judgment. There were, however, various occasions, even in her very early years, when, through the visitations of heavenly love, her mind was forcibly aroused to a conviction of the need of redeeming grace. She was particularly impressed by the preaching and influence of William Savery, whose home in London was at her father's house. In some memoranda of this period, she remarks, "Frequently in the meetings appointed by him, I was greatly wrought upon by his living ministry;" and notwithstanding that she subsequently wandered far from the way of peace, there is good ground to believe that the remembrance of those truths which had penetrated her heart through the instrumentality of this gospel messenger, was never altogether effaced.

Being naturally endowed with a lively imagination and a taste for literature, she sought to suppress the upbraidings of conscience in intellectual pursuits, and employed much time in the composition of verses that were merely a transcript of visionary and romantic ideas, afterwards published under the title of "Poetical Tales." This volume obtained but a limited circulation; for, soon after it had issued from the press, the conviction that it had been an unhallowed and unprofitable exercise of her understanding was so impressed upon her spirit, that, although the sacrifice was considerable, she caused all the unsold copies to be destroyed. It is interesting to observe how, in later years, this talent for metrical rhythm, which had been so misapplied, became consecrated, as were all her faculties, to the promotion of piety and virtue.

During the long period in which her mental energies were thus misdirected, a cloud of darkness enveloped her spirit. She had, when about nineteen years of age, imbibed sceptical views in reference to the truths of revealed religion; and as she seldom read the Holy Scriptures, and was almost a stranger to their sacred. contents, her imagination pictured an easier way to escape from the power and the consequences of sin than in that self-renunciation which the Gospel enjoins. In some memoranda of her experience, she says, in reference to the snares by which her mind was entangled :—" I was led to a love of metaphysical studies, and fancied I discovered, with clearness, that human vice, and consequently human misery, sprang from ignorance of the nature of virtue, and that if mankind would become instructed they would become good; and that it was only necessary to behold virtue in its native beauty, to love it and to practise it. O how fallacious was this reasoning! 'The world by wisdom knows not God; the natural man receives not the things of the Spirit of God, for they are foolishness to him, neither can he know them, because they are spiritually discerned.' "

At length, however, when, in 1811, Martha Savory had completed the thirtieth year of her life, she became deeply impressed by the conviction that she was wandering on the barren mountains of doubt and error;

and through the renewed visitation of divine love, the light of the Sun of righteousness again shined into her heart, and its humbling influence brake the rock in pieces. Some circumstances occurred that were instrumental in promoting this great change. She was introduced into frequent communication with some honored servants of the Lord, particularly with the late Mary Dudley, and her daughter Elizabeth. An attack of indisposition prostrated her bodily strength, and afforded opportunity for serious reflection. Whilst from this cause confined to her chamber, a young person (Susanna Corder), with whom she was only very slightly acquainted, but to whom she was ever afterwards united in an intimate and confidential friendship, was attracted to visit her. The interview was a memorable one; the overshadowing wing of goodness and mercy being permitted to gather their spirits under its blessed influence. On her recovery from this illness, Martha Savory paid a short visit to her new friend, which afforded an opportunity for the manifestation of continued deep Christian interest; and, on her quitting the house, Susanna Corder put into her hand a copy of the "Olney Hymns." When she had proceeded a few steps towards home, she opened the book, and without noticing even the title, instantly cast her eyes on the lines, "The rebel's surrender to grace," commencing—

"Lord, Thou hast won; at length I yield;
My heart, by mighty grace compelled,
    Surrenders all to Thee ;
Against thy terrors long I strove,
But who can stand against thy love ?
    Love conquers even me."

She was deeply affected by the remarkable application of the whole of the hymn to the experience which
11

she was then passing through; she could not refrain
from weeping, and to avoid the observation of passers-
by, she walked through secluded streets, giving vent to
her emotion; and she afterwards repeatedly expressed
her belief that there was, in this apparently casual incident, a divine interposition and guidance; "for," said
she, "*every word* of that hymn appeared as if purposely
written to describe *my* case, so that I could scarcely
read it from the many tears I shed over it. It is no
exaggerated picture."

She now spent much time alone, almost constantly
reading the Bible; and so precious was the influence
that operated on her spirit, whilst thus employed, and
so wonderfully were the blessed truths of the gospel
unfolded to her understanding, that, as she expressed
it, "every page of it seemed, as it were, illuminated."
Sustained by the joy and peace of believing, she was
enabled to follow in faith the leadings of the Holy Spirit,
and, through divine strength, to become as a whole
burnt sacrifice on the altar of that gracious Redeemer,
who had, in his rich mercy, plucked her from the pit of
destruction. Having had much forgiven, she loved much,
and shrunk not from the many and deep humiliations
which were involved in such a course of dedication to
her Lord. Even her *external* appearance strikingly
bespoke her altered character. There had always been
in her countenance an expression of benevolence, but it
had not indicated a gentle or diffident mind. In her
demeanor and personal attire, she had conspicuously
followed the vain fashions of the times; but now, humility, with a modest and retiring manner, marked her
conduct; everything merely ornamental was discarded,
and the softening effect of a sanctifying principle im-

parted to the features of her face a sweetness which, impressing the beholder with a consciousness of the regenerating power that wrought within, was, to more than a few of her acquaintance, both arousing and instructive. She changed her residence from Finsbury to the borough of Southwark, and settled near her friend Susanna Corder, with whom she united in the formation of a philanthropic association, "The Southwark Female Society for the relief of sickness and extreme want." The late Mary Sterry, and several other estimable members of Southwark meeting, together with benevolent individuals among the different religious denominations of the district, soon joined them, and the society became a highly influential channel through which assistance has been variously rendered to many thousands of the indigent poor; and it still continues, though with a reduced scale of operations, to be an important source of help to the sick and destitute.

Martha Savory devoted to this work of mercy much time and personal exertion; but a more important service was also designed for her. She felt constrained to give evidence of her love to Christ by a public testimony to the grace which had been vouchsafed to her through Him who is "the way, the truth, and the life." Deep were the conflicts of spirit which she endured ere she could yield to this solemn requirement, but "sweet peace" was, she says, as she records the sacrifice, the result of thus acknowledging her gracious Lord. "This step," she continues, "appears to me to involve the greatest of all possible mental reduction, but I reverently believe it was necessary for me, and more, perhaps on my own account than on account of others; for, without this bond, and the necessary baptisms attending this vocation, I should have been in danger of turning back, and perhaps altogether losing the little spiritual life which has been mercifully raised." She adds a fervent petition for preservation and guidance, and that, by whatever means, however suffering to nature, the vessel might be purified, and fitted for the Master's use. She first spoke as a minister in the year 1814. The humiliation and brokenness of spirit which marked these weighty engagements, were felt by many, especially among her youthful friends, to be peculiarly impressive, as tokens of the soul-cleansing operations of omnipotent love, and as an awakening call to yield to the same regenerating influence.

She was acknowledged as a minister by Southwark Monthly Meeting, in the year 1818, when she had reached the age of 36; and in 1821, with the cordial approval of the meetings of which she was a member, she commenced that course of missionary labor in the gospel, to which she was subsequently so much devoted. Her mission, on this occasion, was to Congenies, where, and in the surrounding villages, she remained twelve months.

A letter to one of her sisters, written a few years after her marriage, so fully represents her religious sentiments, and the doctrine she was concerned to preach and maintain, that it may not improperly conclude this outline of her mental and religious character.

Burton, 13th of Twelfth Month, 1830.

I read thy remarks, my endeared sister, on the present state of things amongst us, with much interest, from having had corresponding feelings frequently raised in my own mind in this day of general excitement on religious subjects.

It remains to be a solemn truth that nothing can draw to God but what proceeds from him; and whatever may be the eloquence or oratory of man, if it be not the gift of God, and under his holy anointing, which always has a tendency to humble the creature and exalt the Creator, it will in the end only scatter and deceive. It has long appeared to me that true vital religion is a very simple thing, although from our fallen state, requiring continual warfare with evil to keep it alive. It surely consists in communion, and at times a degree of union, with our Omnipotent Creator, through the mediation of our Holy Redeemer. And seeing these feelings cannot be produced by eloquent discourses or beautiful illustrations of Scripture, but by deep humiliation and frequent baptisms of spirit, whereby the heart is purified and fitted to receive a greater degree of divine influence; seeing it is produced by daily prayer, by giving up our own will, and seeking above all things to do the will of our Heavenly Father, surely there is cause to hope that those who are convinced of this, and who have tasted of spiritual communion through this appointed means, will never be satisfied with anything however enticing which, if not under the influence of the Holy Spirit, may well be compared to "sounding brass or a tinkling cymbal."

I am far from confining this influence to the ministers of our little Society, but assuredly believe that those who are brought under the immediate teachings of the Spirit, under every profession, will be more and more convinced that they cannot preach to profit the people, in their own will and at their own command; and that as true and spiritual religion prevails they must in this respect come to us, and not we go to them. Yet still it is certainly a day of much excitement, and of danger especially to the young and unawakened, and there never was a time when the members of our Society were more loudly called upon to watch unto prayer both on their own account and on account of others, humbly to implore, not only that the Holy Spirit may not be taken from us, but that a greater effusion of it may be poured upon us as a body, that so we may all be made and kept alive in Him in whom is

life, and the life is the light of men. I believe this would
be much more our experience, if the things of this world were
kept in subjection by fervent daily prayer and the obedience
of faith, which remain to be the means pointed out by our
gracious Redeemer, of communion with the Father through
Him. What can be more pure than the profession we make,
to be guided by the Holy Spirit? and if we really are so, we
shall be concerned to maintain this daily exercise of heart
before the Lord, and yet become what I reverently believe is
his gracious will respecting us, and *all* under every name who
are thus guided and have become living members of the
Church of Christ, even that we should be as lights in the
world, or a city set upon a hill which cannot be hid:

--------

The dwelling which John and Martha Yeardley
occupied was on the highest ground in the village,
commanding a wide and cheerful prospect, and overlooking, on the western side, the valley of the Dearn
and the conspicuous town of Barnsley, which, notwithstanding the smoke that envelopes it, stands out in fine
relief on the opposite hill. Their cottage adjoined the
Friends' burial-ground; and just on the other side of
the wall reposed the remains of Frances Yeardley, on
the site formerly occupied by the meeting-house.*

* This is one of the earliest burial-grounds which belonged to Friends.
Over the gateway was a curious inscription on brass, now removed to
Barnsley. It is as follows :

"Anno Domini 1657. Though superstitious minds doe judge amisse
of this buriall place, yet lett them know hereby that the Scripture saith,
The earth, it is the Lord's. And I say soe is this, therefore seeing we,
and by his people also sett apart for the churches use, or a buriall place,
it is holy, or convenient and good for that use and service, as every
other earth is. And it is not without Scripture warrant or example
of the holy men of God to burie in such a place; for Joshua, a servant
of the Lord and commander in chiefe or leader and ruler of the people

The house, says Martha Yeardley in a letter to her sister R. S., is warm and comfortable, though at best what Londoners would esteem a poor place. We feel quite satisfied with it; and when we get our garden in order, and a cow and a few chickens, it will be equal to anything that I desire in this world. To-day the snow has disappeared, and John is very busy with his garden.—(1 *mo.* 7, 1827.)

John and Martha Yeardley did not remain long idle in their new position. In the First Month, 1827, they received a "minute" for visiting the meetings in their Monthly Meeting; and in the Second Month they commenced a tour amongst the meetings in some other parts of Yorkshire. These duties occupied them until the 19th of the Fourth Month. We may extract from the Diary recording the former of these engagements, a brief note of their visit to Ackworth School.

1 *mo.* 20.—Lodged at J. Harrison's. On First and Second-day evenings had some time of religious service with the young people at the school, and felt much united in spirit to this interesting family. On Fourth-day, Robert Whitaker accompanied us to Pontefract, and we were comforted in his company, for we felt poor and weak—much like children needing fatherly care.

of God, when he died was neither buried in a steeple-house, now called a parish church, nor in a steeple-house-yeard, but he was buried in the border of his inheritance, and on the north side of Mount Gaash, as you may read; see Joshua, the 24th chapter, and the 29th and 30th verses. And Eleazer, Aaron's son, who was called of the Lord, when he died, (they buried him not in a parish church, nor a steeple-house yeard, but) they buried him in the hill of Phinehas, his son, which was given him in Mount Ephraim, as you may read, Joshua, the 24th, the 33rd v. And these were noe superstitious persons, but beloved of the Lord, and were well buried. And soe were they in Abraham's bought field, Genesis, the 23rd chapter, the 17, 18, 19, and 20 verses: though superstitious minds now are unwilling unto the truth to bow, who are offended at such as burie in their inheritance or bought field, appointed for that use."

Among John Yeardley's notes made during the more
general visit, we meet with a memorandum which may
be taken to mark a stage or era in his Christian experience.   The daily record of religious exercise and feeling
which is so useful to many in the hidden season of tender growth and preparation for future service, is less
likely to be maintained—and, it may be, less necessary
—in the meridian of life, when the time and strength
are taken up with active labor.

3 *mo.*—I could write much as to the state of my mind, but
have of late thought it safer not to record all the inward dispensations which I have to pass through.   I feel strong desires
to be wholly given up to serve my great Lord and Master, and
that I may above all things become qualified for his service;
but the baptisms through which I have to pass are many, and
exceedingly trying to the natural part.   Nothing will do but
to rely wholly on the Divine Arm of Power for support in
pure naked faith.

# CHAPTER VIII.

## 1827–28.

### PART I.—GERMANY.

AETER John and Martha Yeardley had visited their friends at home, their minds were directed to the work which they had left uncompleted on the continent of Europe; and, on their return from the Yearly Meeting, they opened this prospect of service before the assembled church to which they belonged.

(*Diary*) 6 *mo.* 18.—Were at the Monthly Meeting at High-flatts, where we laid our concern before our friends to revisit some parts of Germany and Switzerland, and to visit some of the descendants of the Waldenses in the Protestant valleys of Piedmont; and, on our way home, our friends and some other serious persons in the Islands of Guernsey and Jersey. Our dear friends were favored to enter most fully and feelingly into our views, and under a precious solemnity, a general sentiment of unity and concurrence spread through the meeting, which constrained them (as the certificate expresses it) to leave us at liberty, accompanied with warm desires for our preservation. Hearing the certificate read brought the concern, if possible, more weightily than ever upon me, and a secret prayer was raised in my heart that we might be enabled to go through the prospect before us to the honor of Him who has called us into his work.

They attended the Quarterly Meeting in the latter
(161)

part of this month, and returned by way of Ackworth, where, says John Yeardley,

We had a comfortable parting with dear Robert and Hannah Whitaker, in their own room. R. W. has passed with us through the deeps, and has indeed been a true spiritual helper to us under our weighty exercises of mind.

On the 8th of the Seventh Month they set out, and on the 17th attended the Meeting of Ministers and Elders in London.

The Morning Meeting was a precious and refreshing time to our poor tried minds. There was a very full expression of near sympathy and entire unity with us in our intended religious service. It is a strength and encouragement not only to have the concurrence of our friends, but also to know that we have a place in their prayers for our preservation and support in every trying dispensation.

On the eve of their departure from London, a circumstance occurred of a very disagreeable character. The shop of their brother, A. B. Savory, in Cornhill, was broken open; many valuable articles were taken, and their travelling trunks, which had been left there, were ransacked. Although their loss was trifling, the annoyance of such a contretemps may easily be conceived. J. Y. says:—

It is far from pleasant thus to be plundered of any part of our property; but I consider it as much the duty of a Christian to bear with becoming fortitude the cross-occurrences of common life as to be exercised in religious service.

They left London on the 22nd, for Rotterdam. On their arrival, a disastrous occurrence happened which gave a shock to their feelings. The manner in which J. Y. mentions the event evinces his tenderness of mind in ·commencing a long journey, in which his vocation was to be to sympathise with the poor and afflicted.

Since we landed safely on shore a circumstance has occurred which has brought a gloom over us. One of our shipmen being busy about the sails, part of a beam fell from the top-mast and struck him on the head. He never spoke more, but died instantly. He has left a widow and two children, not only to weep for him, but also to feel bitterly his loss in a pecuniary way. We intend to recommend their situation to some of our benevolent friends in London. My heart is much affected in having to commence my journal on a foreign shore by recording such an afflicting event. And, as it regards ourselves, how much we have which calls for thankfulness that we have so mercifully escaped.

From Rotterdam they directed their course to Pyrmont, passing through Gouda, Utrecht, Arnheim, and Münster; at the last place they were laid by from the heat and weariness. They reached Friedenthal on the 4th of the Eighth Month, and John Yeardley makes the following reflections on re-entering his German home:—

As I find myself again in this country, many thoughts of former days spring up in my mind. Since I was last here I have passed through much; nevertheless the Lord has guided my steps, and I have cause to give Him thanks.

They visited Minden and the little meetings around, bestowing much labor on them; but at Pyrmont, to suffer, rather than to do, was their allotted portion.

It sometimes seems to me, writes J. Y., that we have in this place little to do and much to suffer. I am often cast down, and have to sit in silence and darkness. This state of mind is an exercise of faith and patience, through which much may be gained if it is turned to right account.

Of the Two Months' Meeting, he says:

On the whole a favorable time. But I am not without my fears that the little Society in this place will lose ground, in a religious sense, if more faithfulness is not manifested in little things.

Soon after their arrival in Germany they turned their steps towards the north-west corner of that country, and the borders of Holland. The object of this journey was to visit some places on the shores of the North Sea, near Friesland, where the inundations of 1825 had caused great desolation, and where a new colony had been formed by the government from among the ruined families. This little journey was so emphatically, an act of faith, and the course of it lay so much through a part of Europe seldom visited by travellers, that we shall transcribe the diary of it without much curtailment.

9 *mo.* 4.—Having for sometime felt an impression to visit Friedrichgroden and other places on the shore of the North Sea, near the confines of East Friesland, we set out from Pyrmont in company with our dear friend Louis Seebohm, travelling with extra-post in our own carriage. We found this a pretty expeditious way of travelling for this country, being able to make about fifty-five English miles a day. Between Oldendorf and Bückeburg, we experienced a remarkable preservation from danger. Our postillion being a little sleepy, had not sufficient care of the reins, and the horses suddenly turned off towards an inn, but missing the turn, instantly fell into a deep ditch, one horse quite down, and the other nearly so; the carriage wanted only a few inches further to go, and then it would have come upon the horses, so that a few plunges must have upset the whole concern. We sprang instantly out, and set the quiet animals free. The man was so frightened he could scarcely step from the box. The whole affair did not last more than a few minutes, when we were on our way again, with great cause for thankfulness

to the Preserver of our lives. The driver was so honest in acknowledging his fault, that I gave him his *trinkgeld*, and our friend L. S. gave him some advice. We got well on through Minden to Diepnau and lodged there.

Next morning set out about seven o'clock, and that day travelled late to reach Oldenburg, which we accomplished at about one in the morning. Next morning we were in a dilemma which way to take to find our place of destination. The landlord was kind in sending out several times to gain information, but in vain : at length there came into the room a deaf and dumb man who frequented the house, and who, when he knew our inquiry, immediately wrote down the particulars of the place, and explained it by signs on the table. We left two books for this intelligent man for his kindness, and set forward. Dined at Varel, and had two poor tired horses and an awkward driver to Jever. We gave him several severe lectures without much effect ; at length we came to a small inn on the road, where he made a stand, and said he could go no further without two more horses, which we really believed was true, for if he had not got them we must have stuck in the sand. The horses being procured we got to Jever about eleven o'clock.

Here was a good inn, and we rested pretty well ; but in the morning discouragement took hold of my spirits in a way that I have seldom experienced. I was ready to conclude we were altogether wrong and out of the way of our duty ; but forward we must now go to see the end of this exercising journey. The country about Varel and Jever is remarkably fertile in pasture. The cows handsome, rolling in abundance of grass, and pretty much the whole country had the appearance of ease and plenty ; in Varel we saw the poor-house, a building capable of containing 400 persons, and only four individuals were there. The inhabitants live in simplicity, but also in the general in ignorance and indifference as to religion. I was exceedingly low in mind on the way, but felt once more that we were in our right place, and my precious M. Y. encouraged me by saying we should not go there in vain. On opening the Bible, I was comforted in turning to Psalm lxxviii. 12–14.

After having thus travelled some days, as it were in the dark, we arrived at Friedrichen Siel, near Carolinen Siel, in which neighborhood, on the border of the North Sea, lie Friedrichgroden, New Augustengroden, and New Friedrichgroden. It is a tract of land gained from the sea of about ten or twelve hundred acres, banked round in three divisions, and made arable, on which are built about twenty farmhouses, which form almost a new world. This land is the property of the government; a small sum is paid on entering, and a yearly ground-rent, and then it is the property of the purchaser for ever.

As soon as we stepped on the banks of one of these *grodens*, and I set my eye on one of these retired abodes, I felt no longer at a loss where we should go or what we should do. It opened suddenly on my mind as clear as the sun at noonday, that we must remain here a day or two and visit these new settlers in their dwellings. Accordingly we drove to the inn at Carolinen Siel. On asking for a map of the surrounding country, one was put into our hands containing a plan of the places which had suffered so severely by the floods in the spring of 1825; which rendered those people much more interesting to us.

After dinner we commenced our visit, and called on a young man and his sister who live on one of the farms, and have about seventy acres of land. They received us with a hearty welcome, and entered into friendly conversation. The house was one of the first on New Augustengroden, built in 1816, [swept] down by the water in 1825, and rebuilt the same year. He was an intelligent young man, and answered many inquiries which we made.

Finding the distance might be too great to walk, next morning we procured horses, and started about seven o'clock, taking from our small stock of books one for each family. We commenced intercourse with them by first interesting ourselves about their families and domestic concerns, not unmindful of every suitable opportunity to turn the conversation on the subject of religion, which is too much neglected by most of them. They are of the Lutheran profession; but the church being at some distance, they do not regularly

attend.  Most of them have as many as six children, and
some eight, with fine countenances.  We felt deeply interested, particularly for the mothers, some of whom are
tender-spirited, amiable women, and wept much in the opportunities we had with them.  Their late afflictions have made
on some a deep impression, and it was a time when, I trust,
such a visit might be of advantage.  In the floods, several
had their houses swept away; and one lost thirty-six head
of cattle, and had to drag his children out of the water naked,
and take refuge on the tops of the houses.  But the most
touching case was that of a man who lost his wife and five
children, his father, mother, and servants.  They were sent
away in a waggon, as a means of escape; but the waggon
was swept away by the torrent, and all perished.  The husband, who was left alone in the house, got to land on some
boards, part of the wreck of the house, and expected to find
his family safe; what must have been his feelings when he
found they had all perished in the deep!  We felt truly
prepared to sympathise with them, and think they were
sensible of our visit being in the sincere love of the Gospel.
Their kindness towards us exceeded description.  In going
from house to house, one of them seeing us in the field, and
not knowing our errand, thought we had missed our way,
and came running almost out of breath to set us in the road.
When he found that our visit was intended to him, he seemed
overjoyed, and conducted us to his home and his interesting
wife.  His name is Friedrich Fockensllammen.  He soon
showed us all that was in his house and barns; and I may
say he was equally ready to tell us all that was in his heart.
We could not get away without taking coffee with them.

Having felt much towards seeing them together, the way
seemed open to propose to this man to have a meeting.  He
readily undertook to consult with a few others; and he came
to our inn next morning with another, when he said, the good
work must have a small beginning, and although he himself
was quite willing, the others did not see the necessity of it,
or were too cautious.  This person told us that, with respect
to temporals, they could never have got forward again in the

way they had done, had it not been for the kind and effectual
assistance received from England. After an interesting conversation with these two, we parted in much affection. My
M. Y. drew up a short epistle, which was signed by us all,
and forwarded to them: this was an entire relief to our
minds.

Understanding the fair was to commence on First-day
morning, we found it necessary on Seventh-day evening to
seek fresh quarters. The First-day is worse kept in the terri-
tories belonging to Hanover than in any part of the Continent that I have seen, and the greatest religious ignorance
prevails there. The cause may rest with the Government in
giving too much power to the Church: the ecclesiastics are
fond of keeping in their own hands all things relating to
religion, and will not suffer the light to shine that the people
may see for themselves. The Edict of Stade has lately been
renewed, prohibiting religious meetings; no unauthorised
persons (as they call it), are permitted to preach or hold
meetings, on pain of imprisonment; all foreign missionaries
to be immediately sent beyond the boundaries. The settlement we were visiting was partly in Hanover, and partly in
Oldenburg.

Besides these colonies on the reclaimed strand of the
ocean, John Yeardley had another object in undertaking
this journey, which was to inspect the Industrial Colony
at Fredericks-Oort, in the province of Drenthe, in Holland. Towards this place the party now directed their
way.

Between Wittmund and Aurich (continues J. Y.) is a moor
called Plagenburg, about six English miles square, on which
are some of the poorest mud-huts I ever saw. People who
intend to settle here from any part receive a grant of land
for ten years free, and afterwards pay a yearly ground-rent
of about five shillings an acre. The idle and burdensome
poor are also sent here; and by this means the whole neighborhood is relieved from poor-rates, except for the support

of a few individuals who spin, &c., in the poor-house.  We were informed that near Norden there is a colony for thieves and gipsies, who are sent to this place and compelled to build themselves huts and cultivate the land.  They are strictly watched by the police, and severely punished when they attempt to go away without leave.

We had a long and tedious ride, through deep sand, to Leer.  On our arrival we made inquiry about Fredericks-Oort, but could obtain no intelligence, nor could we find it on the maps which we borrowed for examination.  This was very discouraging; for I had hoped, if it was right for us to go, we should find some one to give us certain directions to it.  I slept but little, and next morning set again to work, and found there was a Jew in the town who travelled much in Holland.  I desired he might be sent for; he came, and immediately gave us directions where to find the places we wanted.

I ought not to omit remarking the comfortable feeling that I was favored with, riding from Wittmund to Aurich [on the way to Leer].  In reflecting in stillness where we had been and what we had done, I felt not only peace and inward satisfaction, but thankfulness filled my heart that we had been thus far enabled to do what we believed to be in the way of our duty.  This Scripture language passed through my mind: "Blessed are ye that sow beside all waters, that send forth thither the feet of the ox and the ass." (Isa. xxxii. 20.)

11th.—Left Leer about eleven o'clock in the morning, and expected to arrive at Assen at eleven or twelve at night, but to our great disappointment we travelled the night through, and only reached Assen at seven next morning.  At Wehndam on our way we rested the horses.  Our friend L. S. went for an hour to bed, and my M. Y. and self sat in the carriage and would have slept, but there came so many admirers of our vehicle that we could not sleep for their almost continual remarks about its elegance, convenience, &c.

This part of Holland is fruitful; the houses are clean and neat; and the dress of the women very singular.  Their caps

12

have a plate of silver or gold on each side almost like a helmet, and sometimes very costly. At the inn at Nieuweschans [on the borders of Germany and Holland], the cook had one of these golden helmets which had cost about 150 florins.

In these flat countries they have no spring water; the land lies so much below the sea that all is impregnated with salt. Rain water is used for drinking, and the method of preserving it is in a deep reservoir lined with boards and puddled with clay. I was surprised to find it kept good so long: it is seldom known to go bad. One of the farmers on the Grodens drew water out of his well and handed me a glass to drink; it had a yellowish tinge, but except this I never saw clearer and have seldom tasted pleasanter spring water, and the best tea I ever drank was made from rain water so preserved. One thing which contributes to its quality is the great surface of tile which it has to run down, and which tends to filter it.

The mode of manuring the land is similar to that practised in Brabant, and the produce proves that it is excellent; for no better meadows, or corn land in a higher state of cultivation are to be seen than in some parts we have lately passed through.

The cows, when fresh in milk, are milked three times a day, by which means more milk is obtained than in the common method; any one wishing to make a fair experiment of this must try it not for two or three days only, but for a week or ten days.

John and Martha Yeardley found the institution at Fredericks-Oort of a deeply interesting kind. It was established by private benevolence to improve the condition of the poor, and to relieve the country from beggars, and was commenced in 1818. The poor families which are placed there are employed, some in manufacture, some in cultivating the soil, and every means is made use of to encourage industry and provident habits. When our friends visited the colony, it

comprised 2900 souls, including the staff by which the
institution is worked, and which is necessarily numerous.
They thought the method of instruction in use in the
schools excellent, and found that religious liberty was
strictly respected.

From Fredericks-Oort they went on to Ommershaus,
where is the poor-house and penal colony belonging to
the former institution. Thirteen hundred beggars, orphans, and criminals were then in the colony.

How much, remarks J. Y., such an institution is wanted in
England; every inducement is held out for improvement in
civil society, and a most effectual check placed against vice
and idleness.

The travellers fared badly in Holland, and they were
rejoiced to "set foot again in honest Germany, where
they know how to use strangers with an honest heart."
They returned through Bentheim and Osnabrück, and
arrived at Pyrmont on the 19th. Here they spent ten
days in resting, and in preparing to pursue their journey
through South Germany.

On First-day, the 30th, they took leave of their
friends.

First-day, says John Yeardley, was a solemn time, both at
meeting and at the reading in the afternoon; I hope both my
M. Y. and I were enabled to clear our minds. In the evening
we took an affectionate and affecting leave of them all; it was
to me particularly trying. I could not refrain from weeping
much.

Not much occurs in the diary to claim attention, until
they reached Friedberg, not far from Frankfort.

10 mo. 7.—Sat down to our little meeting, after breakfast, and reading, on First day morning. It was to us both

a season of deep feeling. My dear M. Y. was so filled with
a sense of our own weakness, and the Almighty's goodness
towards us in a wilderness travel through a dark country,
that she knelt, and was enabled to pour forth a heart-felt
supplication for a precious seed of the kingdom in the hearts
of the people among whom we were; and also that He would
in his tender mercy remember us his poor instruments, and in
the right time cause light to break forth on our path, preserve
us in the way we ought to go, and make us willing to suffer
for the sake of his suffering cause: to which my heart said,
Amen!

At Frankfort they formed acquaintance with J. H.
von Meyer, ex-burgomaster of the city, a learned and
pious man, who had made a new translation of the Bible
into German, and had stood firm for the cause of real
Christianity in the midst of much declension. In the
afternoon they drove to Offenbach to see J. D. Marc, a
Christian Jew, who had earned experience in the school
of suffering. He said, amongst other things, that he
could never preach but when he believed it to be his
duty, and then he could declare only what was given
him at the time; this he considered to be the only
preaching that could profit the hearers. His views on
the inutility of water baptism were so decided, that
when converted Jews asked him to administer to them
this rite, he told them he could not recommend it, for it
would do them no good. He gave them many names
of awakened persons in the Palatinate :—

Where, says John Yeardley, there is still a lively-spirited
people who hold meetings for religious improvement; perhaps
the descendants of those who were visited by W. Penn in
former days.

The next day they returned to Frankfort, and made

the acquaintance of Pastor Appia, a Piedmontese, who, with his wife, was very friendly; and when he heard that they had left their own land to visit his native country, marked out a route for them, and gave them letters of introduction. "When I am with such good people," observes J. Y., in relating their interview with Appia, "I am always uneasy in my mind that I am not more worthy. May the Lord strengthen me!"

On the 10th, they went to Darmstadt, where they met with several enlightened Christians. One of these, Leander van Ess, had been a Roman Catholic priest; and although a zealous promoter of Christianity in the face of persecution, and favored with a more than ordinary degree of spiritual light, he had thought it right not altogether to forsake that communion, but remained amongst the Romanists to do them good. He had translated the New Testament for their use. At parting with his new friends he embraced them, gave them his blessing, and wished them a prosperous journey. "I felt myself," says J. Y., "comforted and strengthened by this visit."

On the way to Heppenheim, he continues, (to which place they next directed their course), I felt quiet in mind, and was once more assured that we were in the way of our duty. As I thought of the difficulties which might await us, these words were brought to my remembrance, "Touch not mine anointed, and do my prophets no harm."

Crossing the Rhine, at Mannheim, they stopped, on the 12th, at Dürkheim, where they became acquainted with Ludwig Fitz, a man of a frank and inquiring disposition.

For three years, writes J. Y., he has held meetings in his house; in the commencement he had to suffer no little per-

secution. On his entering our room he observed that it was
the Lord who had thus brought us together. I have scarcely
been half an hour with you, he said, after a while, but it
seems as if I had known you for seven years. He, with his
wife and daughter, took us to call on a Mennonist, a pious
man, who holds firmly by Baptism and the Supper. He soon
began to speak on these points. I replied to what he said as
well as I could, maintaining that in Scripture there are two
baptisms spoken of; that, as the soul of man is spiritual, it
can be reached only by that which is spiritual, and that
therefore I did not see the necessity of maintaining that
which is outward. He said he desired to possess the former,
and not to neglect the latter. As to the Supper they both
advanced in proof of the observance being good, that often,
whilst using it, they experienced inward joy and refreshment.
I said we must not limit to a certain time or place this joy
in the Lord, as if the use of the Supper only were the cause
of it. The gracious Lord is ready at all times to sup with
us, and to refresh the sincere and cleansed soul, and make
it joyful in him. We took leave of each other in love; I
said we did not travel for the purpose of turning people from
one form to another, but with the desire only that they might
all be brought nearer to the Lord. It was pleasant to me
that Fitz's wife was with us; during the conversation she remained still and weighty in spirit.

We inclined to attend the evening devotion at Fitz's, but
prefaced our request with the hope that they would not be
offended if we did not take part in their observances. This
was immediately granted; and Fitz said, I feel that your
spirit is true and sincere, and I have unity with it. When
their service was ended, we asked them to remain a while in
silence, and I trust I may say we were enabled to utter what
was required of us in testimony and supplication.

In Dürkheim there are eleven converted Jews, who dare
not meet except in secret for fear of the rabbins. One night
the rabbins attempted to take away their bibles and other
books, but they received a hint of their intention, and sent
the books to Fitz's house. One of them, a servant girl, as

soon as she heard that some Christian friends were come into
the town, went to Fitz's, and took up one of the books we had
given him. She read a little in it hastily, put it in her bosom,
and ran home. Her curiosity and love of the truth impelled
her to come to our hotel, and wait unobserved in the hall to
catch a glimpse of us as we came out. We felt much for
these awakened ones of Abraham's offspring; their oppressed
condition rested much upon our hearts; but as we had no
opportunity of conversing with them, I wrote a few lines from
Friedelsheim to the young woman, and sent them with some
books by Fitz, who accompanied us to that place. *Tuke's
Principles* finds much entrance among the awakened Jews.

Travelling through Spires, Carlsruhe, and Pforzheim,
they came on the 16th to Stuttgardt, where they found
Henry Kienlin, of Pforzheim, who, as the reader will
remember, had won so large a place in their love and
esteem on their former journey.

He not only, says John Yeardley, professes our principles,
but bears a clear and fearless testimony for them. His wife
is of the same mind with him, although she does not yet show
it in the simplicity of her dress.

On the 18th, we set out in company with our good friend
to Ludwigsburg to see the prison. There are about 600
prisoners, of both sexes, for the most part employed in labor.
Order and cleanliness prevail, and the food is good. The
governor, Kleth, is a worthy, pious man; he himself reads
the Holy Scriptures to the prisoners, and endeavors to
promote their spiritual improvement. When we entered a
room in which were a number of men, they rose, and stood
serious and quiet as though they expected we should address
them; and for a short time the love of God was felt amongst
us in an impressive manner; but nothing was given us to
utter.

It will be recollected that when John and Martha
Yeardley were at Stuttgardt in 1826, they met with the

Pastor Hoffman, and that they desired to visit the institution at Kornthal, of which he was the director, but were obliged to forego this visit in order to hasten forward to Basle. They now prepared to discharge this debt of Christian love. Kornthal is situated four miles from Stuttgardt; it was founded in 1819 by dissenters from the Moravians and Lutherans, and consisted in 1825 of about seventy families. J. and M. Y. went there on the 19th.

We were received, says the former, in a brotherly manner by the Director Hoffman. On entering the room we were informed that their pastor had died the night before; but instead of sorrow there seemed to be joy. This society holds it for a religious duty to rejoice when any of their members are favored to enter a state of endless bliss. This is religious fortitude which but few possess, but I believe it is with them sincere, for in going over the institution with the Director, I observed they spoke of it as a matter of holy triumph.

No meeting was held with the members of the establishment during this visit; it was left for J. and M. Y. to attend the usual evening assembly on First-day, the 21st; and they were informed that it would be an occasion on which any present who were moved by divine influence might freely relieve their minds.

At three o'clock, J. Y. writes, we set off to Kornthal under most trying feelings; I do not know when I have suffered so much from discouragement. On account of the death of the pastor, many were come to attend the interment which was to take place the next day. This caused the meeting to be large; not less than 700 persons were present, and among them six or seven pastors. The service commenced with a few verses; the first words were these:—

> "Holy Spirit come unto us,
> And make our hearts thy dwelling-place."

I can truly say I was awfully impressed with their meaning, and a secret prayer rose in my heart that it might be experienced amongst us. After the singing, a silence truly solemn ensued, and I intimated that I felt an impression to say a few words. When I sat down our kind friend the Director summed up the substance of what I had said, and repeated it in an impressive and becoming manner. He did this with the idea that some present who only understood Low German might not have clearly got the sense; however, we were told afterwards that they had understood every word that I had said. Hoffman generously acknowledged to the hearers that what had been delivered was strictly conformable with Scripture doctrine, and that he united most fully with it.

Next morning the children being assembled for religious instruction, at the conclusion I requested they might remain awhile, and I had a few words to say to them, which was a relief to my mind. Hoffman asked if they had understood; they almost all answered, Ja, ja, ja.

This visit has afforded an opportunity of our becoming acquainted with many serious characters out of the neighborhood who were come to the interment; many of them felt near to me in spirit. Hoffman's wife is a precious, still character; there is much sweetness in her countenance. All received us heartily in Christian love; it felt to me as if it were the night before one of our Monthly Meetings, and I was at a Friend's house, so much freedom was to be felt. The inn is kept by Hoffman; they would make us no charge, saying love must pay all. We were most easy to make a present to the box for the institution, but they would have refused it, saying feelingly, Travellers like you have many expenses.

The cause for J. Y.'s peculiar discouragement in the prospect of this meeting was the want of an interpreter. Any one who knows the difficulty of public speaking or continuous discourse in a foreign language, will comprehend the anxiety which he felt when he saw no alternative but that of committing himself to preach in German. Though very familiar with the language, he never completely overcame the want of early and of thoroughly grammatical instruction in that difficult and intricate tongue. It was with feelings of this kind that he penned the following memorandum before going to Kornthal :—

18*th.*—Extremely low in mind and in want of faith. No creature can conceive what I suffer in the prospect of having to speak in a foreign tongue in a religious meeting.

At Stuttgardt they took leave of their endeared friend, Henry Kienlin.

It is, says J. Y., hard to part; but every one must follow his calling, and mind only the direction of the Lord.

On quitting Stuttgardt, John Yeardley makes a few remarks regarding the religious state of Würtemberg.

22*nd.* — Würtemberg is a favored land. In Feldbach, three hours from Stuttgardt, there are about 800 Christian people who hold meetings in each other's houses : some of them belong to the Kornthal Society. Years ago, many emigrated to America and Russia, to gain religious liberty ; now it is granted them by their own Government.

On the 22nd, they journeyed to Tübingen, where they visited the worthy Professor Streundel.

He was surprised and shy when we entered, as if he wanted to say, The sooner you take leave the better. But as soon as he knew where we came from, his countenance changed, and he received us heartily. He had his wife called —a very polite person. He asked many questions as to our church discipline, &c.; the order of our Society pleased him much. He had undertaken the study of divinity from an apprehension of duty, and said that it was only by the assistance of the Holy Spirit we could be made instrumental in the ministry.

On the 25th they came to Wilhelmsdorf, on the Lake of Constance, where is a branch of the Kornthal Association. They found the director "a man of great simplicity, but of inward worth."

He was, continues John Yeardley, six years in Kornthal, and seems to be sensible of the importance of the situation he fills, and of his incapability to be useful to others unless assisted by divine grace. He read our certificate attentively, and said, in a weighty manner, Yes; one Lord over all, one faith, one baptism. We found they have no regular preacher, but meet for worship every evening and on First-day mornings. We were desirous of seeing them together, and they were pleased to find such was our intention. The bell was rung, and in a few minutes the whole colony assembled, about two hundred, with children. Much liberty was felt in speaking among them; and some of them appeared to be sensible of the value of true silence, and from whence words ought to spring; many shed tears under the melting influence of divine love which was so preciously to be felt amongst us. We took an affectionate leave, well satisfied in visiting this little company, to strengthen them to hold up the cause of their Lord and Master, in the midst of darkness. Within about thirty English miles there are none but rigid Roman Catholics, not one Evangelical congregation. At our departure my wife said: "These words arise in my mind for thy comfort: Thy faith hath saved thee; go in peace."

At the inn where we stopped at Wilhelmsdorf, we were spectators of an occurrence rarely to be seen. Among the laborers who dined there, the one who had finished first read a chapter from the Bible to the rest. When all had done eating, one offered a prayer; and then all went quietly back to their work. This practice shows at least the sincerity of their hearts.

# CHAPTER IX.

### PART II.—SWITZERLAND.

ON the 27th of the Tenth Month John and Martha Yeardley crossed the Swiss frontier to Schaffhausen, where their presence was welcomed by several pious persons. Amongst these were a young woman, Caroline Keller, who from a religious motive had altered her dress and manners to greater simplicity, and John Lang, Principal of the United Brethren's Society. In a social meeting convened on the evening of their arrival, J. L. directed the conversation to the principles of Friends, and J. and M. Y. explained the views held by the Society on silent worship, the ministry, and the disuse of ceremonies.

The [French] language, says J. Y., was difficult to me; but by the grace of God I was helped, and they were quite ready to seize the sense of what we endeavored to convey. The love of God was felt among us, and the Principal said, at parting, that he had not before been so impressed with our views. I sent him Tuke's "Principles," and he told me yesterday he was attentively studying it. My dear M. Y. told me it had been given her to believe we were in our right place, and that we were called by religious intercourse to bear witness for our Lord and Master and his good cause.

I am afraid, he remarks in a letter in which he describes their service at Schaffhausen, I am afraid thou wilt think me too minute in my details; but really when I enter into the

( 180 )

feeling which accompanied us in these visits, it seems as if I
could scarcely quit it.

They spent the 29th at Schaffhausen in close Christian communion with two pious families.   To C. K.
particularly, at whose house they dined, they felt so
nearly united, that they scarcely knew how to part from
her.

We have cause to be thankful, says J. Y., for our visit to
Schaffhausen; but if we were more faithful we should be more
useful.   Our friends were quite inclined for us to have had a
meeting with them, but we were too fearful to propose it.   O
vile weakness!

On the 31st they saw the Agricultural School for poor
children at Beuggen.   Amongst the boys were twelve
young Greeks, who were being instructed in ancient
and modern Greek, and in German.   They had been
sent to Switzerland by the German missionaries, and
most of them had been deprived of their parents by the
cruelty of the Turks.   It was the intention of their
benefactors that they should return to Greece to enlighten their countrymen.   Their religious instruction
was based simply upon the Bible, without reference to
any particular creed.

In the Greek school, writes John Yeardley, we observed a
serious man about thirty years of age, who had the appearance of a laborer, learning Greek.   This was a little surprising, and led us to inquire the cause.   The inspector readily
gratified us: and gratifying indeed it was to hear that this
poor man had given up his work of ship-carpenter, from pure
conviction that he was called to go and instruct the poor
Greeks at his own expense.   He is intending to spend the
winter in learning the modern Greek, and to proceed in the
spring to Corfu.   He intends to provide for his own living

by working at his trade, and he will take for instruction about four boys at a time, and as soon as he has brought them forward enough, set them as monitors over others. Some time ago two young men were sent out by the Bible Society to Corfu; but before they reached the place of their destination they were deterred by the missionaries on account of the unsettled state of the country, and dared not proceed further for fear of losing their lives. It is remarkable that, at the juncture when these two young men were turned back by discouragement, this poor man should receive the impression to go to the same place. We desired to have an interview with him, and he was instantly sent for to the Inspector's room. After a few remarks which opened for us to make to him, he confessed he had no peace but when he thought of giving up to this feeling of duty, and that when he looked towards going he felt happy in the prospect of every hardship. It was remarked that, as this call was made from above, the great Master alone could guide his steps; he appeared fully sensible from whom his help must come. He is beloved by his employers, and has an excellent certificate from the pastor, of his moral and religious character.

On the 2nd of the Eleventh Month they went to Zurich, and the same day drove out over a very bad road to Pfäffikon to visit the Herr von Campagne.

We had a cold wet journey, but the good old man gave us a hearty welcome to his house. He is seventy-six years of age. He asked us pleasantly how we came to think of visiting an old man who was on the brink of the grave. He had heard much of Friends, and wished, he said, to become personally acquainted with some of the Society. He is a most benevolent character, but we could not unite with all his religious views; he does not think it necessary to meet for religious worship; in short, his principles are much the same as those held by Jacob Böhmen.

We slept at his house, and next morning returned to Zurich, where we called on our particular friend Professor

Gessner and his family, and we rejoiced mutually to see each other again.

In the afternoon they called on Pastor Koch, tutor to the young Prince of Mecklenburg, who was at that time in Switzerland, and the next morning, First-day, as they were holding their little meeting for worship, the Prince himself, with Herr Koch and the Herr von Brandenstein, gave them a visit. The Prince spoke English; and J. Y. says:—

I had a strong impression to speak to him in a serious way, which I was enabled to do at some length. On parting he held me with both his hands in mine, and said, "I thank you, sir, for your kind and instructive communication; I shall never forget it so long as I live."

A little before twelve o'clock, he continues, came our kind young friend, Hannah Gessner, to accompany us to the ancient and worthy Bishop Hess. He is in his eighty-seventh year, but lively in spirit and active in mind. He is uncommonly liberal in his religious opinions, and his enlarged heart seemed to overflow with Christian love towards the followers of Christ under every name. He treated us as a father, and I felt instructed in being in his company. He gave us his portrait as a token of respect and friendship.

In the evening we took tea with Professor Gessner's sister, Lavater, in company with seven of the professor's daughters and sons, who are all serious persons. After some conversation on the order and ministry of our Society, it was proposed by dear Hannah, through her aunt, whether we would like to have a Meeting or the Scriptures read. After a portion of Scripture had been read silence ensued, in which my dear M. Y. and I said what was on our minds in testimony and supplication. It is a time of precious visitation to some of them. We felt sweet unity with Pastor Gessner, and believe him to be a gospel minister. On parting he took me in both arms, and said, in such a feeling manner that the words went to my very heart, "The Lord bless thee, and put the words of his wisdom into thy mouth."

On the 6th they went to Berne, and the next morning they inspected Fellenberg's institution at Hofwyl.

It is, says John Yeardley, what it professes to be, for education in the fullest extent of the word, to give to those committed to their care an education suited to their circumstances and their future prospects in life. There is a first-rate boarding school, for young gentlemen; a middle school, for tradesmen, &c.; a [boys' and] girls' poor school of industry, for those who can pay nothing.—(*Letter to Josiah Forster.*)

To J. Y. the most interesting department of this institution was the school of industry for poor children, in which at that time a hundred boys were clothed and educated. He describes at some length, and with evident approbation, the system on which the school was conducted; but adds, "I cannot say much as to religious instruction."

From Hofwyl they proceeded through Lausanne to Geneva, where, being desirous of improving themselves in French, and the season not permitting them to travel, they hired a lodging, intending to remain two or three months.

As on their former visit, they held frequent intercourse with pious persons, several of them well known in the Christian world; such as Gaussen, Bost, and L'Huillier. Of Theodore L'Huillier, minister of the New Church, John Yeardley says:—

Though a moderate Calvinist, he embraced us at once on the broad principle of Christianity. We became acquainted with him two years ago, but think him now much deeper in the root of real religion.

11 *mo.* 19.—We called yesterday evening on our dear friend Owen, and met there a pious lady, Fanny Passavant. We

had much serious conversation, I hope to profit, at least to our own minds; for we were given to see a little the importance of the situation in which we stand, and the necessity of being, in our intercourse with these religious persons, wise as serpents, and harmless as doves.

1828. 1 mo. 13.—We have had much satisfaction in becoming acquainted with Ami Bost. He was one of the first who bore testimony to the light which broke forth in the corrupt church of Geneva, and he suffered much in defending the doctrines of the New Church. In Germany he was, with his wife and six or seven children, driven from town to town by the police, for holding religious meetings in his house, and for refusing to have his children baptised. His sentiments in the office of the ministry and the appointment of preachers, are in perfect unison with those of Friends; also on the ordinances of the Supper, &c.

1 mo. 20.—During the greater part of our stay at this place I have felt my mind extremely poor, but a secret desire and prayer has been maintained to be preserved in patience, believing it to be as necessary to learn to suffer as to do. And although it is apparently little we can do here, we have felt repeatedly the assurance that it is the ordering of Best Wisdom, and as such we are well satisfied.

After our little morning meeting we went to dine with dear Captain Owen, and spent the remainder of the day with a few religious friends there. When the evening reading was finished, we had a solemn time under the seasoning influence of divine love. Our hearts were too full for any religious communication, except supplication, which was offered both by my dear M. Y. and myself.

Martha Yeardley also gives an account of this meeting, and of a visit they paid to the Female Prison.

Before our departure for Lausanne and Neufchâtel, a relation of Mary Ann Vernet's kindly attended us to the female prison, and introduced us to others of the committee; and in the evening we had a religious opportunity with the few confined there, during which they evinced much feeling.

13

Our interesting companion told us the next morning that she trusted the circumstance would be blessed to them. We had also a very interesting opportunity at Charles Owen's the evening before we left, at which was present, as often before, a very precious friend of ours, of the name of Fanny Passavant, a single woman, very rich, yet who lives in great self-denial, and gives almost all she has to feed the poor. She is what they call in this country a very *interior* character; which means one that cherishes the inward life. In her company we often felt baptized together, and she gave us strong recommendations to some of the same class at Neufchâtel, who are desiring to learn in the school of Christ. —(*Letter to Elizabeth Dudley.*)

At the expiration of their sojourn in Geneva, they did not, as they had expected to do, proceed to the valleys of Piedmont, but, as the last extract intimates, turned their steps towards Neufchâtel. The motives which influenced them in this change of purpose are described by John Yeardley, in a letter to his brother, of the 11th of the Second Month, 1828.

In my last to thee I signified our intention of departing for the valleys of Piedmont, which did not take place. After due consideration of the subject for more than two months, in a state of humble resignation to be directed aright in this important matter, we did not feel it press with sufficient weight on our minds to warrant our moving in the face of so much difficulty as is at present in the way. We have always considered our safety in such engagements to depend on taking step by step in the fresh light afforded; and it is a favor to know when and where to stand, as well as when to go forward.

While the way to Piedmont was thus for a time obstructed, a door was set open for them in a part of Switzerland which they had not yet visited. From John Yeardley's reflections before they left Geneva, it would appear that in the discouragement they felt in the prospect of a long journey through France, they were little aware of that plentiful repast of spiritual food which was to be served to them before they would have to cross the Jura.

In looking towards the long journey before us, writes J. Y., I have been much discouraged, almost fearing to depart from this place without first being favored with more quietude of mind, which I was this morning favored to feel in a greater degree than has been the case for a long time. In my last solitary walk to La Traille, I was led to pray in secret for preservation on our journey, and almost to ask an assurance of protection, but received for answer, "Go, in faith."

On the 21st of the First Month, they left Geneva and went forward to Lausanne, where they were again refreshed with the society of some spiritually-minded persons.

*23rd.* — We visited several of the pastors. We found M. Févaz, minister of the Seceders in this place, very interesting, humble, and spiritual. He related to us, in much simplicity and candor, that in the commencement of their separation they were strenuous to preach doctrinal sermons, but now they had been favored to see the necessity of preaching purification of heart through the operation of the Spirit.

Called on —— Gaudin, who keeps a boarding-school in a beautiful situation near the town. We had not been long in the company of him and his dear wife, before we felt much contrited together, and had a precious religious opportunity. At parting, the dear man, with myself, was quite broken into tears. We left with him, as well as with the others, Judge Hale's "Testimony to the Secret Support of Divine Providence," which we had translated, and had got printed at Geneva.

On the 24th they proceeded to Neufchâtel. This was a memorable visit.

We soon found cause, writes John Yeardley, to believe the Great Master had been before us, to prepare the way in the hearts of many to receive the doctrine he has mercifully enabled us to preach. Our dear F. Passavant had given us a letter of introduction to Auguste Borel, a man of few words, but of a remarkably weighty and sweet spirit, who received us with the greatest affection. He has lately separated from the national worship, and retires in silence in his own chamber. He soon made us acquainted with a few others of a similar turn of mind.

Martha Yeardley, describing the commencement of their religious service in this place, says:—

We were invited to a meeting which we felt most easy to attend, and my husband was given full liberty to speak if he felt inclined; but for a while the usual activity of their meetings—such as singing, commenting on texts with Calvinistic explanations, &c.—entirely closed our way. But before they separated I ventured to request, in the name of my husband, that such as inclined would favor us with their company a while longer, and rest a little in silence. Nearly all remained, and under a solemn covering he addressed the company, while I translated in much fear, yet ventured at the end to say a few words for myself. Several of the company attended us home, and expressed much satisfaction: and from this time a door was opened to us at Neufchâtel in a very remarkable manner. They flocked to our inn at all times in the day, and in considerable numbers, many acknowledging, in the course of very interesting conversation, that they thirsted for something more satisfying than mere doctrines continually repeated — something that would preserve from evil, that would cleanse the heart, that would bring into nearer communion with the Saviour.—(*Letter to Elizabeth Dudley.*)

On the 27th, continues the Diary, A. Borel conducted us

to a meeting with some *interior* persons, about three miles from town. It was a time of close exercise of mind, but ended to satisfaction, and, I hope, to the edification and strength of some present. The master of the house, Professor Pétavel, said that never until that evening had he been able to see clearly the beauty and advantage of pure spiritual worship, contrasted with outward forms.

After having taken tea with a large company, our kind guide conducted us through woods and over mountainous and bad roads to a village, where a large concourse of people were assembled for worship. A schoolmaster was speaking on a chapter which had been read: we had full unity with what he delivered, which was accompanied with a power which convinced us that he really preached the gospel. After he had done, we were introduced as religious strangers from England; and silence ensuing, opportunity was given for us to express what came before us.

*28th.*—Some of the most *interior* told us they had long been exercised about spiritual worship, and had often wished to see some of the Society of Friends. On hearing of our intended visit two years ago, they said if we had come then [we should have found them] wrapped up in doctrines, but now they were given to see they could not live on the letter alone, they must be born again, and partake of that bread which cometh down from heaven. Many of these awakened persons came to our inn at all hours, and our hearts were filled with love towards them as a cup overflowing; so that it was given to us to minister to them almost individually as they came to us.

On the 29th they went to Berne, and the following morning walked over to Wabern, where some of A. Borel's friends resided, who received them with open arms.

After dinner M. Combe drove us in his car to Scherli. We alighted at the house of one of the peasant-farmers, situated quite among the mountains, with the Alps fair in view. They received us in the name of disciples with every mark of love and respect. They were more disposed to sit in silence than to ask questions. On my asking if they had seen or heard of any of our Friends, in these parts, one of them innocently replied, No; we do not know anything of your religious principles. I then began to explain them; and when I spoke of our manner of worship, belief, &c., and of some of our peculiar tenets respecting Baptism, the Supper, &c., it is not possible to express their emotion; their eyes turned first towards one and then towards another, and seemed to sparkle with joy, without their uttering a word till I had done. These were entirely the principles they held, and about a year ago they separated from the church, about twenty in number, and attempted to meet for religious worship. This was prevented by the police; for although they live in a very remote situation, they are strictly watched by the pastor, who wishes to compel them to come to his worship. We were there only an hour or two, but a number of these innocent-hearted people came flocking to the house, and immediately settled into a silence truly solemn. We could indeed say our hearts burned with love towards them.

Two of these young men came to us the next day, and spent most of the day with us. One of them, Christian Speicher, told me he did not know how to express the satisfaction he felt to hear of a body of professing Christians in a distant land, who held the same religious principles as they in their isolated situation had been long seeking after and had been made willing to suffer for.

During our stay under this hospitable roof [M. Combe's at Wabern] it was an open house for all comers, and they were not few. Our spirits were so united with many of them we did not know how to leave them; but our great concern was to recommend them to remain with Him who had so mercifully and powerfully visited them.

On the 31st they returned to Berne, and the next day called upon a pious chimney-sweeper, waiting whilst he changed his sooty clothes.

We were not a little surprised to hear him of his own accord, without knowing who we were, declare the same doctrine as we are concerned to preach.   There are a few *inward* persons who assemble at his house, and hold the same sentiments. About a year and a half or two years ago, there was a remarkable awakening in the canton of Berne, and a few here and there of a more spiritually-minded sort seceded.   There is a ferment to prevent their meeting together, and to compel them to go to the usual place of worship; but in vain, for nothing but spiritual food can satisfy their hungry souls.

On their return to Neufchâtel they visited the celebrated school of the Moravians at Montmirail, where, says Martha Yeardley—

We soon felt quite at home with a precious, spiritually-minded man, the master, and his agreeable English wife.  This is an excellent institution, for females only, and several English are there.   We were about seventy in company at dinner, and much sweet feeling prevailed.   The master of this interesting family was delighted to hear something of Friends to whom he had never before been introduced.

At Neufchâtel, on First-day (2 mo. 3,) they met large companies in the morning and evening, and the next morning took leave of their friends in that city, "deeply humbled under a sense of the great Master's work among them."   They went to Locle under the conduct of A. Borel, whose "kindness exceeded all description."

On the way, writes John Yeardley, we took refreshment at a pious man's house in the morning, and dined at another friend's, with whom we had a precious religious opportunity. It reminded me of the mode of visiting our own dear Friends in England; we find in the hearts of these visited children of the Universal Parent genuine hospitality; they hand us of all they have in their houses in the name of disciples.

At Locle they were met by Mary Anne Calame, with whom their hearts became instantly knit in the strongest Christian friendship.

She came before we were well alighted. We had heard much of the character and benevolent exertions of this dear woman but could say in truth the half had not been told us. Her countenance is strong and impressive, her hair jet black, cut short, and worn without cap; her dress of the most simple and least costly kind. Her sole desire seems to be to do the will of her Lord and Master in caring for 170 poor children, who are in the institution at bed, board, and instruction. The forenoon was spent in looking over the schools and hearing the children examined. The house is a refuge for the lame, blind, deaf, dumb, and sick. Peace and contentment prevail through the whole. This establishment was commenced about twelve years ago with five children, and has prospered in a remarkable manner. M. A. C. is one with Friends in principle, and, as well as some others of the family, entirely separated from the usual forms of worship.

Martha Yeardley, in a letter from which we have already quoted, describes the origin of the asylum.

About twelve years since M. A. Calame believed herself called to form an institution for orphans and unfortunate children. She associated some others with her for this object, but having peculiar views on religious subjects, and more perseverance than her colleagues, she was soon left nearly alone, with means entirely inadequate to the increasing demands, viz., about three francs yearly from a very limited number of persons. The children daily augmented, and she dared not refuse admission: when in necessity she was encouraged to trust from unexpected donations. This increased her faith; and after some years, a boys' school was added. In this way the institution has been supported without any regular funds.

Her faith is still often very severely tried, but they have never yet been suffered to want. Her refuge in times of extremity is prayer, and it has been in some instances very evidently answered, so that she has severely reproached herself for daring to doubt. In speaking on this subject she said to me: "I am at times much beset with temptations when I consider the number I have thus collected without any visible or certain means of support; but how can I dare to doubt after so many proofs of the care of the great Master? He knows our wants; he knows these dear children have need of food and clothing, and he provides it for them; and he knows that all I desire is to do his will."

On remarking to her the sweet tranquillity and order which reign in, these schools, she said, "It is the Master's work; they are taught to love him above all, and to do all for his sake." We felt very nearly united to her and to an intimate friend who resides with her: they are both what are called deeply interior characters, and have long withdrawn from the places of public worship, but fully unite with our views.

She is really a very extraordinary character, extremely simple and cheerful in her manners, possessing great natural talents, and evincing in her conducting of the institution, not only the Spirit, but the understanding also.—(*To Elizabeth Dudley*, 2 *mo.* 7, 1828.)

With Locle, John and Martha Yeardley's mission to Switzerland for this time terminated. They crossed the frontier into France, and made the best of their way through that country, in order to proceed to the Channel Islands.

This morning (2 mo. 5,) writes J. Y., Mary Anne Calame and her friend Zimmerling, with A. Borel, accompanied us two leagues to the ferry, and saw us safe over into France. This last parting with friends so dear to us in a foreign land, was very touching; our hearts were humbled under a sense of the Heavenly Father's love.

*6th.*—Passing the custom-house made us late at our quarters, where they are not accustomed to receive such guests. Their curiosity to see and know who we are is very great. To prevent French imposition, my M. Y. was to bargain beforehand for what we had. On asking what the meal would cost, we were answered they could not tell, for they did not know how much coffee we should drink. This simple but appropriate reply so amused us that it put an end to our bargaining.

I shall not soon forget the sensation I felt on passing the river into France. I could not forbear drawing the discouraging contrast of quitting those to whom we had become united in the gospel of peace, in a country the most beautiful that Nature can present, with a long journey in prospect through a dreary country whose inhabitants wish only to get what they can from us. These discouraging fears could only be silenced by reflecting that the same protecting Providence presides over all and everywhere.

Travelling with their own single horse, their favorite *Poppet*, the progress they made was necessarily slow, and they did not reach Paris till the 19th. After spending a few days in that city, they proceeded to Cherbourg, and arrived there after six days of hard travelling. At this place John Yeardley writes:—

3 *mo.* 2.—In looking back on our late travels, a degree of sweet peace and thankfulness covered my mind in the humble belief that our weak but sincere desires to do the great Master's will was a sacrifice well-pleasing in his holy sight. In looking forward to the dangers we had still to encounter, I was led closely to examine on what our hope of preservation was fixed. Should it please Him who had hitherto blessed us with his presence and protecting care, to put our faith again to the test, how we could bear it, how we should feel at the prospect of going down to the bottom of the great deep. I felt a particular satisfaction that our great journey had first been accomplished; if this had not been the case it would have been a sting in my conscience. But now an

awful resignation was experienced, and it came before me as
an imperious duty to be resigned to life or death; and the
joyful hope resounded in my heart, All will be well to those
who love not their lives unto death.

The presentiment of danger which this passage describes was speedily fulfilled, as was also the hopeful
promise by which it was accompanied.   They were
detained at Cherbourg until the 13th, waiting for a
vessel.   Leaving port early that morning, they landed in
Guernsey the next day; and it was in going ashore that
they were exposed to some danger of their lives.   John
Yeardley thus relates the occurrence:—

I descended first into a little boat, and standing on the
side to take my M. Y. down, the man not holding the boat
secure to the ship, our weight pushed it from us, and we
plunged headlong into the sea.   My dear M. Y.'s clothes
prevented her from sinking, and she was first assisted again
into the boat.   I went overhead, and had to swim several
turns before I could reach the boat.   The salt water being
warm, and the time not long, we received no further injury.
What shall we render unto the Lord for all his mercies to
us, his poor unworthy servants!   how often has he made bare
his mighty arm for our deliverance.   In the midst of danger
fear was removed from us, and we were blessed with the
unspeakable advantage of presence of mind, and enabled
to use the best means under Divine Providence to save our
lives.

They visited the Friends and a few other persons in
Guernsey and Jersey, and then proceeded to Wey-
mouth, and on the 25th to Bristol.   At Bristol and
Tewkesbury they were deeply interested in the state of
the meetings, and had some remarkable service in both
places.   Taking also Nottingham and Chesterfield in
their way, and being "well satisfied in not having

overrun them," they arrived at the cottage at Burton on the 8th of the Fourth Month, having been absent about nine months.

In the retrospect, say they, of this long and arduous journey, we have this testimony unitedly to bear,—that the Arm of divine love has been underneath to support and help us; and although we have had many deep baptisms to pass through, especially when we beheld how in many places the fields are white unto harvest, and were fully sensible of our own inability to labor therein, yet He who, we trust, sent us forth was often pleased to raise us from the depth of discouragement, to rejoice in him our Saviour. If any fruits arise from our feeble efforts to promote his cause, it will be from his blessing resting upon them, for nothing can possibly be attached to us but weakness and want of faith. But, blessed be his holy name, he knew the sincerity of our endeavors to do his will, and has been pleased in his condescending mercy to fill our hearts with his enriching peace. Amen.

# CHAPTER X.

## 1828—1833.

ON their return home Martha Yeardley was attacked with a severe illness, consequent probably on hard travelling and bad accommodation during the journey.

Under date of the 18th of the Fifth Month, J. Y. writes :—

How circumstances change! Last Yearly Meeting we were in London with the prospect of a long journey before us, and now my dear Martha is on a bed of sickness, and I have myself suffered; but through all there is a degree of peaceful resignation in the belief that all is done well that the Great Master does, and that what He keeps is well kept.

Later in the day he thus continues his Diary :—

This has been a day of great trial on account of my dear Martha being much worse. My poor mind has been distressed at her weak state: I should sink under discouragement, did I not consider that He who sends affliction can support in it, and he who brings low can raise up in his own time, if it be his blessed will, to which all must be submitted.

In the Seventh Month he took her to Harrowgate, where her health became very much restored, and soon after their return they paid a religious visit to Ackworth School and to the families of Friends in Barnsley.

Some of the opportunities at Ackworth, writes John

Yeardley, were seasons of much contrition of spirit; feeling deeply humbled under a sense of Divine goodness and mercy in restoring this large family to usual health after a time of deep affliction.

In the latter part of this year they were much occupied in establishing an Infant School at Barnsley; and also in collecting and remitting subscriptions to Mary Anne Calame for her Orphan Institution. In acknowledging to Martha Yeardley one of these remittances, M. A. C. writes thus:

May our Heavenly Father render thee a hundredfold what thy charity has prompted thee to do for my numerous family of children; and may his blessing rest on all those who have contributed to it.

We think of you every day, and we desire to live only to do the holy will of our God. Your visit has been a testimony of his love towards us; he has permitted that it should be blessed to us; for the remembrance of you carries us towards Him who is the finisher of our faith, where we mingle with you in the unfathomable sea of the divine mercy.

My large family is much blessed; good and happy tendencies manifest themselves in many, and in general peace reigns through the house. The assistant masters and mistresses walk more or less in the presence of the Lord; the governess [M. Zimmerling] especially grows deeper in the divine life: she is often ill, but she bears this cross, by the help that is given her from above, with much submission and faith.

Last month we had the pleasure of making a little journey to Berne and the neighborhood, to visit our friends there who love you so much. We heard that you had both fallen into the sea, and that thou wast ill in consequence. Thou mayst understand how the wishes of our hearts encompassed thee; I have felt my soul for ever united to thine in the Lord; and it seems to me that if my eyes should never again meet thine in this land of exile, I should speedily recognize thee in the happy mansions where the goodness of the Redeemer has prepared us a place. O, my sister, may he bless thee, may he bless John whom he has given thee to accomplish his work; may he open thy mouth and direct all thy steps, and give seals to thine and thy husband's ministry, and make you increase together unto the stature of Christ.—(12 mo. 14, 1828.)

The entries in the Diary at this period are not numerous: we select from them the following short memorandum:—

1829. 4 mo. 9.—In our usual reading this morning, I was struck with these words: "If two of you shall agree on earth as touching anything that they shall ask, it shall be done for them of my Father which is in heaven." (Matt. xviii. 19.) A fervent desire was raised in my heart that we might unitedly ask for faith and strength to do the will of our Heavenly Father, and that his blessing and preservation might attend all that concerns us.

In the Fifth Month they attended the Yearly Meeting; and John Yeardley was present at the anniversary of the Peace Society.

5 mo. 19.—Attended a meeting of the Peace Society, much to my own satisfaction. It was truly gratifying to hear from those not in profession with us, such strong and decided sentiments against all war, as being not only inconsistent with the spirit of Christianity, but also contrary to sound policy. I am convinced *public* meetings are necessary to keep alive *public* feeling, as well as to excite individual interest. As it regards myself, I can say, before attending the meeting I felt but little concern with respect to this great question.

Soon after their return home, they were comforted by the intelligence that a few of those persons at Neufchâtel who had so joyfully received their gospel message, had found strength to establish a meeting for worship. This information was contained in a letter from Auguste Borel, from which the following is an extract:—

He who tries the heart, and who knew the sincerity of my desires, deigned to hear my prayer on the 24th of February, when, without any previous understanding, we met four in number at my house at ten o'clock in the morning. This day is called with us *Torch Sunday*, and is a day of rejoicing in the world; and, if I ought to say so, during my carnal life it was to me a day of true pleasure, which I always looked for with impatience, because of the great bonfires which are then lighted, and which are seen from our city, illuminating every point of the wide horizon. It is my hope that the God of love, in the analogy of the spiritual order of things, may have kindled in our hearts his sacred fire, and will condescend to maintain and increase it in time and in eternity. Since that time we have continued our meetings without interruption: our number has not yet exceeded six or seven. We do not force the work, but, recognising that it is the Lord alone who has begun it, I feel daily more and more that He alone ought to direct it.

A portion of this summer and autumn was occupied by John and Martha Yeardley with holding public meetings for worship within the compass of Pontefract and Knaresborough Monthly Meetings. Amongst the notices in the Diary of these meetings, are the following:—

8 *mo.* 16.—A public meeting at Wooldale, to which came many more people than could get into the house. The Friends said they never saw so large a meeting in that place. Many of those present expressed their satisfaction by saying they could have sat till morning to hear what was delivered. It is an easy matter to become hearers of the word; but it was the doers of the word that were pronounced happy.

*23rd.*—Meeting at Otley, in the Methodist chapel. It was not very full, but very solid and satisfactory. The last public meeting in this place was held in silence, which might probably be the cause of a small attendance on this occasion. It is hard work to bring the people to see and feel the advantage of silent worship : the time is not yet come, and perhaps never may. We must be willing to help them in the way pointed out, and try to strengthen the good in all; for if they are only brought to the Father's house, it matters not in what way or through what medium.

In the Eleventh Month they returned to the Monthly Meeting the minute which had been granted them, and received at the same time a certificate to visit some meetings of Friends in the midland and south-western counties.

Before they left home for this journey, they received intelligence that John Yeardley's early and intimate friend James A. Wilson was no more.

11 *mo.* 24.—My heart, says J. Y., is pained within me, while I record the loss of one with whom I have been for many years on the most intimate terms. He has long had an afflicted tabernacle and a suffering mind, which, I believe, contributed to his refinement, and prepared him for the awful change. He had been recommended to go to a warmer climate, and had taken up his residence at Gloucester, where he died, which prevented us from attending him in his last moments. He possessed much originality of character, joined to sincerity and genuine piety; and I doubt not he experienced the fulfilment of this promise: "Behold, I have caused thy iniquity to pass from thee, and I will clothe thee with change of raiment." (Zech. iii. 4.)

On the 11th of the Twelfth Month they left home, and during the next two months were closely occupied in visiting various meetings from Yorkshire to Devonshire.

14

Their service commenced with an encouraging meeting at Monyash, in Derbyshire.

*13th.*—The first meeting we attended was at Monyash. It was larger than we had expected, in consequence of strangers coming in, and proved rather a lively commencement to our spiritual course of labor.

On the 14th they held a meeting in the Potteries, in a cottage belonging to one of the few Friends in the place. Word having got abroad that strangers were expected, many of the neighbors came in, so that the rooms below-stairs were filled: it was a refreshing time. They found in the woman to whom the cottage belonged a bright example of piety and charity.

She has been, says J. Y., a cripple from her childhood; but is able to maintain herself by keeping a school for little children; she is not unmindful, also, to help her poorer neighbors out of her small earnings.

At Bristol, where they arrived on the 1st of the First Month, 1830, they rested a few days at H. and M. Hunt's.

We had, says J. Y., much pleasure in being in this family. Bristol is the largest meeting we have in our Society in England, and to me it was a very trying one on the First-day morning. I was much cast down after meeting; but we staid over the Monthly Meeting on Third-day, which afforded me relief of mind, and I left with as much comfort as I could well desire.

At Plymouth John Yeardley found an object of lively interest in Lady Rogers' Charity School, established to fit girls for becoming household servants. He was gratified with the good order, simplicity, and economy, which pervaded the institution. Martha

Yeardley suffered much during their journey in Devonshire, from the inclemency of the weather; and a heavy
fall of snow on the night of the 17th prevented their
leaving Plymouth at the time intended. In consequence
of this, they hired a lodging, and employed themselves
in visiting the Friends from house to house, and in
organising an infant school, which the Friends had long
desired to see established.

On their return from Plymouth they stopped at
Sidcot, where they spent some time at the Friends'
school. Here the subject of offering prizes to children
came under the notice of J. Y., and like all other
subjects connected with education, engaged his serious
reflection.

It would certainly be better, he says, if the basis of good
actions could be laid in the children's minds on a principle
of rectitude and justice, so that they might be taught to do
well from a love of truth, and not from a fear of punishment
or a hope of reward; but so long as human nature remains
unchanged, a check against the one and an incitement to the
other seem to be necessary, as a help to overcome the evil in
the mind, until that which is good shall become predominant.

They returned to Yorkshire through Warwick and
Leicester, and on reviewing the journey John Yeardley
has the following reflections :—

2 mo. 22.—Almost all the meetings we attended on this
journey of 800 miles are very small, except Birmingham and
Bristol, and the life of religion is low among the members in
general; which is not much to be wondered at, when we
consider that many of those meetings are constituted [chiefly]
of a few individuals who have had a birthright in the
Society—born members but not new-born Christians, without
the power or form of religion, no outward means to excite
them to faith and good works. If they neglect the spirit of

prayer in themselves, it is not surprising they should grow
cold in love and zeal for the noble cause of truth on the
earth. But in the lowest of these [meetings] there is something alive to visit, and in going along we felt the renewed
evidence that we were in our right allotment in thus going
about, endeavoring to strengthen the things that remain;
and though we have had to pass through much suffering,
both outward and inward, yet we have also experienced times
of rejoicing in doing the will of our Lord and Saviour Jesus
Christ.

After the Quarterly Meeting in the Third Month
they visited each of the meetings within their own
Monthly Meeting, "thinking," says J. Y., "a little
pastoral care was due to our Friends at home, seeing
we are often concerned to go abroad."

In the Fifth Month they went up to the Yearly
Meeting, viâ Lincolnshire, taking several meetings in
the way. Among the subjects which occupied Friends
in their annual conference this year was that of missions to the heathen, which, it was proposed by some,
should be taken up by the Society.

The subject, writes John Yeardley, was fully entered into,
and the interest was very great. Many Friends spoke their
sentiments freely and feelingly, and the subject was taken
on minute to be revived next year. If this important matter
were brought home to each individual of us, there would be
more missionaries prepared and sent forth to labor; but we
love ease and our homes, contenting ourselves with reading
and talking about what is going forward in the great cause of
religion and righteousness in the earth.

They returned home through the midland counties,
visiting most of the meetings in Oxfordshire, and in the
parts adjacent; which they had been unable to do the
previous year in returning from the West.

.It was comforting to us, John Yeardley says, to be with Friends in Oxfordshire, whom we had so long thought of. Many of their meetings are small; but there are a few individuals among them precious and improving characters, who, I believe, are under the preparing hand for greater usefulness in the Lord's church. With these we were often dipped into near union of spirit, which sometimes caused the divine life to rise among us to the refreshing of our spirits.

In the Sixth Month they again left home, being minded to see how the churches fared in the eastern part of Yorkshire. The point which most interested them in this tour was Scarborough, where they were attracted both by the town itself and by the little society of Friends. "It felt to us," says J. Y., "very much like a home. We lodged at Elizabeth Rowntree's, a sweet resting-place." (7 *mo.* 4.)

At the same time that they reported to their Monthly Meeting the attention they had paid to this service, they received its sanction to undertake a journey in Wales.

It is truly humbling to us, writes John Yeardley, in describing this occasion, thus to have to expose ourselves, poor and weak as we are; but the cause is not our own, but is in the hands of our great Lord and Master. May he help us!  (7 *mo.* 19.)

They left home on the 7th of the Eighth Month, and spent the 11th at Coalbrookdale, in the company of Barnard Dickinson and his wife. From thence Samuel Hughes accompanied them as guide into Wales, and continued with them a week.

He proved, says J. Y., a most efficient helper in this wild country, knowing the roads well, and he was kind and attentive to us and our horse. The stages are long and hilly, and

we are often obliged to go many miles round the mountains
to make our way from one place to another. The road to
Pales is over the moors; we scarcely saw a house for miles,
except here and there a little cot, on a plot of ground obtained
as a grant to encourage industry. These little dwellings were
generally surrounded by a few acres of well-cultivated land
enclosed from the moor. It is much to be regretted that
the plan of cottage culture is not more generally promoted;
wherever I see it practised I view it with pleasure, as tending
to increase the comforts of the poor.

On the 19th they attended the Half-year's Meeting
at Swansea. A Committee of the Yearly Meeting was
present. Elizabeth Dudley was also there, with a certificate for religious service; and she and John and
Martha Yeardley, finding that the errand on which
they were come was the same, resolved to join company
and travel together through South and North Wales.
They were accompanied throughout the journey by
Robert and Jane Eaton of Bryn-y-Mor.

As there are very few meetings of Friends in Wales,
the chief part of their service was beyond the limits
of the Society. They met with great openness in many
places from the Methodists and other preachers and
their congregations. From the notes which John
Yeardley made of their religious labors in this journey,
we select several passages.

9 *mo.* 13. Aberystwith.—Our first object was to inquire
for a place of meeting. We found they were all engaged for
that evening, which detained us here a day longer than we
had expected; but this little detention enabled us to make
acquaintance with two of the Independent preachers, to whom
we became much attached in gospel fellowship, A. Shadrach
and his son. The father preaches in Welsh, and the son in
English. It was comforting to us to meet with two such
pious, humble-minded Christians, laboring diligently to

forward the cause of religion.  They kindly offered us their chapel for the evening, and after the meeting they both expressed much satisfaction in having been favored with such an opportunity.

9 *mo.* 15.—We arrived pretty early at Machynlleth, which is a clean little town.  We did not know but that we might have proceeded on our journey after having refreshed ourselves and our horses; but, E. D. feeling much interested for the people of the town, it seemed best to have a meeting with them.  I walked out, and seeing a good meeting-house, inquired to what persuasion of people it belonged, and found it was an Independent chapel, and that the minister lived about a mile and a half in the country.

The prospect of being unable to make the people understand us was discouraging; for in the streets there was nothing to be heard but Welsh.  However there was no time for reasoning, it being near twelve o'clock, and all must be arranged by seven in the evening.  After some difficulty we found the preacher, a kind-hearted pious man, who readily granted his chapel, and undertook to act as interpreter should occasion require.  This was the only place where we adopted the vulgar mode of giving notice by the town-crier, so common on all occasions in this country; but the time was short, and many of the people were not able to read our English notices, which we generally filled up for the purpose.

The meeting was pretty fully attended, and the people were mostly quiet, considering there were many who could not understand.  When E. D. sat down the minister repeated in substance what she had said; for, not being used to speak through an interpreter, she declined his giving sentence by sentence.  When he had done, I felt something press on my mind towards the poorer classes present, who I was sure could not understand English: so I stepped down from the pulpit, and placing myself by the minister, requested he would render for me a few sentences as literally as he could.  This he did kindly, and, I believe, faithfully, to the relief of my mind.  He then addressed a few words on his own

account to the assembly and dismissed them. We regretted
the want of the native language, as we could not have the
same command over the meeting as would otherwise have been
the case.

At Barmouth, instead of convening the people to hear
the word, they had to exercise a Christian gift of a different kind—the gift of spiritual judgment.

9 *mo.* 19.—On entering Barmouth we thought of a meeting
with the inhabitants; but on feeling more closely at the subject the way did not appear clear; there was something which
we could neither see nor feel through. This power of spiritual discrimination is very precious. How instructive it is
to mark our impressions under various circumstances and at
different times!

9 *mo.* 25.—At Ruthin we obtained information respecting
the few individuals at Llangollen who profess with Friends,
and set off to pay them a visit. We arrived at the beautiful
vale of Llangollen to dinner, and alighted at the King's Head
Inn, at the foot of the bridge, which afforded us a fine view
of the Dee. There are at present only four or five persons
who meet regularly as Friends. They live scattered in the
country, and are in the humbler walks of life; but we thought
them upright-hearted Christians who had received their religious principles from conviction. We saw them on First-
day morning in the room where they usually meet, and again
in the evening at our inn, and were much comforted in being
with them. The room where they meet is in such [an obscure
situation] that we should never have found it without a guide.
We thought it right to procure them a more convenient room,
which we did.

27*th.*—In the evening we had a public meeting in the
Independent Chapel, which was crowded; there is much
openness in the minds of the people to receive the truths of
the gospel. Before the assembly separated, we proposed to
them to establish a school for poor children; several present
expressed their conviction of the want of such an institution,

and the minister was so warm in the cause that he proposed their commencing without delay.

28th.—We went to Wrexham, and had a meeting in the evening. The notice was short, but the people came punctually, and a precious time it was. After it was over several bore testimony to the good which had been extended to them that evening, and were ready to cling to the instruments, inviting us to have a meeting with them when we came again that way.

This favored time, at the close of our labors among a people whom I much love, seemed like a crown on our exit from long-to-be-remembered Wales. My heart was humbled in reverent thankfulness to the Father of all our mercies, who had graciously preserved us in outward danger, and sustained us in many an inward conflict.

At Coalbrookdale they bade an affectionate and gospel farewell to the Friends with whom they had been so closely united in this long journey, and returned to Burton on the 20th of the Tenth Month.

In the Eleventh Month they made a circuit through Lancashire, taking all the meetings of Friends in course. They found " several meetings chiefly composed of such as had joined the Society on the ground of convincement, mostly in places where no ministering Friend resided." In visiting one of these small meetings, John Yeardley relates a circumstance in the gospel labors of his friend Joseph Wood:—

We visited a little newly-settled meeting at Thornton Marsh, near Poulton in the Fylde. Our worthy friend Joseph Wood had the first meeting of our Society that was ever held in this part. It is so thinly inhabited that the Friends wondered at his concern to request a meeting; but one was appointed for him at an inn, I think a solitary house; a good many poor people came, and it was a most remarkable time. J. W. said afterwards he believed there would be a meeting

of Friends in that neighborhood, but perhaps not in his time.
It has now been settled about eighteen months.

This journey occupied them about two weeks, and on
returning home John Yeardley makes the following
animating remark:—

The retrospect of this journey in connexion with that of
Wales afforded a sweet feeling of peace. We were often low
and discouraged, but help was mercifully extended in the
time of need. I often wish I had more faith to go forth in
entire reliance on the Divine Arm of power, for truly in the
Lord Jehovah is everlasting strength.

On the conclusion of this engagement followed a
month of quiet but industrious occupation at home.

12 *mo.* 25.—A month has been spent in the quiet, in
reading, writing, and many other things in course. Leisure
being afforded, I have spent a good deal of time in reading
diligently and attentively the Holy Scriptures, I trust to some
profit.

After this seasonable pause, John and Martha Yeardley were much occupied with a projected change in their
place of residence, which issued in their removal, in the
spring of 1831, to Scarborough. The motive which
induced them to make choice of this place, and the
feelings under which the change was accomplished, are
fully unfolded in the Diary.

We have for some time been on the look-out for a change
in our residence. Inclination would have led us to remain
in our own Monthly Meeting, but a strong impression that
it might be right for us to remove for some time to Scarborough, has remained with us ever since we visited that
place in the Seventh Month, and has always stood in the way
of our fixing elsewhere, although very often have we tried to

put it from us.  We were so desirous to settle at C. [near Pontefract], that only five pounds a year in the rent saved us from taking the step.  It was my prayer at the time, and always has been, that we might be rightly directed, and I had a hope that if it was not right for us to go to C. something might turn up to prevent it.  And since we could not agree for the house which was offered us in that place, we concluded to go for a short time to Scarborough, and try the fleece there, under the belief that we should then be enabled rightly to determine.  This I hope has been the case, for we had not been many days, I may say hours, in the town, before we were fully convinced it was the place for us to settle in.

Having made trial of Scarborough, they returned to Burton to arrange for their removal, which took place on the 7th of the Fifth Month.

We have now seen John Yeardley for many years in the devoted exercise of his calling of a gospel minister. It is instructive to follow him, as we are able to do soon after his removal to Scarborough, into his chamber, and see how, when alone with the gracious Giver, he was wont to regard the precious gift; how he lamented that he had not used the talent more diligently; and how his mind was enlarged to see the grace and power which the Lord is ready to bestow on those who seek and trust him with their whole heart.

6 mo. 8.—The important duty of a gospel minister has this day been brought closely under my consideration.  It is most assuredly the imperious duty of those who are called to feed the flock, to labor diligently for the good of others.  With respect to myself, I feel greatly ashamed; and it has occurred to me that should I be cast on a bed of sickness, or otherwise be deprived of an opportunity of exercising this gift, it would be an awful consideration, and cause of deep regret, that I had not better improved the time.  The hardness of heart

in others, as well as in one's self, is difficult to penetrate;
nothing but the power of divine grace can reach it, and this
requires not only waiting for, but also laboring to overcome
the wandering and unsettled thoughts to which the poor
mind is subject. Merciful Father, give me more confidence
in the gift which thou hast bestowed on me, and favor me
with a greater portion of strength to minister thy word faithfully. "Who then is that faithful and wise steward whom
his Lord shall make ruler over his household, to give them
their portion of meat in due season? Blessed is that servant
whom his Lord when he cometh shall find so doing."—(Luke
xii. 42, 43.)

Tenderly mindful of the religious wants of those
whom they had lately left, so early as the Seventh
Month John and Martha Yeardley revisited the several
congregations in Pontefract Monthly Meeting. They
were both humbled and comforted in the course of this
visit.

We were, says J. Y., united in sympathy to many dear
friends within the circle from whence we have removed, and
I was strengthened to labor according to the ability received
from day to day.

Since this little journey, he continues, we have been pretty
much at home attending the meetings in course in the neighborhood. We are comfortably settled in our new abode,
which feels to us really a home as to the outward in every
respect; and in a religious sense we entirely believe it is our
right allotment for the present.

In this new halting-place of his earthly pilgrimage,
John Yeardley experienced an increase of freedom of
spirit, and of faith and joy in his Saviour.

10 *mo.* 7.—For a few days past I have felt my mind raised
above the earth and fixed on heavenly things. I desire that

the blessed Saviour may more and more be the medium through which I may view every object as worthy [or unworthy] the pursuit of a devoted Christian. I humbly trust this quietude of mind is in answer to prayer; for I have long supplicated for a renewal of faith, and that a little spiritual strength might be given me to rise above the slavish fear of man. My heart was almost sick with doubting; but on Fourth-day last a bright hope livingly sprang in my soul that I should yet be favored to attain to greater liberty in the exercise of my gift in the ministry, if I were faithful in accepting the portion of strength which is offered. Grant that this may be the case, dearest Saviour!

10 mo. 23.—My heart is filled with wonder, love and praise, in contemplating the goodness of Almighty God to his poor, unworthy creatures. When we have done all that is required of us, we are unprofitable servants; but how often we come short of doing this. And yet so gracious, so good, and so just is our Divine Master, that he suffers not the least act of obedience to lose its reward, but is continually encouraging and stimulating us to greater devotedness of heart.

The persuasion which he and Martha Yeardley entertained of the need there was in the Society for increased means of scriptural instruction, led them, soon after they removed to Scarborough, to propose the establishment of a Bible class. The plan was for questions on the Scriptures to be given in anonymously in writing by the members, and answers to be returned in the same way at the next meeting. The scheme was at that time almost, if not quite, a novelty in the Society, but it was accepted with pleasure and confidence by the Friends of Scarborough, and the meetings were maintained for many years. There is an intermission in J. Y.'s diary at this period, but he makes allusion to the class soon after its establishment in a letter to his sisters S. and R. S.

By way of a relaxation from haymaking this charming morning, I have been again perusing your affectionate notes, which you were so kind and thoughtful as to forward us by our dear brother and family. I felt the deprivation exceedingly of not attending the last Yearly Meeting, but quite think it may have been all for the best.

But I will proceed at once to the real object of my now addressing you, which is to say we cannot be satisfied without your paying us a visit this summer. We think we have much to invite you to. I think you would feel some interest in our Bible class: it becomes increasingly instructive and agreeable to all engaged in it. I so highly approve of this mode of Scripture instruction, that I think the time is not far distant when they will become more general. We meet once every two weeks when nothing intervenes to prevent.

The autumn of this year was taken up with a series of public meetings, mostly in the East Riding, in the greater part of which J. and M. Y. had the company of Isabel Casson of Hull.

In the Eleventh Month, at the same time that they returned the minute which had been granted them for this service, they laid before their friends the prospect of more extensive travel in the work of the Gospel than any they had undertaken before. The time was come for John Yeardley to pay that debt of Christian love to the benighted inhabitants of Greece which he had felt to press for years upon his mind; and at the same time he and Martha Yeardley believed it to be required of them to revisit some of the places of their former service, and to take up their abode for a while with companies of persons whom they should find like-minded with themselves; and also to perform the unaccomplished duty of visiting the Piedmontese valleys. Considering the extent of country over which they travelled, the varied nature of their labors, and the large number of serious-minded and sympathizing persons with whom they were brought into relation, this journey may perhaps be regarded as the most active and fruitful period of their lives. We are able, as we have so often been before, to read their impressions of duty, and their feelings, their hopes, doubts, and aspirations, in J. Y.'s simple and faithful Diary.

11 mo. 7.—Yesterday was our Monthly Meeting at Pickering, and to me a very memorable one. We stated to our friends the prospect of a visit to some of the Grecian Islands and the Morea, the Protestant valleys of Piedmont, and some parts of Germany, Switzerland, and France. It is about five years since I first received the impression that it would be my religious duty to stand resigned to a service of the above kind. For the last nine months it has not been absent from my thoughts for many hours together. It has cost me not a little to come at resignation; but my Heavenly Father has been very gracious, and has brought me into a willingness to do his will. If I know my own heart I have one prevailing desire, and that is to devote the remainder of my days to his service; and my prayers are very fervent that he may be pleased to give me faith, patience, and perseverance to do and to suffer all that his wisdom may permit to befal me. I am often ready to covenant with him to go where he may be pleased to send, even to the ends of the world, if he will strengthen me with his strength, enlighten me with his light, guide me by his counsel, and prepare me for glory. "If thy presence go not with me, carry us not up hence."

They left Scarborough in the Second Month, and spent the time which intervened before the Yearly Meeting in social visits in London and the neighborhood, in pre-

paring for the journey and studying the modern Greek
language.

Nothing, says J. Y., could exceed the interest which our
friends take in doing all in their power to forward our
views with respect to the important mission before us.—
(3 *mo.* 4.)

A chief desideratum had been to find a Greek who
should accompany them as guide into his native country. "Ever since," says M. Y., in a letter of the
Twelfth Month, 1832, "we have resigned ourselves to
this arduous mission, my dear husband has frequently
said, 'If we are to go into Greece, how I wish we might
find some companion for the journey, some *Greek* to
conduct us into his country, to us altogether strange
and unknown!'" A letter from Stephen Grellet to
William Allen, which was sent down to J. and M.
Yeardley, was the opportune means of supplying this
want. It spoke of a Greek girl then at the school at
Locle, named Argyri Climi, who was exceedingly desirous of returning to Greece, and whose simple and
teachable character recommended her at once to their
attention. "When," continues M. Y., "we came to this
part of Stephen Grellet's letter, we were both deeply
moved, believing that thus the way might be prepared
before us."

They communicated their thoughts on this interesting
subject to M. A. Calame, proposing when they visited
Locle to take A. Climi as their companion into Greece.
During their sojourn in London they received a letter
from A. Climi, written in French, in which that amiable
young person signified the pleasure and gratitude with
which she accepted their proposal.

Locle, 29th of April, 1833.

Excuse the liberty which I take of writing to testify my great gratitude for your kind intention to take me with you and bring me back to my country. How could I have ventured to hope that I should have the happiness of being with such kind and beloved friends. I cannot express the joy I felt when Mademoiselle Calame made your proposal known to me. How great is the mercy of God! How often might he have turned away his face from me and cast me off; but instead of forsaking me he has looked upon me in mercy, and shown me that he wills not that sinners should perish, but that they should have eternal life. Was it not he who saved me from the hands of the Turks, and brought me to Switzerland, and placed me with charitable protectors, who are never weary of doing me good? And now he has crowned it all, by giving you to me as guides and protectors in my long journey, and that I may settle again in my own country.

Your grateful

ARGYRI CLIMI.*

The meeting in London at which their prospect of foreign travel was ratified, was a time of spiritual favor. With such credentials, and with a sense of the divine commission and guidance, clear and unmistakable, like that which John Yeardley enjoyed, many may be ready to exclaim, Who would not go forth on an errand like this to the ends of the earth! Such may be reminded, for their consolation, that if the will is laid as an unbroken offering at the foot of the cross; if all their powers are consecrated to the Lord, and his Spirit is suffered to penetrate and transform every part of their being; though a field of labor such as that which

---

* This young person, under the name of Amanda, is the subject of No. 7 of a series of small tracts published by John Yeardley in the latter years of his life.

was appointed to John and Martha Yeardley may not be appointed to them, they will, in an equal degree, inherit the blessing of doing their Lord's will, and may rest in the promise, "They that wait upon Him shall not want any good thing."

5 *mo.* 21.—Yearly Meeting of Ministers and Elders. Third-day morning. Our visit to the Grecian Islands, &c. claimed the attention of the meeting. It was a very precious time; a sweet solemnity prevailed; several Friends said afterwards, they thought they had never known quite so full an expression of unity and encouragement on any former occasion. What a favor it is to have the sympathy and concurrence of the church in such important concerns! My heart's desire and prayers are that we may be preserved humble and watchful, relying for help and strength on nothing short of our Divine Master, the holy Head of his own church. Whatever may befal us on our intended journey, I wish once more to record my firm conviction that it is the Lord's requiring, and come life, come death, I desire that my heart and soul may be given up fully to follow Him who laid down his own precious life for my sake,—a poor unworthy sinner.

# CHAPTER XI.

## 1833–4.

PART I.—THE JOURNEY TO ANCONA.

JOHN AND MARTHA YEARDLEY left London on the 21st of the Sixth Month, 1833.

Travelling through France they found in the places where they halted more of simplicity and Christian life than they had expected. In Paris, especially, they were quickly brought into contact with a number of pious persons to whom their society and their doctrine were welcome, and they visited many benevolent institutions conducted on broad Christian principles. This was in the early part of Louis Philippe's reign, and under the administration of Guizot. In reading their account of these institutions, we are painfully reminded how much the rising tide of religious liberty has been checked and driven back by the hands of priestcraft and arbitrary power.

Here, and elsewhere during their journey, they wrote letters to members of the Foreign Committee of the Meeting for Sufferings, descriptive of their religious labors, from which, after their return, a selection was printed for the use of Friends. Besides these letters, John Yeardley kept his usual Diary, which often enables us to add to the narrative, traits of character and reflections not to be found in their joint epistles.

(219)

Amongst the first persons upon whom they called in Paris, were the Protestant bookseller Risler, and Pastor Grandpierre: the former they found to be devoted heart and soul to the diffusion of evangelical religion; the latter they had known on their former journey, and he received them as his Christian friends. He introduced them to Mademoiselle Chabot, a lady who spent her time in translating religious and useful books into French, and had a class of children in the First-day school. Respecting this lady, they say:—

Our introduction to this precious character was much to our comfort. We rejoiced together in contemplating the wonderful work which the Lord has in mercy begun, and is carrying on in this great city. On First-day afternoons she attends a school, to which the children of the rich go, as well as the poor, to be instructed in the Scriptures. The young persons in her class learn texts, and are questioned to see if they thoroughly understand the subject. On our asking whether the children answered the questions from what they had learnt by heart, she replied, " No ; it would be of no use, you know, for the dear children to repeat merely by rote ; we want the great truths of the gospel to sink into their hearts."

After this visit, which refreshed our spirits a little, we called on Madame D'Aublay, sister-in-law to Brissot, who was executed in the time of Robespierre. She is a Roman Catholic, and thinks the groundwork of true religion to be in their church, but that their customs and the mass are nothing worth. We left her some tracts, and amongst them one of Judge Hale's, which struck her so forcibly on reading it, that she followed us to our hotel, to say how much it was suited to her state of mind.

6 *mo.* 30.—After our little meeting this morning with the few friends resident here, and some others, we went to the Protestant Chapel, in the Rue Taitbout, to hear the children examined in the Scriptures. Many of the parents were

present. The class which we attended was conducted by
Mademoiselle Chabot. The subject was the crucifixion of
our Saviour, the 27th chapter of Matthew. The children
repeated the portion they had learnt, and then Mademoiselle C.
questioned them in a simple, sweet, and instructive manner,
calculated to impress the great truths of Christianity on their
minds. A gentleman examined a class of boys; and after
this course of exercise was finished, De Pressensé gave them
a lecture from the Old Testament. The subject was the
healing of Naaman, and the manner of proceeding was simple; the child called upon stood up and answered pretty much
as they do at Ackworth; he repeated a few verses directly
bearing on the subject, and the application which was made
was admirable. We were really edified in being present.
How much this kind of instruction is wanted for many of
our poor children in England! How delightful it is to see
a large room filled with Roman Catholic children and parents,
all receiving Christian instruction together! The Roman
Catholics no longer object to send their children to Protestants, because they know they will be well instructed. The
chapel is a beautiful room, with a circular gallery supported
on pillars, and a dome top; and it is the identical place where,
only two years ago, the Saint Simonians held forth their
doctrines:—

> . . . . . . Oh reformation rare,
> The den of modern infidels is become a house of prayer!

7 *mo.* 2.—We had a long walk to the Rue St. Maur, to
meet by appointment our kind friend De Pressensé to visit
the schools for mutual instruction. At this season of the
year the children are more busy with their parents than
usual; but in winter there are 200 boys, 200 girls, and 200
children in the infant school, with an evening school for
adults. Scripture extracts are made use of, and also the
Scriptures themselves. We were struck with the quiet and
good order of all these schools. I have seen very few in
England where the same stillness is observable. With the
exception of some three or four, all the children are Roman

Catholics; and on First-days, particularly in winter, the room
is filled with Roman Catholic men and women, mostly parents
of the children, who come to hear them examined in the
Scriptures and to receive instruction themselves.   Our conductor showed us the boys' gardens.   On the walls were
grapes hanging in large bunches, belonging to the master.
The boys are so far from stealing them, that if they find any
on the ground, they take them to him.   Of the children who
attend at the school, forty-six are provided with bed, board,
and clothing, at a neighboring establishment.

One of the most interesting men with whom J. and
M. Y. became acquainted was Pastor Audebez.

He was, say they, formerly minister at Bordeaux, but
received a strong impression that it was his religious duty to
come to Paris.   Soon after he left Bordeaux, a great awakening took place in that neighborhood under the ministry of
his successor, while with himself at Paris all seemed darkness
and discouragement.   This induced him to think he had done
wrong in removing, and he was much distressed ; but as he
persevered in doing what presented as his duty, his way for
usefulness in this great city opened in a remarkable manner.
He first opened the chapel in the Taitbout, and then one in
the Faubourg du Temple, where his labors have been crowned
with success.   He told us with great simplicity that he never
premeditated or wrote his sermons, but after reading a portion
of Scripture proceeded to speak from what he felt to impress
his mind at the time.   He said some of the ministers considered their discourse before delivering it, and he believed their
mode of preaching was also blessed.   Being accustomed to
arrange their thoughts in methodical order, perhaps such might
not perform so well in any other way, and the people were
used to it ; but he preferred speaking from a more spontaneous
spring of thought, though not so well arranged as to theo-
logical order.

We felt much inclined to hear him for ourselves, and
attended in the Rue St. Maur on First-day evening; and

we have this testimony to bear,—that we heard the *gospel* preached to the *poor*. He first read the 25th Psalm, and then part of the Epistle to the Romans, which formed the basis of his exhortation. It reminded me of [what I have read of] the preaching of the early Christians. My very heart went with his impressive exhortation to believe in the Lord Jesus as the only means of salvation, and of the necessity of bringing forth fruits unto holiness.

7 *mo.* 5.—Pastor Grandpierre came to pay us a visit with four of his missionary students. We had a precious religious opportunity with them. The Pastor expressed his belief that the power and presence of the Saviour had been evidently felt among us. The young men were much tendered; one of them was a grandson of the late Pastor Oberlin, and had been sensibly affected by what Stephen Grellet had said in a meeting at his father's place of worship in the Ban de la Roche. Three of the young men who were in the institution at our last visit to Paris are now in Africa. We admire the principle on which this establishment is conducted; the inmates are not sent out unless they believe it to be their duty to go; if this be not the case at the expiration of their term, they return home.

On the 7th John Yeardley, accompanied by Joseph Grellet, brother of Stephen Grellet, visited the Sabbath-school in the Rue St. Maur. Martha Yeardley was indisposed and unable to leave the house.

When the classes had finished, says J. Y., De Pressensé proposed to give a lecture on a subject from the Old Testament, and bestowed great pains to make it clear to the infant capacities of the children. I had intimated to my worthy friend a desire for liberty to express what might arise in my mind when he had done, which was most readily granted, and after I had spoken to the children, there seemed great liberty in addressing the teachers, parents and young persons present. There was much seriousness the whole time and a precious sense of divine love was over us. Our kind friend,

J. Grellet, interpreted for me in an impressive and clear manner.

The name of Mark Wilks has been for many years identified with the cause of evangelical religion in Paris. John Yeardley had an interview with him, and makes an interesting note in his Diary regarding his opinions on the state of religious parties at this period.

7 *mo.* 9.—This morning I had an interview with Mark Wilks. He received me very cordially, and, as I expected, I found him full of religious intelligence; he is just returned from a tour in Switzerland, and speaks encouragingly of the state of the Christian church in general. He has resided in Paris fifteen years, and of course seen many changes. He assured me that the arm of infidelity is weakening; nothing like the same exertion is made to spread the vile doctrine. The fact is, in some degree, the people are too indifferent to trouble themselves about it, and would not spend a sou for its promotion; on the other hand, zealous Christians are doing all in their power to promote the spread of gospel truth.

On the 15th John S. Mollet, who had arrived in Paris after them, accompanied J. and M. Y. to Madame d'Aublay's.

We met, they say, several of her relations who professed to be Catholics, but were rather of the philosophical school. They were interested in the conversation, though nothing of a religious nature occurred. Madame d'Aublay has distributed many of our books and tracts. The next day she took us to see more of her friends, much of the same character. We have a hope that our drawing some of these to the really Christian characters may do good, since each class expressed surprise to hear us speak to them of the other. It will be no small satisfaction if any of our Society here should be like the mortar to bind parties together, and weaken prejudice, that the one true knowledge may increase.

*21st.*—Attended the chapel at the Taitbout this morning. Heard a discourse by Pastor Grandpierre; he preaches the gospel in its purity, with much of the right unction. We did not feel out of our place in being present, and I trust it may have its use both on ourselves and others. This kind of Christian liberty seems to open our way among the people. In the evening we had quite a large meeting in our room; several of the attenders at the Taitbout coming in, together with the Friends in Paris. It was, adds John Yeardley, a precious tendering time, and I trust strength was given to preach the gospel; the sick and afflicted were not forgotten by my M. Y. in supplication.

By "the sick" in the foregoing passage was probably intended Rachel, wife of Dr. Waterhouse of Liverpool, and daughter of David and Abigail Dockray. This young Friend, who was ill in the neighborhood of Paris, was about to be removed to England, but at the very time when the carriage was at the door she was struck with paralysis. This happened two days before the meeting just described, and J. and M. Y. had hastened to offer their sympathy and aid to her afflicted husband and mother. They deferred their departure from Paris in order to remain with the family, and they both took turns in assisting to watch by the bed-side of the sufferer. She survived only a few days, and expired, in the hope and peace of the gospel, the day after they quitted the city.

We may conclude the narrative of this interesting visit to Paris with a short reflection by Martha Yeardley.

I have been renewedly confirmed since being in Paris that our first religious awakening proceeds from the immediate influence of the Spirit on the heart of man, and this is the doctrine preached and maintained by the writings of the

truly devoted Christians in this place, who are brought to
profess living faith in our Lord Jesus Christ as the Alpha and
Omega, the Beginning and the End.

They found the country on the road to Nancy very
agreeable.

29*th, evening.*—The white houses among the trees, and
the vines on the hill-sides, form a picturesque landscape. The
reapers were busy in the harvest fields; and the ground that
is cleared of its burdens gives proof of the diligence of the
French farmer; the plougher, if not the sower, literally over-
takes the reaper. In the forepart of the route we saw much
wood and water, hill and dale, with cattle feeding in the
peaceful pastures, which is a lovely sight. As we advanced
towards Chalons, it became less interesting, more flat, with
fewer trees and meadows. Everywhere the harvest more
forward than in England, but the crops much more light and
thin.

They entered Nancy under a feeling of gloom, and it
was some time before they could find relief to their
minds; but by patiently pursuing the paths of intercourse which opened before them, they were enabled to
deposit with some serious individuals their accustomed
testimony to the simple spiritual nature of the gospel.
In allusion to this trial of their patience John Yeardley
remarks:—

I cannot, I dare not, complain, when I think of the difficulties some of our Friends had to encounter who travelled
on the Continent years ago, when darkness prevailed to a
much greater extent. The want of the language, &c., which
some of them experienced, must have been very trying. It
is to me an unspeakable comfort to be able to understand the
language of the country where we travel.

Travelling by the Diligence being too rapid for
Martha Yeardley's state of health, they hired a carriage

and horses to take them to Strasburg, and found this
mode of travelling 'less expensive, as well as much less
fatiguing, than the public conveyance.

8 *mo.* 5.—Left Nancy at 6 o'clock in the morning, and had
a delightful journey. I feel particularly peaceful in spirit,
and a degree of resignation pervades my heart to be given
fully up to do the will of my Heavenly Father.

Our mode of travelling afforded us an opportunity of calling
at Phalsbourg, where we found a handful of Protestants,
about twenty-six families, mostly German settlers. On
inquiring for the minister, we found he was engaged with his
class at the college. His wife appeared surprised at seeing
such strangers, thinking from our dress and our speaking
French, we were no doubt Roman Catholics. We soon perceived the family were Germans, and I then addressed them
in their native tongue, which immediately opened the way to
their hearts. Nothing would satisfy the good woman but
that we must call at the college to see her husband. He was
embarrassed on being so suddenly called out of the class, and
appeared a little fearful; but when he understood who we
were, and our mission, he became almost overjoyed to see us.
There has been a little awakening in this place, and a desire
to obtain the Scriptures. One of them said, "I have been
accustomed to smoke tobacco, but have now left it off, and I
will put the money into the box to save for a Bible." Another
said, "I have been accustomed to take snuff, but I will now
save the money for a Bible." And another said, "I have
drunk more wine than I need; I will take less, and subscribe
for a Bible." This little account in such a dark place was
quite cheering; for they are surrounded and oppressed by
the Roman Catholics, in whose presence they are afraid to
speak.

On entering Alsace, the view of the country was enchant-
ing. We dined at Sarrebourg, which appeared at a distance
like a town in the midst of a wood.

At Strasburg they were received in an ingenuous

manner by some enlightened Roman Catholics, who did
all in their power to forward their object; but it was
not until they fell in with the Protestant Professor
Cuvier, that they found the proper channel for the work
of the gospel. In few places did they find brighter
tokens of inward spiritual religion.

8 mo. 6.—Called on Professor Cuvier and delivered the
letter which Mark Wilks had kindly given us. We found
the professor an humble-minded Christian, kind and affectionate. He conducted us to Pastor Majors, who was born
in Prussia, and speaks German and French well. We soon
became united to him in spirit. He is one of the *inward*
school, and a diligent laborer in the Lord's vineyard. He
has been here about three months as pastor of a little handful
of Christians. He is fully sensible of the necessity of a right
preparation of heart before acceptable worship can be performed. He said when the people came to their place of
worship they were full of the world, and the word preached
did not profit, because it did not sink into their hearts. I
believe he fully comprehends the nature of true silence; and
he is acquainted with many *interior* persons whom we wish
to see in Switzerland, &c. This dear man was nine months
in Corfu, preparing to be a missionary there; but he was
taken ill, and suffered much in body and mind. The way in
which he mentioned the wonderful dealings of the Lord with
him was to me very instructive. He told me he had not been
sufficiently careful to seek divine counsel before he undertook
the mission; and it had pleased the Almighty to bring him
into the deeps, and instruct him in the school of affliction;
and he can now most fully acknowledge there is no safety but
under the guidance of the Holy Spirit. He and a few others
have united for the purpose of printing and circulating small
tracts, purely Scripture extracts. They are now engaged in
forming a selection for every day in the year, from the Old
and New Testament. I accord much with their work; it is
just what I have thought of for a long time.

Pastor Majors conducted us to Professor Ehrmann, a worthy Christian, simple-hearted and spiritually-minded. His two daughters are precious young women; the older of them recollected to have seen us at Kornthal, in 1827. She knew us instantly, and appeared overcome with joy and surprise, though we could not recollect her. It is no wonder we should have felt so much attraction to this place, though on entering the town I was, as usual, extremely discouraged, and I feel unworthy to be employed in the least service of my holy Redeemer.

On the 7th they dined at the La Combes, a Catholic family, who took them to see the House of Correction, where John Yeardley interrogated the boys in the prison school, and afterwards addressed them. In the evening they were present at Pastor Majors' Bible-class.

It is composed, says J. Y., of ten young men, who meet once a week at his lodging, and he instructs them in the Scriptures. I rejoiced to meet with them. Before the conclusion we had a religious opportunity, in which I was strengthened to express what was on my mind. The pastor offered a prayer in which our hearts truly united. The Saviour's love was very precious to our souls, and I trust we were edified together in the Lord.

8th.—The Pastor Majors called for us to pay a few visits. He is so spiritual and *interior* in his walk with God that it does me good to be in his company. Passing along the street, he said, We will just speak to a man who has been in England; he will be pleased to see you. He was alone in his meal and flour shop, which is apart from the house. He received us heartily; and on our coming away he pressed us to go up and speak to his daughters. After hesitating a few moments we went to the room and to our surprise found a little company of young females met to work for the missionaries, and to read. After sitting a while with them, one of the girls in much simplicity handed the Bible to our friend, and he read a chapter in the First Epistle of Peter, which was followed by a Friends' meeting with these dear young persons. I felt great openness in addressing them, and thankfulness filled my heart to the Father of mercies for having given us this casual opportunity of preaching the gospel.

In the evening we went to meeting with Pastor M.'s flock. He has taken the first floor of a good house, and appropriates three rooms opening one into another for a meeting-house, placing his pulpit, which is on wheels, in the doorway, so that when the meeting hour is over he can put the pulpit aside and make the rooms his dwelling. The rooms are fitted with long benches; the men and women sit separate and enter by different doors. The worship is conducted with much solemnity; they have for the present discontinued singing. They sat in silence some time at the commencement, when Majors offered a short prayer, and then read and expounded a small portion of Scripture. When he had finished he introduced us as English friends. He had told me previously that if I felt anything to say, I had only to intimate it to him. This liberty was acceptable to me, for I had felt much exercise of mind for the people; and after we had rested some time in silence, I was strengthened to speak with great freedom, and the power of the Most High was over us. Many thirsty souls were present, who, I believe, know the value of true silence. The two rooms for the women were crowded, and the stillness which pervaded was remarkable. A military man addressed me after the meeting, in English, expressing his great satisfaction and joy in being present; he is a regular attendant at this place of worship. The pastor said he was comforted and thankful that the Spirit of the Lord had been with us, and divided his word to the state of the people.

On the 9th, Professor Krafft and Pastor Majors conducted them to the Agricultural School for destitute children at Neuhoff, four miles from the city. This

well-known institution was founded by a man who had
been taken as a child out of the streets, and whose wife
had been brought up in an orphan-house. John Yeardley says:—

The arrangement of the farm-yard, &c., and the cropping
of the land are pretty much the same as at Beuggen, near
Basle, and what is now practised at Lindfield; and it is just
what we want Rawden to be—at least what I should like to
see it. Before leaving the premises, we had the children assembled in the schoolroom, and held a meeting with them,
with which we were well satisfied. There is a sweet spirit of
inward piety in the master and mistress.

On First-day, the 11th, they attended Pastor Majors'
meeting in the morning, and in the afternoon appointed
a meeting of their own in the same place, at which some
hundreds were present.

It was a precious tendering season; much openness was felt
in preaching the word, and I trust many hearts were reached
by the power of the Holy Spirit. At 7 o'clock we held our
usual meeting in the room at the inn, to which came many
of our friends; and I trust we were again favored with the
presence of the Divine Master. To conclude the evening, we
went to Professor Ehrmann's, where we partook of tea, fruit,
wine, &c. It felt to us a true feast of love.

This has been a day of much exercise; but best help has
been near in the time of need, and I feel sweet peace. There
is a great awakening in this place; thirty of the young women are preciously visited. In accompanying them home,
some of them expressed to me that it had been a blessed and
happy day, they hoped never to be forgotten. These dear
lambs are near to us in gospel love, and I am glad they have
such a minister in Pastor M.: he stands quite alone, not
being connected with any other Society.

In reading of days spent like that which has just

been described, we see in a striking manner what was the nature of that work of the ministry for which John Yeardley was prepared at Barnsley and Bentham by so many deep baptisms and sharp trials of his faith and obedience. The stage on which he was called to act was not the most public; the part which he had to perform was unobtrusive; but when the value of strengthening the weak, comforting the afflicted, and, above all, skilfully dividing the word of truth in the anointed ministry of the gospel, comes rightly to be estimated, it cannot be said but that the fruit was in some sort commensurate with the power of the call and the extent of the preparation.

The next day and the succeeding were occupied by John and Martha Yeardley in an excursion to the Ban de la Roche, of which the former gives the following account in his Diary.

*12th.*—In company with Majors, we set off at 6 o'clock to the Ban de la Roche. We had a most delightful drive by the side of the river, flowing along the fertile meadows: the hills on each side variegated with trees of almost every color, and occasional vineyards added to the richness of the scene. After travelling twelve leagues, we arrived at Foudai, where we met with an affectionate and hearty welcome from the whole family of the Legrands. The two families live together in one house, with their lovely children. We took tea with them, and then proceeded up Steinthal to Waldbach, to the house of the late pious Oberlin. Pastor Raucher's wife and daughter were out when we arrived; but we spent a little time with the dear old Louise, who is lively in spirit, and though she could not speak much, it was refreshing to us to be near her. The pastor's wife and daughter came home in the evening, and received us with open arms. We spent the night there, and they accompanied us the next morning to the Legrands' to breakfast, about a league in distance. After we had breakfasted, we requested a chapter might be read, and then had a precious meeting with them. We were so knit together in spirit, that we could hardly separate from one another. They accompanied us, on leaving, all the way up the hill, when we again took an affectionate farewell.

The conversation of our dear friend Majors has been to me truly instructive, and I trust our being thus thrown together is in divine wisdom. We have gone very fully into the nature of our church discipline, and have had much spiritual conversation to the refreshment of our souls.

We arrived at Strasburg about .7 o'clock, and I attended the class of his young men, which afforded me once more an opportunity to speak to them of the things that belong to their eternal peace.

Their religious service in Strasburg finished with a visit to the family of Professor Ehrmann, in which Martha Yeardley ministered to the company, and they commended one another in solemn supplication to the safe keeping of Israel's Shepherd.

Both the German and French languages are spoken in Strasburg. In their religious communications to those who spoke German, J. and M. Y. sometimes availed themselves of the interpretation of Pastor Majors, who they found was never at a loss, and who said, "It is no difficulty for me to interpret for you, because you say the very things that are in my heart."

From Strasburg they went on to Colmar and Mülhausen. The latter place, particularly interested them, from the number of persons recently awakened there, and they held several meetings in the town. John Yeardley says :—

In the whole district of Alsace there is a great deal of spiritual religion among the different professors; but in some of the ministers there is great deadness, or else infidelity.

16

The next halting-place on their route was Basle. This city, and the little canton of which it is the capital, were then in a state of civil war. The great political eruption of 1830, by which half Europe had been convulsed, continued to agitate Switzerland long after it had spent its force elsewhere. On the 3rd of the month, a little more than two weeks before the date at which we are arrived, a large body of the citizens, under arms, went out to reduce the peasants to subjection: the latter gave them battle amongst the hills and entirely defeated them, killing 200 of their number. The ferment was gradually subsiding when J. and M. Y. were in the city.

They found the town pretty quiet, though full of soldiers. A general sentiment seemed to prevail amongst serious persons, that the judgments of the Lord were upon the country.

Poor Switzerland, exclaims J. Y., what an awful judgment is come upon thee! Is it to be wondered at? within the last six months they have persecuted and banished twenty ministers from the Canton of Basle, simply because they preached the gospel, and the unbelieving inhabitants could not bear it.

They visited the Mission-House, and held a large meeting there with the students and others; Pastor Majors, who was present, from Strasburg, interpreting for them. "It was," says J. Y., "a season long to be remembered."

From Basle, they took the Diligence direct to Locle, where they spent two days with M. A. Calame's large and interesting family. They were introduced to Argyri Climi, whom they describe as a girl of " pensive character and genteel manners." On the 26th they descended the slope of the Jura to Neufchâtel.

About 5 o'clock, says John Yeardley, we came in sight of the snow-capped Alps. I saw them for some time through the trees, but the sun shone so bright that I did not for a moment imagine they were any other than clouds; but coming out from the wood I soon discovered my mistake; and a most majestic, sublime sight, indeed it is.

At Neufchâtel they took a lodging a little way out of the town, by the lake, and remained there a month, receiving and making calls and holding meetings for worship at the houses of their friends, as Professor Pétavel's, ———— Châtelain's, and in their own rooms. At the close of a day spent in this manner J. Y. says:—

I feel this evening a degree of sweet peace, and a strong desire to become more united to my Saviour, who died that we might live. When the mind is fixed on eternity, how little do all other things appear! Lord, redeem me from the world, and grant me power to live for thee alone!— (9 mo. 1.)

His observations on another similar occasion mark the religious state of the deeply interesting company in this place, amongst whom they went about in the liberty of the gospel.

9 mo. 24.—In the afternoon had a long walk with our dear friend Pétavel's family, quite to the top of the mountains, from which we had the most delightful view possible. In the evening we took tea with them; and, a few others coming in, we had a religious opportunity before parting. It is extraordinary how great is the desire to hear the word in its simplicity; they love the simplicity of the gospel, but probably are not prepared, as yet, to hold silent meetings alone. They all say it is remarkable we should be sent among them in this time of war in the land with the message of peace.

The little meeting which had been begun by Auguste Borel had been discontinued in consequence of his removal into the country. He visited them, and they found him alive in the truth and full of affection as before.

Amongst a number of new acquaintances, one of the most interesting was a Polish Countess. She lodged near them, with her husband and child, and sent to desire the liberty of calling on them. Martha Yeardley had often longed to become acquainted with her; and she, as she told them afterwards, had felt so strongly inclined towards them when she met them on the promenade that she could not rest without seeking their acquaintance.

At the time fixed, say J. and M. Y., the Countess came alone, her husband being unwell, and asked a few questions respecting our views in travelling. She is a Roman Catholic by profession, but has been brought up in great ignorance of her religion, and quite in the gaiety of the world. She deeply lamented the state of her unhappy country, to which a fatality seemed to attach, and spoke of her own particular trials, having lost four of her children. Whilst we were endeavoring to make her sensible of the mercies which are often hid under the most painful dispensations, an English missionary, who had been engaged in preaching to many of the Polish refugees in the country, came in with Professor Pétavel. They became much interested for the Countess, and in reply to some of her questions, the missionary explained the truths of the gospel in a clear and satisfactory way. We rejoiced in the unexpected meeting; several others came in, and it proved a memorable visit.

When again alone with the Countess she continued her history, opening her heart to M. Y. with the greatest confidence. In former years, she said, she had been drawn to seek the Lord, but for awhile affliction seemed to harden her heart, and she lost the religious impressions she had received; but now she felt again a desire to become acquainted with her Saviour, for she was miserable and felt the need of such a refuge.

22nd.—In the afternoon the Count and Countess paid us a visit. He is a man of strong mind, weary of the disappointing pleasures of the world, and happily turned to seek comfort in the substantial truths of religion. The Countess was delighted to find that we were of the same Society as William Penn, whose name her father much revered. They desired permission to attend our meeting; and a little before the hour we called on them, and they accompanied us to Professor Pétavel's, where we had a room quite filled and a good meeting. At the conclusion M. Y. made some apology to the Countess for the imperfect manner in which the communication was made; but she replied, "It comes from the heart, and it goes to the heart." After the meeting none seemed disposed to move, and the Countess commenced asking questions directing to passages of the Scriptures, apparently desirous to confirm the practices of the Romish Church, but sincerely seeking to have the conviction of her own heart confirmed that they were errors. It is not easy to describe the interest which this scene presented. ·An accomplished Roman Catholic lady proposing questions of the deepest moment, and the learned but pious and humble Professor Pétavel answering them with the Bible in his hand, while a roomful of attentive hearers were, we trust, reaping deep instruction.

Argyri joined them on the 27th at Neufchâtel,[*] and they left that city the same day for Geneva.

Here they tarried nearly a fortnight, were received

---

[*] She brought an affectionate epistle from M. A. Calame. The felicity of style and beauty of penmanship which distinguished the letters of this extraordinary woman agreed with the rest of her character. We have the epistle in question now before us, exquisitely written. It ends with these words :—

"Il nous eût été bien doux de prolonger les moments de la voir

with much affection by their old friends, and had a few
religious meetings.   Martha Yeardley says:—

We met with several very interesting persons at Geneva,
and had three religious opportunities with them; at the last
meeting the number was much increased, but the place is
not like Neufchâtel.   The different societies make bonds for
themselves and for one another, so that love and harmony do
not sufficiently prevail amongst them.

Our stay in this place, writes John Yeardley, has been a
time of distress of mind and perplexity of thought, arising
probably from the great weight and importance of the journey
before us, and the anxiety of providing a conveyance through
a strange and dark country.   After much difficulty, we have
concluded a written contract with an Italian *voiturier* to take
us to Ancona.   May our Divine Keeper, in his infinite mercy,
grant us protection and safety, even in the hands of ungodly
men!

The journey to Ancona took them seventeen days;
they crossed the Alps by the Simplon, and traversed
Italy through Milan and Bologna.   Martha Yeardley
touches upon a few points of the journey in a letter to
Elizabeth Dudley.

Ancona, 11 mo. 4.

We had much to do before we could meet with a suitable
conveyance, and at length trusted ourselves with our Italian
coachman, who could not speak French.   For a certain sum
he was to give us three places in his coach, and provide us
with food and lodging by the way.   The other passenger

encore, mais la sagesse demande que tout se fasse avec ordre; voilà
pourquoi notre chère enfant vous est confiée plus tôt; que le seigneur
l'accompagne et vous aussi, precieux amis; nous vous confions tous
trois à la garde divine, et nous vous assurons encore ici de l'affection
Chrétienne qui unit nos ames aux vôtres en Celui qui est le lien
indissoluble.

"M. A. CALAME."

Locle, 24 du 9 mois, '33.

inside was an Englishman, who spoke very little French and no Italian, and another Englishman outside was in the same situation. We could not but feel ourselves a very helpless company when arriving at the inns, which were quite of an inferior class, and little or no French spoken. We did pretty well, however, till we got to Milan, where we rested some days; and our Englishmen were exchanged for an Italian priest who spoke no French, and a Swiss who was a little useful to us as far as Bologna; after this place we travelled five days alone. The inns on this side of Milan are much worse, and from the detention of our passports in the towns we passed through, we were often prevented from reaching the place of destination, and obliged to lodge at villages, where we suffered much in the way of food and lodging; yet through all we were favored to bear the journey much better than I expected. My J. Y. was rather poorly for two days, and I was extremely anxious about him; but the sight of the Gulf of Venice seemed to help to restore him.

At Sinigaglia, a town eighteen miles from this, they told us that we should just meet the vessel which was to sail on the 30th. Judge then what was our disappointment when, on arriving at the inn here, we found that it was gone.

This disappointment was a severe trial of their patience; but they consoled themselves with reflecting that "good in some shape might arise out of the seeming evil."

Ancona, says John Yeardley, is beautifully situated on the side of a high hill, in appearance at a distance a perfect model of Scarborough. There are in the place a good many Greeks, one of whom Argyri recognised as we inquired at his shop the way to the Post-office. On returning she made herself known to him, and he shows us every attention; he is a fine looking man, with a countenance as strong as brass. We are comfortably lodged, with a delightful view of the harbor, but our hearts are in Corfu.

Our young companion, adds M. Y., is amiable and very

quick, but not of much use to us respecting her native tongue,
which she retains but very imperfectly, and is not at all fond
of speaking it.

The houses are high, and many of the streets narrow and
offensive, for want of cleanliness and from an immense population; such numbers are continually in the streets, that
there is no quiet or good air in the town. The darkness is
extreme, and the dissipation apparently very great; the
oppression of our spirits at some periods is almost insupport-
able; and yet I am at times very sensible of the calming
influence of divine love, with a sense that, having acted to the
best of our judgment, we must resign ourselves to wait for the
return of the steam-packet from England.

When on arriving here we found there were no letters, and
that probably they were sent to Corfu, my heart sank within
me. We have, however, been since cheered by receiving a
very kind letter from dear Robert Forster; nothing could
have been more in season than this token of remembrance.

Finding no suitable vessel for Corfu, with the assistance of their Greek friend they hired a lodging, and
gave their time to the study of Italian and the Modern
Greek. Religious labor was hardly to be thought of;
the government of the town and every public office was
under the direction of the Roman Catholic priests, of
whom there were more than 400. However, they were
enabled to hold improving intercourse with some individuals, mostly Greeks; "for whom," says Martha
Yeardley, "we felt much interest, and some, I believe,
became attached to us; we gave them a few books."

Before commencing with their visit to the Ionian
Islands, it will be interesting to glance at the circle
of Friends whom they had left in England. From
the letters which have been preserved, we select
the following extract: the first is from the pen
of one who may be described as sound in heart and

understanding, of extensive knowledge and large Christian charity.

Scarborough, 10 mo. 16, 1833.

MY DEAR FRIENDS,

Accept my grateful acknowledgments, and through me those of all your friends in this neighborhood, for the copies which I have received of your interesting journals. It is indeed a cause of rejoicing to us that you have been so favored in meeting with so many pious persons with whom you could hold Christian fellowship, and among whom there is strong reason for believing your labors have not been in vain. It is to me very gratifying that you feel and exercise so much Christian freedom in mingling among persons of various denominations, whom, though owing to education and to various circumstances, they may differ considerably in opinion on subjects of minor importance, yet conscious of one common disease—that of sin, and looking for or experiencing the only remedy—reconciliation with God through one Saviour,—you can salute as brethren and sisters in the truth, and feel your spirits refreshed whilst you enjoy the privilege of refreshing theirs; and like Aquila and Priscilla, with Apollos, are made the instruments, I trust, of "expounding unto them the way of God more perfectly." My dear mother thinks that the persons you meet with must be more spiritually-minded than Christians in this country. They have, perhaps, from external circumstances, experienced deeper baptisms, and have made greater sacrifices, than many amongst us have been called upon to make; and we know that ease and outward prosperity have not been favorable to the interests of the true Church: but, without doubt, they are exposed to similar dangers to those in this land whose minds have been awakened to the importance of religious truth.

After speaking of a journey which he had made with Samuel Tuke and Joseph Priestman for re-arranging some of the Monthly Meetings in the West Riding, the writer continues:—

On the journey I received intelligence of the decease of Hannah Whitaker; the account produced a strong sensation in the minds of Friends generally, who felt much for our dear afflicted friend Robert Whitaker, and for the loss which the institution at Ackworth has sustained. I have had a note from R. W., written evidently under very desponding feelings; yet he knows where alone consolation is to be sought, and I still cherish the hope that his valuable services will not be lost to the establishment in which they have been so long blessed.

We intend to meet as a Bible class on Second-day evening: our number will be small, but I hope we shall persevere. Your house and garden look much as usual; but I scarcely like to look at them, since I cannot go to spend such pleasant evenings as I used to do there. However, I believe you are in the way of your duty, and I know it would be wrong in me to repine at the loss of your company.

I trust you do not forget our poor little company in your approaches to the throne of grace. You are, I believe, the subjects of many prayers: O that the parties who offer them were more worthy!

Your affectionate friend,<br>JOHN ROWNTREE.

This letter was endorsed by one from J. R.'s mother (the Elizabeth Rowntree whom the reader may remember as the hostess of J. and M. Yeardley on their first visit to Scarborough,) from which we extract a few lines.

The accounts I have received have often helped to cheer my drooping mind, to hear how many you have met with in various places, who could sit down with you in worshipping the Father in spirit and in truth. I have thought of the privileges many of us have had, yet I think many you have met with may make us ashamed of ourselves; and the desire of my heart has often been that we may be more deepened.

John Rowntree's letter contained the information that Richard Cockin, of Doncaster, a Friend universally known and respected in the Society, had been physically disabled by a stroke of paralysis. R. C. himself wrote at the same time to John and Martha Yeardley, describing his affliction, which he received with childlike resignation as a message of love from a Father's hand.

I have, he says, no expectation of getting again to meeting, and it does not appear probable I shall be able again to get down stairs. With respect to the state of my mind, it was an occasion of grateful admiration to me that such a poor unworthy creature as I felt myself to be, should be so favored as to have my will entirely subjected, as to become resignedly willing either to live or die; and, for a time, the prospect of not continuing long appeared to be most probable. I, however, felt no reliance upon anything that I had done or could do; my dependence was entirely upon the unmerited mercy of God through Jesus Christ.

# CHAPTER XII.

## 1833–4.

### PART II.—GREECE.

ON the 21st of the Eleventh Month John and Martha Yeardley left Ancona, and had a safe but suffering voyage of two days to Corfu, the capital of the island of that name.

The atmosphere in this place, writes J. Y., soon after they landed, is different from Ancona in every respect. It has to us a feeling of home, and our minds are clothed with peace and, I trust, gratitude to the Father of mercies. What we may find to do is yet a secret to us, but He who has brought us here will in his own time open the way before us.

Isaac Lowndes of the London Missionary Society received us with much affection and kindness, and his wife and daughter are very desirous to promote our comfort. They took us to see a furnished house in the town, a part of which will suit us remarkably well. We think it a providential thing to have such comfortable quarters to come to.

Some extracts from the Diary and the Journal letters will show in what kind of service they were engaged during their three months' residence in this island.

11 *mo.* 24.—I went with J. L. to the First-day school in the village about a mile from the town. A delightful morning, and a delightful sight to see about sixty fine Greek children reading the New Testament in the modern language. Their countenances are lovely and interesting, and their

( 244 )

anxiety to hear and answer questions is great; their aptitude in comprehending the subjects offered to them exceeds all I have hitherto seen in any class of children of similar standing. The little group was composed of nearly all girls, clean and neatly dressed in the costume of the country.

*27th.*—To-day we received a long visit from Lord Nugent, President of the Ionian Government, who had heard of our arrival on the island, and was anxious to see us. He is very kind and extremely open with respect to his plans for the improvement of the jail, and for cottage cultivation. He desired me to go and see some unoccupied land without the gate.

*28th.*—According to appointment we went to the palace, and were received by Lady Nugent with marked simplicity and kindness. We were introduced to Lord L. and other persons of influence, took tea, and spent a most agreeable evening, and I hope a profitable; for all our conversation was on the subject of bettering the condition of the poor and destitute children.

*12 mo. 3.*—This morning we received a visit from a roomful of Greeks. We are desirous to cultivate the acquaintance of the Greeks as the object of our visit of gospel love. Yesterday we were visited by several of the military officers and their wives, who will I hope co-operate with our plans of benevolence. Lord Nugent's taking us by the hand opens the way to all others of rank and standing.

*11th.*—This morning we had a visit from Dapaldas, Greek professor of theology in the university. He is a pleasing and enlightened man, and speaks French well, which gave us the opportunity of conversing with him pretty freely. I feel to love him much. He is one of the laborers in translating the Old Testament.

*13th.*—To-day we have received letters from England. Many of our beloved friends have been called from this state of being to another world. How much my heart feels humbled; how unworthy I am of the least of the mercies daily received at the hand of a bountiful Creator. Since we have been here I have been favored with a strong conviction that we are here in the ordering of Divine Providence. What

may in time open before us in the way of gospel labor I
know not. It requires time, caution, and much perseverance,
to find a way to the hearts and best feelings of the Greeks.
I greatly desire that we may be found in humble watchfulness
and prayer; and that, if found worthy to be the feeble instruments of declaring the way of salvation to the natives of these
islands, we may embrace every opportunity to preach repentance towards God and faith in our Lord Jesus Christ, for this
is the great object for which we have left our native land and
all that is dear to us in this world.

*26th.*—Argyri left us and is gone to Syra. She was very
sorrowful, and the parting to us all was painful. Although
reserved and timid, she has become extremely attached to us,
and we trust the three months we have passed together will not
soon be forgotten. Her company has often been sweet and
cheering, and in our little meetings for worship her heart has
not unfrequently been tendered with religious feeling. She
is desirous of being useful in schools, and of making a stand
against the many superstitions which prevail, influencing
others by her example, and through the aid of divine grace
leading them to that vital religion in which she was instructed
at Locle, and which is now a strength and comfort to her own
mind.

1834. 1 *mo.* 6.—To-day we received a visit from the young
Count François Sardina. We had much conversation with
him on the subject of the intercession of saints. He could
not admit that they practiced the adoration of saints, they
only meant to hold them up as examples of piety and virtue,
and to induce others to follow them. We pointed out to him
the importance of taking Him for our example who spake as
never man spake, and has left us an example that we should
follow his steps. This young man is very inquisitive and
inclined to be sceptical, but under all has serious impressions.
Many of the Greeks who are not entirely built up in their
superstitions are inclined to doubt respecting the truths of
Christianity. We were glad to put into his hand J. J.
Gurney's *Evidences.*

*23rd.*—This evening we had another long visit from the

Count. We entered very fully into Church discipline, and left few points of faith and doctrine untouched, either in his Church or ours. I do not remember ever to have been more closely questioned; but I think this young person sincere in his inquiries. I believe it is a precious time of visitation to his soul; he is very amiable and affectionate, and acknowledges the evils and vanity of the world.

27*th.*—This evening we have had a long conversation with Pathanes, our teacher in the language, and a deacon in the Greek Church. He is much attached to the rites of his own Church, but acknowledges the necessity of regeneration. They have a fatal error in the ceremony of baptism, positively asserting that when the child (or individual) has received this, he is really born again, and a fit heir of salvation. Such is the efficacy which they attach to this ceremony, that their creed sets forth, in the most unqualified manner, that whoever receives not the form cannot enter the kingdom. We could not forbear lifting up our testimony against the injurious effects of such a creed.

28*th.*—We have had a ride to-day with I. Lowndes and family across the island, sixteen miles, to the sea on the other side. Our road led us through a perfect wood of olive-trees, thickly planted and loaded with fruit. The hills are often variegated with the cypress, &c., and near to the sea are beautifully romantic. We dined at the fortress of Paleocastazza, on the top of a high hill, on provisions we took with us,—the air good, and the prospect delightful. This place was formerly a convent; the church still remains in use, and we visited two of the old Greek priests. One of them is ninety-five years old; he was lying on a dirty hard couch in a miserable apartment; the other performs the liturgy. I. L. gave him the book of Genesis, which he could read but very indifferently. He was besides extremely cross, full of complaints of the soldiers who were stationed there. What a proof that to those who are in the gall of bitterness there is no peace, even in such a remote place.

2 *mo.* 1.—Another long and pleasant visit from Count Sardina. He is mild and condescending, but close in argu-

ment.  His mind appears gradually to become impressed
with the truths of the gospel; and I trust the notions he has
received from sceptical writers are giving way to a hope of
salvation through Christ Jesus our Lord.  Fearful of doing
anything to make the members of his own Church his
enemies, he comes to us by night,—not for fear of the Jews,
but for fear of the Greeks.

9th.—How often our hearts are ready to sink within us in
the midst of this dark and superstitious people.  We have
now been here nearly three months, and have not had one
opportunity of publicly preaching the gospel.  The power of
prejudice in favor of their own superstitious rites, and the
overwhelming influence of moral evil, seem entirely to close
our way in this line.  We have had much conversation with
our friend, Isaac Lowndes, who has resided on this island
thirteen years, on the subject of publicly preaching the gospel
to the people; and he says that such is their attachment to
the ceremonies of their own church that they cannot be prevailed upon to attend the ministry of any other denomination.
I. Lowndes is a character with whom we feel much Christian
unity, and his family is like a little lamp shining in the midst
of gross darkness.

This darkness, adds Martha Yeardley, is increased by the
dissipation of the greater part of the English.  The military
have great influence here, and their practices tend greatly to
demoralize the unhappy people.  We have just heard that they
have obtained leave of the Senate to hold a ball in the new
school-rooms, and to break down the partition-wall between
them for this purpose, which will prevent the school from
being opened for another month.

On the 23rd John Yeardley continues:—

To-day my drooping spirit has been refreshed by six precious letters from England, expressing the interest of our
dear friends in our mission; but oh, how my heart is humbled
in the sense of how little we do.  During our stay here I
have been closely engaged in translating Judson's Questions

on Scripture. The correction is nearly finished, and we propose having a number printed for the school.

Ignorance of the language was a perpetual hindrance in their way. Although they devoted a very large portion of time to acquiring it, the difficulty was almost insurmountable. They learned to read and translate; but to converse in Greek was for a long time almost entirely beyond their power.

Although to preach and teach the gospel was the primary object of John and Martha Yeardley's errand, the temporal improvement of their fellow-men was by no means foreign to their mission; and we have often seen that plans for the promotion of industry and self-support were to the former objects of peculiar interest. During their residence at Corfu no small portion of his time was occupied with the establishment of a model farm, which seems to have been a joint scheme on his part and that of the administration. A grant of land was obtained from the Senate, and the prisoners, with some of the poor, were set to work to cultivate it. Some of the landowners watched the progress of the experiment, with the intention, if it should be successful, of introducing the plan upon their estates.

We may conclude this account of their residence in Corfu with some general remarks on the religious character and condition of the inhabitants.

We trust, say they, our sojourn in Corfu may not have been in vain: if we may only be permitted to prepare the way for the further enlargement of the Saviour's kingdom on the earth, we may well be content. Preparing the way it may truly be called, for there is a great deal to be done among a people just emerging from barbarism, and bringing with them all the fixed habits of ignorance and superstition,

17

before a door can be opened for the direct preaching of the
gospel. Their mode of reasoning is strong and wily, and they
ask questions which can only be answered in private conversation and by Scripture proof. A great means of affording
help must be by educating the rising generation and by the
diffusion of Scriptural knowledge. Many of the priests are
extremely ignorant, and some of them have only learned by
*rote* the service of their own church in the ancient Greek;
their knowledge, therefore, cannot be founded on their own
search for Scriptural truth, seeing they have not had the
opportunity of examining for themselves. In some instances
when we have presented to them the New Testament in the
modern language, they have said, with a look of anxious
gratitude, This is what we want; we priests teach in the
churches what we do not ourselves understand.

On the 26th of the Second Month they crossed the
sea to Santa Maura, having a delightful passage of eight
hours. Captain McPhail, the governor, a friend of
William Allen's, met them himself with a boat, and
conducted them to his house. He showed them every
attention during their short sojourn, and introduced
them to those persons whom they desired to see. They
made an interesting call on the bishop;—

A nice old man, who was many years priest in a village in
the mountains, and, what is a wonder, he has been promoted
on account of his virtuous life. He was a good example in
his own village, and a great promoter of schools. The old
man is candid enough to confess that he was happier among
his rustic peasants than he is now in more refined society.
We gave him the book of Genesis in Modern Greek; and it
was highly gratifying to us to see the surprise and pleasure
of his countenance on being presented with an account of the
Creation and works of the Almighty in his native tongue.
We thought the opportunity favorable for proposing the
Scriptures to be read by the clergy in the modern instead of

the ancient language. He made no objection, and appeared to see the great utility which might arise from it.

Something has been said about the semi-barbarism of the Greeks. What our friends learned respecting crime and violence, whilst in this island, places the manners of the people in a very strong light.

Nothing can show more strongly the demoralized state of these islands than the frightful acts of cruelty done to the cattle out of pure revenge. One shudders to think of the skinning of beasts alive, cutting off the ears of asses, breaking the legs of horses; yet of these sorts of cruelty not less than 500 acts have been committed in the last four years, and the offenders have escaped being brought to conviction!

This dark picture is happily relieved by some traits of moral beauty. The narrative of a ride into the mountains of Santa Maura, which J. Y. made under the escort of the governor, proves to how great a degree virtuous and gentle manners grew and flourished in the remoter parts of this island.

3 mo. 1.—This morning we set out for a ride about nine miles up the mountains to a village called Carià, which contains about 1200 inhabitants, and in the surrounding hamlets there are about the same number.

About half-past 9 o'clock we started; Captain McPhail and myself on his two sure-footed horses, and another English gentleman on a fine mule. After we had left the newly-made road, we pursued a track perfectly unequalled in any part where I have travelled; rugged precipices, shelving rocks, and large loose stones, which assailed the feet of the poor beasts every step they took. However, for my part, I was well rewarded; it gave me an opportunity not only of seeing the interior of the island, but also a specimen of the disposition of the natives. Before we reached the village, I observed, with some surprise, a tribe of people assembled on the top of the cliffs to see us come in, and on ascending a few more paces of rock, we found the children of the boys' school arranged like a little army, with myrtle branches in their hands to welcome us to their sequestered hamlet. After greeting us with great respect, they followed us to the country-house of our English friend.

The mountain multitude waited with patience until we had made our repast, when a few of the leading villagers were introduced to our room. And what was their request? —A school for their daughters. They were asked what they would give towards its support. They answered, Whatever we can afford; we that are able will pay for the poor, and they shall go free. It was then intimated to them, that their friends would assist them in establishing a school; but that they themselves must join in the effort, and that it would be well to consult together, and put down their names and the number of children they would send. Here the town-crier came forward, and said he had for the last twenty years cried everything the government wished to be made known in the town, free of cost, and he would now go round and cry for the benefit of the school. Next came forward the father of the young woman proposed for the mistress, who it was proposed should be further instructed in the village, and then sent to the town to learn the system. We asked them if they were sensible of the advantages of a school for girls, of having them brought up to be good wives, capable of managing their households, and able to read the precious things in the New Testament. One of them replied, Without instruction what are we?—we are like the beasts. One peasant had been so anxious for his daughter to learn to read, that he had made interest to send her to the boys' school. When we asked why he did so, he said, Because I had no other means, and I wished to have her read the New Testament to us; now I have the advantage of hearing that precious book read to me by my own daughter. It was delightful to witness a feeling like this in a people so uncultivated; surely the friends of education in Greece have encouragement to go on and prosper.

After this pleasing interview we proceeded to .the boys' school, followed by as many as could get into the room. When the boys had read, I desired that questions might be put to them on what they had been reading, but soon found that this important mode of instruction was neglected ; the master promised to introduce the questions which we are having printed, if we would send him the books.    On returning to our quarters, we found among the crowd who were still present, the three priests, come, I suppose, to pay their respects to the governor.    We were glad of an oppor· tunity of conversing with them.    On asking their opinion as to a school, one of them said, in Greek, It is good, blessed and honorable.    I could not let this favorable opportunity pass without impressing on them, through McPhail, the advantage of reading the Scriptures to the people in the modern tongue which they could understand, telling them that the book of Genesis was already printed in Modern Greek.    They could hardly believe me, and on my showing them a new copy of this and of the Psalms, their eyes sparkled with pleasure.    Our friend the governor read aloud a portion of Genesis, and one of the priests a little out of the Psalms.    The long-robed, patriarchal looking man said, Ah, this is what we want !    We priests read in the churches what we don't understand ourselves, and how can we explain it to others.    They modestly asked if they might have the books for a while ; and when we said they were given to them, there was a little jealousy who should have them ; this we removed by saying that more should be sent.    Many of the kind-hearted people accompanied us to the precipice, and ran before to clear the way ; and, through divine mercy, we reached the dwelling of our kind host in safety ; not without a steeping of mountain rain.

When the good Bishop of Santa Maura heard the result of our interview with the peasants, he sent one of his most influential priests with a subscription book for his people to put down their names towards a fund for the schools, thus promptly giving his sanction to general education.

3 *mo.* 2.—First-day.  After breakfast we read a chapter
and held our meeting with Captain McPhail and his wife,
and felt a little comfort in holding up the standard of religious
worship.  Something was given us to utter, both in testimony
and supplication.

The next evening we dined with the governor.  It was a
state dinner, given to the judges and persons of rank in the
town; about twenty of us sat down; the repast was splendid
and the dishes innumerable.  At the head of the table was
Captain McPhail in full uniform; on his right our hostess in
a rich Greek dress; on his left a young lady in the full
Italian style; my M. Y. and myself were not the least singular
in appearance.  All was done in good order, and a sweet
feeling prevailed.

4*th.*—We are like prisoners at large, not being able to
leave the island till the steamer returns.  Captain McPhail
has kindly proposed our paying a visit to the continent to
see a little colony of the natives who live in wigwams.  These
people like many others suffered greatly from the Turks, and
took refuge in Santa Maura, which has excited in them
a feeling of gratitude for the protection of their English
neighbors.

About 9 o'clock we started in the Captain's boat, a family
party, not leaving even the baby at home.  We had a pleasant
sail of less than an hour, and found seven ponies waiting for
us at the landing-place.  The ponies were brought into the sea,
and we mounted the pack-saddles; some of our company being
carried from the boat on men's backs.  Thus arranged we
set out, one by one, along the narrow goat-paths, accompanied
by our retinue, some going before, and some following with
the baggage.  We winded our way among bushes of myrtle
and mastic till we reached the willow-city.  It consists of
about sixty perfect wigwams of one room each, with no other
light but what is admitted by the doorway, four feet high,
with here and there a glimpse that makes its way through the
wattles.

The people having received notice of our visit had made a

general holiday, and were all assembled, with lively good-humor in their countenances, to greet our arrival. This is the first year that they have been left to enjoy their lands in peace since the destruction by the Turks of their little town, which stood at about half an hour's distance. Some of them possess property in land and cattle, and all live on the produce of their own farms, and produce their own clothing. These simple-hearted people show their good sense by avoiding all lawsuits, so common among the Greeks. They choose one upright old man, with two assistants, to govern them, to whose judgment they submit, and the greatest punishment is to be shut up for two or three days in a solitary room in the convent.

The wigwam where we alighted was soon filled with visitors. We were served with coffee by our hostess,—an interesting woman, with much expression of mildness in her countenance. After conversing a while with the villagers, and satisfying their curiosity as well as we could, I thought it a suitable time to bring about the primary object of our visit, and inquired who among them could read. A young man came forward who had been educated in the school at Santa Maura ; we gave him a New Testament, and he read the greater part of a chapter in the Gospels. Those who were in the room listened with surprise and attention, and many without looked eagerly in at the doorway to hear what was going on. This was probably the first time they had heard the gospel in their own language. We gave them a few copies of the New Testament and some tracts, for which they hardly knew how to express their gratitude ; and we requested the reader to continue the prac-tice he had commenced.

When this scene of interest was over we took a turn round the other huts. They are situated on the side of the hill, among myrtles, and command a delightful view of the valley. We passed by the common oven, and on looking in saw our dinner preparing. The table was spread in the hospitable wigwam which we first entered, a clean white tablecloth and napkins on a large board, with cushions around on boxes for chairs. The repast consisted of a whole lamb, well roasted, and two sorts of Yorkshire-pudding, one of which was particularly good.

This patriarchal repast being finished, we again went forth, and visited the convent of Plijâ, distant from the wigwams about ten minutes' walk. Many of our new friends accompanied us, the judge with great solidity of manner leading the way. We passed a beautiful fountain at the head of the glen, and entered the monastic edifice, which is built of stone. The abbot, a fine old man, met us at the door with a pleasant countenance. He invited us into his cell; we had to stoop very low to save our heads, and the door-case was rubbed bright on all sides by the friction of this solitary inmate passing in and out. The hermitage consists of one room with a bed in the corner, screened by a slight partition; a lattice-window admitted a peep into the rich and lovely vale below, and the pure air of the mountain was not obstructed by glass. I had often heard of the Eastern custom of sitting cross-legged, but never till now experienced it in reality. We were desired to sit on cushions spread on the floor for our reception, and were served with the finest walnuts and honey I ever tasted; and while we partook of this hermit-like repast, there was a precious feeling of good, and I believe we had the secret prayers of the good abbot, as he had ours. When we presented him with the New Testament, Genesis, and the Psalms, he kissed the books and pressed them to his bosom, expressing his gratitude for the treasure.

Our next visit was to the habitation of the judge, which is of the same description as the rest, where we were served again with coffee. What pleased us was the sweet feeling of quiet which prevailed, of which I think some of them were sensible; one woman, our first hostess, put her hand to her heart and said very sweetly, "I love you."

They would not let us depart without showing us their ancient custom of taking hold of hands and dancing round, singing meanwhile a sort of chant. Many of them came with us to the water's edge, and prayers were raised in our hearts for their good, and thanksgiving to our Divine Master for the comfort and satisfaction of the day.

3 *mo.* 8.—Under the hospitable roof of Captain McPhail we
have felt much at home. His wife said our coming had been
a blessing to her; she is near to us in gospel love. The captain accompanied us in his boat to the steamer.

From Santa Maura they proceeded to Argostoli, the
chief town of Cephalonia.

We arrived about five o'clock in the morning. The entrance to the town for a considerable distance is like a perfect
lake: the white houses along the side of the harbor, and the
craggy hill with the olives growing out of the rocks, had a
pretty appearance at the break of day. Our young Greek
interpreter, Giovanni Basilik, was with us. We had to call
up the inhabitants of the only inn in the place before we could
get shelter. At first the host refused to receive our little
company, but after some explanation he consented to arrange
the desolate-looking rooms into habitable order.

They visited the schools and the prison, and they
received from the Resident, H. G. Tennyson, and the
schoolmaster and mistress, a friendly reception; but the
islanders are generally careless of instruction, and progress of all kinds is slow.

From Cephalonia they traversed the sea to the beautiful island of Zante. Though they had ten men to row,
the passage occupied thirteen hours.

Contrary wind, writes John Yeardley, compelled us to
approach the island slowly, which gave us an opportunity of
viewing the villages and scattered houses at the foot of the
mountain. The town of Zante is very long; the main street
has piazzas on each side for a considerable distance. In many
of the windows (I suppose a Turkish custom) there are something like cages, through which the women peep without
being seen, under the pretence of modesty; but it is horrid
to hear of the wickedness committed in-doors. However,
I am glad to find the custom is dying away, and that the
young women are now permitted to walk in public more than

they were a few years ago. This island is by far the finest
we have visited; it is very fertile and well cultivated, and
supplies England with currants; but, like their neighbors,
the people have the character of being immoral, treacherous,
and revengeful. It is sorrowful to think that, under the
system of picture-worship, there is scarcely a sin of which
the poor Greek is not guilty to an enormous extent. With
God all things are possible—he can change the hard heart of
man by the power of his Divine Spirit; but, morally speaking, it must be some great convulsion that can work a real
change in the nation. W. O. Croggon has labored here
more than seven years, and knows not of one conversion
among the rich Greeks—not one attends the service for worship. He is the Methodist missionary here, and is called the
friend of every man: he has been a real friend to us.

The Governor and his wife have paid us marked attention.
The former took us to see the prison, which is well conducted,
and the prisoners are classed. We suggested the benefit
likely to result from the prisoners being employed, and Major
Longley [the Governor] intends to introduce basket-making.
We have, in addition to the public schools, visited several
private ones, and are pleased to find so many children receiving education: this is really the chief source of hope for improving the morals of the Greeks, and dispersing the gross
darkness which surrounds this people, whose long servitude
and sufferings under very hard masters have almost driven
them back to barbarism.

17th.—There was a shock of earthquake, more violent than
has been felt for some years in this place. Our room shook
almost like a ship at sea; the walls, beds, tables, and glasses
were all in motion, and the sensation, while it lasted, was that
of sea-sickness. The noise may be compared to the rolling
of a carriage with many horses coming at full speed, and suddenly stopping at the dwelling. (See *Eastern Customs*, p. 78.)

Having thus explored the four principal islands of
the Ionian Archipelago, John and Martha Yeardley
turned their course towards the Morea.

30th.—At 6 o'clock in the morning we put ourselves once more at the mercy of the waves of the Mediterranean, and had a quick passage of fourteen hours. The landing at Patras was frightful; a sudden squall threw us off the shore, and caused us to lose part of the rudder, so that we were obliged to get into a very small boat, which threatened to upset every moment. We were, however, favored to land in safety on a projecting rock: it was nearly dark, and the whole had a terrific appearance.

The plains near Patras, once beautifully planted with currants, olives and vines, are now perfectly desolate. The castle was in possession of the Turks eight years, who made continual sallies from it for provision and firewood; while, in order to disappoint them, the Greeks themselves assisted in the destruction of all vegetation; so that there is scarcely any green thing to be seen. The old town is a scene of ruins; the site of the new town is near the sea, where temporary shops and houses have been erected.

It was difficult to find a shelter for the night; but a kind fellow-traveller assisted us, and at length we were pressed into a miserable dirty room, with only a board for a bedstead.

At Patras we had abundance of consultation, whether to undertake the journey to Corinth and Athens by land, or to encounter the gulf. We concluded to venture on the latter, and contracted with the captain of a little boat to depart at five the next morning. He deceived us by not sailing at the time proposed; but we made an agreement with other sailors to go off in the evening, hoping to get to Corinth the next morning: but, after tossing all night, we found in the morning the ship had only made twenty miles; and about mid-day the captain declared he could not get to Corinth, and must put into a small port on the opposite side of the gulf, called Galaxidi, and wait for better weather. We were so exhausted as to feel thankful in the prospect of being once more on land. Nothing can be more comfortless than these small Greek vessels; in the cabin you can neither stand nor lie at full length.

After some difficulty in getting on shore, we were led to the khan, a very large room with a fire in one corner for boiling water, and a wine store; and round the side were benches which served for sitting by day, and on which the traveller spreads his mattress for the night, if he has one; if not, he must go without. We were desired to mount a ladder to a loft like a corn-floor, badly tiled in, and divided into four parts by boards about five feet high. The one division of this place assigned to us had no door, and when the windows were shut, which were of wood, there was no light but what shone through the tiling or was admitted between the boards. The place was soon furnished, for the boy brought us a mat and spread it on the floor, which was all we had a right to expect; but as we seemed to be visitors who could pay pretty well, they brought also a rough wooden table and three wooden stools.

*2nd.*—Galaxidi is in ruins, presenting only mud cottages and temporary wooden houses; ships also are in building.

*4th.*—This morning we walked among the huts of the town, and found an old man keeping school near the ruins of his own school-room, which had been destroyed by the Turks. It happened to be his dinner-time, and he was seated cross-legged on a stone, with a footstool before him, enjoying a few olives and a morsel of bread. Around him stood his ragged pupils, reading from leaves torn out of old books, some of which were so worn and dirty that the poor boys could scarcely discover what they had once contained. The weather was by no means warm, yet we could not wonder at his choosing the open air for the place of instruction, when we saw his dwelling, which was a mud hut not quite nine feet square, with no opening for light but through the doorway. In this hovel he taught his forty scholars when the inclemency of the weather did not permit their being out of doors. The grey-headed father was surprised that his humble company had attracted the notice of strangers; but, seeing the interest we manifested in his calling, he inquired for a New Testament, which we gladly furnished, with the addition of some tracts to such of the children as could read them. This sight was gratifying to us as showing a disposition to teach and to learn, even under the most disadvantageous circumstances.

Our quarters at the khan became more uncomfortable; the people were so uncivil they would hardly give us cold water without grumbling. The second night we witnessed one of the most dreadful storms we ever remember to have seen. Violent gusts of wind shook our desolate abode, while the rain poured down in torrents and found entrance in various parts of our apartment.

They intended, as we have seen, to go to Athens by way of Corinth, and when they were disappointed of sailing to that city, and thrown upon the opposite shore of the gulf, they still seem to have supposed it impossible to reach the capital by any other route.

5th.—Being, says John Yeardley, on the contrary side of the gulf, and thus deprived of helping ourselves by means of horses, we gave up all hope of reaching Athens, and thought we must of necessity return to Patras. We therefore inquired for a vessel to take us thither; but never shall I forget my feelings of horror while trying to contract with a man for a boat. I said in my heart, O that I might be permitted to try the fleece once more in turning our faces towards Athens. The man was exorbitant in his demands, and it was too late to reach Patras without risking the night on the sea. To stay where we were was next to impossible without serious injury, especially to my dear Martha. Strong indeed was our united prayer for direction and help in this time of distress, and ever-blessed be the name of our adorable Lord who heard and answered our prayer. Out of the depths of distress a little light sprung up, and we thought if we could take a boat and cross over to Scala, a little port on the opposite side of the creek, we might then take mules to [Castri the ancient] Delphi, and if not able to proceed further on our way, the change we hoped would be useful to M. Y. We did make the effort, and were favored to get to Scala, where we found only a few scattered mud houses; but on landing, there was a change of feeling immediately experienced. We were rescued from ship-builders and sailors, the vilest of the vile, and placed among a simple country people.

The master of the custom-house, to whom we had a few lines of recommendation, invited us to his house and gave us coffee. He provided us with four mules; three for the interpreter and ourselves, and the fourth for the baggage. It was about eight miles, or two and a half hours' ride, to Delphi; and no sooner had we begun to feel the mountain air than my dear M. began to revive. We had to climb precipices where nothing but mules could have carried us. At the foot of the mountain we came in company with two camels, which was a new sight to us.

The situation of Delphi is the most beautiful that eyes can behold: mountains of rock, such as we never before saw, and in the back ground the far-famed Parnassus, covered with snow. The village consists of about one hundred cottages, some of them built in the rock. We were conducted to one of the best of these rustic dwellings, and met with a very friendly reception from the inmates. The house consisted of two rooms, and we were offered the use of one of them; they furnished us with mattresses laid upon a sort of dresser, where we slept much better than for many previous nights; even the hen and her thirteen chickens under our bed did not disturb us. The novelty of the visiters soon brought in several of the neighbors, who did not leave us, even while we took our tea. As there was a good feeling, we thought it well to improve the opportunity, and inquired who could read. The master of the house, a sensible man, said there were only about twenty in the village who know anything of letters, but that he could both read and write, for his father was a priest.

After tea we produced a New Testament and the book of Genesis, and our interpreter read aloud the first two chapters of Genesis. Our host had never seen the Scriptures in his own language, and we think we never beheld a countenance more full of delight and intelligence than his was during the reading. After a short explanation of what had been read,

and a word of exhortation, we thought to close; but the
company were so pleased with hearing the account of the
creation and fall of man [from the sacred record itself], that
they requested us to read more. I desired them to ask any
questions on the subject they might wish; and the first which
our host put was, What kind of tree it was, the fruit of which
Adam was forbidden to eat? We answered that it was translated in our language *apple*. He said they thought it was a
*fig*. We told them it might be a fig, or it might be an apple;
but that the object of the Almighty was to try Adam's
obedience. They at once agreed to this; and the master of
the house wisely observed, Jesus Christ came to restore to us
what was lost by Adam's transgression. He then said, It
would have been better if Adam, after his transgression,
instead of hiding himself, had confessed his sin to God, and
begged his forgiveness. We all agreed that it was a natural
act for man, in his fallen state, to wish to seek excuse, rather
than to confess his sin and repent. We then made some
remarks on the prophecy of the Saviour in the third chapter
of Genesis, and ability was given us to preach the Gospel of
life and salvation. All hearts seemed touched, and our own
overflowed with gratitude. We may in truth say, Our
Heavenly Father has plucked our feet out of a horrible pit
and out of the miry clay, and set them upon a rock, and put
a new song into our mouth, even praise to his glorious name.
On considering afterwards our situation, we could not but
behold the hand of a gracious Providence which had led us to
this spot; had we attempted to go by Corinth to Athens, we
should [as they afterwards learned] have been stopped by the
waters, and have missed seeing this interesting people; but
from hence the way was passable, and only four days' journey
by land.

After dinner we walked through the village up to the rock.
We came to a fountain where several women were washing;
one of them, a young-looking person, suddenly left her companions, and with hasty step and entreating air advanced
towards us, as we supposed to ask something; but she
bowed her head almost to the ground, and then kissed our

hands; after which she withdrew in a cheerful and diffident manner. The reason of this salutation was, that the young woman had lately been married, and it was customary for the last bride of the village to kiss the hands of strangers.

The temple of Apollo once occupied nearly half an acre of ground; a great many of its marble pillars are still to be seen, half buried by the plough, and corn growing over them. About a hundred yards from this temple is the cave in the rock from whence the priestess pronounced the oracle. Among the curiosities of this wonderful place, the tombs in the rocks are not the least remarkable. They are built of the most beautiful white marble; the entrance is by a large archway, and round the circle are several recesses in the stone, one above another, where the dead had evidently been deposited. They illustrate the history of the maniac dwelling among the tombs (Mark v. 3.), for these caves formed a perfect sort of house in which persons might dwell.

*8th.*—We were not able to leave Delphi on account of the high wind with some rain. In the evening we again enjoyed our Scripture reading on the hearth. We continued the book of Genesis, and our host inquired whether those who died before the birth of the Saviour were lost. He was informed they were saved through faith in the promise. He had supposed they went into hell, and that when Christ came he released them. We asked him if Enoch, who walked with God and was translated, could have been sent to hell. Of this he knew nothing, never having read the Scriptures.

*9th.*—This morning we procured four mules and four men, and proceeded on our pilgrimage towards Livadia, thirty-three miles from Delphi. Our kind host recommended us to the special care of one of the muleteers, who put his hand to his heart, and feelingly accepted the trust. We were most of the day winding round Parnassus, whose height above us was tremendous. The road was frightful; over rocks, waters, and swampy ground; we could hardly have believed it possible to pass through the places where our mules penetrated. The muleteer performed his trust faithfully, rendering us all the assistance in his power. On parting we presented him with some tracts; he could read, and was much gratified with the gift.

At Livadia we were badly lodged, in a smoky room, and suffered much from extreme fatigue; but we found ourselves with an interesting family, to whom we read the Scriptures, seated with them on the floor; and we could not but feel grateful to our Divine Master, for leading us among those who were thirsting to receive the Holy Scriptures in a language they could understand.

10th.—We travelled on horses through a comparatively flat country, despoiled of all its verdure by the ruthless hand of war. The evening was wet; we reached the once celebrated Thebes in the dark, and were glad to take shelter in a smoky room, in the first house that could receive us. The situation is fine, but the present town occupies only the part which was the fortress of ancient Thebes.

11th.—This day we had much mountain country to pass through. Every tree we could see was either partly burnt or partly cut away. Towards the end of our day's travel we went through an immense wood, difficult of passage, on leaving which the Gulf of Ægina appeared in view. We rested for the night at a little settlement of Albanians near the coast. We obtained shelter in the cottage of an old woman, who seemed a little startled at the appearance of strangers, whose language she could not understand. Concluding, however, that we had the common wants of nature, and having no bread to offer us, she quickly prepared a little meal, made a cake, and baked it on the hearth under the ashes. We made signs to be furnished with a vessel in which we might prepare a little chocolate, our frequent repast under such circumstances; and, at length, a very rough homely-looking pitcher was produced; but the greater difficulty was to find something in which to boil the milk and water. After waiting till their own soup had been prepared, we obtained the use of the saucepan. These difficulties overcome, we enjoyed our meal; and offered some to a Greek woman who had walked beside our mules for the sake of company, on her dreary journey to Athens; but she refused, with thanks,

18

saying, I am not sick; for the Greeks seldom take beverage of this sort, except when they are indisposed. As the inmates of this homely cottage, as well as the neighbors, who usually come in to see travellers of our uncommon appearance, did not understand Greek, we were deprived of the opportunity of reading the Holy Scriptures to them, or of conversing with them on the subject of religion. All that we could do was to prepare for rest, of which we stood in great need, having had a very fatiguing ride through the woods to this place. The room in which we had taken shelter was also to be our sleeping-place, in common with the old woman and her family and the Greek traveller; in another part of the room were also a sheep and several other animals. We swept as clean as we could a space in the neighborhood of the quiet sheep, and spread what bedding we had upon the mud floor, surrounding it with our baggage, except our carpet-bags, which served us for pillows; and after commending ourselves and the household to the protecting care of the great Shepherd of Israel, we obtained some refreshing repose. (See *Eastern Customs*, pp. 17–19.)

*12th.*—We started with tired bones. After a pleasant ride of four hours the Acropolis of Athens burst upon our view. The city is beautifully situated in a plain bounded by mountains, and near to a rich grove of olive-trees, which has been spared amid the ravages of war. I felt, says John Yeardley, low and contemplative; many and various thoughts crowded into my heart. Every foot we set in Greece, we see desolation. I can scarcely believe that I am in the place where the great Apostle of the Gentiles desired to know nothing but Christ crucified; and in sight of Mars Hill, from which the same apostle preached to the Athenians the true God.

We reached the only inn in the town, much worn by fatigue and bad accommodation, yet very grateful for having been preserved from any serious accident during our perilous journey, and under a precious sense that it was in right ordering we persevered in coming to this place.

We introduced ourselves to the American missionaries, Hill and King, and met with a hearty reception. The schools under their care are the most gratifying sight we have seen. J. Hill and his wife have nearly 500 children on their list. We were much pleased with the arrangements of the schools: the classification is the best I have ever seen, and the children exhibit intelligence and thirst for instruction. The effect of Scriptural instruction on the minds of the Greek children is very gratifying. A young girl whom the directors had taken into the school as an assistant teacher, entered the family with a mind fortified in the superstitions taught in her own church, observing scrupulously the feast and fast-days, the making the sign of the cross before eating, and the kissing of pictures. The mistress wisely avoided interfering with what the girl considered to be her religious duties; but after she had attended the Scriptural reading and the family worship for a short time, the light of divine truth broke in upon her heart; and as she embraced the substance of the religion of Jesus Christ, her attachment to the superstitious forms became gradually weakened, until at length she left them altogether. The mistress one day said to her, I observe you do not keep the fast-days, nor cross yourself before eating, nor kiss the pictures. No, replied the child, I am convinced that making the outward sign of the cross cannot purify the heart from sin; and as to meat and drink, I read in the Scriptures, that it is not that which goeth into the mouth that defiles the man.

15th.—Visited the schools under the direction of Jonas King, of the Boston mission. He has an academy for young men, and a school for mutual instruction, containing together 150. I think the mode of Scripture lessons particularly efficient. The instruction given in the schools at Athens seems more complete than in any we have visited during the journey. J. K. has service in modern Greek three times on First-days, at which some of the young men attend, along with other Greeks, but not many.

During our stay in this city we visited many Greek families, and distributed among them religious tracts and portions of the Holy Scriptures, and exhorted them to the observance of their religious duties, often calling their attention to those points in which their own practices are at variance with the doctrine of Holy Scripture.

The ancient ruins are exceedingly grand, and raise mingled feelings in the heart not easily described, but tending to humble the pride of human greatness. We saw the Temple of Theseus, the prison of Socrates, the famous Temple of Minerva; but the spot that most nearly interested us was Mars Hill, whose rocky mount was in view from our lodgings, where we sat and conversed together of the Apostle Paul preaching the true God; and in the sweet stillness which covered our spirits, earnestly desired that the pure Gospel might again be freely preached and received throughout this interesting but desolated country.

There are not more than sixty really good houses built in the town; but, including great and small, there may be 1500 dwellings. It is settled that Athens shall be the seat of the Greek government; and the young king, Otho, laid the foundation-stone of the new palace in his last visit to this place.

18th.—Being anxious to get to Patras in time to sail by an English packet to Corfu, we set off for the port. J. Hill met us, to see us embark in a boat for Kalimichi. The Greek sailors have a superstition against sailing at any time but in the night; but after being deceived by one captain, we prevailed on another to set sail [in the daytime], in the full hope of reaching Kalimichi the same evening. A favorable gale wafted us on for some time, but a slight storm coming on, the cowardly captain ran us into a creek, and kept us tossing all the night in his open boat. About eight o'clock the next morning we were favored to reach Kalimichi in safety, where we procured mules and reached Corinth to dinner.

Here there are only a few houses standing in the midst of ruins. We took up our abode at the only inn, from the windows of which we looked upon the busy scene of a fair. Our hearts were not enlarged, as the great Apostle's was; for our spirits were clothed with mourning in contemplating the darkness of the place. Many persons to whom we spoke could not read; and on offering a Testament to the man of the inn he refused to receive it.

We pursued our travels, and at mid-day met with a trying detention from the muleteer having neglected to obtain a permission. We were at length suffered to proceed, but arrived late at a miserable khan, where we passed the night in a loft. This poor place could only furnish two mules and a donkey, with a man to attend them; but we were encouraged to hope we should find four horses about two hours further on; but here we were disappointed, and could get no horses to proceed. We felt truly destitute, and took refuge in a loft from the scorching rays of the sun. We had very little food with us, and saw no probability of quitting our desolate abode till the next day at any rate. Thus situated we were endeavoring to be reconciled to our allotment, when most unexpectedly, about two o'clock, we espied a small fishing-boat sailing towards Patras, and immediately ran down to the shore, a considerable distance, to make signals to the boatman, and inquire whether he would convey us to Vostizza, a place within a day's journey of Patras. We directly procured a mule to convey our baggage to the shore, and descended by a very rough path to a creek where the boat lay to. Here we were again detained by the guard making great difficulty in allowing the boatman to take passengers without a permit, which could only be obtained in the town, so strict and per-plexing are the regulations for travellers under the new government. However, after detaining us an hour and causing us to lose most of the fair wind, he suffered the man to take us. We sailed along pretty well for a time, when the wind suddenly changed, and the boatman told us we could not get to Vostizza that night, but added they would put us on shore where we should be within an hour's walk of it, and that we could readily find a mule to carry our baggage. This we gladly accepted, and were soon landed and on our way.

Although sick and weary on board, we seemed to receive new strength for our walk, and arrived at Vostizza at about eight o'clock. Here our accommodation for the night was

much like our former lodging ; for this large town has also
been burned by the enemy, and presents a scene of ruins.
We engaged horses for the next day to convey us to Patras,
and were a little cheered with the prospect of being near that
place of attraction. The man of the house where we lodged
could not read, but informed us there was a school in the town
of fifty boys. We saw a person in the next shop writing, and
offered him a Testament, which he very gratefully received,
and sent for the schoolmaster, who seemed much pleased with
our offer to send him books and lessons. We also gave books
to several we met with, who began eagerly to read them
aloud, and soon obtained hearers, so that it became a highly
interesting scene : boys who received tracts from us showed
them to others, and numbers crowded about us, even to the
last moment of our stay. If we had had a thousand books
we could have disposed of them. What a difference between
this place and poor Corinth !

Our trying journey through Greece has given us an opportunity of judging of the state of things, and I hope will enable
us to relieve some of their wants. It is cause of humble
thankfulness to the Father of mercies that he has preserved
us in the midst of many dangers, and brought us in safety so
far back on our way with hearts filled with love and praise.

They arrived at Patras on the 22nd, but found that
the English steamer had sailed two days before. They
employed the interval before the sailing of another
packet in establishing a girls' school, which was commenced soon after their departure. At Corfu they
received information of the opening of the school, conveyed in a letter from the sister of the English consul
in the following encouraging terms :—

I am sure you will be gratified to hear that the school
which was established by your benevolent exertions has been
opened under the most favorable auspices. The first day
we had twenty-two girls ; we have now forty-eight. Nothing

can exceed the eagerness shown by the children to be admitted, and their parents seem equally anxious to send them;
with very few exceptions they come clean, and on the whole
are attentive and well behaved.  Of the forty-eight there are
only nine who can read.  The little Corfuot you recommended
is first monitor, and of great use.

They reached Corfu on the 12th of the Fifth Month,
and were kindly accommodated at the office of the Commissary Ramsay.

Immediately on our arrival at Corfu, our young friend the
Count Sardina renewed his visits.  We saw him almost daily;
our conversations were often truly spiritual; he opened his
heart to us, and we rejoiced to believe that he had attained to
a degree of living faith in his Redeemer.

It will be recollected that their inability to collect the
inhabitants in a meeting for worship was a source of
discouragement to John and Martha Yeardley in their
former visit to Corfu.  Now, on revisiting this island,
they had the satisfaction of holding two meetings for
worship with Isaac Lowndes' congregation.

6 *mo.* 1.—Isaac Lowndes had now obtained leave to hold
his meeting for worship in the large school-room, and I felt at
liberty to propose having an opportunity to address the congregation.  This he gladly accepted, and gave notice of our
intention.  It was pretty well attended, but not full; a good
feeling prevailed.

15*th.*—We had another meeting with the little company
who meet in the school-room.  The room was better filled
than on the former occasion : it was a precious season of divine
favor; utterance was given to preach the word, and I trust
there were some into whose hearts it found entrance.

A few days before we left the island, I. L. took us to visit
the Jewish Rabbi, who, though full of argument, appears

extremely dark and bewildered, dwelling on mysterious words
whose interpretation is confined to the rabbinical office.   He
said they looked for a temporal king, who should give a
temporal kingdom to Israel.   It was a truly painful visit, and
we left him with the desire that he might be instructed even
out of his own law, which, if properly understood, would
prove as a schoolmaster to bring him to Christ.

After spending about five weeks at Corfu on this
second visit, they again crossed the Adriatic to Ancona.

# CHAPTER XIII.

## 1833–4.

PART III.—THE RETURN FROM GREECE.

OF the numerous letters which John and Martha Yeardley received from England during this long journey, very few have been preserved. We shall extract short passages from two which came to their hands not long before they left the Islands. The first is from John Rowntree, and is dated the 13th of the First Month, 1834.

On my own account, and on behalf of the Friends of our Monthly Meeting, I feel grateful for the information respecting your proceedings. There is some difficulty in satisfying the eager anxiety of my friends to know all that is to be known about your engagements, and I may truly say that the kind interest which you feel about us is reciprocal. Often do I picture you to myself, laboring in your Master's cause, receiving as fellow-partakers of the same grace all whose hearts have been touched with a sense of his love, who are hoping to experience salvation through Him alone.

Our reading meetings are pretty well attended this winter. We have been reading James Backhouse's journal: he was still engaged, when he sent the last account of his proceedings, in Van Diemen's Land. Like you, he and his companion rejoice at meeting with those to whom, although not exactly agreeing with us in some respects, they can give the right hand of fellowship as laborers under the same Master. Like you, too, they devote considerable attention

(273)

to the improvement of schools, and the improvement of the temporal condition of the poorer classes among whom they labor.

In a letter from William Allen, written the 31st of the Third Month, occur the following words of encouragement :—

I have heard, through letters to your relations and others, that you have been much discouraged at not finding a more ready entrance for your gospel message; but really, considering the darkness, the sensuality, and the superstition of the people in those parts, we must not calculate upon much in the beginning. If here and there one or two are awakened and enlightened, they may be like seed sown, and in the Divine Hand become instruments for the gathering of others. Should you be made the means of accomplishing this, in only a very few instances, it will be worth all your trials and sufferings. And again, you must consider that, in the performance of your duty, seed may be sown even *unknown by you*, which may take root, and grow, and bring forth fruit to the praise of the Great Husbandman, though you may never hear of it. Be encouraged therefore, dear friends, to go on from day to day in simple reliance on your Divine Master, without undue anxiety for consequences; for depend upon it, when he has no more work for you to do, he will make you sensible of a release.

The passage to Ancona was tedious.

We embarked at noon, and had a long passage to Ancona of twelve days. We landed on the 29th, and soon found ourselves occupying an empty room in the Lazaretto, without even the accommodation of a shelf or closet. The term of quarantine is fourteen days, but four days are remitted by the Pope. The heat is oppressive, and the mosquitoes annoy us much, but we are preserved in a tolerable degree of health; and in taking a review of our visit to Greece and the Ionian Islands, we are still sensible of a very peaceful feeling, under a belief

that we have followed the pointings of the Great Master, and
a hope that the day is not far distant when the way will be
more fully opened in those countries to receive the gospel.
The preaching of John in the wilderness has often appeared
to us to be applicable to this people,—Repent, for the kingdom
of heaven is at hand.

7 *mo.* 6.—We left Ancona, and took the route through
Foligno and Arezzo to Florence.  That part of the Pope's
dominions through which we have passed is highly picturesque; hill and dale continually, and the whole country
cultivated absolutely like a garden.  Most of the towns are
on the hills, and nothing can exceed the beauty of their
situation.  But as to vital religion, the spirit of those who
desire the promotion of the Redeemer's kingdom, on the
broad and sound basis of common Christianity, must be
clothed with mourning in passing through this superstitious
and illiberal country.  What we have seen of Tuscany is not
so fine, but the appearance of the peasants is much superior.
The inns are much more agreeable than we found them on the
road from Geneva to Ancona.

We arrived at Florence on the 10th.  The persons to whom
we had recommendations were absent, on account of the heat
of the season, except the Abbot Valiani, a spiritually-minded
man, who showed us great kindness.  He has refused many
advantageous offers of promotion, choosing to be content
with a little, rather than to be hampered with fetters which I
believe he thinks unscriptural, and not for the good of the
Church; he is of the opinion that it would be better for the
common people to have the Bible, and to be more acquainted
with its contents.  He conducted us to see the School for
Mutual Instruction, founded under the patronage of the
Grand Duke, about twelve years ago.  The school-room is
very large, airy, and well lighted; it was formerly a convent.
The system of education differs a little from that practiced
in England; but the children, about 240 in number, are
apparently under an efficient course of instruction and discipline.  The younger boys have a string put round the
neck, which confines them to the place during the lesson, but

I observed it did not confine their attention. We were much pleased with the countenance and manners of the director, the Abbot Luigi Brocciolini; his heart appears to be in his work, which is by no means easy.

We left Florence early on the 13th, and had four days' hard travelling to Genoa. From Sestri to Genoa, a day's journey, is by the sea, and under the mountains, some of them of a tremendous height, and beautifully covered with olives, vines, and figs: the houses hang quite on the sides of the mountains amidst the olives; I do not remember to have passed through any country equally picturesque.

We had packed as many books and tracts as we well could in our wardrobe trunks, which were not once opened at the different custom-houses, but the surplus tracts, &c., we were obliged to put into a spare box by themselves, and this box was not suffered to pass the frontier of Sardinia. The first officer was embarrassed, not knowing how to act, and sent a gendarme with us to the bureau of Sarzana, the next town. The officer there was remarkably civil, but told us the law is such that books cannot enter except on conditions to which we could not in our conscience submit. We therefore left them in the bureau, desiring that they might be made useful: a person in the office said, in a half-whisper, These are the books to turn the people's heads. We were glad this loss did not prevent us from distributing others out of our remaining store, at the inns, and pretty freely on the road.

Their object in returning by Genoa was to visit the valleys of Piedmont. They reached Turin on the 19th, and proceeded on the 22nd to Pignerol. From this place they visited most of the valleys, went into all the families where Stephen Grellet had been, and had frequent religious conversation with the pastors and some of the people.

We spent, says J. Y., five days amongst them. The old pastor Best died soon after the time that Stephen Grellet was

there. We met his son, lately appointed chaplain to the
Protestant congregation at Turin. He is a young man of
talent, lively and intelligent, and desirous of being useful in
his new sphere of action. He came to us often at our little
inn, and made many inquiries as to the nature of our religious
principles; our conversation mostly turned on the necessity
of the assistance of the Holy Spirit in the exercise of Christian
ministry. This he fully admitted, but was not prepared to
dispense with the necessity of an academical preparation. I
fear that sending the young men to Geneva for this purpose
has not always had a salutary effect.

We thought it right to attend their worship on First-day
morning at La Tour. The congregation consisted of about
900 clean and well-dressed peasants, many of whose countenances looked serious. The short discourse of Pastor Peyron
was orthodox, and the application impressive and edifying.
He afterwards dined and spent the afternoon with us at the
widow Best's, with several branches of her interesting and
pious family. I humbly trust this day was spent to mutual
comfort.

They were disappointed to find that strangers were
forbidden by law to hold public meetings, or preach in
the assemblies of the Protestants; and although they
met with many pious individuals, they thought the life
of religion on the whole at a low ebb, and deplored the
prevalence of the forms and ceremonies used by the
Church of England. The schools, too, they found to be
in a very poor state; the masters deficient in education
and badly paid, and the schools conducted without
system. The ministers showed them great kindness,
and on their quitting La Tour, Pastor Best encouraged
them by the expression of satisfaction with their visit.
They returned to Turin on the 28th.

Passing over Mont Cenis, they directed their course
to Geneva, where they arrived on the 3rd of the Eighth

Month, rejoiced to be once more on the English side of
the Alps.  On their outward journey their sojourn in
this city had been short, but now they found it needful
to make a longer visit, and were thankful in being
permitted to mingle again in intimate communion with
those who understood the language of the Spirit.  They
paid and received many visits, and held two religious
meetings at their hotel, at the latter of which about fifty
persons were present.

One of the most interesting occasions of which they
speak was a Missionary Meeting, in which the minister
Olivier unfolded his experience of a divine call to leave
his country, and go abroad on the service of the gospel.
The voice which he described as having been sounded
in his spiritual ear, and the manner in which he received
it, must have struck John Yeardley as singularly in
accordance with the call to a similar service which he
himself had heard so distinctly in his younger days, and
which, like Olivier, he had for a long time hidden in his
heart.

8 *mo.* 4.—In the evening I attended the Missionary Meeting in the Chapel de l'Oratoire.  Pastor Merle [d'Aubigné]
opened the meeting by a short prayer, and singing, and then
gave a narrative of the liberation of the slaves in the English
colonies, according to the account received from England.
Pastor Olivier, from Lausanne, was present.  He is about to
depart for Lower Canada, and he spoke in a very touching
manner of the way in which the mission had first opened on
his own mind.  When the concern was made known in his
heart, he kept it there in secret prayer to the Lord for
direction, and whenever he heard what he believed to be the
same voice, it was always—Go, and the Lord will go with
thee.  A real unction attended while he gave us this account;
the way in which he spoke of it resembled the manner of
one of our Friends laying a concern before a meeting: many

hearts present felt the force of his words. His exhortation to the young persons was excellent. Pastor Gaussen concluded the meeting with an address and lively prayer.

Among the friends with whom they had religious intercourse were Pastors L'Huillier, Gallon, and Molinier. The last was a "father in the church" to them. After some conversation on the state of religion in Geneva, he proposed their sitting awhile in silence, well knowing the practice of the Society of Friends in this respect. John and Martha Yeardley had each a gospel message to deliver to him, after which he took them both by the hand, and offered up prayer for their preservation and the prosperity of the Society to which they belonged. "It was," says J. Y., "the effusion of the Holy Spirit, accompanied with power, and refreshed our spirits."

With Pastor Gallon John Yeardley had a long conversation on the principles and operations of the Société Evangelique.

I find them, he says, more liberal in their views than had been represented, and their extent of usefulness is already considerable. In their Academy they instruct young men with a view to their becoming ministers, missionaries, schoolmasters, &c., as the prospect for their future usefulness may open under the direction of Divine Providence. In a place like Geneva, such an institution may be well: while we regard it with some caution lest it should run too high on points of doctrine, we cannot but hail with peculiar satisfaction such a favorable opportunity of educating young men in the sound principles of Christianity, that they may happily prove instruments in the Divine Hand to check the spread of infidelity.

From Geneva they went to Lausanne. Their old friend, Professor Gaudin, took them to see several pastors, and other pious persons, and on First-day, the 17th, he and his family, with some other serious-minded individuals, joined them in their hour of worship at the inn.

It was, says J. Y., a time of a little encouragement to our tried minds, for we had been brought into doubt as to the utility of resting here, although we had seen, as we believed, in the true light, that we ought to seek out a few who could unite with us in our simple way.

On the 18th they went on to Neufchâtel, where they were received as before with much affection, and where they proposed to settle down for the winter, after making a tour in some neighboring parts of Switzerland.

On the 20th they went to Berne, and hired a lodging, for the purpose of devoting themselves to religious intercourse with persons of the *interior* class. As soon as it was known they had arrived, their acquaintance rapidly increased, and they found it difficult to receive all who came. One of their first acts was to renew their intercourse with the Combe family at Wabern, where their visit in 1828 had left a sweet remembrance.

They spent a fortnight in Berne and the neighborhood, and some passages from John Yeardley's account of this interesting visit may properly find a place here. The continual flow of Christian sympathy which it was now their happiness to experience, formed a strong contrast to the dreary spiritual wastes they had traversed in Italy and Greece. It was at this time that they contracted or renewed a friendship with Sophie Würstemberger, since well known to many other English Friends.

8 *mo.* 24.—How greatly I feel humbled under the prospect before us in this place; many thirsting souls are looking to

us for help, and we feel poor and weak; we can only direct
them to Him from whom all strength comes. O my Saviour,
forsake us not in this trying hour; give us the consolation of
thy Holy Spirit, and a portion of strength to do thy will!
Our meeting is appointed for this evening; enlighten our
understanding, O Lord, that we may be enabled to instruct
the people in the right way.

*25th.*—More came to the meeting last evening than we
expected. They were still, and a good feeling prevailed;
there were those present who knew something of inward
retirement with their Saviour.

Madame Combe called yesterday to ask some questions on
the Supper and Baptism. I believe it would be an advantage
to these pious people, if they were to read and compare one
part of the Scripture with another more diligently. She left
us well satisfied with the explanation given to her questions.
We never touch on these points, unless we are asked questions upon them.

The various visits received this day have closed with one
of no common interest from Dr. Karl Bouterwek, a young
man from Prussia. He told us he had received much benefit
in the church of the Dissidents, but was on the point of
separating from them, because he could not agree in acknowledging they were the *only true* visible church. After
some observations on the Supper, &c., we observed that there
were individuals in this place whom the Most High was
calling into more spirituality and purity of worship. He
asked why we thought so. Our reasons were given, and he
made no reply; but a most solemn and precious silence came
over us, which it was beyond our power to break by uttering
words. Our hearts were filled with love, and the dear young
man went away to avoid showing the feelings of his heart by
the shedding of tears.

*28th.*—Took tea at the Pavilion, a pleasant country walk
of twenty minutes from town, with Mad<sup>e</sup> de Watteville and
her daughter. She had invited a number of friends to meet
us. We passed a couple of hours, pleasantly conversing,
mostly on religious subjects. It is a little extraordinary,

19

with what openness some of these dear people speak to us of
the state of their minds. When the circle was seated, we
formed a pretty large company. The daughter of Mad⁰· de
W. whispered to my M. Y., Are we too dissipated to have
something good? We told her it was always good to endeavor to retire before the Lord in humility of soul. I trust
a parting blessing was felt amongst us.

30th.—From 9 o'clock till half-past 12, we received visits
in succession, I think not fewer than fifteen. At half-past 2,
Mad⁰· de Tavel accompanied us to the Penitentiary prison.
For cleanliness and order, I think, it exceeds all I ever saw
of the kind. I fear the religious instruction is very superfi-
cial; none but formal prayers and written sermons are used.

31st.—Attended Mad^lle· Berthom's Scripture class, at the
Institution for the Destitute. There are eighteen girls in
the house to bed and board; it has been established about six
years. M. B.'s method of examining the children is the most
simple and spiritual of any that I have seen; she has an extraordinary gift for the purpose.

9 mo. 2.— Attended the Monthly Meeting in the missionary room. Many of the company were peasants from
some distance. The singing excepted, it resembled a Monthly
Meeting for worship in our Society; for all had liberty to
speak one after the other, five or six speaking by way of testimony: the doctrine was sound, and the way in which they
coupled this with their Christian experience was really excellent. I had much unity with the concluding prayer by
Pastor Merley.

2nd.—The evening was spent at Mad⁰· W.'s, with a pretty
large company. —— proposed for a few verses to be
sung; afterwards he read a chapter, and gave a long expo-
sition, somewhat dry. When this and a prayer were gone
through, it was late; neither my M. Y., nor myself, were
able to express what was on our minds. Some uneasiness
and disappointment were expressed by several; and two of
these dear friends came to our lodgings the next day, with
whom we had a precious time. My M. Y. had to speak
a few words to the particular state of M. B., and at the

close she acknowledged, in brokenness of spirit, that it was the truth.

There is a remarkable awakening in the town and canton of Berne, both among those of the higher walks of life and the peasants; but there is not strength enough to come out of the forms. There are thirty females to one man among those who are lately become serious.

From Berne, J. and M. Y. proceeded to Zurich, arriving there on the 5th of the Ninth Month. They spent three days in the city, chiefly in the company of the Gessner-Lavater family, and renewed with the various members of it the intimate friendship of former years. A short passage descriptive of this sojourn is here appended.

9 *mo.* 7.—We attended the worship of the National Church, and heard the pious Gessner. What he said was excellent, but I never enter these places without feeling regret that good Christians can be so bound by book-worship; it certainly damps the life of religion in the assemblies. How much we ought to rejoice in being delivered from the forms.

I was instructed yesterday evening by hearing a reply of one of the first missionaries of the Moravians [?]. He had labored diligently for twenty-five years, and when asked how many souls had been turned to the Lord by his means, he modestly answered, Seven. The person expressing surprise at the smallness of the number in so many years, he replied, How happy shall I be to stand in the Lord's presence at the last day, and to say, Lord, here am I and the seven children whom thou hast given me. We ought to labor in faith, and not expect to see fruit.

The next town where they halted was Schaffhausen, like Zurich, dear to them in the recollections of past visits. Here they examined the school for poor children in the town, and that of Buch in the neighborhood. They were delighted with both these institutions. The mistress of the former possessed an extraordinary natural talent for her office ; she was originally a servant, when, instead of seeking her own pleasure on the First-days of the week, as other servants did, she would take a few children to teach them to read and instruct them in the Bible. Their visit to the school at Buch is described by John Yeardley in No. 10 of his Series of Tracts, *The Six Secrets.*

On the 13th they went to Basle, where they conversed with most of the pastors, and several other individuals of religious character.

Serious, retired persons, says John Yeardley (9 mo. 21), frequently come to us and open the state of their minds with great freedom and confidence. If we are of any use to their thirsty souls, it is the Saviour's love that draws us into sympathy with them, and his good Spirit that enables us to speak a word in season to their condition.

As usual, they visited the Mission House. Inspector Blumhardt informed them that the translation which had been made of J. J. Gurney's "Essays on Christianity," and of which 2000 copies were printed, had been productive of great good ; they had been distributed chiefly among those who were connected with the German universities.

They remained at Basle until the 1st of the Tenth Month, and then returned by way of Berne to Neufchâtel. At Berne a sudden diversion was given to the current of their thoughts by the intelligence of the death of Thomas Yeardley. J. Y. has left a memorandum of the occurrence, and of the singular foreshadowing of it upon his own mind which took place at Zurich.

10 *mo*. 2. *Berne*.—We found many letters from England
waiting for us here, one of which, from my nephew John
Yeardley, brought the sorrowful intelligence of the sudden
and unexpected removal of my dearly-beloved brother Thomas,
of Ecclesfield Mill. This took place on the 6th of the Ninth
Month, about 20 minutes past 2, without sigh or groan, even
as a lamb. These are the expressions of J. Y.; he adds several
sweet expressions of my precious brother's, which show that
the solemn change to him was a joyful one: and I do believe
his tribulated spirit is now at rest. On recurring to the 6th
ultimo to see where we were, and what were the contempla-
tions of my mind, I find we were at Zurich. That morning
the following lines which I heard when a child, and had not
repeated for the last twenty years, came forcibly into my
mind:—

> "It's almost done, it's almost o'er,
>   We're joining them that are gone before;
>   We soon shall meet upon that shore
>   Where we shall meet to part no more."

I not only repeated them to myself the whole of the day, but
even sung them aloud so often that my dear M. Y. said to me,
"Whatever can be the meaning that thou so often repeats
these lines?" I replied, "I do not know that I have repeated
them for the last twenty years, but to-day they are continually
with me." This can have been nothing but the spirit of
sympathy with the soul of my dear departing brother, for the
awful impression of sorrow and solemnity in my mind on that
day will never be forgotten; I mourned with the bereaved
family without knowing it. My M. Y. had opened her portfolio to begin a letter to our sister Rachel, and I wrote the
verse on a piece of loose paper, and she slipped it into her
papers, and said to herself, Surely these lines are not prophetic
of something that is going to happen? Last evening she
handed me out of her portfolio the piece of paper containing
the lines.

At Berne they received also the tidings that "the
excellent" M. A. Calame was no more; the Christian

mother of 250 orphan children was taken from the
scene of her labors and the conflicts of time to the
heavenly rest in her Saviour. The following appear to
be among the last words which she wrote; they were no
doubt addressed to her faithful companion Zimmerlin :—

In my numerous shortcomings I have enough constantly to
humble me, and without being surprised at it, since evil is my
heritage; but my help is in the Lord, who delights in mercy.
I have hope also for all my brethren whom I love, whatever
name they bear. There are twelve gates by which to enter
into the Holy City, and if they have passed through the great
gate, which is Christ, I am sure that those who enter from the
east, as well as those who have been brought in by the west,
will be there; but those who enter with me are better known
to me than the rest whom I shall meet in that celestial
Jerusalem, whither my sighs daily carry me, yet in submission to the heavenly decrees, desiring only that the will of
God our Saviour be done.

You think my task is light? Ah, no! the love which the
Lord has given me spends itself on so many hearts closed to
their true interests; I see the hand of the enemy in their
souls; I am so often deceived in my hopes, that my work is
watered by my tears. From time to time, however, the Lord
gives me hope; a soul awakes from sleep, and is kindled into
light by the torch of the gospel.

And now, dear sister, have no longer any esteem or consideration for me; only let the love of Christ live in thy
heart for me: the desires of my heart carry you with it to the
feet of Him who is Love.

When they returned home, John and Martha Yeardley printed a short memoir of this extraordinary woman,
whose name, though comparatively little known upon
earth, is doubtless enshrined in the hearts of many who
still survive, and shall one day shine with a lustre

which the most brilliant of her sex, whose ambition it
is to adorn the court, the concert or the drawing-room,
will desire in vain to wear.

At Berne J. and M. Y. commenced a Bible class,
similar in kind to the Scarborough réunion, which was
continued until their departure, and was the source of
much pleasure and profit to those who attended. Before
quitting Berne, thinking it might perhaps be the last
opportunity they should have of meeting with their
numerous and beloved friends in that city, they invited
them to join them in worship in their apartment.

Many, says John Yeardley, gave us their company; much
tenderness of spirit was felt, and through the mercy of Divine
Love many present were, I trust, comforted and refreshed.

We quitted Berne on the 30th. We had become so
affectionately attached to many Christian friends, that parting
from them was severely felt. But what happiness Christians
enjoy even in this world! those who love the Saviour remain
united in Him when outwardly separated.

Neufchâtel, for the sake of those who resided there,
was equally attractive to them as Berne.

We arrived at Neufchâtel, writes John Yeardley, on Fifth-
day, and on Seventh-day (11 mo. 1) settled into a comfortable lodging on the border of the lake. It feels to us the
most like home of any residence we have had during our
pilgrimage in foreign lands. Our suite of cottage-rooms
runs alongside the water, with a gallery in front, and the
little boats on the lake, and the mountains in the distance,
covered with snow, are objects pleasing to the eye. What
gives us the most satisfaction is the feeling of being in our
right place, and to meet with such a warm reception from our
dear friends.

This feeling was succeeded by some religious service

of an interesting character, in reviewing which John
Yeardley says :—

23rd.—Among those who meet with us, a little few know
how to appreciate true silence, others are not come to this.
But for what purpose are we here? If it may please our
Heavenly Father to make use of us as feeble instruments of
drawing a single individual into nearer communion with the
Beloved of souls, we ought to be content; and, blessed be his
Holy Name, his presence is often felt in our hearts.

As has been already said, they looked forward to
spending the winter at Neufchâtel. This intention, and
their ulterior project of visiting Germany in the spring,
were frustrated by the alarming illness of Adey Bellamy
Savory, Martha Yeardley's only brother, the news of
which reached them on the 29th of the Eleventh
Month.

This day's post, writes John Yeardley, brought us the
sorrowful news of the severe illness of our dear brother A. B.
Savory. The family at Stamford-hill have expressed a strong
desire for us to return, if we could feel easy so to do, and
seeing that we have pretty much got through what we had
in prospect in Switzerland, we are, on the whole, most comfortable to go direct for London, and leave Germany for the
present. Our great Master is very gracious to us, giving us
to feel sweet peace in the termination of our labors, and to
look forward with hope to seeing our native land once more.

The next day was First-day; the parting with their
Neufchâtel friends was very affecting.

11 mo. 30.—A precious meeting this morning. The presence of Him who died for us was near, to help and comfort
us; our hearts were much tendered by his divine love. The
taking leave of our dear friends here was almost heart-
rending. There is a precious seed in this place, which I

trust, is a little deeper rooted since our last visit, and it is the prayer of my heart, that the Saviour may water and watch over it, and that it may produce abundance of fruit to his praise.

They took their departure on the 2nd of the Twelfth Month, and arrived in London on the 13th, travelling through the north of France twelve days and six nights.

Through divine mercy we arrived safe in London, on Seventh-day evening, and lodged with our beloved relations at Highbury, who received us with all possible affection. Our spirits on meeting, mingled in silent sorrow, while we were enabled to rejoice in God our Saviour. On First-day morning we went over to Stamford-hill, and soon were introduced to our beloved brother, who was perfectly sensible, but extremely weak. The peace and serenity which we were favored to feel by him was an inexpressible comfort to our sorrowful hearts.

A. B. Savory died the next Third-day evening, and his remains were interred on the First-day following.

21st.—This was the day fixed for the solemn occasion of accompanying the remains to the tomb. The body was taken into the meeting-house at Newington, and the company of mourners and all present were, I believe, comforted and edified through the tender mercies of our Heavenly Father. J. J. Gurney's communication was particularly precious; he also paid a consoling visit to the family after dinner.

We shall conclude this chapter with some reflections made by John Yeardley, on reviewing the changes which death had produced in the circle of his relations:—

1835. 1 mo. 31.—Waking this morning, I took a view of the great ravages death had made in our families; when this exhortation pressed suddenly and with peculiar force on my heart,—Be thou also ready. My soul responded, Thou Lord, alone, canst make me ready. O gracious Saviour, who died for me, be pleased to redeem me from the bond of corruption, and purify my heart from earthly things.

# CHAPTER XIV.

DURING the seven years comprised in this chapter, the materials which exist for delineating John and Martha Yeardley's history are meagre. Of the numerous journeys which they made in the course of this period, the record kept by the former frequently consists of a mere itinerary.

After attending the Leeds Quarterly Meeting in the Third Month, they returned to their home at Scarborough, but soon left it again to be present at the Yearly Meeting in London. The Society of Friends began about this time to be agitated by differences of opinion, chiefly on points of doctrine. John Yeardley not only kept himself sedulously free from the spirit of party, but, whether from a natural aversion to public life, or from the fear of exceeding the limit of his own calling and abilities, he abstained from taking a prominent position, and left it very much to others to sway the affairs of the Church. But he was not unmindful of the dangers by which the Society was assailed, and he bent the force of his mental vigor and Christian experience towards the promotion of individual growth in grace and faithfulness to the divine call, and the diffusion of clear and comprehensive views of Scriptural truth; and when the hour came for sympathising with those who were harassed by doubts, or such as were subjected to trial by the effect of religious dissension, he was ready,

(291)

with his beloved partner, to share the burden of the afflicted, to probe the wounds of those who had been bruised, and to pour in the oil of heavenly consolation.

His note regarding the Yearly Meeting is short:—

The business was of a most important nature, and some-times very trying. We had strong proof that many spirits professing to have made long progress in the Christian life were not enough subdued by the humbling power of divine grace; but through all, I trust, our heavenly Father dealt with us in mercy, and sent help and wisdom to direct and strengthen his poor tribulated children.

On returning to Scarborough, he writes:—

I humbly trust our hearts are truly grateful to the Author of all our mercies, who has granted us once more a little rest of body and sweet peace of mind; but, as it regards myself, I must say that inward poverty has prevailed more since my return home than it has done for the last two years of absence. It is well to know how to suffer want, as well as to abound.

Want of occupation was not one of John Yeardley's trials, even when " standing," as he expressed it, " free from any prospect of immediate service, and feeling much as a vessel not likely to be brought into use again." Scriptural inquiry, the study of languages, and of the history of the Church, watching the progress of religious light and liberty on the Continent of Europe, his garden, the binding of his books—these were the employments of his industrious leisure. To these must be added the time bestowed on several small publica-tions from his own and his wife's pen (the latter chiefly poetical), of which the " Eastern Customs," a volume which was the product of their united labor, and the materials for which were supplied by their journey to Greece, is the best known.

But there was another object which drew largely on John Yeardley's time during his residence at Scarborough. This was the unsectarian schools established in the town for the education of the industrial classes. Of these the Lancasterian School for girls was his favorite, and the deep and steady interest which he manifested for the improvement of the children, as well as the peculiar talent which he evinced for attracting and developing the youthful mind, are shown in an affectionate tribute to his memory by the late mistress of the school:—

For many years he was a visitor at our Lancasterian School, where it was his delight to impart knowledge to a numerous class of girls. He had a happy method of communicating information. The children used to listen with the greatest attention and delight; they never wearied of his lessons. Scriptural instruction was his first object; the children were questioned on what they had read, and it was delightful to watch their countenances whilst he explained portions of Scripture, which he frequently illustrated by the manners and customs of Eastern nations; and this he did in a way that rendered his teaching valuable, as he did not fail to make an impression and gain the affections of his hearers.

One little girl we had whom he used to call the *oracle;* and indeed she was not inappropriately so-called; for whenever any of the girls were at a loss for an answer, they invariably turned to her, and seldom failed to receive a response to their silent appeal. This gifted child died between the ages of sixteen and eighteen; he was a frequent visitor at her bedside during a lingering illness, and it was his privilege to see that his labors had not been in vain.

I shall *never* forget him, not only for the important instruction I derived from him, but also for his valuable assistance. During my labors of more than twenty-five years, I had none to help me as he did. When at home he never failed to visit us every afternoon: no matter what the state of the weather was—snow, wind or rain—he was to be seen at half-past two, with his large cape folded round him, bending before the blast, toiling up the hill near the school. So accustomed were we to him that his coming was deemed a matter of course.

After our Scripture lesson a portion of time was devoted to geography, particularly Bible geography; then he would talk to them of places where he had travelled: his descriptions of the Ionian Islands, the people and the schools he had visited there, used to be a favorite theme, and very interesting. In this way our afternoons were passed, and truly they were times of profitable instruction.

He seemed to care less for the boys' school; he did occasionally visit them, but the girls were his pets. I have sometimes thought his knowledge of the ignorant and degraded state of the females in Greece was the cause of his taking so much interest in the education of the females in his own land.

In addition to J. Yeardley's labors at the Lancasterian School, some of the older girls and a few others who belonged to the school assembled at his house one evening in the week, whom he instructed in reading and Scriptural knowledge. Some of these still speak with gratitude of the benefit they then received.

In the Ninth Month of 1835, John and Martha Yeardley visited Settle Monthly Meeting, and Knaresborough, under appointment of the Quarterly Meeting. On their way thither they took up at York their aged and valued friend Elizabeth Rowntree of Scarborough, who was on the appointment.

Her company, says J. Y., was a strength and comfort to us; she exercised her gift as an elder in a very acceptable manner, in many of the families we visited, as well as in the meetings for discipline.

This notice is succeeded almost immediately by the record of Elizabeth Rowntree's sudden decease :—

On the 25th of the Eleventh Month, we were introduced into deep affliction by the sudden removal of our precious elder, E. Rowntree.  Her dependence for salvation was fixed on her Saviour, the Lord Jesus Christ, through the help of whose Spirit she had been enabled to lead a life of godliness and of usefulness to her fellow-mortals, and was always con· cerned to give the praise to Him to whom it was due,—the Lord of Lords.

This event, with the removal of another pilgrim to become an inhabitant of the world of beatified spirits, and the pressing subject of the divisions in the Society, form the topics of the following letter from Martha Yeardley to Elizabeth Dudley :—

Scarborough, 12 mo. 5, 1835.
During our long sojourn last spring, in and about my native city, my spirit was deeply oppressed, nor did the con· flicts endured appear to produce much benefit either to myself or others.  Here the way is more open, and, although we also deeply feel the effects of the storm which has been permitted to assail our little Society, we are more able to endure it; and desire to abide in our tents, except when called upon to defend that immediate teaching of the blessed Saviour, upon which we depend for our little portion of daily bread. I can truly sympathise with thee, my beloved Betsy, as having to bear more of the burden and heat of the day, and I do fervently believe with thee, that the more, as individuals, we commit and confide the cause to the Great Master, in humble prayer, the sooner it will be extricated from the perplexities which now harass and distress those who are truly devoted to it.

We have deeply to mourn for our endeared and highly valued E. Rowntree, suddenly taken from us about ten days

since. She and her sister R. S., from Whitby, had spent the
preceding evening with us; she was in usual health, and
sweetly cheerful, rejoicing that she had been enabled to
assist dear Sarah Squire in a family visit to Friends of this
meeting, though she did not sit with her in the families.
I heard of her illness and hastened to her; she appeared
sensible but for a very few moments after having been got
to bed; yet was heard begging for patience under extreme
agony; then added, We had need live the life of the righteous,
for it is an awful thing to die. Then she suddenly sank into
a slumber, and lay till a little after nine at night, when her
purified spirit was peacefully liberated.

We have got through Pontefract and some meetings in
the neighborhood to our comfort, and on the journey had
an opportunity of sitting beside the dying bed of dear Sarah
Dent, which was indeed a peaceful scene. She was perfectly
sensible, and so animated that I could hardly give up hope
of her restoration. But she had not herself the least prospect of life, and said that, although she had found it a hard
struggle to give up her husband and children, she had,
through the mercy of her gracious Redeemer, attained to
perfect resignation. This was about a week before her death,
and we have heard since, that a little before the close, she said,
The Lord Jesus is near, I want you all to know that He is near
indeed!

Dear Ann Priestman has united with us in visiting this
Monthly Meeting: it seems now best for us to remain at home
for a short time, under the bereavement which our own meeting has suffered.

In 1836 they again attended the Yearly Meeting;
of which John Yeardley thus speaks:—

The Yearly Meeting was, I think, on the whole, satisfactory, much more so than many Friends could look for,
considering the discouraging circumstances under which we
came together. The main bent in all the important deliberations on subjects of great moment to the well-being of our

small section of the universal church, was to adhere to the
long-known principles of the Society, and to turn aside the
sentiments of opposing individuals in the spirit of gentleness,
forbearance and love.

They visited many meetings in going from and returning to Scarborough. The most interesting of these visits
was at Thame, in Oxfordshire, which John Yeardley
thus describes:—

6 mo. 14.—Went in the evening to Thame, and had a
meeting with a few who have met in the way of Friends for
about five years at Grove End. There are only seven or
eight who meet regularly, but they are often joined by a few
others. No notice had been given to their neighbors of
our coming, but on seeing us go to the meeting many
followed; the room was quite filled, and a precious meeting
it was. Their hearts are like ground prepared for the good
seed of the kingdom. The nature of spiritual worship was
pointed out, and testimony borne to the teaching of the Holy
Spirit.

This little company reminded us of many such which we
met with in foreign countries, particularly in Switzerland
and Germany. We had a good deal of conversation with William Wheeler, who was one of the first to meet in silence. He
was a leader in the Wesleyan congregation, and became uneasy with giving out hymns to be sung with those whose states
he knew did not correspond with the words. He would then
sometimes select a hymn most suited by its general character
te the company; at other times he would leave out a few
verses, and select others which he thought might be sung
with truth by the whole congregation; but the thing became
so burdensome that he was obliged, for conscience' sake, to
leave it altogether, and sit down with a few others in silence.
At first they met with opposition, and even persecution, from
persons who came to their meeting to disperse them. On
one of these occasions a few rude young men had banded
together to beset them the next meeting-day, and disperse

20

them. W. W. was strongly impressed that it was right for
him to proclaim an awful warning to some—that the judgments of the Almighty awaited them, that eternity was nearer
than they were aware and he wished them to consider and
prepare for it. One of the disturbers was taken suddenly ill,
and died before the next meeting-day ; which produced such
an effect on the others that they never more molested the little
company in their worship.

In reviewing this journey, J. Y. says, under date of
the 25th of the Sixth Month :—

I trust my faith is afresh confirmed in the gift of the
Holy Spirit to lead in the way of religious duty, and to give
strength to do His will. Lord, grant that the remainder of
my days, whether few or many, be entirely devoted to the
holy cause of endeavoring to promote the Saviour's kingdom
on earth.

In 1837, John and Martha Yeardley were occupied
with making circuits in the service of the gospel through
several counties of England. They were attracted to
Lancashire, which they visited in the autumn, by the
peculiar state of some meetings in that county, an extensive secession having taken place not long before. The
difficulties which they had to encounter on this journey
are represented in a letter from Martha Yeardley to her
sisters, written at Manchester the 4th of the Ninth
Month, 1837.

I do not recollect that, in my little experience, I ever had
more preparatory exercise of mind to pass through; and I
believe it has been the same with my dear J. Y. We have,
however, in many of our visits, been much comforted under
the belief that those who remain firm in the testimonies
given us to bear are in a more lively state, and more banded
together, than has been the case heretofore, and that, through

the mercy of our holy Head and High Priest, there is a renewed visitation to many. In the public meetings, of which we have had many, there has been a rather remarkable openness to receive the truths of the gospel, united with our view of the spirituality of this blessed dispensation.

We approached this place in deep prostration of spirit; and truly we feel that all the previous baptism has been needful, in order to enable us in any degree to perform our duty here. There has been a sore rending of the tenderest ties, and the wounds are not yet healed. There are a few who entertain ultra views, and their over-activity tends to keep up excitement in those who are wavering and have not yet left the Society : this makes it very difficult for moderate people to stand between them, and calls for very deep indwelling with the blessed source of love. On the other hand there are, I fear, very many who rejoice in the delusive suggestions of our unwearied enemy—that the cross of Christ is not necessary—that they may speak their own words and wear their own apparel, and still be called by the name of Him who died for them. I think we never have had more to suffer than in some of the meetings we have attended, from a disposition, perhaps in some degree on both sides, to criticise ministry : still there are, I believe, many precious individuals among the young and middle-aged who are under the forming hand for usefulness. There is indeed a loud call for laborers in this large and mixed meeting ; and we are ready to weep over the vacant seats of those who have deserted their post, and, I greatly fear, are seeking to warm themselves and others with sparks of their own kindling.

Another letter from M. Y., written at the conclusion of this journey, supplies a few more traits of the Christian service into which they were led in the course of it.

Scarborough, 10 mo. 7.

We remained nearly a month in our lodgings at Manchester, receiving and paying visits, some of which were very interesting.   Dear H. Stephenson and family were extremely attentive, and her daughter Hannah was our constant guide in that large place.   We spent First-day at Rochdale, and in the evening a large number of young Friends took tea with us, between thirty and forty.   This has mostly been the case on First-days, both at Manchester and elsewhere, and these opportunities have tended to our relief.

After this we bade farewell to Lancashire, under feelings of thankfulness which I cannot describe, for having been mercifully helped and preserved through such a warfare.

In the autumn of 1839 they again travelled south-wards, directing their steps through the eastern counties of England, and London, Surrey, and Hampshire, to the Isle of Wight, where they spent five weeks exploring its coasts and corners, in search, not of the naturally picturesque, but of the beautiful and hopeful in the moral and religious world.   They returned home by Bristol and Birmingham.

So attractive to their spirits was the Isle of Wight, that the next year they repeated the visit, going thither after the Yearly Meeting.   In the Seventh Month they attended the Quarterly Meeting at Alton, and on their return to Newport were accompanied by Elizabeth and Mary Dudley and Margaret Pope.   They remained in Newport and the vicinity several weeks, during which time, amongst other engagements, they conducted a Scripture class with some young persons three evenings a week.   In a letter dated the 27th of the Sixth Month, J. Y. says:—

My dear Martha feels deeply for the Unitarians in this place; we sometimes think the way may open for us to help them a little.   Their great stumbling-stones are, the want of clearness in the mystery of the oneness in the Godhead, and of faith in the practical influences of the Holy Spirit, as operating on the heart of man. Our morning reading opens a suitable door of communication for those whose curiosity prompts them to seek our company.

In company with Elizabeth Dudley they held several public meetings at various places on the island. They have left no record of this service, but we have a notice of the meeting at Porchfield, in a letter from E. D.

The meeting was very satisfactory, sweet and refreshing to our spirits. The road was rough and hilly. We were behind time, and our friends being punctual, the house looked full when we got there, though more followed, until not only within but outside the walls there was a crowd of orderly, attentive people. Many of them were happily acquainted with the power of religion in their hearts, and prepared for spiritual worship. The assembly was composed of various denominations from a straggling village and more remote habitations. The chapel was built many years ago, by a pious man, now above eighty years old, who was with us, and who enjoys to have the place used by any who from love to Christ and the souls of men are attracted to visit them. The simplicity and openness to be observed and felt that evening was a comforting indication of freedom from party spirit, and those vain disputations which in so many instances keep Christians at a distance, and mar their individual peace as well as usefulness.

Before they left Newport, they provided, with the help of several friends, suitable accommodation for the little meeting of Friends in that town. On taking leave of the island, which they did in the Eighth Month, John Yeardley remarks:—

We have had much comfort and satisfaction in our sojourn in this place: a strong evidence is felt in our hearts that it has been ordered by the Lord. We have cause to acknowledge that our labors have been owned by the Divine

Presence in our various exercises for the promotion of the Saviour's kingdom.

In the spring of 1841 they repeated their visit to the Isle of Wight, spent great part of the summer in religious service in Essex, and visited afterwards Bristol, Bath, and other parts of Somersetshire.

At Bath they remained for some weeks.   Soon after their arrival in the city, they were introduced into sympathetic sorrow on account of the death of John Rutter, whose guests they were, and who was suddenly removed, by an accident, from time to eternity.   This event is described in a letter from John Yeardley to his sister R. S.

Bath, 9 mo. 24, 1841.

The affectionate family of the Rutters gave us a hearty reception, and we remained under their hospitable roof until Second-day, when they were plunged into deep distress by the awfully sudden removal of their beloved father.   He went out before breakfast, and called at his son's wharf.   A cart of coals being about to be weighed, he was leading the horse on to the machine; the animal, being a little unruly, suddenly rushed forward and pushed down J. R., and the wheel passed over his body.   He was immediately conveyed to his own shop, when the spark of life became extinct, and he ceased to breathe, without apparent pain or emotion.   We were nearly ready to leave our room, about half-past 6 o'clock, when one of the sons knocked at our door, and related the awful occurrence.   I went down immediately : the scene may be more easily imagined by you than described by me.   We endeavored to calm them as much as possible ; and, though deeply afflicted, they bear the stroke with sweet resignation. I wrote letters at their request to most of their near relatives; and as we could not think of leaving the sorrowing family to go as proposed to Bristol, we immediately procured a lodging and settled in, in the evening.

On Third-day afternoon we went to the Quarterly Meeting at Bristol, and returned to Bath on Fifth day, not wishing to be long absent from the dear sorrowing ones. We have a pleasant situation on the hill-side, called Sidney Lodge, from which, when the gas is lighted, the city is presented to our view like a beautiful panorama.

Their minds had been for some time in preparation for renewing, on the Continent of Europe, Christian intercourse with some of their old friends, and for exploring new veins of religious life in countries which they had not yet visited. Accordingly, in the Fourth Month of 1842, they acquainted the Friends of their Monthly Meeting with the prospect of missionary service which had opened before them, informing them that from the conclusion of their last European journey they had believed it would one day be required of them to re-enter that field of labor. The Monthly Meeting accorded its full and sympathetic approbation, which was endorsed by the Quarterly Meeting at a conference of men and women Friends, of which John Yeardley says:—

The great solemnity which prevailed was truly refreshing to our spirits, and I believe to the spirits of many others. Our friends gave us their full unity, *encouragement, sympathy,* and *prayers.*

Martha Yeardley thus expresses the feelings with which she contemplated this arduous journey, in a letter to Josiah Forster:—

It is indeed an awful engagement, now in the decline of life, and, with respect to myself, under increasing infirmities; but I believe it best for me not to look too far forward, but simply to confide in the mercy and guidance of that blessed Saviour who has been our support and consolation under

many deep trials, humblingly believing that whether enabled
to accomplish the important prospect or not, it was an offering
required at our hands, and that we must leave the event to
the Great Disposer of all things.

In the same letter she mentions their having heard
of the death of Louis A. Majolier of Congenies, which,
she says, although a cause of rejoicing as it regards him,
was read by us with mournful feelings, from the recollection of his fatherly kindness in days that are past, and
also from renewed solicitude for the little flock in that
country.

Before their departure they went once more into the
West Riding, to see how their brethren of J. Y.'s earliest
acquaintance fared.   They were joined by William Dent
of Marr, near Doncaster, with whom they were " sweetly
united in the fellowship of the gospel;" and they returned
to Scarborough with " grateful and peaceful hearts."

# CHAPTER XV.

## 1842-3.

In the journey which now lay before them, John and Martha Yeardley were about to explore a part of Europe hitherto untried, — the province of Languedoc, conspicuous in past ages for its superior enlightenment, but now, owing to the temporary mastery of error, wrapt in ignorance and gloom. In this mission, the opportunities which they found for reviving and gathering together the scattered embers of truth, were nearly confined to social intercourse; in seeking occasions for which, they availed themselves of introductions by pious Protestants from place to place, whilst they were careful, as had always been their practice, to wait, in every successive step, for the direction of the Divine Finger. The mission was performed in much weakness of body, and under frequent spiritual poverty; yet it will be readily acknowledged that theirs was a favored lot, to be able, with the clue of gospel love in their hand, to trace the pathway of Christian truth, and the footsteps of true spiritual worship, and of a faithful testimony for Christ, through the midst of a degenerate and benighted land.

They went to London on the 2nd of the Eighth Month, and spent the time before they sailed in gathering information and counsel for their approaching journey, and in social visits. Speaking of one of these visits (to their nephew J. S., at Clapton), John Yeardley says :—

(305)

Before parting we had a religious opportunity, in which a word of exhortation flowed in gospel love, and ability was granted to approach the throne of mercy in solemn supplication. I often wish we were more faithful in raising our hearts to the Lord before separating from our friends when met on social occasions; a blessing might attend such simple offerings.

In a vist they paid to Thomas and Carolina Norton, the subject of establishing a school for the children of Friends in the South of France came under consideration; a project which, as we shall see, they were able in their visit to that part of the country to carry into effect.

They left London on the 16th, and on the 19th arrived at Amiens, where they halted for a few days. They found in this city a movement among the Roman Catholics, a number of whom had joined the Protestant worship. The Protestant Pastor, Cadoret, was very friendly to them; when he heard that they belonged to the Society of Friends, he pressed John Yeardley's hand and said, I am very glad to make your acquaintance; it is the first time I have seen any of your Society, of whom I have heard much.

On the 20th J. Y. writes, in allusion to the spiritual darkness which so generally covered the land of France :—

My soul is cast down, but when I am afflicted because of the wickedness of the people, I call to remembrance these words: "Fret not thyself because of evil-doers. Trust in the Lord and do good; so shalt thou dwell in the land, and verily thou shalt be fed."—Psalm xxxvii. 1, 3.

A large number of workmen of various nations are employed at Amiens in weaving. J. and M. Y. visited several of these in their cottages, and before they left the city invited the people of this class to a meeting, especially intended for their own countrymen, but open to all who were willing to come. The meeting, says J. Y., was an occasion precious to our souls; the Lord gave us ability to declare his word. I spoke in English and my dear Martha in French.

At Paris, whither they proceeded on the 22nd, they were disappointed in finding that the majority of the persons at whose houses they called were in the country, and some with whom they had taken sweet counsel in former years had been removed by death. Pastor Audebez was at home, and received them with a cordial welcome. They were detained in Paris longer than they had anticipated, by the illness of Martha Yeardley, and did not leave till the 9th of the Ninth Month. The morning after they had entered Paris the words of Job were brought to J. Y.'s recollection in a forcible manner:—" Thou hast granted me life and favor, and thy visitation hath preserved my spirit." (Job x. 12); and in going out of the city he was refreshed with the joyful language of David,—" How excellent is thy loving-kindness, O God! therefore the children of men put their trust under the shadow of thy wings. They shall be abundantly satisfied with the fatness of thy house; and thou shalt make them drink of the river of thy pleasures. For with thee is the fountain of life: in thy light shall we see light."—Psa. xxxvi. 7–9.

Some letters which John and Martha Yeardley received from England during their sojourn in Paris show the strong sympathy which accompanied them in their journey, and contain, at the same time, references to events which will be interesting to the reader.

South Grove, Peckham, 8 mo. 12, 1842.

Numbers vi. 24–27:—"The Lord bless thee and keep thee; the Lord make his face shine upon thee, and be gracious unto thee; the Lord lift up his countenance upon thee, and give thee peace. And they shall put my name upon the children of Israel, and I will bless them." To be pronounced by Aaron the high priest and his successors, as the type of Him by whom all blessing and favor are bestowed on the church and her children.

The above portion of Holy Scripture, with the 121st Psalm, has been so sweetly in my remembrance since parting with my beloved friends John and Martha Yeardley, that, before retiring for the night, I transcribe the words which convey, so much better than any language of my own, the renewed and abiding desire under which they are committed to the care and guidance of the Good Shepherd, in humble but confiding belief that he will equally watch over, guard and keep, those who go and those who stay; causing each, amidst all variety of circumstances, to realize the soul-cheering truth that, at the throne of grace, mercy is obtained and grace to help in time of need. May the peace which passeth all understanding keep our hearts and minds through Jesus Christ, prays your nearly-attached friend and sister,

E. DUDLEY.


THE SAME TO MARTHA YEARDLEY.


Peckham, 8 mo. 21, 1842.

While in the sick-chamber of my sister, instead of at meeting, it feels pleasant to devote part of the evening to thee, my beloved friend. I have enjoyed the thought of your having a good Sabbath at Paris, where, no doubt, a sphere of duty will be found, and perhaps many exercises of faith and patience attend the labor of love which may await you there; while, in the spirit of true dedication and acquiescence so mercifully bestowed upon you, no commandment will be counted grievous, nor any service for your Lord too hard or painful. His words come sweetly to my mind as really the portion of a brother and sister dear in the bond and power of an endless life,—"Blessed are your eyes, for they see, and your ears, for they hear."

Accounts from various parts of this land continue to indicate much unsettlement, and there have been large companies of Chartists in the immediate vicinity of London; but happily the civil power proved equal to their dispersion. One would hope the abundant harvest, now ready to be gathered, may turn the current of feeling, and induce the desire rather to praise the Lord for his goodness, than to spend time and strength in murmurings and disputings with their fellow-mortals. The destruction, not only of property, but of life, in some recent contests, is quite appalling, and we certainly live in very eventful times; the tendency, however, both of the good and evil, is so obviously towards an increase of light and knowledge, that it seems warrantable to expect *all* will be overruled to better views and practices becoming more general, and the kingdoms of this world being thankfully surrendered to the righteous government of the Prince of Peace. But alas! deep and complicated may be the sufferings yet behind for the church and her children to endure, whether in being sharers in, or but the witnesses of, what is pronounced upon the world of the ungodly.

FROM JOHN ROWNTREE.

Scarborough, 8 mo. 29, 1842.

The account of your proceedings at Amiens has been particularly interesting to me. Whether manufacturing employments are unfavorable or otherwise to moral and religious character; or whether it is merely the larger earnings which artizans receive, enabling them more glaringly to gratify their natural and corrupt inclinations than agricultural laborers, can do; whether the passive ignorance of the country laborer, or the more active and intelligent habits, yet combined with moral darkness, of the manufacturing operative, most retards the diffusion of religious truth, are serious questions for us in this country. Our manufacturers

have been alarming the whole nation, and threatening us
with something like political revolution; but they have
received a severe lesson, and many of our jails are filled with
the victims of unprincipled agitators. Considering how little
of the Christian spirit is generally found in the operations of
government, the treatment of these poor creatures has on the
whole been lenient, and no very severe punishments are anticipated.

Whether the people of this nation have learned more of
righteousness from the judgments of the Lord, which have I
think evidently been made known in this part of his earth, is
perhaps known only to Him who knoweth all things. I often
fear;—for surely there is very much of darkness and wickedness among us—yet I can not unfrequently hope that light is
spreading, and that although the powers of evil are active
and strongly developed, yet the active diffusion of the means
of good more than keeps pace with them. "Greater is He
that is in you than he that is in the world," is still a consoling
assurance to many dejected yet hoping believers. Our dear
friend Hannah C. Backhouse is strong in the faith that light
is increasing, that the fields are white already for harvest, and
that the Lord of the harvest is preparing and sending forth
laborers into his harvest.

The Protestants whom you found at Amiens, and in some
other places, would probably remain totally unknown to
ordinary travellers, and perhaps we do not enough consider
how little known in a great nation the salt that preserves it
may be. The reports from the agent of the Bible Society in
France seem to me more than usually encouraging. I hope
you may be enabled to impart some spiritual gift or knowledge to many hidden ones who appear to be hungering and
thirsting after righteousness in that vain-glorious nation, and
that your faith may be strengthened by meeting with such.

John and Martha Yeardley arrived at Lyons on the
13th, and, after making some calls, intended to proceed
to Nismes the next day. But not feeling satisfied to
leave the city so soon, they concluded to remain there

one day more; and they had cause to be thankful in having taken this course.

For, says J. Y., we have made the acquaintance of several religious persons. An evangelist and colporteur named Hermann Lange, a German Swiss, took us to see some Protestant converts, amongst whom we have found much of the interior life. The Lord gave me a word of exhortation for them, and helped me to utter it in French. We had a conversation with our friend Lange respecting the ministry in our Society. Like many other persons he supposed we had no recognized ministers; we explained the usage of Friends, and showed him our certificates, with which he was pleased. He admired the good order in use amongst us, and said that he had for a long time desired to be informed respecting the principles of Friends; that he thought as we did, that an express call of the Holy Spirit was necessary to the ministry, and that women as well as men ought to be allowed to preach. I felt intimately united to him in spirit: on parting we gave him some tracts explanatory of our principles.

Lyons is the head-quarters of popery; the Jesuits here exert a strong influence with the government against the Protestants. We visited a good man named Elfenbein, who with his wife, is very useful to the awakened Protestants. He is a colporteur, and introduces the Holy Scriptures into families to whom he speaks concerning the things of God. He and his wife called upon us in our hotel. On parting he proposed we should pray together. This gave us the opportunity of explaining our sentiments regarding prayer; and we proposed remaining a while in silence, and if it should please the Lord to put words of prayer into our heart, we would express them with the help of the Holy Spirit. After a time of silence, Elfenbein prayed for us with unction in a few words: it was a favored time; thanks be to God.

On the 15th they resumed their journey, and passing through Nismes proceeded to Congenies. They found there Edward and John Pease, who were travelling on a religious errand, and were about concluding their labors in those parts. The meeting was a source of comfort on both sides. The next day, which was First-day, was a solemn season: the gospel message was largely delivered in the little meeting-house, and Christine Majolier interpreted for those who spoke in English. The Two-months' Meeting was held, and here, as well indeed as on every other occasion, the English Friends missed the company and help of their valued friend, Louis A. Majolier.

After residing for a while at Congenies, they removed to Nismes, where they preached to the strangers who attended the usual meetings for worship, distributed religious tracts in the city and its environs, and insti-tuted a Scripture Reading Meeting for the young. But the object which most strongly engaged their attention at Nismes was the foundation of a boarding-school for the daughters of Friends. Louis Majolier, during a great part of his life had conducted a day-school at Congenies: this school was, of course, not accessible to the children of those Friends who lived at a distance; and soon after L. M. died even this was given up, and the means of education in the Society failed altogether. In their project for supplying this deficiency, John and Martha Yeardley found the parents and other Friends ready to second their efforts; and at the Two-months' Meeting in the Eleventh Month, it was resolved to establish in the first place a school for girls only at Nismes, and a committee was appointed to carry this resolution into effect. A mistress was found without much difficulty in Justine Bénézet, a valuable Friend, who had had for sixteen years the superintendence of the Orphan Asylum, and whose health had in some degree given way under the too onerous charge.

In reference to the accomplishment of this undertaking, J. Y. writes:—

12 *mo.* 14.—*Nehemiah* i. 11:—" O Lord, I beseech thee, let now thine ear be attentive to the prayer of thy servant, and to the prayer of thy servants, who desire to fear thy name; and prosper, I pray thee, thy servant this day." I often think of these words of the prophet, and they [have supported me] when my soul has been cast down on account of the school.

During their abode at Nismes they visited the little congregations of Friends which lie to the westward of that city, and had to record that the presence of their Divine Master went with them, giving them his word to declare, and inclining the hearts of the hearers to receive it.

A letter from John Rowntree, which reached them towards the end of the year, contains some observations on the work they had found to do in their journey, with an interesting notice of what was passing in England.

Scarborough, 11 mo. 14, 1842.

My dear Friends,

. . . . . The plan of your meetings for Scripture instruction seems to me particularly good; you will, through them, have numerous opportunities for impressing on the minds of your hearers the inestimable value of the Holy Scriptures, when properly received, and made available by the enlightening influence of the Holy Spirit, and the worthlessness—nay, the danger—of resting satisfied with a mere knowledge of their words. The words of our Lord were "spirit and life" to those who would receive them as

21

such; yet how many who heard them were to be judged by them at the last day, because they believed not.

We still hear sad accounts of distress in the manufacturing districts of the country. Some of your friends have probably informed you that at our last Quarterly Meeting much sympathy was expressed for the destitute artizans, and a liberal subscription was commenced, and was to be carried forward in all our meetings for their relief: a few days ago it amounted to £800—I hope it will exceed £1000: but what is that, it may be said, among so many? yet I hope much good may be done by it, and Friends in other parts of the nation seem to be considering whether they ought not to make some efforts for similar purposes. At Liverpool we hear that upwards of £200 has been raised.

You will probably have heard of the very sudden death of Jonathan Backhouse, whilst his wife was laboring under a religious engagement in the north of our county. His change seemed a translation from that state of strong but imperfect love which a member of the militant Church might feel here below, to that fullness of love which his Saviour had purchased for him above.

In the Third Month, 1843, they quitted Nismes, taking their young friend Jules Paradon as their companion.

The parting, says J. Y., from the dear family at the school was sorrowful. Before taking leave, we had a religious opportunity with the children, in which all hearts were touched.

They arrived at Montpélier on the 7th. The pious characters to whom they were introduced in this city were mostly of the upper class—bankers, doctors, lawyers, and professors. They found that the principles of the Society of Friends were very little known there, but that many were desirous of being acquainted with them.  Being pressed in their spirit to propose a meeting for worship with such as were disposed to give their company, their new friends readily agreed to it, and about thirty-five persons sat down with them at their inn.  The assembly was, as they believed, owned by the great Master, who showed himself to be their strength in the time of weakness, and gave them power to preach the gospel and explain the nature of true worship. Pastor Lissignol and Dr. Parlier were amongst those to whom they were the most united.  The latter filled the office of mayor when Josiah Forster and Elizabeth Fry were at Montpélier.  He told John and Martha Yeardley that the meeting they had just held had been strengthening to his faith.  That the Lord by his Spirit should move the hearts of his children in a distant land to visit his heritage in other countries, he regarded as a proof of his love; and he spoke of the unity of spirit which is felt by those of different nations who love the same Lord, as a precious mark of discipleship.

The town of Montpélier, say J. and M. Y., is built with taste and elegance, and the situation is most delightful: there are 4,000 Protestants in a population of 36,000.  On Sixth-day (the 10th) we left this place of deep interest, with hearts grateful to the God and Father of all our sure mercies, in that he had enabled us to bear a testimony to the spirituality of worship as set forth by our Saviour himself.

After leaving Montpélier, they continue the narrative of their journey as follows:—

We lodged that night at Passanas, a dark Roman Catholic town.  Inquiring if there were any Protestants, the chambermaid replied, "Protestants! what is that?"  When we had made her understand, she said there were a few, but they went to Montagnac to *mass*.

11*th.*—We slept at Narbonne, an ancient town of 10,000 inhabitants. No openness to receive even a tract; the inquiry for a Protestant excited an evident bitterness in the reply.

On the 12th, held our little meeting with our faithful friend Jules, in which ability was granted to supplicate for the spread of divine light over this benighted district. At 9 o'clock we set out to make a Sabbath-day's journey: the wind extremely high and always in our face, which fatigued Nimrod [their horse] as well as ourselves. We dined at Lesengnan: not a Protestant in the place, yet we met with a circumstance worth recording. Jules, who is ever watchful to find out who can read, gave a few tracts to some boys in the stable-yard. When I went out, writes J. Y., to see our horse, several rather bright-looking boys followed me, asking for books. After ascertaining that they could read, I supplied them. This was no sooner known, than boys and girls came in crowds, soon followed by many of their parents. As our visitors increased, I ran upstairs to fetch my dear M. Y., and we embraced the opportunity to speak to them on the importance of religion. No doubt curiosity drew many to us, for we were a novel sight there, and the mingled multitude was not less so to us. Among our auditors was a messenger of Satan to buffet us. He was a good-looking man, who expressed a seeming approval of what we had done, saying we made many friends. We told him they were all children of the same Almighty Parent, and that there was but one true religion and one heaven. This observation drew off his mask, and he began to express doubts whether either heaven or hell really existed, and brought forward the threadbare argument of not believing what he could not see or prove. We asked him if he had a soul: he said he had. We asked him how he knew that he had a soul, for he could not see it: he replied, he believed that he had a soul, but that his soul would die with his body. We then asked him why two and two made four: he said he could not tell, and yet acknowledged he was bound to believe it. The countenances of many around beamed with joy at seeing this darkling perplexed; and we did not shrink from exhorting him to repentance and faith in Christ, who died for him and for all men.

On returning to our room the landlady entered with a fine-looking girl, for whom she begged a book. This opened our way to speak to her of things connected with salvation. She said,—"We have not much of religion here." "Why so?" we asked. "Because the people do not like to confess to the priests." "And what is the use," said we, "of confessing to man?" "Because," she replied in somewhat trembling accents, "we think it eases our consciences, for the priests are the appointed ministers to take charge of our souls." "What," we replied, "a man take charge of immortal souls! God never committed the power to forgive sins to man: Jesus Christ alone can pardon sins; he died to save us!" I shall never forget the countenance of this dear woman, which seemed to express her long-shaken confidence in her spiritual guides. We exhorted her to come to the Saviour, who intercedes for us without the aid of man, and gave her a New Testament, which she said she would read.

*12th.*—Went to Maux to sleep. The landlady was communicative: she told us that some travellers like ourselves some time ago had given her a New Testament, which she had lent about the village, together with tracts, and that she wished for more. We inquired if there were any persons in the village who would like to come to us for books. She soon sent us an interesting young woman, a schoolmistress, to whom on her entrance we presented some tracts. She regarded them with an air of thoughtfulness which seemed to measure the quantity to be taken by the price she would have to pay for them. When she found they were to be had gratis, her countenance brightened, and with it the brightness of her mind showed itself. On speaking with her of the responsibility of her profession, and the importance of imbuing the minds of children with just principles, she said, "I am desirous of instructing the children in the religion of the heart. Religion," added she, "though a good thing, is badly put in practice in our church; the people do not like to confess to the priests,

and there is a great desire for instruction and to receive
books."

They saw again at the Inn at Maux the man who
had opposed them at Lesengnan, and found him much
better disposed than he had been the day before. He
told them he had been a Romish priest, but being dis-
gusted with the practices of his church, he had left it
and joined the army: he promised to read the books
they gave him.

Our present mode of travelling (with our own horse), they
continue, though somewhat slow, affords opportunities of
endeavoring to do a little good, which we should miss in
travelling by Diligence or extra-post. It is curious and
instructive to observe the various dispositions of the people
in the dark places through which we pass: sometimes they
are so fanatical as to tear a tract before our face; others
receive them with joy. During a half-hour's rest for our
horse at a village near Castelnaudry, my M. Y. made the
acquaintance of an aged woman at the door of her cottage,
who really did us good. On inquiring if she could read, "It
is my consolation," said she, "to read the Scriptures." "And
we have great need of consolation," we answered. "Yes,"
said she, "I am a widow of near eighty years, and have had
many cares; but I pray to God, and he grants me the consolation of his Holy Spirit, and if I confide in him he will
never forsake me."

At Castelnaudry they left the main road and crossed
the mountains to Saverdun, in order to visit the Orphan
Institution in that place.

By not going first to Toulouse, remarks John Yeardley,
we saved about thirty miles of travelling; but it was ill-spared,
for one part of the road was so bad that it required a forespan
of two oxen to drag the carriage through the deep mire and

over the dangerous ditches. After a little dinner at a poor
place in the mountains, we procured a mule as a reinforce-
ment; for we stuck so fast in the mud that I never expected
we should be able to extricate ourselves. My poor M. Y.
had to walk a great part of the way; I am quite sure extra
strength was given us for the emergency. We lodged at
Mazères, where we called on the Protestant minister Bésière,
a most open-hearted Christian. He knew some of our Society,
and wherever this is the case it insures us a welcome. On
our telling him the dangers we had encountered on the road,
and that we had escaped unhurt, he sweetly said,—"The
Angel of the Lord encampeth round about them that fear
Him, and delivereth them."—Psal. xxxiv. 7.

On arriving at Saverdun, on the 17th, we immediately
pursued the object of our visit, and proceeded to the Institution, where we delivered our letters of recommendation,
and received a cordial reception from the director, Pastor
Enjalbal. When the *little porters* opened the door, they
cried one to another, "Voilà des Anglais!" The director
seems to be wonderfully fitted for the post he fills. He was
once a captain in the army. After his conversion, his heart
was penetrated with gratitude to his Saviour for bringing
him to a knowledge of the truth, and he desired to devote
the remainder of his days in doing good to his fellow-
creatures, particularly in the instruction of youth. The
project of the Saverdun school was then in agitation, and a
manager was wanted. The excellent Pastor Chabrand applied
to him, knowing him to be the man for the office if he would
only undertake it. When he visited him for this purpose on
behalf of the committee, he found him in his chamber
weeping, and, as his confidential friend, he asked him what
was the matter. "Why," said he, "my heart overflows
with love to the Saviour, for all that he has done for me, and
I seem to live without doing anything for his cause in
return." "Well," said the pastor, "but the way is now
open for you; I am come with a proposal from the committee
for you to accept the government of the Saverdun Institution; but I will not have an answer from you at present:

weigh the matter for a fortnight, and I will come again and receive your decision." A sense of duty decided him to accept the offer.

The superintendent conducted us to the members of the committee, to whom we had brought a kind introduction from Pastor Frossard of Nismes. The supporters of this institution, are the most influential in the town, rich, and withal pious characters. The Mayor, their secretary, is very active: he with his wife, an excellent woman, and several members of the committee, met us in the evening at our inn; they appeared to be greatly interested in works of benevolence, and in everything connected with religion and education.

*Toulouse*, 3 *mo.* 20.—We arrived in this great and busy city on Seventh-day evening. Our first call was on the brothers Courtois, to whom we had letters of introduction from our Christian friends at Nismes. They received us in a most cordial manner and were very open and communicative.

On First-day morning, after our little meeting, we called on Professor F. Barnier; he was rejoiced to see my M. Y., whom he knew at Congenies twenty years ago. He was then a Roman Catholic; indeed, in name he is not changed; but he is become very spiritually-minded, and much attached to Friends and our principles, believing them, as he said, to be the nearest in accordance of any with the doctrines of the New Testament. He has been, with his wife, several times to our hotel, and we feel sweet unity with his quiet exercised spirit. His situation here is important, having a boarding-school for the children of Protestants, with a few Roman Catholics, his piety and sincerity securing to him the confidence of both parties, which is matter of wonder in this day of religious conflict. He is one of those characters, more of whom we are desirous of finding; one who wishes rather to enlighten than to censure the dark prejudices of men.

We spent the evening with our kind friends the Courtois, and attended worship in their house. F. C. read the parable of the great supper (Luke xiv.), and made some remarks in explication of it; after which Pastor Chabrand spoke with much feeling on the influence of the Holy Spirit, the gradual operation of the Spirit in the secret of the soul, and the preciousness of dwelling in Christ, as the branch in the vine, in order to bear fruit.

Pastor Chabrand told us in conversation that the first time he really saw the state of his soul and his need of a Saviour, was in the meeting-house at Westminster during half an hour's silence. After this time of precious silence a minister arose* and spoke in so remarkable a manner to his state, unfolding the history of his life, that he was melted to tears. Ever since that time he has appreciated the principles of our religious Society, and particularly our practice of waiting upon God in silence. These remarks opened our way to speak on a subject which has often given us pain in our intercourse with pious people, viz., the practice of going suddenly from one religious exercise to another. We expressed our opinion that Christians, in general, in their worship, would derive more edification from what is spoken, if they were to dwell under the good feeling which is sometimes raised, before passing so precipitately to singing, or even to prayer. With this he entirely agreed, and thought it a point of the utmost importance; he wished it could be put in practice, for their church in general suffered loss for want of more quiet gathering of spirit before God.

John and Martha Yeardley did not go further towards the west than Toulouse; on quitting that city they turned northwards to Montauban.

For several days, so they write, before reaching the extent of our journey westward, we travelled through a fertile country, having the Pyrenean mountains on the south, covered with snow, a magnificent sight for those who travel to see the beauties of nature, but our hearts are often too heavy to enjoy them.

---

* We believe Joseph John Gurney is here referred to.

*Montauban, 3 mo.* 23. — Last evening we reached this pretty town, part of which is built on a high cliff overlooking the river Tarn, and commanding an extensive view over a fertile plain. Our first call was on Professor Monod; his wife is an Englishwoman; she was pleased to see her compatriots, and introduced us to Professor de Félice and some other pious individuals. Professor Monod invited us to spend the evening at their house, along with a number of persons who join in their family reading, and we did not think it right to refuse the invitation. A pretty large company assembled in the professor's room at 8 o'clock, among whom were some students of the college. The eighth chapter of the Epistle to the Romans was read, and some remarks made by the professor; he then kindly said, if we had any word of exhortation in our hearts, e hoped we should feel quite at liberty to express it. We felt it right to make some observations with reference to the fore-part of the chapter, which sets forth that state of Christian experience in which the mind is prepared to participate in the many precious promises contained in the middle and latter portions; ability was also given us to express our faith in the one Saviour and Mediator, and in the influence and guidance of the Holy Spirit, and his office in the sanctification of the soul. This favored opportunity closed with supplication. We are well satisfied with our visit to this place; it has removed some prejudices from our minds, and perhaps may have shown to those with whom we have had intercourse that Friends are sound in the faith. The short time we spent with Professor de Félice has left a sweet impression on our minds. He mourned over the want of spiritual life among the Protestants of Montauban, amid, as he said, "much preaching, and many appeals to conscience."

At Castres, where they stopped on the 26th, they visited the Orphan House, and held intercourse with the pastors, and with a pious lawyer.

On our journey, says John Yeardley, we had heard of a

man near this town who bore the name of Quaker, and we
inquired of the lawyer if he knew whether he was sound in
the Christian faith. The lawyer spoke with respect of the so-
called Quaker, but thought that in his opinions he favored
Arianism. "If so," said I, rather hastily, "we will not seek
him or recognize him." "Why," said the advocate, "it is
the very reason you should go to see him, and try to do him
good." At this reply my conscience was stung on account of
my hasty conclusion; and after reflecting on the matter, we
walked next morning five or six miles into the country in
search of the new Friend. He received us with joy, and we
soon satisfied ourselves as to his soundness in the Christian
faith; but. he was rather ardent in his expectations of the
reign of Christ on the earth. Twenty years ago he refused to
take an oath on a jury; the judge told him he must go to
prison, to which the Friend replied, "I am willing to go to
prison, but I cannot swear to condemn any person to death;
if you place me as juryman I shall acquit all the criminals."
The judge, believing his scruples to be sincere, dismissed him
without further trouble. This dear man attached himself to
us in such a manner that it was difficult to part from him; he
pressed us to remain some days in his house, but this our duty
did not permit.

From Castres they returned through Béziers to
Nismes, visiting various little companies of Protestants
by the way, and arrived in the latter city on the 1st of
the Fourth Month. They found that the school had
increased in numbers, and the scholars had made good
progress.

On entering the school-room, says J. Y., the girls all flocked
to us, their black eyes sparkling with joy, while they clung
round us with their little arms to be embraced. The harmony
and peaceful feelings which pervade the family are truly
comforting to our hearts.

In taking a retrospect of what they had done up

to this time, they write thus to their Friends in England :—

The manner in which our gracious Lord has condescended
to open the way for a portion of labor in this part of his
vineyard, adds a grain to our faith: the service which has
hitherto fallen to our lot on this journey is of that nature
towards which we had a view before we left our native land;
and we are bound gratefully to acknowledge, amid many
conflicts and discouragements, that sweet peace is sometimes
our portion. But our dear friends in England will readily
conceive that our baptisms are various and deep, during our
separation from the bosom of our own little visible church;
and we hope to retain a place in their sympathy and prayers,
when they are favored with access to the throne of mercy.
Our love flows freely and unceasingly to all our dear friends,
from whom it is always comforting to hear. Brethren, pray
for us, that the word of the Lord may have free course and
be glorified.

On the 18th of the Fourth Month they again left
Nismes, and commenced their journey towards Switzerland, accompanied, as before, by Jules Paradon. On
their way to Grenoble, they had opportunities of
spreading many copies of the *Scripture Extracts*, which
they had with them, among the Roman Catholics; and
they had also some interesting conversation with individuals of that profession.

At Tullins, they write, the eagerness to receive books was
so great, that a crowd soon assembled around us, and we
found it difficult to satisfy them; again, at the moment of our
departure, they pressed round our carriage, and we could
hardly separate ourselves from them.

On the 22nd (to continue their own narrative) we arrived
at Grenoble, with a view to spend First-day there. A letter
from one of our acquaintances at Nismes to Pastor Bonifas
procured us a kind reception, and he invited us to spend

First-day evening at his house, where a meeting was to be
held. We did not, however, feel quite at liberty to attend, as
we found the regular church-service would be performed. The
next day we received another invitation from the Pastor to a
meeting where only the Scriptures would be read. We
thought it best to accept it, and by going a little before the
time proposed, we had a very interesting conversation with
the Pastor, his wife, and a young Englishwoman, on our
peculiar views. The meeting was an assembly of various
classes, with a preponderance of young persons, and was a
very interesting occasion: many of the young people were
deeply affected. In the morning of this day we had been to
see an aged Catholic woman of the Jansenist persuasion: she
appeared to have no dependence but on her Saviour, and,
full of faith and love, to have her conversation in heaven; she
gave us a sweet benediction at parting.

They left Grenoble on the 25th, and pursued their
way by Chambéry to Geneva, taking care to dispose of
most of their French tracts by the way, lest they should
be stopped at the Savoy custom-house. They arrived
in the city of Calvin on the 27th.

Here, as on former occasions, they found much to
interest them. Several of the ministers and professors
whom they had known before, seemed to have become
more spiritually-minded; and with the flock of the
deceased Pastor Monnié, in particular, "of precious
memory," they were united in near Christian fellowship.

It seems to us, they write, that the feeling is spreading of
the necessity of the immediate guidance of the Holy Spirit;
and we believe that this view of the gospel, with that of the
universality of divine love, is much more calculated to win
upon unbelievers, and to enlighten Romanists, than the high
Calvinistic doctrines which have so generally prevailed, and
which impede the growth of Christian humility and daily
dependence on divine help.

At our little meeting on First-day morning, we had the company of a widow and her daughter. The former is like a mother to those around her who are seeking spiritual things, and we were much comforted together. She invited us to tea, and to have a meeting in her house the next evening: a considerable number were collected, among whom were a pastor, several professors, and many females. The pastor read a chapter; and when, after a time of silence, the way opened for communication, it was like casting seed into prepared ground, and the retirement of spirit before the Lord which we recommended seemed really to be experienced before we separated; it was a silence to be felt better than expressed.

Amongst other pious persons in this city, they had an introduction to the Countess de Sellon.

She received us, says J. Y., with open heart, saying, "I am fond of the principles of your Society, believing they have the real substance of religion, stripped of its forms." She asked us many questions, and we felt sweet unity with her.

On the 3rd of the Fifth Month they went to Lausanne, where they renewed their friendship with Professor Gaudin, and had interviews with several other seeking persons.

We were, they say, most interested by a pious magistrate, Frossard de Saugy, near relative to a dear friend of ours at Geneva. He inquired respecting the education of children, of whom he has many—by what means he could make them sensible of vital religion. We replied that all we could do was to represent to them the love and mercy of our blessed Redeemer, and recommend them to cherish the convictions of his Holy Spirit, which are very early bestowed upon us all: he entirely united in our views.

From Lausanne they went to Yverdun, and the day after to Neufchâtel. Since their last visit in 1834, some who were very dear to them had been summoned to eternal rest, which cast a shade of natural sorrow over their entrance into the place: and they were called upon, in addition, deeply to sympathise with some of those who remained.

The family of Professor Pétavel has sustained a great loss in the death of his eldest son, accompanied by circumstances peculiarly striking. This young man was about nineteen years of age. He had been very serious for some time before his illness, and wished much to be employed as a missionary. Early instructed by his mother in the importance of seeking divine influence, his mind was prepared to receive the baptism of the Holy Spirit; and he had a deep conflict to pass through, which he confided to his mother, and which he seemed to think was the presage to suffering. In performing some gymnastic exercises he received a fall on the head, which after some time was followed by a paralytic affection of the whole body, so that he became entirely helpless, and his speech was taken away. It was only his tender mother who could ascertain his wants and administer to them, which she did with unceasing assiduity. After about six months his speech was almost miraculously restored, and he used it in praising the Lord for the remarkable support and consolation of his Spirit. He said he had been sensible of all that had passed, and that he had been abundantly confirmed in the belief that true religion consists in hearing the voice of our blessed Redeemer, and seeking to do his will. After some time the capability of speaking much again forsook him; yet he lingered some months longer, and when M. Y. beheld him soon after our arrival, he appeared like a precious lamb purified, and waiting to be gathered to the everlasting fold. The resignation of his parents was truly edifying: they proposed that we should both come the next day, and sit quietly beside him for a while. This proved a deeply impressive time; the presence of the Great Shepherd was evidently with us, and called forth thanksgiving for the mercies received and the deliverance anticipated.    While listening to a few words addressed to him at parting, he fixed his dying eyes upon us with an expression not to be forgotten, and before midnight the precious spirit was received into the arms of its Saviour.    As we left for Locle early in the morning, we did not hear of this until our return the day following.

Their visit to their favorite orphan-institution was, as ever, very interesting.    They thus describe the state in which they found it :—

Our dear German friend M. Zimmerlin, the associate of dear M. A. Calame, still lives : she received us with over-flowing affection.    After tea, which we took there, she hastened to show us the improvements in the premises, which, she said, our kind friends in England had contributed to procure by their donations through us.    The institution appears to be now in excellent order.    In the evening, the children, 138 in number, were collected with the mistresses and family, and we had a very satisfactory opportunity with them.    The same precious influence seems to prevail which we have noticed heretofore.

They returned to Neufchâtel the next evening, where they heard that the remains of Paul Pétavel were to be interred the next day.

His father, they add, was desirous that the meeting we intended to hold with our friends should be held at his house that evening.    When M. Y. went to see the family, she found the parents full of gratitude and praise.    The funeral was attended by the students from the college, and a large number of others ; for the professor is much beloved, and the affecting situation of his son has been a lesson of instruction to the young people who used to associate with him, and

seems to have had an effect on the whole town.  The evening
of this day proved to be a memorable time: a considerable
number were collected, among whom were several pastors
and a number of young persons.  I seldom, says J. Y., remember to have attended a more solemn occasion.  The
Saviour's presence was near, to console and instruct.  After
my M. Y. and I had relieved our minds in testimony and
supplication, the professor and the other pastors spoke with
much feeling; I think it was evident they were constrained
by the Spirit.  We parted (to resume the words of their joint
epistle) from the family under a strong conviction of the
support and consolation which those experience who depend
in living faith upon their blessed Redeemer.

From Neufchâtel, John and Martha Yeardley went
to Berne, where they renewed the bond of friendship
with those to whose spiritual state they had ministered
in former years.  With these they united several times
in worship and in social religious intercourse.  At the
close of one of these meetings, the lady of the house, an
active and benevolent character, acknowledged, that she
was sensible of the truth of what they had heard, and
believed that in the present day the Lord was leading
many of his devoted children to listen to his voice, that
they might be brought more under the teachings of
his Spirit, and from this would flow their consolation.
" This (they observe) is the more remarkable, as, when
we were here before, she held views on election and
the *finished* work of grace, almost to the exclusion of
the work of ' regeneration and the renewing of the Holy
Ghost.' "

We find in some here, writes John Yeardley in his Diary,
a desire for food of a more spiritual nature: they really
enjoy waiting on the Lord in silence; but the customary
activity is strong, and not easily broken through.  I trust

22

the day will come when silence will more prevail in the assemblies of the people. We left Berne with feelings of peace and of much affection for many in that place, and thankful to our Heavenly Father, in that he had prepared the hearts of his people to receive the invitation to feed on that spiritual food which alone can nourish the soul to eternal life.

They arrived at Basle on the 17th. Since they had visited this city in 1834, Hoffmann, the director of the institution at Kornthal, had succeeded Blumhardt in the superintendence of the Mission-house. He received them with his usual kindness, and one evening they supped with the students, and had a religious meeting with them. They spent another evening with a pious family, where several missionaries and pastors were present. In speaking of this occasion, John and Martha Yeardley were led into a reflection which deserves to be pondered by Christians of every name.

Before separating, they say, the Scriptures were read, and some of the missionaries spoke on the importance of uniting in desire for a more general outpouring of the Spirit: J. Y. also spoke much to the same effect. It was, we trust, a profitable season; but the reflection arose on this occasion, as it has done on some others when among serious persons not of our profession, that if they would but suffer the degree of divine influence mercifully afforded thoroughly to baptize the heart with the true baptism, much creaturely activity would be done away, and the light of the gospel would shine in them and through them in much greater purity.

We paid and received visits, they continue, from some of the *Intérieurs* whom we had known before, and had to lament something of a visionary spirit in the midst of right feeling. We recommended simplicity, and close attention to the Scriptures and to the Shepherd's voice.

One day John Yeardley went into the mountains to
see an establishment called the Pilgrim Mission Institution, where he was interested in meeting three young
men from Syria, who had come there to escape the
scenes of war in their own country, and with the desire
to be rendered capable of instructing their countrymen.

They left Basle on the 22nd, and entered Germany.
They were, for a time, a good deal embarrassed with
the change of language from French to German, having
had little or no occasion to use the latter tongue during
their journey. They stopped at Carlsruhe, where they
called, with an introduction, on the Princess of Würtemberg.

She received us, they say, very kindly, and we had a
satisfactory interview with her, and also with an interesting
female who has the charge of her children. After much
conversation with the princess in French, she introduced us
to her three lovely children, and asked J. Y. to give them a
word of exhortation. We remained silent awhile, and, under
a precious feeling, offered prayer for the divine blessing on
this family and all its branches; after which the word of
sympathy and exhortation flowed freely. At parting, the
princess took a cordial leave of us, and said she received our
visit as a blessing from the Lord.

The next day they pursued their way towards
Pyrmont. Being weary with travelling, and their
horses also needing rest, they tarried two days at Frankfort. Here they saw their old friend Von Meyer; and
spent much of their time in the company of Dr.
Pinkerton. " I was instructed," says J. Y., " with
seeing the charity and Christian meekness in which he
daily lives."

On the 3rd of the Sixth Month they reached

Pyrmont, where they remained a few weeks. They
attended on the 2nd of the Seventh Month the Two-
months' Meeting, at Minden. Many peasants were
present in the meeting for worship, and on John and
Martha Yeardley's return to Pyrmont, some of them
came to the meeting there on First-day, and begged
the Friends to go to Vlotho to meet a company of their
brethren. They gave the peasants liberty to call a
meeting at that place for Third-day, the 18th.

On Second-day, as they were setting off, an accident
happened to John Yeardley.

He had left the horse's head, writes M. Y., to attend to
placing the baggage, when, hearing another carriage drive
rapidly up, our horse set off, and my J. Y., in attempting to
stop him by catching hold of the reins, fell, and was much
bruised, but through mercy no limb was broken. We applied
what means were in our power, and I urged our remaining at
Pyrmont, and sending to defer the meeting; but he would go
on to Lemgo. His whole frame was much shaken, and we
passed a sleepless night, so that the meeting next day was not
a little formidable. It proved a much longer journey to
Vlotho than we had expected; when we arrived we found
a large number assembled. Five of our Friends came from
Minden to meet us, and it was a remarkable meeting, notwithstanding we had gone to it under so much discouragement:
we have cause to bless and adore our Divine Master, who
caused his presence to be felt amongst us. August Mund-
henck interpreted for J. Y. and for me. J. R. also suffered
his voice to be acceptably heard in testimony, after which the
meeting closed in solemn supplication. We pursued our
way that night to Bielefeld and the next day towards the
Rhine.

On their way home they stopped at Düsseldorf.
The ten years which had gone by since they had visited
the Orphan Asylum at Düsselthal, near this town, had

wrought a great change in the physical condition of Count Von der Recke. He looked worn and ill, the effect of care and anxiety for his numerous adopted family; but he evinced a spirit of pious resignation, and had a hearty welcome ready for his visitors. They returned to England through Belgium, and arrived in London on the 8th of the Eighth Month.

They did not at once return to their home at Scarborough, but spent a month in Hertford, Oxford and Buckinghamshire, attending the meetings of Friends in these counties, and visiting that of Berkhamstead several times.

# CHAPTER XVI.

## 1843–48.

THE tour which John and Martha Yeardley made in
and around Buckinghamshire, and which is mentioned
at the conclusion of the last chapter, was undertaken in
quest of a new place of abode.   In a letter from Martha
Yeardley to her sister, Mary Tylor, written on the 3rd
of the Eleventh Month, she says :—

Thou art aware that we have thought, if way should open,
of going nearer to you, and of pitching our tent within the
Quarterly Meeting of Buckinghamshire.   We offered to purchase a cottage at Berkhamstead, but for the present that
has quite fallen through : we therefore intend to rest quietly
here for the winter, in hopes that in the spring or summer
something may offer, either at B. or in that quarter, to which
we feel attracted ; yet desiring to commit this and all that
concerns us into the all-directing hand of our great Lord
and Master, who has a right to do with us what seemeth
him good.

Not long afterwards they purchased a house at
Berkhamstead, called Gossom Lodge, to which they
removed in the Fourth Month, 1844.

Very soon after they had taken possession of their
new dwelling, they made a circuit through the meetings
of Buckinghamshire and Northamptonshire, holding a
few public meetings by the way: and the next summer

(334)

they undertook a more extensive religious visit—viz.,
to the six northern counties of England.

In the course of the same year we find them meditating a further removal, into the immediate vicinity of
London. One of the few entries in his Diary which
were made by John Yeardley during this period,
speaks of the apprehension of duty under which they
contemplated this change: it was written after their
removal.

For some years past I have often thought the time might
come when we might see it right to settle within Stoke
Newington Meeting. This feeling now began (1845) to
fasten more strongly on our minds than it had done before,
and we thought it right to make an effort to let Gossom
Lodge, and seek a residence at Stamford Hill; and we have
reason to believe that in this important step our prayer has
been answered, and that all our deliberations have been
guided by that wisdom which is from above. Very strong is
my conviction that our Heavenly Father is not unmindful of
the outward circumstances of those who seek his counsel, and
desire to act under the guidance of his Holy Spirit. We
were favored to let our house at Berkhamstead without
trouble; the very first person to whom we made it known
took it off our hands: and with equal ease we found another
dwelling at Stamford Hill, which I consider as a proof that
our prayer was heard and answered in this serious step: the
signs I had asked were granted.

They removed to Stamford Hill on the 2nd of the
Twelfth Month, 1845. As soon as they had settled in,
John Yeardley became seriously indisposed with his old
complaint, which ended in the jaundice. In the course
of the spring and summer of 1846 he repaired with M.
Y. to Bath, and afterwards to Harrowgate, to seek a
restoration of his health.

The waters of the last-named place proved, he says, very efficacious both to my beloved M. Y. and myself. My precious dear, he continues, suffered much in her health through the fatigue of nursing me during the winter. How my soul overflows with gratitude to my Heavenly Father that he has united me to such a partner, who takes more than a full share in all my sorrows; and, thanks be unto our God, we have often to rejoice also together in Him!

On their return from Harrowgate they visited many of the meetings in London and the vicinity,—a service which they had always had in view, in looking towards a residence at Stamford Hill; and from the Eleventh Month, 1846, to the First Month, 1847, they were occupied in a religious visit to the families of the members and attenders of Gracechurch-street Monthly Meeting, in which their service was very acceptable.

The friends appointed to arrange the visits, says J. Y., have done so with willingness and efficiency, and we have, I believe, the help of their spirits. In passing from house to house, we are made sensible of our inability to render aid to others unassisted by the Spirit of our Divine Master. Wherever we have gone we have been received with kindness and Christian cordiality; and in thus being permitted to mingle our feelings with those who are bound up with us in religious profession, we feel sweet peace and comfort, and our hearts are filled with thankfulness to the Lord, that he has enabled us to do that which we believe he put into our hearts.

They returned the minute which had been granted them for this service on the 6th of the First Month. Many who read this Memoir will remember how the tidings of the death of Joseph John Gurney, who suddenly expired on the 5th, spread through the Society, and produced wherever it came an impression of sorrow-

ful but heavenly solemnity. The event is referred to
in the notice of this meeting which is contained in the
Diary.

The meeting for worship was particularly solemn. The
spirit of our dear departed friend J. J. G. seemed present
with us. The event had impressed our minds with the
awful uncertainty of time. My dear M. Y. ministered to our
comfort, and so did dear ——. I was constrained, under
a sense that the Lord had withdrawn many laborers from
his vineyard, to lift up a prayer for the remnant that is left,
to crave prosperity for the blessed work of grace in the hearts
of all present, and to ask for more devotedness to the Lord's
cause.

The next day they received intelligence of the decease
of one of their Scarborough friends, whose dying words
are worthy to be preserved in lasting remembrance.

1 mo. 7.—On returning from meeting we found a letter
informing us of the sudden decease of Isaac Stickney of
Scarborough. When the doctor attempted to give him brandy
in his sinking state, he said, Doctor, don't cloud my intellect;
if this be dying, I die in the arms of Jesus. These last words
of my beloved and long-known friend are sweetly consoling
to my spirit.

In the Second Month of 1848, John Yeardley again
prepared to go forth and preach the Gospel in several
countries on the Continent of Europe. He was accompanied by his beloved wife, partly in the character of a
fellow-laborer, constrained by the force of Christian love
to the same field of service, and partly as his companion and helper in countries where she did not
otherwise feel herself called to labor. The course
of their anticipated travel is described in the following
extract from the Diary. They were unable, as it proved,

to obtain admission into the Russian Empire; and this part of the mission was accomplished by John Yeardley alone, and at a later period.

1848. 2 mo. 8.—At our Monthly Meeting at Gracechurch street, I proposed my concern to visit some parts of South Russia, particularly the German colonies; also some places in the Prussian and Austrian dominions, parts of Switzerland and France, particularly Ardèche, and a few places in Belgium, and to revisit parts of Germany. My precious M. Y. also was constrained in gospel love to tell her friends that she had long thought of a visit to France and Belgium; and, if health permitted, should think it her religious duty to accompany me to South Russia. We had the full unity of our friends, who expressed much sympathy and encouragement, to our great comfort. It is about twenty years since I first thought seriously that I might have to visit the Crimea, and for thirty years I have had a prospect of some parts of Bohemia. Truly the vision has been for an appointed time; and if the period be now come, I trust it is the Lord's time, and that his presence may go with us. Many have been the conflicts and deep the baptisms through which I have passed, before coming to a willingness to offer to do what I believe to be the will of my Divine Master. Feeble as are my powers, I desire they may be devoted to his cause for the remainder of my days; and I do esteem it a great mercy to have arrived at a clear pointing in this important prospect. May the blessing of preservation rest upon the beloved partner of my sorrows and my joys, and on myself; and may He whom we desire to serve heal all our maladies of body and mind!

While their attention was thus turned to foreign lands, a storm was gathering in France which in the course of this month burst upon Europe with extraordinary violence, and overturned or endangered half the thrones on the Continent. This convulsed state of the European nations rendered it needful for them to wait a few months before they commenced their undertaking. In the Seventh Month, John Yeardley speaks of having obtained the further concurrence of the church, and of the feelings which the immediate prospect of the journey awakened in his mind.

7 *mo.* 1.—At the Quarterly Meeting, and also at the Yearly Meeting of Ministers and Elders, our friends entered very fully into our proposed visit to the Continent. The expression of sympathy and full unity was abundant; there was a strong evidence of the good presence of the Lord being near during the deliberations, which proved a strength and comfort to myself and my beloved partner. The needful certificates are now all in our possession, and are expressed in terms the most appropriate and encouraging. My mind is deeply humbled at the near approach of our departure, in the present state of affairs on the continent of Europe: but I feel a confiding hope in the divine power for protection and safe guidance. May the Lord Almighty give us strength and resignation to commit our lives into his hand, and to say, Thy will be done. Amen!

This series of travels was the last in which John and Martha Yeardley were to be engaged as joint-laborers in their Lord's work. The health of the latter had been for several years seriously affected; and although she continued to take a deep interest in the spiritual condition of the countries they had visited before, and was enabled to the end to afford her husband the assistance of her strong sympathy and of her religious exercise of mind, the fatigue of constant travelling told more and more upon her enfeebled frame, and she did not long survive the accomplishment of this journey. John Yeardley, less advanced in years, and possessing a hardy constitution, had not yet lost the fire of his earlier days. The same spring and impulse was still strong within him which had animated him in former journeys, and which those who knew him in middle life will not fail to remember. Some of these will have before them the mental image of his person and manner—the fixed resolution, the concentrated mind, the ardent and devoted spirit, which shone through his impressive countenance and his whole figure, when he was engaged in his Lord's work; and perhaps also they may call to mind the very words of faithful counsel, or of encouragement, drawn from the well-spring of gospel sympathy, which fell from his lips.

John and Martha Yeardley did not accomplish the extensive mission which now lay before them at one stroke, but in three stages, returning to England between each. The most prominent object in the first journey was Belgium; in the second, the Rhine country; in the third, they were called to sow seeds of Christian doctrine in lands lying beyond the limit of any former travel—viz., in Silesia and Bohemia.

This was the first time that the Roman Catholic country of Belgium had called forth the exercise of their Christian charity. They left London in the Seventh Month, and spent about three weeks in travelling through the country, resting chiefly at Ghent, Brussels, Charleroi and Spa. They were accompanied as far as Brussels by Robert and Christine Alsop, and through the whole journey, by an ingenuous young man whom they had engaged to assist them, named Adolphe Rochedieu. The religious opening which awaited them at Brussels was very encouraging; few incidents which arose in the course of their numerous journeys were of a more animating character than the acquaintance which they made with the pastor Van Maasdyk and some of his flock. We give the narrative from J. Y.'s Diary and letters.

7 *mo.* 19.—H. Van Maasdyk paid us a long visit this morning. He was educated in a convent in Belgium, and becoming a priest, he exercised the functions which devolved upon him with much credit to himself, and to the satisfaction of his superiors, until the year 1836. He possessed a Bible in Latin, which he never read. He had the cure of a large parish, in which, down to the year above mentioned, there was not a single copy of the Scriptures in the Flemish tongue. About that time the colporteurs introduced the New Testament in Flemish, and some copies of the Bible, which greatly excited the priests, and in particular the bishop, who said the translation was mutilated and falsified, and commanded that the members of the Catholic Church who had received copies, should either burn them themselves, or bring them to the curés for that purpose. Van Maasdyk's parishioners accordingly brought their Bibles and Testaments (five copies) to him to be burned. He was zealous in the Romish faith, and had preached violently against the distributors of the wicked books, as they were called; and he was about to fulfil the command to burn them, when suddenly he felt something in his heart which restrained him, and he thought, I will at least first examine the foundation of the bishop's charges. He took up his Latin Bible, and placing beside it the copy in Flemish, began with the charge of mutilation. He found it not at all abridged. He then went to the charge of falsification, and found the two copies to agree with slight variations here and there; in fact, the modern translation proved to have been made from the Vulgate, which was the one in his possession. He read the denunciation of our Saviour, "Woe unto you Scribes and Pharisees, hypocrites," and it struck him forcibly; he felt that he must say, "Woe is me, I am one of those who deceive the people." He read again, "There is one Mediator between God and man;" and here again his conscience smote him: "Woe is me, I teach the people in their confessions that the saints make intercession." His sorrow was so deep, that he thought he could die a thousand deaths rather than continue a Romish priest.

Now his persecution began. He was beloved by his flock, who entreated him not to leave them. After much conflict of mind, he wrote a decided letter to his bishop, who in the end gave him his dismissal. Still feeling himself called to proclaim the Gospel, he began to assemble the people in little companies, and to instruct them in the Scriptures. At the entreaty of his friends he settled at Brussels, where there was a wide field for labor amongst the poorest of the Roman Catholics, who speak only Flemish. His congregation consisted at first of some fifteen or twenty persons; but such was the success he met with, that they have been obliged four or five times in succession to seek a larger building, and his congregation now consists of 500. He is said to be one of the most powerful preachers in the Flemish language. It is delightful to be in his company; his heart is filled with gratitude, and his eyes sparkle with joy, when he is with those who love the Saviour. Nothing is paid him by his congregation; he has a little property of his own, and sometimes receives a little help from the Adolphus Society.

After a long conversation with him on the spiritual nature of worship, he took us to see some of his flock, with whom we had family sittings from house to house. This is exactly the class our hearts longed to visit; thanks be to our Heavenly Father who has thus opened our way.

*20th.*—The meeting at Pastor Marzial's last evening was much larger than we had expected. Van Maasdyk came in unexpectedly after the service which had been held at his dwelling, and with him a part of his flock. Many of the company were those who had renounced Romanism; some of the young men interested us exceedingly. I had a deal of conversation with them as to their religious experience. There were several young Germans among them, who are residing in Brussels; with these I conversed in their own language, which was highly gratifying to them. As Pastor Marzial speaks English well, I clung to him in the hope of having him for an interpreter; but he encouraged me to speak as well as I could in French, as the natives like it much better, and consider it a compliment to their language. This made me very low, it being a company of well-educated persons, and I asked Van Maasdyk what I should do. I would rather, he replied, hear ten words from your own mouth, than ten thousand through the mouth of another; we shall understand you, and what comes from the heart goes to the heart. This settled the question; I gave myself up to the language, and was helped through. My M. Y. was favored in her communication. After a short address from M., I concluded the meeting with supplication, also in French. I do believe the Spirit was poured upon us from on high; many hearts were touched, and tears flowed freely from many eyes.

The Lord has indeed opened a wide door for us in this place; the dear people follow us from meeting to meeting, entreating us for an opportunity of the like kind in their own houses; but we must be watchful to see our own way. However, if the oil is staid, it is not for want of vessels, for what we have to communicate seems like seed cast into the prepared ground. May the Lord himself be their teacher, and carry on his own work; for it is most assuredly his. To those who are spiritually minded, to hear of a society holding spiritual views, is like marrow to their bones. It is not so much what we are able to say to them, but our being as living witnesses to the truth which these awakened people feel in their own hearts.

21st.—Attended a meeting of Van Maasdyk's in the poorer district of Brussels; about seventy to eighty persons present, consisting of converted Romanists, seeking Protestants, and two awakened Jews. Two of the company were blind men, very pious, who gain their living by selling matches. Our friend read, explained, and applied the tenth chapter of John, in Flemish; he also interpreted for me a few words, which I spoke in German.

On their way to Charleroi, after passing through Mons, they traversed the great Belgium iron and coal

country, where the people speak a patois but understand
French. Here they made a free distribution of the
religious tracts they had taken with them, and found an
able co-adjutor in their postillion. When he understood
what their object was, he allowed few opportunities to
pass by without putting these little messengers into the
hands of his fellow-countrymen.

At Charleroi, where they arrived on the 22d, they
enjoyed Christian association of the most interesting
kind, especially with Pastors Poinsot and Jaccard, and
with Marzial, who followed them from Brussels. They
seem to have found much more of the life of religion
among the newly-awakened in Belgium than they had
expected.

We have, says J. Y., good reason to believe that the burden
we have so long felt for the inhabitants in some parts of
Belgium was laid upon us by our Divine Master, who is now
pleased to make way for us to throw it off; thanks be to his
great name.

From Charleroi they went by Liège to Spa, where
they procured a lodging in order to enjoy a period of
needful rest. The tracts they gave away on the road
were received with eagerness. Adolphe handed them
out freely right and left, and when any one hesitated to
take them, a significant nod from the postillion never
failed to secure a ready reception.

The country from Namur to Liège, writes John Yeardley,
and particularly from Liège to Spa, is beautiful, the road
running along the banks of the Meuse, amid wooded rocks.
These are the works of my Heavenly Father, but I sigh
after the workmanship of his hands, created after his own
image.

Passing over several incidents of religious intercourse and labor, we select a circumstance which illustrates the state of the country, and of their own feelings in relation to it.

Under date of Spa, the 2nd of the Eighth Month, John Yeardley says :—

My M. Y. made acquaintance with an interesting young woman in a shop, and gave her some of the *Scripture Extracts*. She came to us last evening, and remained some time conversing on the Romish religion. She had never seen the Bible. When we asked her what was the nature of the mass, she said she did not understand it, but she attended it because others did. We gave her the Bible used by ourselves, having no other at our disposal. Her eyes sparkled with joy at the newly-acquired treasure. Her heart is touched by the Spirit of God, and I humbly hope her eyes will be enlightened to seek for strength independently of her blind guides. I never saw and felt more sensibly the awful account the priests will have to give for thus deceiving the people in the things which belong to their salvation.

On the 3rd they quitted Belgium, and proceeded to Bonn. Here they had the pleasure of meeting their old friend, Charles Majors, formerly of Strasburg. In a walk which they took with him, they renewed the sweet intercourse of former days.

8 *mo*. 5.—We took a walk with Majors and his family to the top of "Mount Calvary," and mounted a steep hill pitched with sharp stones, on which the poor Romanists go barefooted, repeating prayers at each station, supposed to be as many as the times when our Lord rested when bearing his cross from the gate of Jerusalem to Mount Calvary. Having descended, we sat down at the foot of a cross, and spoke of Him who bore our sins on the cross in his own body. A

23

desire was felt and expressed that the little company might ever dwell near to Him who died on the cross.

At Mannheim, John Yeardley writes :—

I took a walk in the public gardens, opposite the Hotel de l'Europe, where we lodge. All very quiet without, and I felt peaceful within myself, reading a chapter and sitting alone. The Spirit of my Divine Master was near, and I felt assured that there was something in this place with which we could unite.

They found here a little company, who met together without any regular pastor.

They gave us, says John Yeardley, a cordial reception, and their countenances indicated that they had been with Jesus; and, although scattered as sheep among wolves, they appeared to belong to the fold of the true Shepherd. After a few family calls, we were conducted to the house of a pious widow, where the meetings were usually held. As we were in haste, these Christian people kindly appointed a meeting for worship, to be held the same evening, to receive our visit, which, through divine mercy, proved like a refreshing brook by the way : the Saviour's presence being over us, his doctrine dropped like dew on the thirsty ground.*

At Strasburg they found Pastor Ehrmann, and several other pious persons whom they had known in 1833, with whom and with some others they had much conversation on religious subjects, and were called upon to explain the views held by Friends, particularly on marriage, education, and the care of the poor.

Before parting, says John Yeardley, M. Passavant asked for silence, and we had a sweet time of religious communion, in which consolation and encouragement were

* See *The Widow's Mite*, No. 5 of J. Y.'s Series of Tracts.

offered, and thanks rendered for the favor of being permitted to meet together, and for the favor of the Divine
Presence.

Basle was their next halting-place. A letter written
by Martha Yeardley from this city, contains some notice
of the social and religious life by which their tarriance
in foreign cities was characterised, and of her own peculiar position as a gospel minister.

The pious Spittler, she says, has just been with us; he is
still full of faith and good works. M. L., whom we knew as
a nice girl at Corfu, is married to a serious merchant of this
place; a sister of C. Majors' wife at Bonn, with her husband,
also resides here; and we have fixed to take tea with them
and some of their friends to-morrow evening. My J. Y. is
gone with a converted Jew, Spittler, and one who has been a
missionary to Jerusalem, to a lecture this afternoon, where it
is probable he may have an opportunity of speaking to those
assembled. As it is to be all German, I excused myself in
order to rest and continue my letter. I have deeply felt on
this journey, as on others, that it is difficult for females to
make their way as gospel ministers; we have always found
it tolerated, but I am always sensible of a prejudice against
it. On some occasions my J. Y. has explained our views on
this important subject.

*15th.*—Yesterday we went to see a remarkably interesting
institution for missionaries, on the top of a high mountain,
called Chrischona Berg. It was established by Spittler, and,
is well worth the trouble of a little fatigue in getting to it.
Twelve young men of the poorer class, who have offered
themselves from a sense of duty to become missionaries, are
there taught various languages, and retained until some field
of labor opens for them to which they feel bound. It is
also a working institution; they are taught various trades, in
order that when they go out they may earn their living.
After viewing the premises and hearing a lesson in Arabic,
we saw the pupils assembled in the schoolroom. Instead of

a hymn in English, which they had learned, we asked for a
little silence, which was felt to be precious. My J. Y. then
addressed them in German, and was much helped. The
superintendent, a very interesting man, was in England for
some time; and in consequence of a hurt received on the
head in Malta, was sent to the *Retreat* at York, where he
became acquainted with several Friends, Samuel Tuke in
particular. Under the gentle treatment there he recovered,
but he lost his wife and one child at York, and has left two
others in England. I felt much for him, and ventured to
offer him a little consolation, and also to express my interest
for the institution, which Spittler desired him to repeat in
German.—(*Letter to Mary Tylor*, 8 *mo.* 13.)

Whilst at Basle they visited Pastor Lindel, an old
friend of theirs. He related to them that he had been
some time before applied to, to join the Evangelical
Alliance. "I told them," he said, "we have got further
than you have. In looking over your rules, I observe
there is a class of Christians in England whom you
exclude; and we can receive them. Our bond of union
extends much beyond yours; it embraces, without any
distinction, all who love the Lord Jesus Christ."

From Basle they went to Berne and Neufchâtel.
Their visit to these favorite spots was, as at former
times, accompanied by a good measure of the blessing
of the gospel of Christ.

18*th.* *Berne.*—Many of our former friends having heard
of our arrival, came this morning to our inn; and having
called together a few other serious persons, we had a precious
meeting. They have suffered much since our last visit; our
hearts were dipped into sympathy for them, and our tears
were mingled together. The Lord's presence was over us,
and he caused the word of consolation, exhortation, and supplication to flow freely. Some precious souls whom we have

known in this place have been taken to their rest since we last saw them. Soon shall we also be inquired after and not found! Lord, grant that we may be prepared to meet thee at thy coming!

20th. *Neufchâtel. First-day.*—The meeting was held in a saloon at our hotel, (*Des Alpes*). The room was quite crowded; we were surprised to see them continue to come in, by twos and threes together, at so short a notice. The unhallowed thought arose, Where shall we find bread to feed this multitude? But, thanks to Him who is the Bread of Life, he dispensed food to the refreshing of our souls. My M. Y. supplicated for us, and the gospel-word flowed freely: the meeting closed with thanksgiving by me.

Sad reflections on the political and religious state of the country oppressed their minds while travelling through Switzerland.

21st.—In all the times we have visited Neufchâtel, I never saw it look more beautiful. But the place was dull, and a depressed feeling manifested the life of religion to be wanting. Switzerland has suffered through the recent changes in the governments: infidelity is sorrowfully increasing. An abundant harvest has been gathered into the barns, and Nature everywhere smiles on ungrateful man. Woe to the nations when the ungodly bear rule! Persecution still rages in the Canton de Vaud.

Speaking of the great advantage which an acquaintance with the French and German languages afforded them, John Yeardley observes:—

How I long that some of our dear young friends in England might give up their minds and a portion of their time to the acquisition of these languages—and, above all, give up their hearts to be prepared for the Lord's work! How wide is the field of labor!

From Neufchâtel they proceeded to Geneva, and thence to Grenoble. Here they were received in the most open-hearted manner by the Protestant minister, Amand; but their feelings were severely tried by the martial display which the city presented.

*26th.*—On arriving at Grenoble, we inquired the name of the Protestant minister, and called on him without loss of time. So soon as he understood the object of our journey, he offered us his chapel for a meeting; or, if it would be more agreeable to us, he would convoke a meeting in the schoolroom for to-morrow evening with a number of persons who usually meet there. We accepted the latter proposal. It is comforting to find such a brother in the gospel; but O for the morrow! how my heart fails me for fear! Lord, help us, and give us to trust in thee!

*27th.*—This day is a day of suffering. The soldiers, the drums, the trumpets, with the shouting and dancing of the people, is enough to sink the heart of the reflecting Christian beyond hope, had he not a refuge in retirement before the Lord. The whole course of the military system tends to evil, and the corruption of manners.

The meeting was well attended, and they were thankful in being enabled to mingle in spirit with a company of sincere and pious Christians. The pastor called on them the next day. He had succeeded their good friend Bonifas, spoken of in the journey of 1843. Conversing with him on points on which Christians may differ, he observed, "The Church of Christ is like a great house built on a rock. There are different apartments for the various classes of Christians; but they are in the same house, and on the same rock, Christ."

After attending to some other gospel-service at Grenoble, they resumed their journey, held meetings

in Valence and the neighborhood, and crossing the
Rhone, entered Ardêche. A meeting which they held
at Privas was an occasion of remarkable stillness and
solemnity.

31*st.*—There was a room filled with serious persons, who
immediately settled into silence like a Friends' meeting:
indeed, I wish our meetings in England were always times of
as much good feeling. A chapter, the second of the Acts,
was read; after which I supplicated, and my M. Y. spoke in
testimony, as well as myself. M. Y. closed the opportunity
in supplication.

They held another meeting at Vals, a village in the
Cevennes mountains, near the town of Aubenas. Lindley
Murray Hoag, from America, had had a meeting there
not long before. There was no resident pastor, and the
schoolmaster called on John and Martha Yeardley, and
informed them that when no one was present to preach,
the congregation were accustomed to read a sermon,
the liturgy, and prayers. They explained to him their
objection to written sermons, and he appeared to be
sensible of the inconsistency of them with true gospel
ministry, but alleged that the people would not be
satisfied without having the greater part of the time
occupied with " service." As they could not undertake
that this should be the case, it was agreed that they
should be informed when the usual engagements were
concluded, and that the schoolmaster should give notice
of their intention to hold a religious meeting. In the
morning (First-day), unexpectedly, a young man arrived,
who came to see if he could be established in the place
as pastor, and the schoolmaster introduced him to
J. and M. Y. He raised no objection to their speaking

after the service, but the sermon which he preached, as they afterwards found, was on the politics of the day, and when it was concluded, they were still kept waiting ' during a conference which the consistory had with him. This delay, and their persuasion that the members of the consistory were not the men to sympathise with them in their religious exercise, was exceedingly proving to faith, and they entered the chapel under a pressure of mind almost beyond utterance. After a pause John Yeardley rose and spoke in French, in which he felt himself to be much helped; an influence superior to words was spread abroad, lifting up the messengers above the fear of man. Martha Yeardley followed, inviting the people to come under the teaching of the Holy Spirit, through faith in Christ Jesus, and especially addressing herself to the mothers.

They remained at Vals a week.

Our lodging, says J. Y., is situated amid scenery the most romantic: high-planted rocks, deep glens, and purling streams. For reading and writing we spend much time on a spacious open gallery, protected from the penetrating rays of the sun by a roof; and in the interstices are creepers, vines, and flowers, delightful and airy.

11th.—This has been a trying week. I have been low in mind and suffered much in body, but, thanks to a merciful God, I am restored to comparative health, and my beloved one is better. The peasants who inhabit the mountains can only come to the town on First-days; and as they live dispersed in places almost inaccessible, we concluded to wait over another First-day to see some of them at Vals. We had them invited to the schoolroom. A small number only assembled, but it was a feeling time: I hope a few were instructed, and we were satisfied in having done what we could.

From Vals John and Martha Yeardley proceeded to
Nismes, where they had some interesting service, both
within and beyond the little Society of their fellow-
professors. The account given by J. Y. of the way in
which one of their evenings was spent may be transcribed.

15th.—The wife of De Hauteville came to invite us to
spend the evening with a few religious friends, who met at
her house for reading the Bible. We had known the pious
young woman years before, and were most easy to accept the
invitation. The little company mostly knelt down, and
waited some time in silence; and then a young man offered a
short and sweet prayer. The fourth chapter of the Hebrews
was then read, and nearly all present offered a sentiment on
the subject, in meekness and in love, though they did not
agree in their interpretation. They spoke one after the other,
until all seemed tired; looking earnestly at me, as wondering
what I would say, not having spoken on the question. At
length one of the company asked my opinion. I felt freedom
at once to say I found no difficulty in the matter; I could
well understand the text, but I could not understand their
interpretation of it. This remark surprised them, and raised
an air of pleasantness on every countenance. My remarks
on the passage closed the subject, and I think they were
accorded with in the general. Stillness was then had, and
myself and dear M. Y. spoke to the company. There was
a precious feeling, and we were glad in not having missed
uniting with such spirits in passing an hour or two instructively together.

The service which remained for them to do before
returning to England consisted chiefly of religious labor
amongst the Friends of Congenies and the vicinity, and
in printing and distributing a large number of tracts.
They found the Society of Friends in a drooping con-

dition as to spiritual things, and in going round to their little meetings, Martha Yeardley felt it to be her last visit, and she labored to clear her conscience towards those among whom she had long been conversant, and for whose eternal welfare she felt deeply concerned.

They returned to London on the 20th of the Tenth Month.

# CHAPTER XVII.

## 1849–50.

THE disorganized state of Germany presented a serious obstacle to John and Martha Yeardley's resuming their labors on the Continent.

FROM JOHN YEARDLEY TO JOHN KITCHING.

Scarborough, 6 mo. 23, 1849.

We spent two days at Malton with our dear friends Ann and Esther Priestman, in their delightful new abode on the bank of the river: we were comforted in being at meeting with them on First-day. On Second-day we came to Scarborough, and soon procured two rooms near our own former residence. The sea air and exercise are beneficial to the health of my M. Y. and myself. Scarborough is certainly a most delightful place. The changes in the little society here are great: we miss many whom we knew and loved when we were resident here. It feels pleasant, though mournful, once more to mingle our sympathies with the few Friends who are left.

We sometimes sigh under the weight of our burden on account of poor Germany, from which land the accounts continue unsatisfactory. Mannheim, where we had such a sweet little meeting with a few pious persons last year, is now being bombarded ; also in several other parts of the Rhine the insurrection is not yet subdued. Our friend Dr. Murray returned on Second-day last from a tour through part of France, Belgium and the Rhine. He told us he was obliged to return after having proceeded as far as Mayence, as the steamers were interrupted in their course beyond that

(355)

place, south. This is the very line which we had thought to pursue; we cannot tell how soon an alteration may suddenly take place for the better. We must wait in patience, faith and hope.

The political horizon soon became clearer, and they resumed their journey on the 2nd of the Eighth Month. They again passed through Belgium, stopping at several places, and distributing a large number of religious tracts.

On reaching Elberfeld they were received in a very cordial manner by R. Hockelmann, and they held a satisfactory meeting in that city with a company of serious persons, originally Roman Catholics, who had at first followed Ronge, but afterwards separated from him. John Yeardley says of them:

> They are rejected by the Lutheran and Reformed Churches. They have adopted the name of German Catholics to attract the Romanists to them. There is real life of religion with some of them; perhaps with still a little obscurity on some important points of doctrine. Light does not always shine clearly all at once; nor is it always obeyed, so as to be received in its fulness.

Still more interesting was a meeting they had at Mühlheim on the Ruhr, where, it will be remembered, they found an open door for their ministry on their first continental journey. We give the narrative in John Yeardley's words:—

> 8 *mo.* 17.—On our arrival at Mühlheim we received a visit from the three pastors resident here and in the neighborhood, along with Pastor Bochart, from Schaffhausen, whom we had known some years before. One of them, Schultz, immediately asked me if we were not the parties who had held a meeting in a school-room in this place twenty-four years ago. We entered very fully into the

awakening that had taken place in this neighborhood. The spiritual seed of Tersteegen has never died out; and they told us of a person, Mühlenbeck, in Sarn, who represents those who are acquainted with the interior life. The youngest minister said directly, I will fetch him. In an hour's time he came again, accompanied by a middle-aged man, much like a good old Friend. He recollected us again, and spoke of our meeting. When we went to see him the next day in the village, he took us to the house in which he had lived in 1825, and placing me in the centre of the room said, There stood thou twenty-four years ago, and preached the gospel in this room; there sat thy dear wife and her friend, with the young man who interpreted for her.

They soon set about making a meeting for us, which is to be held this evening in a large room in the house of one of the brethren. O, my Saviour, strengthen us for this evening's work, and forsake us not in the time of need!

18th.—The meeting last evening was got well over. There were two rooms filled with men and a few women; their minds seemed sweetly centred on the Source of good. A precious silence prevailed, and I was enabled to address them in German from Acts xi. 23 :—" When Barnabas was come to Antioch and had seen the grace of God, he was glad and exhorted them all that with purpose of heart they would cleave unto the Lord." The nature of silent worship was also dwelt upon, and freedom from sin, through repentance and faith in Christ. My M. Y. spoke a few words in German, and I supplicated in the same language. Many hearts are prepared to receive the doctrine of the influence and guidance of the Holy Spirit : it seemed like marrow to their bones.

After the meeting some came to our inn, and remained till 10 o'clock. They seemed as if they could not part from us. We spoke of our ministry, missionary journeys, baptism and the Supper, in which we seemed to be one in sentiment and heart. Our short tarriance here has excited curiosity to know who and what we are, and a great desire for books; and a liberal supply has been furnished them. Those tracts

on our religious principles are just the food many are prepared to receive.

In coming this morning from Mühlheim to Elberfeld, my
heart was tendered under a sense of the Lord's mercies. I
feel poor and unworthy, but it is impressed on my heart from
day to day that my little remaining strength and my few
uncertain remaining days must be devoted to my Great
Master's cause. I am thankful that we have not through
discouragement been deterred from entering on this part of
our religious service; for, after all we have passed through
on the occasion, I do believe the present time is seasonable.—
(*Diary and Letter.*)

Before leaving the neighborhood, they had a second
meeting at Elberfeld, the holding of which was endangered by the animosity which prevailed between the
different religious parties. After the place and hour
were advertized, it appeared the room would be required
for a missionary meeting. The president of the missionary society was so unfriendly to those who associated
with John and Martha Yeardley, that he not only
refused to let them have the room, but refused also to
let notice be given at his meeting of the alteration in
time and place which it was needful to make in theirs.
They therefore hastily arranged their meeting for another day, and the alteration was announced in the daily
newspaper. The disappointment proved, in the end, to
be a subject for thankfulness on their parts; for just
before the hour of assembly of the missionary society,
an alarming fire broke out, and threw the whole town
into commotion; and the missionary meeting was obliged
to disperse as soon as the opening hymn had been sung.

The Friends' meeting, which took place two days
afterwards, was held in quiet. John Yeardley preached
on a subject which seems to have engaged his mind

ever since he had entered the place,—viz., the Fall of
Man. While in Elberfeld he printed a tract on this
subject; and in a conversation which he and Martha
Yeardley had with a doctor from Charleroi, the
doctor told them it was the very thing which was
wanted, being exactly adapted to the condition of the
numerous sceptics in that part, of whom he had once
been one.

Their sojourn at Bonn, where they arrived on the
31st of the Eighth Month, was exceedingly cordial to
their religious feelings. The persons with whom they
were the most intimately united were two ladies,
Alexandrine Mackeldey and the Countess Stynum; the
latter of whom had come to know the way of salvation
during a visit to England. J. Y. describes the opening
for service which they found in this city, in a letter to
Josiah Forster:—

This morning, the 1st of the Ninth Month, we received an
early visit from a pious young woman, *interior*. On her
entering the room we felt the Spirit of Jesus was near. As
soon as we discovered the piety of her mind, and her sweet
and open disposition, I said to her: Now, tell us who there
are in this place who are really spiritually-minded persons.
She said, I will; and instantly took the pen, and put down
about six or seven names, among which was the name of the
Countess Stynum. This lady, said she, I am sure, will be
rejoiced to see you; she is too weakly to leave her house, but
I am going to her and will tell her you are here.

Our kind helper soon returned with the expression of a
warm desire from the Countess that we would remain to-
morrow and hold a meeting in her saloon in the evening,
and invite any of our acquaintance, and she would give notice
to her own friends. There was so evidently a pointing of the
Great Master's finger in this matter, that we were at once
constrained to accept the invitation.

*9 mo.* 3.—A little before six o'clock last evening the Countess sent for us to take coffee with her, to have an hour of our company before the meeting. She gave us a hearty reception, and in such Christian simplicity, that we soon felt at perfect ease in her company. She has a well-informed and enlightened mind and a strong understanding, and lives, I believe, in the fear of the Lord. She asked many questions about the religious sects in England, as to the state of real piety, their forms, baptism, &c. Then she came to our own Society. I was in poor plight for answering questions; however, I explained the spiritual view we took of those subjects, and asked permission to send her books, in the reception of which she seemed to promise herself much gratification.

Her commodious and elegant saloon was conveniently seated and pretty well filled. Our manner of worship was quite new to every one present. We first explained it privately to the countess, who immediately comprehended our view; there was no wish at all shown to sing or read; a precious solemnity prevailed, and I was enabled to speak, in German, first on the nature of our silent worship, then on what [else] rested on my mind. The young woman abovementioned, A. Mackeldey, interpreted for my dear M. Y., who, I thought, had the best service; and she did it so well and so seriously that the right unction seemed to be preserved, and prevailed over us; and after a supplication in German we parted under a very precious solemnity.

A. M. said afterwards that she had been instructed by what she had heard, and was prepared to appreciate the value of silence. She observed, I think it a marked favor of Providence that you should have come at the present perplexing time, to comfort and confirm the faith of some in this place, and of me in particular.

Speaking of those with whom they had intercourse in this city, John Yeardley says:—

*9 mo.* 2.—Should it be the will of our Heavenly Father, I hope we may be permitted to see those precious souls again, and water the seed the Great Husbandman has deposited in their hearts. I consider such little companies, or individuals, as a little leaven working silently in a corrupt mass.

I never remember, he writes the next day, to have had more satisfaction in distributing Friends' books, or having intercourse with pious persons, than thus far on the present journey. The thinking part of the people, under the tossing of the present moment, are really thirsting for food more spiritual than they have hitherto received.

At Neuwied they were informed that the *Inspirirten* whom they saw there twenty-four years before, had, with the exception of a few families, emigrated to America, and that those whom they visited at Berlenburg had done the same.

From Neuwied they went to Kreuznach. This was a place to which they had no thought of going when they left England; indeed, John Yeardley, though passing near it on former journeys, was not aware of its existence. But when they were at Elberfeld, a swarthy youth from Cape Town, an inmate of the Mission-house at Barmen, mentioned to them that four of his fellow-countrymen had been for a time at Kreuznach. On hearing this place named, it occurred to J. Y. that it would be well for them to take it in their way. They had good reason to believe, before they left the place, that it was the Lord who had directed their steps thither, and that he had prepared the hearts of some who dwelt there to receive them. John Yeardley thus relates what occurred :—

9 *mo.* 6.—On our sending to a tailor named Ott, he could not come to us by reason of bodily infirmity ; but on paying him a visit I found him a meek and spiritual man. He undertook to speak with some others of the same way of thinking, to meet us in our hotel at 7 o'clock. On making it known
24

he found more were desirous of coming than he had expected;
a number of young people asked permission to be present, so
that our commodious saloon was pretty well filled. We read
the fourth chapter of John, and then I addressed the company
with great freedom; my M. Y. also spoke in German, and
was well understood. Friend Ott said, "You may travel
about, and think your journeyings and labors will do but
little good, but they will be blest far beyond what you may
expect. What you have said this evening has gone to my
heart. If we had only some one to whom we could look in
holding meetings, we should grow." He was reminded of
Him, the Head of his church, to whom we must all look. Of
this he was fully aware, but said, as they were mostly of the
lower class, they had no room, and the pastors did not encourage such meetings.

*7th.*—This morning our new-made friend accompanied us
to three of the villages, to visit several of his friends. We
were pleased with the simplicity and real Christian feeling
with which they received us. We arranged for a meeting in
one of these places for First-day afternoon, and one with our
Kreuznach friends in the evening. My poor soul can only
say, Lord, help !*

---

* The visits of J. and M. Y. to Kreuznach, in this journey, form the
subject of No. 8 of John Yeardley's Series of Tracts, *The German Farmer
become Preacher.* We extract from it the following more particular description of their visit to the three villages mentioned in the text :—

" We started on a bright, hot sunny morning ; and a pleasant drive,
through the vines and under the agreeable shade of double rows of
fruit trees, brought us to the place of destination. At the first farm-
house where we alighted the people were busy at their out-door work,
which, however, on hearing of the arrival of strangers, they soon left,
and came to welcome the travellers with outstretched hand and smiling
countenances. They soon gave proof of their hospitality, by ordering
us to be served with fruit, milk, and butter-bread, nor were we allowed
to depart before partaking of a cup of coffee. The master of the house
was an intelligent, pious man, and gave us much information as to the
state of religion among the people. After wending our way from village to village and from house to house, we returned to our lodgings,
favorably impressed with the piety and apparent sincerity of this simple-
hearted people."

*8th.*—Called again on J. A. Ott, and found him looking very serious. He told me he had read further in the books we left with him, and the more he saw, the more conviction was brought into his mind that what they unfolded was the truth; and that he believed it his duty thoroughly to weigh the matter, and then speak with a few of those who united with him, to see whether they could unite in holding a meeting after our manner, but that it was a serious matter, and they required time to mature it. We were quite of his mind in this respect; at the same time I believe if they had strength to meet together it would be advantageous.

*10th.*—Yesterday we met the little company in Horweiler, a room well filled with souls thirsting, I believe, for spiritual food. "All thy children shall be taught of the Lord," was much dwelt upon by me. My dear M. Y. was wonderfully helped in German. It was a precious season; the presence of the Lord was near, uniting our hearts in him.

At 7 o'clock we had the meeting in our room. It was not so lively as the one in the country; but we can thankfully acknowledge the Great Master was near to help in the needful time. It was a day of great exercise of body and mind. Our friend Ott accompanied us throughout the day's labor, and I felt the help of his spirit.

There are several villages around Kreuznach (some of which we have visited), where dwell a good many spiritually-minded people, who meet together for improvement. We have just received a sweet visit from Adam Tiegel of Schwabenheim, who is come to have a little talk with us. He seems to be the first who was awakened in 1805, and was made the means of awakening others, who now hold meetings in an old monastery.*

Passing on to Mannheim, they saw the effects of the revolution in Baden; the fine stone bridge over the. Rhine had been blown up, and not yet replaced. The

* The history of this worthy man is given in the Tract mentioned in the last note, *The German Farmer*, &c.

handful of pious persons with whom they had met in 1848 had been preserved in the midst of the danger; and their meetings had been maintained and were increased in numbers.   One of these, a widow, told them that, during the bombardment of the city, a cannon-ball had entered her house, and had passed by her bedside when her children were in the room, and also that a shell had burst before her door; but on neither occasion were any of the family hurt.*

At Stuttgardt they received the affecting intelligence of the decease of Elizabeth Dudley, who died of cholera on the 6th of the Ninth Month.  The removal of this, one of her earliest and dearest friends, was a severe stroke to Martha Yeardley, and sensibly affected her bodily health.   In a letter to her sisters, of the 14th of the Ninth Month, she thus gives vent to her feelings:—

It would not be possible to set forth in words what we have felt from the affecting intelligence contained in dear R.'s letter.   What shall we do but seek ability at the Divine footstool to bow in humble resignation to this afflictive dispensation?  I have had for some time a strong impression that something of this kind awaited us in our immediate circle; and it was with a trembling hand that I opened the letters. The tie which bound me to her, and which is now perhaps for a very short time broken, as far as relates to earthly things, was sealed upon my heart by a communion of more than forty-eight years, and includes all the various changes of an eventful life, during which my best feelings were ever cherished and encouraged, both by example and precept, and by the tenderest affection.   But I must not dwell upon this subject, lest I become unfitted for the duties which our present engagement daily calls for.

* See John Yeardley's Tract, No. 5, *The Widow's Mite cast into the Heavenly Treasury.*

To these afflictive tidings was added some discouragement in respect to their proposed journey to Russia. The little hope that John Yeardley still entertained of being allowed to cross the Russian frontier was extinguished by the information he received at Stuttgardt. A large number of the German emigrants who settled in the South Russian colonies were from the neighborhood of this city, and John Yeardley inquired of some of their ministers, who had served in the colonies, how far the country was likely to be accessible to a foreigner going thither to preach the gospel. The information he received was unfavorable, and his endeavors to obtain in this city the signature of the Russian ambassador to his passport were fruitless.

They had, however, something to console them under these trials.

In all our former travels in Germany, says J. Y., we never experienced such an open door and spirit of inquiry among the people as in the present journey. It is said that there is scarcely a village in all Würtemberg where meetings for worship are not held in private houses. The late revolutionists declare vengeance against these people, the pietists, as they call them, and that if the war breaks out again, they are to be the first to be cut off. But the present king gives them their liberty and his protection, and has openly said the pietists have saved his country.—(*Letter of* 9 *mo.* 15.)

Before they left Stuttgardt they were refreshed by a social evening's recreation, one of those occasions of the familiar intercourse of friendship, under the canopy of divine love, in which John Yeardley especially delighted.

17*th*.—Our two young friends, Reuchlin, came to conduct us to their garden among the vine-hills in the environs of the town. We there met their precious mother, and were joined by a good many *interior* ones, who had been invited to meet us. We had a precious little meeting in the arbor, after which we gave them some account of the religious movement in Belgium, &c., which pleased them much. We afterwards partook of fruit, biscuits, and wine. I shall reckon this garden visit among the happy moments of my life, because the presence of the Most High was with us.

On the 18th they went to Kornthal to visit the interesting society in that place. Hoffmann's widow, who seems to have returned from Basle after the death of her husband, was there, but so aged and infirm as to be confined to the house. The inmates of the establishment were therefore convened in some apartments adjoining her chamber, so that she could partake in the spiritual repast. Their kind friend Reuchlin had prepared the way for them; and when the assembly took their seats, a solemn silence ensued. John Yeardley and "Brother" Kölne addressed the meeting, and the former supplicated at the conclusion. On their way back to Stuttgardt, Madame Reuchlin interrogated them on the doctrine of election, and was rejoiced to hear from them their full belief in the universality of the grace of God; and as they communicated to one another their convictions respecting this great truth, their spirits were knit together in the love of the gospel.

From another pious person in this city, John Yeardley received a word of timely encouragement. He was anxious about their going into Bohemia, not having, as he thought, a sufficiently clear guidance to determine his course.

9 *mo.* 19.—A very acceptable visit from a worthy brother, Weiz. He introduced himself and commenced speaking on the guidance and consolations of the Holy Spirit, and spoke of his own experience as though he had known the thoughts of my heart. I have, said he, sometimes earnestly prayed to the Lord for direction what way to take, and have received no intimation; all has been dark within; I knew not whether to go right or left, and I have been compelled to go forward. I have then said, Lord, thou knowest my heart, be pleased to prosper my way; I leave the consequence to thee.

The conclusion to which they came in regard to Bohemia was, not to attempt the journey at that time, but to return to England for the winter, and leave the remoter districts of the circuit which they had in prospect till another year. They therefore returned by Heilbronn to Kreuznach, where they again found many opportunities of instructing and strengthening such as had made some progress in the Christian course.

26*th*.—This evening had about a dozen serious persons to tea. After a long conversation, we read a chapter, and made some remarks: there was also a time of silence, with supplication.

10 *mo.* 1. *First-day.*—This afternoon we attended a meeting at Schwabenheim, a few miles from here. Notice had been given of our intention to be present, and the company was consequently larger than usual. They meet in an old convent, the other end of which forms the parish place of worship. After the singing and a short prayer, the good old A. Tiegel read a chapter in the New Testament, and was proceeding to make some remarks upon it, when I stopped him, feeling something on my mind to say to the people. I was led to recommend a patient waiting upon God for the renewed help of his Spirit, and also to speak on the progress of the Gospel Church from Isaiah ii. 2, 3, &c. My M. Y. spoke a

little in German on the "still small voice," and the teaching
of the Spirit. I did not in this instance feel quite easy
to put aside the whole of their service. After meeting
we had coffee with Tiegel, and took back in our carriage
a few of our Kreuznach friends who had walked to the
meeting.*

*4th.*—Yesterday evening we had a few friends with us two
hours, by appointment, to speak concerning the rules, &c.,
of our Society. Many questions were asked, and a pretty
detailed account given by us, as well as we were able. The
company were all satisfied, and wished to come again.

*6th.*—To-day we received a visit from a young English lady.
She came to ask how we understood the passages in Paul's
Epistles forbidding women to speak in the church. We soon
gave her an answer, and handled the matter so fully that she
was quieted down before she left, little thinking, as she
acknowledged, that so much could be said in defence of the
practice among Friends. She even said she thought it to be
a general loss to the Christian Church that women are not
permitted to take part in the ministry. She is a thorough
Millenarian, and said the prophecy in Joel, that the Spirit
should be poured out on all flesh, referred to the coming of
Christ to reign on the earth, until I reminded her of what
happened on the day of Pentecost, when Peter said expressly
that it was the fulfilment of the prophecy of Joel. Two other
ladies were with her. We parted friendly, and she thanked
me for the information I had given her.

*7th.*—Went to Treisen to a meeting. The little company
meet only about eight persons usually, but we found about
thirty assembled in a small room. I thought it one of the
most lively meetings we have had. They wished me to conduct it in our own way. I told them we always commenced
our worship by sitting in silence. They said, We will also sit
still. I was favored with strength to speak to them of the
pool of Bethesda, when the angel troubled the water, and on

---

\* For a fuller description of this visit, see J. Y.'s Tract, *The German
Farmer*, &c.

the nature and advantage of true silence before God.  At the close, none seemed to wish to depart, but entered into serious conversation.  I think I never saw more satisfaction exhibited at receiving books than on this occasion.  After coffee, we returned to our lodgings with thankful hearts.

In the evening came three young women, with an elderly lady, the mother of one of them.  We had much conversation, and a precious little meeting, which concluded with solemn supplication — a nice finish to our sojourn in interesting Kreuznach.

Our friend Ott has accompanied us; he has been to us as eyes in the wilderness.

From Kreuznach they returned to Bonn, stopping at Darmstadt, Wiesbaden and Neuwied.  John Yeardley had allowed some discouragement to enter his mind in regard to the meeting they had had the previous month at the Countess Stynum's.  They found, however, on repeating their visit to this place, that the occasion in question had been one " of peculiar benefit and encouragement."  They renewed their religious intercourse with the Countess and her friends to their great refreshment and joy.

12*th.*—The evening was spent with the Countess, in a quiet and more private interview than she had with us the last time, owing to so many strangers being present.  After tea we had a long conversation on various religious subjects, particularly on some points relating to the principles of Friends, arising from what she had read in the books we left with her in our former visit.  We were glad of an opportunity to answer her questions.  A few of her private friends were present, much to our comfort.  Before leaving, the forty-sixth Psalm was read, and we had a comforting time together: the Lord be praised!  How sweet in him is the fellowship of the gospel!

Writing to Josiah Forster from Bonn, John Yeardley

makes some general remarks on the religious state of
Germany, as they had found it in their frequent intercourse with individuals of various character during this
journey.

There is no doubt that there is in the German character
generally a tendency to the visionary. We have found a
few who hold doctrines on certain points, which it might do
harm to publish; but we find or hear nothing of fanaticism
now as formerly. Those who are spiritually-minded are
more chastened, and more sound and scriptural in their
views of religious truth ; but not without exception.

A meeting at Mühlheim "not large, but a good
time," closed their religious service in this part of their
long and arduous engagement.

They arrived in England on the 20th of the Tenth
Month, "with peaceful feelings, and in gratitude to
their Heavenly Father for all his mercies towards his
unworthy servants;" but "mourning the loss of some
beloved ones who had died in the Lord in their
absence."

After about five months passed in the quiet of home,
they made preparation once more for accomplishing the
work to which they had been called. The prospect of
distant travel was discouraging, both on account of
Martha Yeardley's weak health and of the state of the
Continent; but, writes John Yeardley, "my mind is
peaceful, and I have an abiding conviction that it is
right to proceed, trusting in the Lord for light, strength
and safety."

On their way through Belgium, the same feeling was
strongly impressed upon his mind.

1850. 4 *mo.* 7.—In the train, soon after leaving Brussels,
my spirit was melted under a feeling of the Lord's goodness.

The object of our journey came weightily before me, and I
considered we had left our home and every object most dear
to our natural affections, with the sole view to serve our Lord
and Master, and in the desire to use our feeble powers to
draw souls to Him, that they might partake of spiritual
communion with the Beloved of souls, through his grace.
A degree of precious resignation followed; and, whatever
may be the result as it regards ourselves, I believe it is the
Lord's will for us thus to go forth in his name; and should
I or the precious partner of my bosom not be permitted again
to see our native land, we shall be happy and at rest, through
the mercy of that Saviour who gave his precious life for us.

On arriving at Berlin their first duty was to apply to
the Russian ambassador for his signature to their passport, with permission to enter the Russian territory at
Odessa.  Their application met with an immediate and
positive refusal, and the extinction of his hopes in this
respect was to John Yeardley a grievous disappointment.

The next evening, after they had borne their burden
all the day, dejected in spirit, and uncertain which way
to turn, their hearts were lightened by a visit from
August Beyerhaus, who at once attached himself to
them and offered them help.  He could indeed do
nothing to facilitate their entrance into Russia, but he
was the means of diverting their minds from the consideration of what had now become hopeless, and of
opening to them, in Berlin, a door of usefulness.  Through
his introduction they became acquainted with several
devoted Christians, some of them of wide reputation in
the Church.  These interviews, which were occasions
of heartfelt spiritual communion, are thus noticed in the
Diary :—

4 *mo.* 22.—Samuel Elsner is an aged warm-hearted Christian, full of faith and good works: he gave us important information, and will send me some names of pious persons in Silesia.

Pastor Gossner we found green in old age; seventy-five years of a variegated life have taught him many useful lessons. His refuge now is strong faith in the Saviour. He was at work in his arm-chair, and was much pleased to see us.

23*rd.*—Pastor Knack, successor to Gossner, is a man of a lively spirit, to whom we at once felt united. He very liberally offered us the liberty of speaking to his flock (the Bohemian congregation in Berlin); and also invited us to visit the little company in the village where we propose going this evening.

At 3 o'clock we had a sweet interview with Professor Neander, an aged man of a striking figure and a Jewish countenance, pervaded by heavenly calmness, and illumined by the bright shades of gospel light. His eyes are become dim through excessive study; his heart is very large, full of love and hope in Jesus Christ. He seemed pleased to hear some account of the order of our Society, particularly with regard to the ministry and gospel missions, observing, "With you, then, there is liberty for all to speak when moved by the Holy Spirit, just as in the primitive church." This observation led us to several points of our discipline, and he seemed delighted that a society existed whose practice, in many things, came so near to that of the primitive church. Before parting the spirit of supplication came over us, under which prayer was offered, particularly for this aged servant of the Lord. His disinterestedness is great. The king will sometimes give him money, that he may take relaxation in going to the baths, &c. But so susceptible is his heart for many who are necessitous, that he will often give to others all that he has received. The good king has then to repeat his gift, and send him away almost by force from his labors.

After these choice visits, John Yeardley says:—

*24th.*—A ray of light and hope has broken in upon our gloomy path,—not into Russia; there *Satan* is still permitted to hinder; but in this city.

They spent two days at Rixdorf, the village alluded to above, three miles from Berlin, where was a small congregation of Bohemian Brethren, who took refuge there in 1737. The women of the society held religious meetings by themselves twice a week. These meetings had been instituted many years before by Maria Liestig, to whom John and Martha Yeardley were introduced, and whom they found to be of a meek and intelligent spirit. She gave them a relation of her extraordinary conversion, which John Yeardley published in No. 3 of his Series of Tracts, under the title of the *Conversion of Mary Merry.* They held a meeting in the village, in which they both had to " speak closely on the necessity of silence in worship." They had also a small meeting at their hotel in Berlin, when " the gospel message flowed freely, in speaking of the spiritual dispensation in which we live, and the progress of light."

On the 29th they left Berlin, and went to the beautiful watering-place of Warmbrunn, in Silesia. The dwellings of the laborers in Silesia struck them as being of a wretched description. " What they do," says J. Y., "in a rigorous winter, like the last, I cannot tell; they appeared to be mostly Roman Catholics."

They resided a month at Warmbrunn. Some of the simple incidents which befel them there form the subjects of the following extracts :—

5 *mo.* 10.—Yesterday was a thorough rainy day; but in the afternoon, to our surprise, came in eight men together, who had heard of strangers having arrived in Warmbrunn

to visit those who love the Saviour. We explained to them our religious principles; their countenances brightened when we spoke of the Spirit being poured out upon all—sons and daughters. A sweet feeling was present with us, and supplication was offered under much solemnity.

11*th.*—I have had a long conversation with C. W. Grossner, of Breslau, on the Supper, &c. We opened the Testament, and read the various passages, and I explained our views as well as I could. I think he is brought under serious thoughtfulness, and half convinced of our principles with regard to the rites, which he acknowledges are vain without the substance. "Religion with many, nowadays," he observed, "is like a polished shell without kernel."

13*th.*—The Countess Schaffgotsch sent her butler with a message from the castle that she would be glad if we would call on her. She gave us a hearty reception, and thanked us for taking so much interest about the people. On our presenting her with some books,—But I am a Catholic, she said. We told her that made no difference to us; we loved all who loved the Lord Jesus. She spoke very sweetly of the influence of the Spirit.

14*th.*—The Countess paid us a long visit, and spoke much of the Roman Catholic faith. She has no more faith in the efficacy of the prayers of the saints than I have, and said she had not prayed to them now for four years; their church only *advises,* not *commands* it.

16*th.*—We went to dine with the Countess Reden and her sister, who live at the castle in Buchwald, one of the most lovely spots in the most lovely of countries. It is truly a peaceful abode, whose inmates fear their God, love their neighbor, and greatly esteem their king. We had been announced to the Countess from Berlin a week before; she and her amiable sister received us as a brother and sister beloved in the Lord. I never witnessed more intelligence combined with Christian politeness and real simplicity. The Countess is about seventy-six years of age; she is the president of the Bible Society, and the spiritual mother of all that is good in the neighborhood. She nursed the present king

on her lap when he was a baby, and her great influence with
him now she always turns to good account in serving benevolence and religion.   Both she and her sister spoke with much
affection of dear Elizabeth J. Fry, and her visit with Joseph
John Gurney.

26th.—Our last meeting, on First-day evening, consisted
of all men, several of whom had come from Erdmannsdorf
and the colonies of the Tyrolese.   They seemed to appreciate
the time of silence, and expressed much satisfaction with
having made our acquaintance, and with the meeting.

On the 30th of the Fifth Month, J. and M. Y. quitted
Warmbrunn and proceeded towards Bohemia.

We passed, says the former, through Hirschberg. Gold-
berg, Liegnitz, and to Dresden, Leipzig, and Halle, making
acquaintance in all these places with serious persons, and,
I hope, scattering here and there a little gospel seed; but
truly we may say, It is sown in weakness.   At Halle we were
much gratified with our visit to Dr. Tholuck, but I think, not
less so with his wife, a most lovely person, delighting to *feel*
and to *do* good.

On arriving at Dresden, it became evident that Martha
Yeardley, who had suffered much for some time from
an affection of the windpipe, required repose and medical
care ; and they concluded to rest awhile at the baths
of Töplitz.   The illness of his wife, and some degree of
bodily indisposition from which he himself suffered, did
not prevent John Yeardley from employing the time in
the diffusion of evangelical truth.

He had heard at Berlin that within a few months
several hundred Bibles and Testaments had been sent
into Bohemia, and had been eagerly bought there by
awakened persons.   He thought that if a translation
could be made into the Bohemian language of some
simple religious tracts, much good might be done by

their dissemination; but he supposed that the intolerant laws of the Austrian Empire, which forbad all freedom of religious action, were still in full force. His account of his feelings and those of Martha Yeardley under the burden which this supposition imposed on them, and of the agreeable manner in which permission was unexpectedly granted them to print and circulate their little messengers of peace, must be given in his own words:—

Our hearts yearned towards the people, but we were afraid to give them tracts, which in other places had often been the means to conversation and to making acquaintance. This brought us low in mind; the body was already weak enough before. We thought it would not do to pass through the country in this state of depression, without trying to remove the cause. I went, therefore, the next morning to the head of the authorities, took with me one of our little tracts, mostly Scripture extracts, and asked whether I might be allowed to have the little book, or such as I then presented to him, printed for circulation. He received me politely, indeed kindly, and looked pleased with my tract, saying as he turned over its innocent little pages, Ah, nothing about politics; nothing against the religion of the country: it is very good, it is beautiful. You are quite at liberty to print and circulate such tracts as these. And when he found that the object was to do good to all, without cost to the receiver, he said, That is lovely.—(*Letter of* 6 mo. 23.)

The Bohemian translations were not made until J. and M. Y. went to Prague, which they did on the 22nd. Their feelings on entering this city, and the manner in which they were helped in their work of love, are described in the following diaries:—

6 *mo.* 23.—Last evening we arrived at Prague. Our heart sunk on approaching this great city. The twenty-eight statues of saints, &c. on the bridge, with the many lamps

devoted to these images, the crucifixes, &c., all indicated that superstition rages rampant.

We lost no time in sending to the Protestant pastors, one of whom kindly came to us in the evening, and we conversed till late. I showed him my little *Spiritual Bread for Christian Workmen*, with which he was much pleased. I told him I wanted it translated into the Bohemian language. This afternoon he paid us another visit, and brought his wife to see my M. Y. He produced the translation of the introduction to the little tract. We are to have 2000 printed. Most of the poor people read only the Bohemian language. I have promised to place 1000 at the disposal of the pastor; he is delighted with the opportunity of having anything of the kind *printed in Prague.*

Much, adds J. Y. in a letter, as I have suffered in the long prospect of a visit to this place, I feel a peculiar satisfaction that it has been deferred until there is liberty to print and circulate gospel tracts. Small as such a privilege may appear, until very recently such distribution of books would have been visited with a very inconvenient imprisonment on the individual transgressing the law.—(6 mo. 23.)

24*th.*—I gave Pastor Bennisch for perusal, and choice for translation, William Allen's *Thoughts on the Importance of Religion,* and our tracts on the *Fall, Regeneration and Redemption, True Faith,* and the *Voice of Conscience.* There is a great movement among the Catholics; they have need to be instructed in the first principles of Christianity, and it is very important that the doctrine of faith in Christ should be combined with that of the practical working of the Spirit as set forth in many of our tracts. On this account, I am glad they are likely to take precedence of others in their circulation; for I do not hear that any tracts decidedly religious have yet been printed in Prague.

During their stay in the city, and after they left, there were printed 12,000 copies of the tracts in Bohemian, and 1000 in German.

At Töplitz, which they revisited before leaving

25

Bohemia, occurred the interesting incident of the Bohemian soldier, which is related under that title in John Yeardley's series of tracts, No. 4.

When they finally quitted the country, they took the nearest road to Kreuznach. On the way, they distributed tracts in the villages, at one of which, where they were detained for want of horses, the inhabitants flocked so eagerly to them to receive these little messengers, that they had difficulty in satisfying them. Notwithstanding this circumstance, the reflection with which John Yeardley concludes his account of their travels in Bohemia was, "It will require a power more than human to make the *dry bones of Bohemia* live."

They spent three weeks at Kreuznach, confirming the faith of the brethren, and printing German translations of several tracts. In passing through Neuwied, they intended only to spend the night there; but hearing that much inquiry after the way of salvation had recently manifested itself in the villages around, they decided, after the horses had been ordered for departure, to remain and visit one of these villages. A meeting was called, and so many attended that the room could not contain them all. It was a good season; De Freis, the friend who had made them acquainted with the religious condition of the place, accompanied them as guide, and was a true helper in the work. He had been twenty years missionary in Greenland and South Africa.

They returned home, both of them worn with travelling, and Martha Yeardley exhausted with disease, which was making sure progress in her debilitated frame; but they were supported by the peaceful consciousness of having accomplished all the service to which they had been called to labor in common.

# CHAPTER XVIII.

## 1851–2.

MARTHA YEARDLEY continued very unwell during the autumn, and by the end of the year her disorder assumed a more alarming form. It soon became evident that her dedicated life must at no distant period be brought to a close; and after many weeks of suffering, with confinement to the chamber during the latter part of the time, she expired, full of peace and hope in Christ Jesus, in the Fifth Month, 1851. The following memorandum, touchingly descriptive of her illness and death, was penned by her bereaved husband, probably soon after her decease.

After our return from the Continental journey my beloved M. Y. became more poorly. A severe influenza cold weakened her much; and a second attack she seemed never to recover. It was succeeded by a regular rheumatic fever. From the commencement of 1851, with but little exception, she was confined to the house, and for a little while to her bed, until the 8th of the Fifth Month, when her sweet and purified spirit ascended to her Saviour, and commenced an eternity of bliss.

Thus was I deprived of my only earthly treasure. She was the Lord's precious loan, granted me for nearly a quarter of a century, for which I can never be sufficiently [thankful]. She was his own, bought with the blood of his dear Son, and he saw meet to take her from me. Ours was a blessed

(379)

union, and a happy life, spent, I hope, unitedly in the service of our Lord. In all our imperfections we did desire, above all earthly things, to do the work of our Divine Master, and to labor for the promotion of his kingdom, and for the spread of his knowledge in the earth.

I was her only nurse till within ten days of her happy close. Long had a covenant been made between us, in the time of health, that whichever of us was taken ill the first, should be nursed by the surviving one, if permitted and strength afforded; which it mercifully was to me, and a happy season was the sick-room. We seemed to live together in heaven; never, I think, could two mortals be more favored with the answer to prayer.

In the early part of her illness she spoke much of the satisfaction she had felt in our three last journeys to the Continent, and that she was thankful in having been enabled to go through the whole of the service which her Lord had put into her heart. I have since thought it was a mercy that I did not proceed into South Russia, as, in all probability, my precious one would have fallen on the journey, and never seen her peaceful home again.

During the whole of the illness her delight was to speak of the joy of heaven. My sins of omission and of commission, she said, are all passed by; my iniquities are all forgiven, and washed away in the blood of the Lamb; and now I rejoice in God my Saviour. His love and mercy to me are beyond all bounds; and so strong is my faith in my precious Saviour, that I have scarcely known, the whole of the illness, what it has been to be troubled with an evil thought.

When she expressed a desire to go to Heaven, I reminded her of my loneliness when she should be taken from me. The Lord will care for thee, was her constant reply. He has promised me over and over again that he will care for thee; the answer to my prayer has always been, I will care for him.

Nearly the last conversation she had with any of her beloved relatives was with ———, to whom she observed:

My affection for thee is strong; I believe thou lovest thy
Saviour: I desire that thou mayest keep nothing back
that the Lord may require of thee, but serve him with
greater devotedness of heart; and if ever thou art called to
bear public testimony to his truth, be sure to preach the whole
gospel, faith in Christ, and the necessity of the practical
work of the Holy Spirit to produce holiness of life. To
[another of her near relatives] she observed: Thou hast
often been sweetly visited by the love of thy Saviour, and
be assured thou wilt never find any joy equal to that of
yielding thy heart in prompt obedience to the will of thy
Lord. Her last words to her affectionate sisters were, The
Lord bless you all: Farewell.

Towards the end of the year John Yeardley again
communed with himself in the language of sorrow, but
also of humble resignation. At the same time he
speaks of an engagement of gospel labor from which
he had then recently returned, the first which he had
undertaken alone since his marriage with Martha
Savory. Having seen his faithful and well-tried com-
rade fall by his side, he had now to learn again to gird
himself and enter, as in the days of his youth, alone
into the combat.

1851. 12 *mo.* 13.—How often have I prayed that the
portion of her Lord's spirit which animated her devoted life
may rest on me! Her heart, her tongue, and her pen were
all employed in promoting the cause of her Divine Master,
whom she delighted to serve. All my earthly joy was now
gone to heaven, and I felt alone in the world; but my spirit
seemed never to be separated from her: she seemed to be
hovering over me constantly. My heart does sorrow for the
loss of her sweet society; to me she was a wise and sound
counsellor, and a never-failing consoler in all my troubles.
I do mourn, but I dare not murmur. I hope my merciful
Heavenly Father will keep me in the hour of temptation,

and be with me in the last trying hour, and prepare me to join this precious one and all by whom she is surrounded with her God and Saviour in the centre of bliss.

I had often mentioned to my precious one a prospect of religious service in Ireland, and once since our return home from our last Continental journey; when she replied, "I have no concern to go to Ireland—thou must do that when I am taken from thee." It cost me many tears and prayers before I could be resigned to request a certificate, alone, for the first time since our union; but, looking seriously at the subject, the language was constantly in my heart, The hour cometh when no man can work. Life is uncertain, and I can only expect sustaining grace by faithfully following my Lord: and, blessed be his name, he has kept and sustained me in every trial.

This day would have been the twenty-fifth anniversary of our union. How near it has brought my precious one to me in spirit, and how strong are my prayers that my Lord may preserve me faithful to the end of the race! I can say my desire is, when he cometh, he may not find me idle.

The visit which John Yeardley made in Ireland was general, comprehending all, or nearly all, the meetings of Friends in the island, and including a few public meetings in Leinster province. He has left very few notes of this journey, except an itinerary of the places at which he stopped, but makes frequent mention of the hospitality and kindness of Friends. From Cork he writes :—

I am in the midst of a family visit to the Friends of Cork, and shall have, I expect, from ninety to a hundred sittings. I am lodged a few miles in the country, in a mansion surrounded by beautiful grounds, and all the beloved inmates most affectionate and helpful to me. They send me to my work in or about the city mostly to breakfast; and I return in the evening, and enjoy the refreshing breezes and the quiet: but then I have the family visits to resume next morning. In riding to town to-day, I tried to raise my heart to God; when the language sweetly occurred to me, Bread shall be given thee, thy water shall be sure.—(*Letter of* 8 *mo.* 5, 1851.)

A few days after his return from Ireland, he left home again to visit the Isle of Man, in company with Barnard Dickenson. On his return, he was refreshed by a visit to Dover, where he spent three weeks in the company of his kind and sympathising friend Margaret Pope.

The interval which elapsed before the recommencement of his missionary labors was to be short. In the First Month of 1852, we find him again under exercise of mind for foreign travel; having, this time, to direct his course towards the interesting community of religious persons in Norway, whose principles and practices are the same as those of Friends. The Diary which follows is the utterance of his heart in the prospect of this work.

1852. 1 *mo.* 24.—This has been a precious morning unto my soul; such a season of spiritual comfort I have not been permitted to experience for a long time. I think it is vouchsafed me through the efficacy of earnest prayer, which has brought me to resignation to my Lord's will. I have now no more doubt as to Norway. Light springs on my path. How powerful is the love of God when it fills the heart; there is not a place on the Lord's earth where I think I could not go, if favored with the strength, and blessed with the presence of my God and Saviour.

Unto thee, Lord, do I commit all my concerns, spiritual and temporal; do thou give to thy unworthy servant an answer of peace. Keep me faithful and patient to the end of the race. Lord, grant that my ministry, which thou hast entrusted to me, may proceed purely and entirely from thy love, and be exercised in thy fear and under the unction of thy Holy Spirit. Lord, keep my heart fixed on the last, last awful moment that I may have to breathe; grant that it may be breathed out in the bosom of my adorable Saviour; all sting of death taken away, my robes washed in his blood, and my spirit purified and ready to be united to those beloved ones who are already enjoying a blissful eternity with thee!

The next entry in the Diary was made at Christiania, where he thus speaks of the unity and concurrence which his friends had testified with his mission.

Since I last wrote any notes in this journal, I have passed through many conflicts respecting my long-thought-of visit to Norway. When the subject was proposed to my friends in London, it met with the warm encouragement and sympathy of all, in every stage, to the receiving the full unity of the Yearly Meeting of Ministers and Elders.

I am accompanied by my dear friend, Peter Bedford, whose sweet and constantly cheerful spirits comfort and cheer me. We have already had many proofs that our being joined together in this laborious journey is of the Lord. Our friend William Robinson proves an efficient helper.

John Yeardley and his companions left London on the 9th of the Sixth Month, and went first to Homburg, as he wished to place a young person in whom he was interested, at the school kept by the sisters Müller at Friedrichsdorf, near that town. Whilst at Homburg he was suddenly attacked with a severe and painful disorder, and was reduced to great extremity. After about two weeks of suffering, he was restored to convalescence, when he thus breaks forth:—

How can I sufficiently record the mercy of my God in sustaining me in a time of great extremity, even when there was but little prospect of my ever seeing Norway. He blessed me with resignation and sustaining grace, so that I could rest as on the Saviour's bosom, for life or death. I knew my Lord and Master could do without my poor un-,worthy service in Norway; but if he had work for me to do in that land he would raise me up in his own time; and so he has done.

As soon as he had sufficiently recovered his strength, they set forth for Kiel; but not before John Yeardley had had a religious meeting with the pupils in the school.

I was, he says, enabled to address them in German; a precious feeling was over us, and many spirits were tendered before the Lord. F. Müller expressed her great satisfaction with this parting visit.

They reached Kiel by easy stages in seven days. From this place he writes:—

My very soul pants to be in Norway; had I wings I could fly there. And yet how few are the days since the cloud between me and that land was so dense that I could not see through it. But even then, O, what sweet peace and resignation were the clothing of my humbled spirit. There seemed nothing in my way to heaven, whether from Germany or Norway. I do believe my eye and heart are fixed on my precious Saviour, and he has been my stay in the hour of sore conflict of body, but none of mind. All seemed peace and bliss when I glanced at the happy home above, already inhabited by my precious one and many more who were dear to us on earth.—( *Letter of* 7 *mo.* 2, 1852.)

On the 5th of the Seventh Month they proceeded to Christiania, John Yeardley employing the time on the voyage in adding to the little stock of the Norse language which he had acquired at home in anticipation of the journey. On landing at Christiania they were refreshed by seeing Asbjön Kloster of Stavanger, who had come to meet them, and for two weeks had been waiting their arrival.

At a meeting which they held in this city, both John Yeardley and Peter Bedford were engaged to minister to the spiritual wants of the people; A. Kloster interpreting for them. The company were so much interested, that many of them went afterwards to the hotel to converse and ask for tracts.

The Friends left Christiania on the 10th, and sailed through the rock-bound sea to Christiansand, the passage between the cliffs being in some places so narrow that there was no more room than was sufficient for the vessel to pass.

In this town they enjoyed much freedom in the gospel, and held two public meetings. Regarding the first of these, John Yeardley says:—

7 mo. 13.—Our large room at the hotel was filled half an hour before the time appointed, and it was with difficulty that we made our way to our seats. A little unsettlement prevailed from the desire to enter, which subsided after a few explanatory words. A time of quiet ensued, and there was much openness to receive the gospel message. Before the close of the meeting I became exceedingly thoughtful about appointing another for the next evening; and on intimating the same to P. B., I found he was under the same impression. It was, therefore, announced to the assembly before they separated, and appeared much to satisfy them. The dear people were unwilling to part from us without a shake by the hand.—(*Diary and Letter.*)

At one of the meetings which they held in this town, whilst John Yeardley was preaching, he became sen-

sible that his interpreter had himself received something to communicate to the congregation ; he therefore
stopped speaking, and the interpreter, faithful to his
duty, took up the word until he had cleared his mind
from its burden.   After he had finished, John Yeardley
resumed his discourse.

On the 14th the Friends drove out a few miles into
the country to " pay some family visits."   They had two
double carrioles, or gigs: the road over which they
passed was " steep and rugged beyond description."   In
returning, the carriole in which Peter Bedford rode
struck against a rock at a sharp corner and was overset.
Peter Bedford's right shoulder was dislocated, and he
otherwise bruised.   In conveying him into Christiansand he suffered much from the shaking of the car ;
but the joint was quickly set by a skilful surgeon ; and,
in the evening, the love he felt for the people was so
strong, that he could not remain absent from the
meeting which had been appointed for that time, and he
even took part in its vocal exercise.

It was, writes John Yeardley, a favored time.   Peter
Bedford gave some account of the difference between our
religious Society and other professing Christians.   It opened
the way for me to speak on the peculiar doctrines and practices of Friends at more length than I ever remember to have
done before; after which the glad tidings of the gospel flowed
freely, and the people were invited to come to Christ and
partake of the full blessedness of his teaching by the Holy
Spirit.   A precious solemnity prevailed, and the serious
attention of the company was great.   A good many soldiers,
and some officers, were present; but the expression of our
dissent from all wars and fightings had not displeased them,
for they shook hands with us most kindly.—(Diary and
Letter.)

Besides being interested for the people of Christian-sand in general, John Yeardley and Peter Bedford were especially attracted towards several young men who had embraced the doctrines of Friends, without any knowledge of the Society, and without any instruction from man.  With these persons they met more than once.  John Yeardley writes :—

We had a precious meeting with them.  They were invited to embrace the doctrines of the gospel in living faith, and to give full room to the workings of the Spirit of Jesus, whose voice they had already heard inviting them to come under his teaching.  We encouraged them to meet for divine worship.

On the 16th the Friends proceeded thirty-five miles to Mandal, travelling post.  From thence, John Yeardley and Asbjön Kloster went by the road to Stavanger, leaving Peter Bedford and William Robinson to follow by steam-vessel, the former being unable to bear the motion of the Norwegian carriages.

John Yeardley, in one of his letters, in a lively manner describes the mode of travelling :—

The usual vehicle in this country is the single-seated carriole, made exactly to fit the figure of the traveller, and no spare room except a little well under his feet.  The seat is placed on two crossbars fixed to the long shafts, the spring of which is intended to mitigate the jolting of the road.  We chose double cars on iron springs, which we found *not too easy:* they were like old-fashioned, worn-out, and very shabby English gigs.  The posting is under government regulation, and is performed by sure-footed ponies kept by the farmers, who are obliged to supply them under any circumstances after having had notice.  A *forbud* is sent on with printed notices filled up with the time at which the traveller expects to arrive at each station.  This *avant-courier* is often a little boy, and sometimes, to save the expense of a horse, for which the traveller has paid, he is sent on foot. On one occasion we met a young girl, with bare feet, who had walked sixteen miles with notice papers, as our *forbud*. Now away goes the traveller, accompanied by a man, or more often a boy, or it may be a little girl, to bring back the pony. They run by the side, but down hills always seat themselves behind on the luggage as best they can. The traveller drives himself, and the little horses are so brisk that, whatever the state of the road may be, they run down the mountains as fast as they can clatter, and so sure-footed that they are scarcely ever known to fall; but a person of weak nerves has no business to be the rider.

From Christiansand to Stavanger is about 200 miles, which took us four days. Our road lay occasionally over a wild and stony heath by the sea, sometimes along the river-banks, lakes, or fiords, but more often among and upon the high and rugged rocks; the passing of some of which is, I think, more difficult than crossing the Alps between Switzerland and Italy.—(*Letter of* 8 *mo.* 3.)

On the way towards Stavanger John Yeardley had a public meeting at Flekkefiord, the first time such a meeting had been held in the place. It was "a good time," and so well attended that the town-hall could not contain nearly all who came together.

Immediately on arriving at Stavanger, the Friends commenced visiting the families of the Friends in the town and on the adjacent islands; and on the next First-day held a meeting about eleven miles up one of the fiords, to which so many flocked from all directions that they were obliged to assemble in the open air:—

It was, says J. Y., a lovely sight to see so many clean-dressed peasants, in their mountain costume, with a serious-ness in their countenances which indicated that a motive better than curiosity had brought them together. I was reminded and had to speak of the miracle of our blessed

Saviour, when he commanded the multitudes to sit down on the grass, and fed them with five barley loaves and two fishes.

Since this time, he says in a letter, we hold our public meetings in the open air, and the stillness that prevails is quite remarkable. Last evening we had a solemn opportunity in a plantation belonging to one of our Friends by the sea-side. The hushing of the trees, the gentle rolling of the waves behind a strong sea-wall, and the warbling of the little birds, all seemed to aid our worship; but these would have been nothing had not the presence of our Divine Master been near. After the meeting, as many as could be seated partook of tea, &c. The seriousness, simplicity, kindness and hospitality, are great. All flock together as if they were one family.—(7 *mo.* 28.)

After this the Friends availed themselves of the efficient assistance of Endré Dahl, and of the active peasants who form a large portion of the Society of Friends there, in a more extensive excursion which they made up one of the fiords which in so remarkable a manner intersect the country. John Yeardley gives a graphic description of this voyage.

Our efficient helper prepared his own boat; our ship's company are all volunteers. We set out with seven, but were joined by others on the way, so that this morning we started with ten men. They are a most cheerful and playful company, all interested in the object of our voyage. It does my heart good to see with what delight they bring planks for seats, and run in all directions to give notice of our meetings. Each seems to strive which shall show us the most attention, even anticipating our wants. They enjoy our family readings and worship; their conduct is instructive; and the solemnity on these occasions precious.

On Fifth-day we landed on an island (Findon) sprinkled with trees, and with a park-like bank sloping to the water. This was refreshing to the eye after having seen nothing but

bare rock for many days. The meeting was at our friend's
house who owned the pretty little farm. It was sweet and
refreshing ; and afterwards a number of these people accom
panied us to the boat, and did not quit their standing till
we were out of sight. My heart yearned towards them in
gospel love.

Next morning we started before 6 o'clock, and when we
had rowed fourteen English miles put into a little village,
Ielsom. We were all strangers in the place, and Friends
and their principles unknown. Our friend Endré Dahl had
a pointing that we should try for a meeting, which was
appointed for 2 o'clock. After waiting till 3, only one or
two persons came, and we had a consultation whether we
should proceed on our voyage, but concluded it safer to go
in and sit down. When we were seated (I may say in faith),
first one and then another came in, till the large room and
passage were filled, and a number were outside under the
windows. It was quite a remarkable meeting, and we were
well satisfied in having exercised patience as well as a little
faith. We were informed that it was the custom of the place
not to attend any appointed meeting till an hour after the
time named.

We arrived at Sand about 9 o'clock, after hard rowing,
the tide being against us. Sand is beautifully placed at an
opening in the rocks, at the mouth of a river where salmon-
fishing is good. As soon as we landed, our ship's company
made the object of our journey known, when a serious-looking
man immediately offered to go about six miles to inform a
person who he knew would like to attend. Two individuals
in this place have for some time been in the practice of
holding a silent meeting for worship ; they had no knowledge
of Friends, nor Friends of them.

Fixing the meeting for the First-day evening, John
Yeardley and his companions pursued their way the
next morning, which was Seventh-day, to Sävde,
situated at the head of the fiord, and consequently the
extreme point of their voyage. Before starting they

went a little way up the Sand river, to view one of the grand Norwegian waterfalls, and also to see how the salmon-fishery is conducted.

A hamper of about six feet in diameter, and the same height, made by the fisherman of the roughest wicker-work, is placed in a side stream of the rock, in the bed of the river. The anxiety of the salmon to mount up the stream is so great, that he forces himself through a hole into the hamper, as the easiest way of advancing upwards, from which position he cannot again escape. In this manner, in a favorable season, sixty-three salmon have been caught in one night in a single basket. It is a source of wealth to the little town of Sand.

At Sävde they held a meeting on First-day morning.

We reached the head of the fiord, writes John Yeardley by 12 o'clock, and found but poor accommodation. We three had one room with three beds; Endré Dahl with his willing-hearted and contented men lodged in a barn on straw. There was time enough to arrange for a meeting in the morning, and we applied for a room at the inn; but a little knot of illiberal Haugeans [followers of Hauge], or *Saints*, as they call themselves, persuaded our landlord not to let us meet in his house. But we obtained better accommodation under the rocks in a house containing two rooms connected by a passage, and, seating ourselves in the centre, could be well heard by those outside the door. We had a good meeting.

Returning to Sand, he continues:—

The wind being against us, the men had to work very hard at the oar to bring us in time for the meeting appointed for 6 o'clock at Sand. Some of the Friends from near Sävde accompanied us in their small boat; and some from Sand had gone many miles to attend the meeting at Sävde, and returned to the one at Sand. Their zeal is great and their love fervent. This was a very crowded meeting, and proved a satisfactory time. We found here a few of the *Saints*, but of a more liberal cast; they expressed great grief that their brethren at the head of the fiord had refused the peaceable messengers of the gospel from a far country a house in which to meet. This unwelcome news had reached them long before our arrival.

At a later date, John Yeardley relates an occurrence which happened at Sand, worthy of note in itself, and which must have been not a little confirmatory of his faith. It came to his knowledge after his return to Stavanger.

When we were at Sand, one of the Friends who joins in holding the silent meeting invited several of our ship's company to his house; but the man's wife was so exasperated that she drove them away, saying she would not have such folks under her roof. She had confounded the principles of Friends with those of some wild persons who had gone about the country spreading ranterism, and giving the people the idea that they were of our Society. It was in vain to reason with her, and the husband, for the sake of peace, mildly con-sented to let the Friends withdraw. However, she attended our public meeting, where the gospel doctrine of our Society was pretty fully illustrated; and I felt constrained also to preach on the unreasonableness of persecution for conscience' sake, either by the government, private persons, or families. Conviction seized her heart, and she became broken to pieces. After the meeting she sought up the Friends whom she had driven from her house, and told them she could not be happy unless they would give her a proof of forgiveness by taking up their abode in her family so long as they might remain in the place. Several of them accepted the invitation, which gave them an opportunity for free and satisfactory conversation.

How merciful are the Lord's doings with us in sending help in the needful time! I was so spent when we arrived at Sand, having had nothing from breakfast till 5 o'clock,

26

that I said in my heart, It is impossible to get through the meeting this evening.

The Friends had some religious service at several other places about Stavanger, and on the 6th of the Eighth Month proceeded northward to Bergen, accompanied by Endré Dahl and his wife and Asbjön Kloster. Their chief service in this city was a public meeting, at which there was a large attendance. John Yeardley says of the meeting :—

There was a great mixture of feeling. Many pious, thirsty souls, I believe, were present, and I hope such were encouraged and comforted; but the strong impression on my mind was to call the sinner to repentance.

On their way back to Stavanger, among the passengers were two Finland convicts, for whose peculiar case they felt much sympathy.

On board our steamer were two prisoners on the deck, in heavy irons. They were natives of Finland, and had been sentenced to some months' confinement in irons at Christiania, for having, it is said, committed some outrage on the priest in disturbing the national worship. There has for some time past been a great awakening about religion in Finland and other parts of the North, and the most active among this number, in their zeal not tempered with right knowledge, have transgressed the law. I heartily pitied the two poor creatures, inasmuch as I feared justice had not been done them; the prejudices of the priests and judges are so great in all matters connected with any separation from the national worship. They were chained together, and were clothed in their native reindeer skins, and on their ironed feet were snow-sandals turned up with a long toe. We offered them money, but they turned from it; and when acceptance of it was pressed, their change of countenance indicated anger. They understood nothing but the Finnish language.

On their return to Stavanger, Peter Bedford felt that his share in the work was accomplished, and that it was not his part to accompany John Yeardley in the service which remained for the latter to do in Norway. After being present at another public meeting in Stavanger, and in a parting interview with the Friends of the town, he went with William Robinson direct to Kiel. John Yeardley had two or three more meetings in the neighborhood of Stavanger, where the desire of the people to attend was more remarkable than ever.

On the 11th of the Eighth Month he bade farewell to this interesting place, and, accompanied by Endré Dahl, again crossed the mountains to Christiansand, holding meetings at several places on the sea-coast, where none had ever been held before. His notices of some of these meetings are well worth transcription.

14*th.*—Journeyed about fourteen miles up the fiord, into the mountains, to Aamut in Qvindesdalen. This meeting was the most solemn of any we have had. Many said, in tears, at the conclusion, This is a doctrine that we cannot resist; it goes to our heart, and meets the conviction of our own experience. What shall we do?—our heart burns within us!

15*th.*—We returned to Fœdde to a meeting this afternoon, which was, I think, the largest we have had. There were two large rooms filled, and a number seated on planks on the grass; not less than about 700 persons were present. Many followed us to the lodging, to converse on subjects that lay near their hearts, and to ask for tracts and books. Among them was a man who goes about to exhort the people to amendment of life. He appeared to be a simple, sincere character, and was much satisfied with our meeting, saying, as if from the bottom of his heart, How remarkably, how wonderfully, have the truths of the gospel been opened and explained to us this day!

16*th.*—At Fahrsund we had some difficulty to procure a place for a meeting. It is a brandy-drinking place. No one would hear anything of our business. A rich old lady has a large room which she lets for all kinds of purposes except for anything connected with *religion;* she gave an abrupt refusal to the application. E. Dahl and I went to the English vice-consul, showed him my certificate, and explained to him the object of my visit to Fahrsund. He kindly accompanied us to the old lady, and told her that we belonged to a respectable religious society in England and were not the persons she supposed, come to preach wild doctrines. She consented to let us occupy the entrance-hall, which was good and spacious. The consul then went with me to call on the sheriff; he said he and his lady would attend the meeting, which they did, with a good many of the respectable inhabitants, but the common people would not come near us. One man to whom a notice was offered, when he saw the word *worship*, immediately tore it to pieces. The lady to whom the room belonged sat near me all the meeting, and looked serious before the close ; and she took leave of us with very different feeling from that in which she first met us. The sheriff came to me after the meeting and offered his hand, saying, I thank you for the present occasion—I shall never forget it.

Before the meeting at Fœdde John Yeardley had an opportunity of refreshing his mind with the charms of Norwegian nature.

My friend E. Dahl and I went out for a quiet walk. It was a lovely Sabbath morning; the sky cloudless, and the sun shining brightly on the water as it rapidly foamed down the cliffs. After gathering a few cranberries we seated ourselves on a shady rock to meditate. All was silent around— nothing heard but the shepherd-boy playing his horn; the sound coming from the distant mountains into the wooded valley where we sat, first shrill, then softening into a simple irregular note. My friend asked me what I thought the instrument was. It is made, said he, of a goat's horn, and is blown to keep the fox from taking the young lambs, and as a means of communication with other shepherds when widely separated on the mountains; the sound of this horn also keeps the sheep from straying.

They arrived at Christiansand on the 19th; and Endré Dahl, finding a vessel sailing for Stavanger, engaged a passage in it for himself. After parting with him, John Yeardley writes :—

E. Dahl and I have been closely united in the gospel bond; he has been a truly affectionate sympathizer and efficient helper. I am thus, he continues, left alone in a strange land; but I do feel a peaceful and a thankful heart to my Heavenly Father that he has in mercy blessed me with light, strength, and faith to go through this service in Norway. Imperfectly has it been performed, I know; but I have done what I could, and a song of thanksgiving is due to my Lord.

John Yeardley returned by Germany to England. At Obernkirchen, near Minden, where some persons had not long before been convinced of Friends' principles, he had a meeting, in which he was joined by a number of Friends from Minden. A few years before, Thomas Arnett, from America, desired to hold a meeting for worship in this place, but was prevented by the police. The object was now accomplished by engaging a room without the limits of the state of Bückeburg, in which the town is situated, and within the Hessian frontier, which includes, in fact, a part of Obernkirchen.

A public meeting for worship in that place (says John Yeardley, in a letter written after his return home,) was such a new thing, that on our arrival we found a press of persons whom the room could by no means contain. The landlord readily granted us his barn, which was commodious, and we threw open the large doors into the yard, which was seated ; besides which, the people stood in numbers. We had a solemn meeting. There is a little company who hold a meeting at Obernkirchen ; several of these have suffered on account of their religious scruples in refusing baptism to their children, &c. These we invited after meeting to take coffee with us, about thirty persons, all serious. It was a delightful occasion. After the coffee we had a sweet parting meeting with this truly interesting company. We had been given to expect that, although we had taken the precaution to *pitch our tent* without the limits of the intolerant place, the police would be present, and would most probably disperse our assembly. But no such thing ;—all was quiet.

I was thankful (he adds in his Diary) that the meeting was held in quiet, for there is a bitter feeling of persecution in the neighborhood. I was previously much cast down, but "thanks be unto God who always causeth us to triumph in Christ."

# CHAPTER XIX

## 1853.

THE call which John Yeardley had received to visit the German colonies in South Russia, and which had lain for a long time dormant, now revived. A friend who had watched with regret his unsuccessful attempts on former journeys to enter that jealous country, and who augured from the political changes which had taken place that permission might probably now be obtained, brought the subject again under his notice. The admonition was timely and effectual. After carefully pondering the matter—with, we doubt not, as on former occasions, a childlike dependence on his Omniscient Guide for direction,—he came to the conclusion that it was his duty once more to address himself to this undertaking: and when it was accomplished, and he had returned in safety and peace to England, he alluded more than once to the manner in which the concern had been revived, saying he had been, before he was thus aroused, like *the prophet asleep.*

He re-opened the prospect of this service before his Monthly Meeting, on the 3rd of the Fifth Month, 1853. In a letter written the same day, he says:—

I am just returned from our Monthly Meeting in London, where I mentioned to my friends my concern to visit the German colonies in the South of Russia, which, thou wilt probably recollect, was included in my certificate for religious

(399)

service on the Continent of Europe, five years ago. I received the expression of much sympathy and unity from my friends, and the certificate was ordered, including on my return, if permitted, any service that may present in Constantinople, the island of Malta, and some places in the South of France. Weak as I am, I cast myself once more into the hand of our Lord and Blessed Protector, in holy confidence that he will do all things well.

On receiving a passport from the Secretary of State, with the requisite counter-signature of the Russian Ambassador, he wrote to John Kitching, the 25th of the Fourth Month:—

I want thee to know that, through the kind and efficient aid of our mutually dear friend Samuel Gurney, I have at length been enabled to procure a Russian passport, and also a letter of recommendation to one of the first houses in Petersburg. Thou knowest, my dear friend, for a long time this matter has been heavy on my mind. It is a great comfort to have the ground cleared in this respect.

John Yeardley left London at the end of the Sixth Month, and went to Hull to take the steam-packet direct to Petersburg. In the narrative which follows, we have interwoven with the Diary extracts from his letters to his sisters; and we have been allowed the use of William Rasche's Journal, in relating and describing many circumstances of which J. Y. himself made no record.

*Petersburg.* 7 *mo.* 10.—On the 30th of the Sixth Month I left my peaceful home at Stamford Hill for my Russian journey. At our kind friend Isabel Casson's at Hull I met my young companion William Rasche. We were affectionately cared for by dear I. C. and her daughter, and she and several other friends saw us on board the steamer. It is a fine ship, well ventilated, with good sleeping accommodation and provisions: the captain is a kind, religious man.

On First-day evening, the captain invited us to the ship's service—an invitation which we gladly embraced. When he had finished, I addressed the company, much to my own comfort: great seriousness prevailed. After I had relieved my mind, the captain closed with a few sweet and feeling words. When the occasion was over, he came to me and expressed his thankfulness that I had been enabled to strengthen his hands by throwing in a word of exhortation. He said that sometimes, when he had felt indisposed and unprepared for his religious duty, he had given himself to a quiet dependence on the Lord, and had been mercifully helped, to the benefit of his own soul, in endeavoring to do his duty to others.

There is great uncertainty (he says in a letter written during the voyage), how we shall find things at Petersburg, and whether they will permit us to proceed to the South; but this I must leave. Whatever way it may please Providence to turn the matter, as it regards myself I believe I shall be relieved from Russia in having made this last attempt.

They arrived at Petersburg on the 9th of the Seventh Month, after a safe and agreeable passage of seven days.

Before we reached Cronstadt, to quote from J. Y.'s Diary, we encountered a strong gale, so that the officers from the guardship, who came to see that all was in order, had hard work to get on board. There were eighteen Russian sailors with oars, yet they could not draw the boat, and our steamer was obliged to throw ropes and haul her in. The sight of Cronstadt was formidable; for more than two miles in and near the harbor there was a line of ships of war. At Cronstadt we had to be put on board a smaller steamer, which caused us much detention. At the custom-house all passed off well; they were more civil and less strict in their exami-

nation than in England. The Russian sailors look very
unbright; they are not active in managing a boat. They not
unfrequently received a few strokes from the fist of the helms-
man, or a rope's-end, either of which they took with that
unconcerned composure which showed they were accustomed
to it. We are located at the hotel of H. Spink, an intelligent
Yorkshireman; his wife is very kind and attentive.

13th.—Spent this day at Peterhoff, with W. C. Gillibrand
and wife, with two of their friends. It is the first opportunity
we have had for serious conversation in this place, and I
hope it was to mutual comfort. They took us a drive after
dinner to see several of the Emperor's pavilions, mostly
surrounded by beautiful pieces of water. There was an
intelligent man present, who had spent some time in India,
—— Watson; he now has charge of the British school in
Petersburg. We find the Scripture Lessons are no more in
use in the school; nor is the New Testament in the Russian
language allowed to be circulated in the country. The Bible
Society is just alive, but can hardly breathe; other institutions languish for want of support; party spirit has crept in
to their great injury. The law is still very stringent in not
allowing a member of one religious body to join another;
but the different sects are allowed their own worship and
schools.

20th.—Left Petersburg by the train at 11 o'clock yesterday, and arrived at Moscow about nine this morning. The
road, with but little exception, is flat and uninteresting. The
forests are immense, mostly of firs and birch, which being
thickly set grow small. Many of the stations are superb.
The line of railway did not conduct us near any towns or
villages that I could observe, but by some of the poorest
scattered huts I ever saw in any country.

At Moscow, John Yeardley and his companion called
on Pastor Dietrich, a German, residing a little out of
the city:—

He is, says J. Y., in one of his letters, a worthy pastor of
the Old Lutheran Church, a sweet venerable-looking man

with long white locks. He was at dinner with his family
when we called, but he would not allow us to go away, but
took us up to the attic story to his study; primitive indeed,
but clean, and to him I have no doubt a room of prayer, as
well as of study. He seemed delighted to find our mission
was to the Colonies. "But what will you do about the
language?" said he; "they speak nothing but German." I
wish the dear girls could have seen his countenance lighted
up with cheerful brightness, when he found we could speak
German: "Ah, I need not trouble you any longer with my
poor English!" He knows a great many of the pastors, and
will give us letters of introduction to the little flocks in the
Colonies and the Crimea.

As might be expected, it was with a sinking heart
that John Yeardley contemplated the formidable journey before him; but, as in other times of extremity, he
cast himself wholly upon the Lord, and found his soul
to be sustained, and his courage renewed to undergo
the hardships that awaited him.

7 mo. 21.—Rose this morning much cast down in mind at
the thought of our long journey, and a want of a knowledge
of the Russian language. Poured my complaint in fervency
of soul before the Lord, and was a little comforted in believing that he would still care for us and preserve us in this
strange and long wilderness travel. It is his own cause in
which I am engaged, and I am willing to endure any bodily
fatigue if I may only be strengthened to do the works to which
my blessed Master has called me. The Divine Finger seems
pointing to the place where the people I am seeking are to be
found.

I went after breakfast to the dear Pastor Dietrich. His
heart was filled with love for me, and I felt the sweetness of
his spirit to encourage me; preciously was the divine unction
spread over us. He gave me some information of the religious state of things here. There seems to be about 800 of
the evangelical party in Moscow, including the French and

English Protestants, and the different classes of Lutherans; a small number out of 350,000 souls which the city contains; the rest are Roman Catholics and of the Greek church, mostly the latter. God knows the hearts of all.

*22nd* [?]. "In thee, O Lord, do I put my trust; let me never be ashamed: deliver me in thy righteousness. Bow down thine ear to me; deliver me speedily: be thou my strong rock, for a house of defence to save me."—(Ps. xxxi. 1, 2.) "Hear the right, O Lord, attend unto my cry; give ear unto my prayer, that goeth not out of feigned lips."—(Ps. xvii. 1.) The above sweet words were brought home to my heart with power this morning after a time of conflict in spirit. Lord, grant me faith and patience to the end of the race, when I shall have to say, Now, Lord, lettest thou thy servant depart in peace. Amen.

Providing themselves with food, and with small change of money for the journey—two things indispensable to Russian travel—John Yeardley and William Rasche left Moscow on the 23rd, by *malle-poste* for Orel. They stopped some hours at Toula: the land south of this town they found to be well-cultivated, and the harvest had begun; it consisted mostly of rye. The journey to Orel occupied forty-four hours. Among their fellow-travellers was a resident of Moscow, Charles Uyttenhoven, who spoke English, German, French and Russ, and who, like themselves, was going to Kharkov. He was a pleasant and gentlemanly companion, and was of great service to them in acting as spokesman on the road.

From Orel there was no *malle-poste* in which they could continue their journey, and they were obliged to hire a *tarantas*, or posting-carriage, a very inferior kind of conveyance. In consequence, besides, of the fair at Pultowa, every vehicle of this description had been taken up except one, which was of course the

worst in the town. When they had loaded their luggage and spread hay to lie upon, they started; but
before they were out of sight of the stable the crazy
vehicle broke down, and they were detained till nearly
eleven o'clock at night, whilst it was being repaired.
In this new kind of conveyance they experienced great
discomfort: they could neither sit nor lie with ease, as
the space was much too small for three passengers.
The country they passed through was very rich; it
may be called the granary of Russia; they found the
harvest more advanced the farther they penetrated into
the south.

At Koursk they hired a fresh *tarantas*. The roads
were inferior to those along which they had travelled,
but the country was more picturesque, still fertile, and
producing much wheat; the weather was very hot, as it
had been all the way from Petersburg. On the 27th, at
midnight, they reached Kharkov.

We have travelled, says John Yeardley, four days and
nights in succession from Moscow to this place. The con-
veyances of the country are exceedingly bad; they almost
shook our bones asunder.

The next day they visited Pastor Landesen, to whom
they had a letter of introduction from Pastor Dietrich.
They spent the day with the family of this intelligent
and pious man. Tea was spread in the garden, to which
meal a number of Christian friends were invited.

The pastor's wife, says John Yeardley, is a sweet-spirited
woman. After much social converse our garden-visit closed
with a religious occasion, in which I expressed a few words
of exhortation. I think we were sensible of the nearness of

the presence of our Divine Master, which proved a brook by the dreary way. We met at the pastor's house Superinten-dent Huber, a worthy and experienced Christian, kind and fatherly to us.

The next day William Rasche went with Pastor Landesen to hire a carriage. No such thing, however, was to be had, and they would have been happy if they could have engaged as good a vehicle as their old crazy *tarantas ;* for the only alternative was a *bauer-wagen* (peasant's cart), if we except the very expensive extra-post carriage, with which they would have been obliged to take a conductor. It happened that a young man, an apothecary's assistant, wanted to go to Iekaterinoslav ; his ancestors were German, and he could speak both that language and Russ. By Landesen's recommenda-tion they took him as their companion, and he was very useful to them on the road. The *bauer-wagen* was much more uncomfortable than the *tarantas* had been ; travelling in it was like gallopping over a bad road in an English farmer's waggon ; and, as the vehicle had no cover, the travellers were exposed without protection to the full power of the sun. The floor of the waggon was spread with mattresses, and, thus furnished, it served them for parlor, kitchen, and lodging-room.

They travelled in this way through the night, but the next day were obliged to wait at a small dirty station for horses till the afternoon ; and in the evening John Yeardley became so ill, from hard travelling and exposure to the heat, that they were compelled to alight at another little station near Novomoskovsk, and make the best of the poor accommodation they could procure. The next morning, somewhat refreshed by rest, they went forwards to Iekaterinoslav, where they happily met with a clean inn, the Hotel Suisse, kept by a German.

The same day they went in a boat up the river Samava, to Rybalsk, seven miles, to see a German schoolmaster named Schreitel, to whom they had a letter of introduction. This is a colony of twenty-five families, founded in 1788: the schoolmaster, who was also the minister, received them in a brotherly manner. It was here that their mission properly commenced. From this place a succession of German colonies extend in a southeasterly direction to the Sea of Azov. The villages are all built on the same pattern, being formed of one straight street of neat houses on both sides, adorned with trees in front and gardens behind. The German colonists consist principally of Mennonites and Lutherans. The former are the most numerous and thriving; they were invited to settle there by Catherine the Great, in order to improve the state of agriculture; but their example has not had the desired influence on the surrounding districts. Although his German neighbor is in an infinitely better condition than himself, the Russian peasant will not imitate the husbandry which is practised so successfully before his eyes.

At Rybalsk, John Yeardley had a Scripture reading and a religious opportunity with a few serious persons who came to the house; and the next evening he held a meeting for worship with the colonists.

On the 3rd, they left for Neuhoffnung. They travelled in a covered carriage, which, though without springs, was a great improvement on their last vehicle. They came the first day as far as Konski, where they passed the night, sleeping in the carriage, the air being very mild the night through. In the afternoon they arrived at another Mennonite colony, Schönweise, where they had a short interview with Pastor Obermanz and a few of his flock. These people produce a small quantity of silk. The travellers were now on the Steppes; they found them very thinly peopled, so that all the country out of sight of the villages appeared like a vast desert. On the 4th they passed through three colonies—Grünthal, Priship, and Petershagen. The settlers here are from all parts of Germany, mostly from Prussia and Würtemberg. Next came Halbstadt, the seat of the Bishop, and Alexanderwohl, where the Friends passed the night. They were surrounded by a large number of settlements on all sides.

These were the places where, according to his previous impressions and apprehension of duty, John Yeardley was to have entered on that work of gospel-labor to which he had so long looked forward. But, instead of finding, as on former occasions of a similar kind, his heart enlarged and his mouth opened to preach the word, he seems now to have felt himself straitened in spirit, and to have been obliged to pass in silence from colony to colony, a wonder perhaps to others, a cause of humiliation to himself. Never before, in all his many journeyings, had such a trial befallen him; and it may be supposed that, coming so soon after the copious and unrestrained exercise of his gift which he had experienced in Norway, it would press upon him with peculiar force. The people to whom he was now come, seem, it is true, to have been in a different state from the simple-hearted Norwegians, who thirsted for the "pure milk of the word;" and their comparative indifference to spiritual things may have been a main cause of the silence which he felt to be imposed upon him. With the reserve natural to him, he has left but little clue to the motives and feelings under which he acted. Great must have been the relief when, as happened on several occasions, his bonds were loosened, and the command was renewed to speak in the name of his only-loved and gracious Lord.

On the 5th they passed through several colonies to Gnadenfeld, where, says J. Y. :—

We halted to breakfast with one of the colonists, and found him a sweet-spirited man, and his family pious. His name is David Voote. He appreciated the object of our mission, and spoke of the awakening that had taken place of late; telling us that devotional meetings had been established, but that some of their preachers did not approve of them. We sent for one of the ministers, with whom I was pleased; he invited us to hold a meeting with them on a future occasion if we could make it accord with our journey, which I hope will be accomplished.

We obtained some information respecting the Molokans, and were directed to Nicolai Schmidt in Steinbach, who often has communication with them. We found him a delightful man, quite of the right sort to be useful to us. As the Molokans speak nothing but Russ, we shall be in want of an interpreter in our visit to them. I told him he must go with us; and he immediately said, I will go with pleasure; whenever you return here and incline to go, I will be at home and will accompany you. This seemed an opening of Providence, and removes one great difficulty in the way of a visit to this people, for whom I have felt more than towards any others in South Russia. N. Schmidt is a wealthy farmer, and sets himself at liberty to promote the extension of the Saviour's kingdom; I felt at once at home with him as a friend and brother.

From Steinbach, which lay a few versts out of the direct road, they proceeded to Stuttgardt, and the next

27

day, the 6th, to Neuhoffnung, where they were accommodated at a farmer's, and had the comfort of a good clean apartment and kind attention to their wants. This is the principal seat of the German Lutheran colonists.

On Seventh-day, says John Yeardley, we attended the school-children's meeting, about 200 present. After Pastor Wüst had questioned on or explained the Scriptures, I had an opportunity to address them. On First-day afternoon we held an appointed meeting [with Wüst's congregation], which was not large, on account of many [with the Pastor himself] having to attend an interment in the neighborhood. After the meeting we received a salutation from some of the young sisterhood, who came to us and surprised us with their sweet melodious voices, singing in concert a hymn well suited to our present situation. After they had ended I went out and had a long conversation with them.

In all my journeyings, he touchingly continues, I was never so much cast down as in this scene of labor; I never before so much missed the help and consolation of my precious one as I now do; but, blessed be a gracious God, she is safe with Him, and free from a toil which she could never have endured. I marvel, and praise his great name for upholding me thus far; I am astonished at the way in which I am enabled to bear the hardships of this journey, and am preserved in health. It is the doing of my gracious Saviour, and I thank him out of a grateful heart. Should I never be permitted to return to my earthly home, I have a joyful hope he will take me to a glorious rest with himself and with those I have so tenderly loved on earth.

On the 8th, William Rasche went to Berdjansk, on the Sea of Azov, to change some English money, and to inquire if there were any religious people there. He met with some interesting persons, who seemed at first to oe prejudiced against the Friends but after some conversation became very loving, and desired he would bring J. Y. to see them the next day. Accordingly, on the 9th, J. Y. and W. R. went to Berdjansk, accompanied by Pastor Wüst and several others. The meeting which they went to attend was held in a private house. It commenced in the usual manner, with singing; after which, —— Buller read a chapter, and the pastor commented upon it; and then they asked J. Y. what he had to say regarding it. He answered by giving his view of the subject, and afterwards addressed them in the ministry. Various individuals then related their experience, one after the other, as is usual in the more private religious meetings in these churches.

—— Buller (writes J. Y., in recording this meeting) is an interesting man; I had much conversation with him as to his own conversion. It seems to have been a work of the Spirit, without, in the first instance, any other instrumentality than reading the Bible. I met several pious persons in the meeting-room, and held converse with them to mutual comfort. They are simple and sincere. We took tea in the garden after the meeting, and did not reach our lodging in Neuhoffnung until 12 o'clock the same night.

10*th*.—This morning they started for Elizabethsdorf, accompanied by Robert Lehmkuhle, a teacher from Kharkov. Their way lay entirely through the boundless steppes, where so many ways ran into each other that the driver missed the road, and they wandered about until 10 P. M., when they took shelter at a German colonist's. The inmates, who had gone to rest, rose to give them milk and bread.

The next day they proceeded to Elizabethsdorf, being escorted on the way by hospitable members of the settlements through which they passed. At Elizabethsdorf they were received by schoolmaster Seib, a brotherly Christian man, whose conversation was "seasoned with grace."

After tea, says John Yeardley, we held a devotional meeting, in which I had an opportunity to address the little company; but the people generally in the colonies are busy till late in the evening. Being much weary with our jolting journey, I retired to the waggon for the night, as I supposed; but W. R. soon came to inform me that a number of young persons, men and women, were come, it being as early as they could be liberated from their day's labor, to have some of our company. I sprang from the waggon with joy, and we had a delightful meeting, with a pretty large company. They sang repeatedly, and betweentimes I related to them something of my travels in Germany and Greece, with which they appeared wonderfully pleased. We were all served with tea out of doors, and the company remained together till after eleven o'clock, and then returned joyfully home.

I was much pleased with Seib. He and another schoolmaster, named Kapper, have been dismissed from their office of teacher, because of their holding private meetings and preaching in them, or explaining the Scriptures. Some of the Lutheran ministers are so lifeless that they will not allow the people to meet in private for their edification. The dead persecute the living, and light struggles with darkness. This is even the case in some districts among the Mennonites. The ministers fear that their people should go before them in religious light. The more I see of the *one-man system*, the more I prize the gospel liberty in my own beloved religious Society.

They returned to Neuhoffnung, and on the 13th went to Nicolai Schmidt's at Steinbach.

Attended the meeting there in the morning, and at Gnadenfeld in the evening, in both which places opportunity was given me to communicate what was in my heart for the people.

The settlements of the Molokans, consisting of three villages, each of about a thousand inhabitants, lie to the south of the German colonies. These people are native Russians and seceders from the Russo-Greek church; they receive their name from the word *Moloko*, milk, because they drink milk on fast-days, which is forbidden by the national religion. The Steppes are their Siberia, to which they have been banished. Their worship is simple, commencing with silence and prayer, and they do not use the ceremonies and discipline common among most other Christians; but they are firm believers in the Christian faith, and many of them are spiritually-minded people.

On the 15th John Yeardley and William Rasche, under the conduct of N. Schmidt, left Neuhoffnung to visit the Molokans. The first village they came to was Novo-Salifks, a prosperous colony in worldly matters, but said to be behind the others in spiritual life. At the next, Wasilowkov, they met with Terenti Sederhoff, the apostle of the Molokans, whose remarkable history J. Y. related in a tract called *The Russian Peasant*, forming No. 12 of his series. Here they also met with A. Stajoloff, who remembered William Allen's visit in 1819. Sederhoff accompanied them to the third village, Astrachanka, where they had a conversational meeting with several of the chief men, but the intercourse was carried on at a double disadvantage.

They spoke, says John Yeardley, nothing but Russ. I never regretted more the want of the language. Schmidt had a manifest unwillingness to interpret all I wanted to say, because it did not accord with his own sentiments, and he

feared it might strengthen the people in those views from
which the Mennonites would draw them. There was a precious feeling over us, and I felt assured they appreciated our
motive in visiting them; they often pressed my hand when
comparing Scripture texts on which we were of one mind.
I felt satisfied in having done what I could to direct them in
the right way, and to strengthen them in it. They are well
read in the Scriptures.

The travellers passed the night at this village, sleeping
as usual in their carriage; and the next day, taking a
loving leave of their friends, directed their course over
the steppes into the Crimea. Here they found themselves in the heart of the Tartar country, beyond the
verge of civilized life.

The Tartar villages, says John Yeardley, are the meanest
possible, consisting sometimes of mere holes dug in the earth,
or huts standing a little above the ground. The men wear
wide drawers with the pink shirt over them; the women
have a chemise reaching to the calf of the leg, dirty and
coarse, an apron round the waist, sometimes so scanty or so
ragged that it will not meet, and a handkerchief tied in a
slovenly manner on the head. In these three articles of dress
they drive the horses and oxen; the sun burns them to a dark
brown, almost black. The children we saw were quite naked.
Various attempts have been made to civilize and instruct them,
but without success. One missionary pursued the work so
far as to feed and clothe the children, and collect them for
instruction, which they received for a while, but all at once
and with one consent it was at an end. When I see the Tartar galloping over the steppe as if riding on the wind, it constantly makes me think of the wild Arabs. When we are
anxious to find a well of water where we may take our meal,
and when we see travellers assembled to water their cattle
and flocks, and the camels running loose on the steppes—which
they do till autumn, when they are sought up for work,—all
reminds us of the customs of the East.

This evening they halted at a Tartar village, where the occupant of the *traktir*, or house of entertainment, persuaded the driver to take out his horses for the night. The conduct of this man and his companions was suspicious; they eagerly examined the mattresses of the travellers, which were of superior quality; and when William Rasche came to make the tea, which he did by the moonlight outside the hut, the boiling water which he poured in to rinse the teapot came out into the tumblers a white liquid; and after the tea was put in the innkeeper held up the pot against the moon, and looked curiously into it. Instead of retiring early, as the Tartars always do, the men in the hut kept a watch upon the travellers; and the suspicions even of the driver were awakened, when one of them came to him, as he was lying by his horses, to borrow his knife. His horses, however, were so weary, and he himself so unwilling to move, that the travelers contented themselves with harnessing the horses, and making ready to depart in case of necessity. Soon after midnight, finding they were still watched by the Tartars, and apprehending that these waited only till they should all be asleep, to carry off their horses or to rob their persons, they decided to make the best of their way out of their hands. The driver being slow to move, W. R. jumped into his place, seized the reins, and drove quickly off, thankful to have effected a safe escape. It is very common for the Tartars to prowl about in the night, and steal the horses and waggons of their more settled and thrifty neighbors.

After about three hours' driving, the moon shining so bright that they could see to read by it, they arrived at another village, of a less suspicious character.

On the 18th they reached Simpheropol, where they

were glad to rest. The next day they wished to visit Pastor Kilius of Neusatz, to whom they had an introduction: as they were considering how they should get to him, he opportunely came to the hotel. He introduced them to several estimable persons, and took them the next day to his dwelling, situate in a picturesque mountain village, twenty versts from the city. At Neusatz commences another chain of German colonies, settled by the Evangelical Lutherans. The next morning they attended the public worship, and in the afternoon the Scripture-teaching for the children. On the 22nd they went to Zürichthal, a village formed of well-built houses, but where they found the school in a very low state. The 23rd they started early for the Sudag colony, intending to spend the time there until the departure of the steamer for Odessa; but they found nothing to interest them in this settlement, and accordingly proceeded to Feodosia, (or Kaffa,) a watering-place on the south coast of the Crimea. The German inns in this place were all full, and to procure a wholesome lodging, they drove the next day four miles among the hills, where they hired a large apartment at the house of a German. The situation was romantic, with an extensive prospect over sea and mountains; and on the hill-side was a thicket, forming a delightful bower, where John Yeardley and his companion "live by day, walked, talked, reposed, and wrote." In this retreat, breathing cool air and quietude, J. Y. received the physical refreshment he so much needed, while he reviewed the course of his laborious journey. Notwithstanding his discouragements, he was able to cast all his burden upon his Saviour, with whom he seems to have dwelt in nearer communion as his day on earth went down.

8 *mo.* 26.—This morning I felt more sweet union with my God in spirit than for a long time; and a strong desire has arisen to live in closer communion with Jesus, the beloved of my soul, the only access to the Father—the only place of rest, safety, and true *peace.* I long more than ever not to be troubled with cross occurrences over which I have no control, and which have too long perplexed me and disturbed my inward peace. I long more than ever to spend my few remaining days on earth as with my God in heaven, to refer everything to him, and to pray more earnestly and diligently for his grace to preserve me near to himself under *all* circum-stances, until he shall have prepared me to be taken to heaven, to join the happy company there in a blissful eternity. "Thou wilt keep him in perfect peace whose mind is stayed on thee, because he trusteth in thee."—Isa. xxvi. 3.

On the 1st of the Ninth Month they sailed to Odessa, where they had to remain eight days. In this city they received a visit from a pastor, who conversed with them on the work of the heavenly kingdom then going on in the East, especially in Constantinople and Asia Minor.

The Saviour's kingdom, writes John Yeardley, in allusion to this conversation, is spreading, and many instruments are being raised up in various nations to help forward the great work. The kingdom of Satan is in danger; he sees it, and stirs up the jealousy of men, setting them against one another, and, by their seeking through party-spirit to exalt their own particular religion, hindering the Lord's work. Into what-ever nation the beams of the Sun of Righteousness shine, the inhabitants begin to inquire the way to Zion, and turn their faces thitherward. This alarms the rulers whose king-dom is of this world.

From Odessa to Constantinople they had a quick and safe passage. At Constantinople John Yeardley was deeply interested in the institutions which the American missionaries have founded for the religious and temporal improvement of the Armenians.    He visited two of these, the high school at Bebek and the girls' seminary at Has-keuï, both beautifully situated on the shores of the Bosphorus.    In the former they found forty-eight young men,—sixteen Greek and thirty-two Armenian. The industrial part of the education was particularly gratifying to him.

Cyrus Hamlin, he says, who has the superintendence of their studies and labor, is wonderfully adapted for his vocation.    He is assisted only by native teachers.    The young men looked serious: some of their countenances were peculiarly impressive, indicating that they had been with Jesus. I saw them assembled in the school-room, and addressed them for some time; and C. Hamlin most willingly interpreted into Armenian what I said.    It was a sweet and memorable time.    The Armenian teacher would scarcely let go my hand after the meeting, he had been so touched with the power of divine love.    In the girls' boarding-school we found twenty-five girls, all Armenians, with the exception of two or three Greeks.    It was a lovely sight to see so many of this class under a course of religious and useful instruction.    Many of the countenances were marked and pleasing, and were *fixed* on me with great apparent seriousness while I addressed them, along with some of the neighbors.    —— Everett (the conductor of the school) kindly and most willingly interpreted what I had to communicate.    He and his wife have also a day-school for boys and girls.    I consider these institutions as bright and hopeful spots in the East, from which much good may arise.

The persevering and well-directed efforts of the American missionaries for the evangelization of the Armenians, and the field of Christian labor which was thus opened, took firm hold of J. Y.'s mind; he longed to visit the schools and congregations in Isnik and

Brusa, and probably only abandoned the journey at this time in the hope of undertaking it at some future day. John Yeardley describes Constantinople as—

Built entirely on the hills which slope from a considerable eminence down to the Bosphorus. The trees towering among the houses, the high spires and gilded domes, have a most imposing effect; but what is the astonishment of the traveller when he commences his ascent up steep, narrow, clumsily-pitched streets. I could only compare them to the worst-constructed bridle-roads in England which the packhorses traversed centuries ago. The three days we were in the city I only saw one or two carriages,—the most curious vehicles; indeed, there is scarcely a street in which two carriages can pass. Donkeys are the chief carriers. As to dogs, they are born and bred in the streets and are the property of the town, and in the day-time lie by dozens in the streets, young and old, are always under the feet of the traveller, and he must constantly poke them out of the way with his stick; by night they are furious. The shops present a jumble of all kinds of wares; and the Turks sit cross-legged in the window, or work at their trade inside.

They left Constantinople on the 15th, and on the 17th went on shore at Smyrna, where, at the house of the American missionary Ladd, they met with another missionary, named Stacking, returning with his family from Persia, where he had labored sixteen years among the Nestorians. The account which he gave John Yeardley of the creed and condition of the Nestorian Church, and of the schools which had been opened in Persia, aroused his deep sympathy and produced an abiding impression on his mind.

Smyrna, like the other Turkish cities which they saw, vividly impressed the travellers with its Oriental character.

Like Constantinople, says J. Y., it is a town of all nations.
The streets are narrow, with a run of dirty water down the
middle.· We met docile camels in great number, bringing
figs from the interior. In the fig-market were thousands of
boxes being prepared and packed for exportation. It is a
sight of interest to see Turks, Greeks, &c., huddled together,
walking, talking, or sitting cross-legged and smoking their
long pipes. We took donkeys and ascended the hill, where
we obtained a good view of the town, and then examined the
ruins where the ancient city stood, and saw the place where
the message from Heaven was received by the angel of the
church of Smyrna. The church of Polycarp stood not far
from that of John the Baptist. After a visit of peculiar interest, I returned to the steam-ship and read the message to the
church of Smyrna, which gave rise to more reflections than I
can here record.

Steaming on the sea of Marmora, (to continue J. Y.'s
narrative of his homeward journey), the Bosphorus and the
Greek waters, was very pleasing. We had a good sight of
the walls of ancient Troas, where the apostle Paul received
the message in vision from the man of Macedonia, to come
over and help them. The quarantine prevented us from
landing at Syra; but I conveyed a note through the English
Consul to my old friend Hildner, who came alongside our
steamer. I learned from him that Argyri Climi was five
years in his school, and usefully filled the office of teacher of
the higher classes; had been married about ten years to a
lieutenant in the army; had three children, and was living
happily with her husband at the Piræus. It appears she
retains her religious principles.

21st.—Arrived at Malta. Ours is the first steamer that
has reached the island since the removal of the quarantine;
we went on shore directly after breakfast. Isaac Lowndes
was rejoiced to see me. We met in the street, and he conducted us to his house. He has been in Malta seven years,
acting for the Bible Society; he gives no bright account of
progress among the Greeks, as to spiritual religion, nor of
things in the island generally. The present governor has

admitted the Jesuits into the island, who are doing mischief;
privileges are being granted to the Romanists to the prejudice of the Protestants; and a regulation has been proposed
which would subject a Protestant to six months imprisonment
for not taking off his hat when he meets the procession of the
Host.

Isaac Lowndes took John Yeardley and William
Rasche to visit Selim Aga, or, as he was named after
baptism, Edward Williams; who with his wife, sister-
in-law, and four children, formed an interesting Christian household. J. Y. published the history of this man
in No. 13 of his series of tracts, *Turkey and the Converted Turk*, where also he has depicted several scenes
from the latter part of this journey.

Arriving at Marseilles, they proceeded quickly on to
Nismes. It was with a gush of natural sorrow that
J. Y. revisited a place where he had often sojourned with
his beloved wife.

The thought, he writes, of the difference in my circumstances now and when last in this place fills me with sorrow.
The beloved one of my bosom, then the stay and solace of my
heart, is no more with me to help and comfort mé in the toils
of life. Yet when I consider what a large amount of suffering she has escaped, I cannot but rejoice that she is at rest
with her God and Saviour, where I humbly hope soon to
meet her. Lord, prepare thy unworthy worm for that awful
but joyful day!

John Yeardley held a small public meeting at
Nismes, and the next day, the 3rd of the Tenth Month,
set out for the bathing-place of Bagnères de Bigorre,
in the Pyrenees. His principal reason for going there
was to recruit his shattered health. " On our arrival
at Nismes," he says, "and during our few days' sojourn
there, I began to feel the effects of my long, toilsome

Russian journey; and, in the hope of preventing a
return of my suffering complaint, I thought it justifiable
to make trial of the sulphur baths and water of Bagnères." But he had also another object in view: "I
had long thought," he adds, in a letter from Bigorre,
" whether there was not a seeking people in this neighborhood, and now I think there is."

His first care on arriving at Bigorre, was to call on
Pastor Frossard, formerly of Nismes, who feelingly reminded him of the changes which had happened to each
of them since they had met before. He proposed
to John Yeardley to meet some Christian friends at his
chapel. This was just what J. Y. had been wishing for.
The meeting was held; and after it was over he gave
the company an account of his travels in Russia, with
which they were highly gratified.

In a letter to his sister, Mary Tylor, which he wrote
from this place, is the following characteristic sentiment:

> Thy welcome letter duly reached me at Nismes, and drew
> forth my tender sympathy for thee and your whole circle in
> the loss of a kind and beloved brother. It is another link
> taken from the family chain, and the shorter it becomes the
> nearer we are drawn together in the bond of affection. How
> the spirit seems to ascend with those loved ones who are
> taken from us, and from earth to heaven! Our desire for a
> blissful eternity becomes more ardent, because they have
> already entered upon it; but above all, we desire to be with
> Him in whom we shall be one, and all will be glory.

Returning to Nismes, he occupied himself with
holding meetings in many places in that neighborhood.
In some meetings which he attended in the city, he had
for fellow-laborers Eli and Sybil Jones, from the

United States, with their companions. Amongst the
audience at one of these meetings were three soldiers,
who, with two others, had been awakened at Lyons, and
who manifested the progress they had made in Christian doctrine by refusing to kneel before the procession
of the Host. Their officer observing their disregard of
this required practice, held his sword over the neck of
one of them, saying he would strike off his head if he
did not bow down. The man was firm in his refusal,
and was sent to prison. To encourage one another in
their new profession, these men were accustomed to
keep religious meetings. They were in consequence
accused of sedition, and when they asserted the simply
religious character of their meetings, one of them was
required to swear to the truth of his statement; he
refused to take an oath, pleading that the New Testament commanded him not to swear. A second was
then called upon in the same way; he also refused;
and their stedfastness was reported to the commanding officer as an act of contumacy. The officer happened to be a Protestant, of an enlightened and pious
disposition; he said that soldiers were called upon to
vindicate the innocence of their companions, not to
procure their condemnation, and that if they did not
choose to give evidence the law would not compel them.
Two of the five received their discharge from the army;
the rest were removed to Nismes. John Yeardley had
some conversation with these three after the meeting,
with which he was well satisfied. They told him that
when they were awakened they wrote and received so
many letters that it excited suspicion, and that the
police who examined the letters took the texts of
Scripture, or rather the figures that referred to the

chapters and verses, for a secret language, used to deceive their vigilance.

On the 8th of the Eleventh Month, J. Yeardley and W. Rasche, accompanied by Jules Paradon, went to Valence, and visited Bertram Combe, at Pialoux, where they remained a few days, B. C. had fitted up a commodious room adjoining his own dwelling, where he held meetings regularly:—

And where, says J. Y., we had several solemn and edifying occasions; and as our being there became more known the attendance increased, so that the last gathering was quite a large one, and peculiarly quiet and satisfactory. Among some meetings which we appointed in the neighborhood two were held in the *temple* of the Protestant Church, which was a mark of great liberality; these two occasions were peculiarly favored. In the latter B. C. alluded to the persecution he had had to endure on account of the disuse of the Supper and Baptism. He boldly avowed the conviction he felt as to the non-use of these things, and that the preaching of the gospel ought to be free. I have seldom been in a district where there is more openness for the gospel message in its simplicity, than in this mountain region.

From Valence, John Yeardley returned direct to England, only stopping at Friedrichsdorf, where he visited the boarding-school.

I reached my home, he says, on the 24th of the Eleventh Month, with a thankful heart to my Heavenly Father for his merciful preservation.

# CHAPTER XX.

## 1853—1858.

JOHN YEARDLEY had scarcely returned to England before war was declared with Russia. The confirmation he received from this lamentable event, that his journey had been made at the opportune time, filled his heart with gratitude. The work he had been able to do had been small, but he had the satisfaction of knowing that it had been accomplished at the only juncture in which it would have been practicable.

The year 1853, he writes, closed with many mercies to a poor unworthy servant. I consider it a great blessing to have accomplished the visit through Russia and to Constantinople before the horrible war broke out. What a frightful state are things in at the present moment!—no access could be had to those countries.

In the Spring of 1854 he spent some time at Bath. He attended, whilst there, a public meeting appointed by Sarah Squire, in which he had a testimony to offer in the gospel. Hearing afterwards that a military man who was present had been brought to conviction by the doctrine which had been declared, J. Y. noted in his Diary the subject on which he had preached.

4 *mo.* 2.—I recollect, he says, alluding to the awful state of the times in which we live, and the need of a refuge in God, and the blessedness of the consolations of the Holy Spirit in a time of trouble. That the Spirit of God was the

28                                        (425)

first agent in the work of man's salvation, bringing to the Saviour who died for sinners: the Father drawing to the Son, the Son perfecting the work, and presenting each member of the living church without spot or wrinkle to the Father. Blessed unity of Father, Son, and Holy Spirit! The Father creating, the Son redeeming, the Holy Spirit sanctifying.

In making a brief note of the Yearly Meeting this year, John Yeardley takes occasion to record his sentiments on a subject which then, as now, strongly engaged the attention of the Society.

The Yearly Meeting has been a precious time; it has strengthened the bond of love and unity. There is, under all discouragements, a love to the Society manifested in the young people of both sexes. It is true there is a great want of bearing of the cross, and many are seeking for excuses to persuade themselves that many of those things that have long distinguished our Society are now no longer of use. But I still think there is more religion in many of our young members than their outward appearance would authorize us to believe. I love to cleave to the good, and to hold out a helping hand to encourage the tender budding of grace, and for the good to overcome the evil. I want them to be brought to conviction, and to be told that they are not required to wear plain clothes, and to use plain speech, because our Friends have done so, but because Christianity leads into simplicity, and the language of Scripture is that of truthfulness, and to follow the changing fashions of the world is too low for the notice of the Christian whose heart is placed on heavenly things, and whose time is too precious to be spent on trifles. There is no peace to the regenerated heart equal to a devotedness of life in promoting the extension of the Saviour's kingdom upon earth.

He soon after alludes to the Memoir of Joseph John Gurney, then just published, and to the sharp stimulus which he received from its perusal—a stimulus which minds fixed upon improvement always receive from the vivid representation of time and talents diligently employed.

6 *mo.* 16.—Many of my solitary moments are cheered, and I am greatly edified, in reading J. J. Gurney's Memoirs. It is a real privilege to be introduced into the daily walk of the life of a Christian man with such an enlightened and enlarged mind, whose expansive heart is filled with love for the whole human race. Strengthened by faith, and filled with the unction of the Spirit, his life was devoted to doing good to the family of man, laboring for the conversion of sinners, and comforting believers.

The diligence of J. J. Gurney in study, &c., has stimulated me to renew the reading of the Greek New Testament, but I sink into the dust when I see what he accomplished in comparison of my own insignificance. It is, however, a comfort to know that I have a merciful Lord, who will not require of me the exercise of gifts that I have not received. O that I may be more faithful in the employment of the capacity which has been entrusted to me, for the good of souls and the honor of my Lord!

The reflections which follow add another to the numberless testimonies of the saints' experience, that the Christian life is a continual warfare.

I am sensible of having lost ground for some time past for want of more diligence in watchfulness and prayer. I have been deeply sorry for it, and I do hope my compassionate Lord has forgiven me. As a proof of his forgiveness, I am permitted to enjoy once more the smiles of his countenance, which cheer my lonely walk. How greatly do I long for more intimate communion with the Beloved of my soul, the precious Saviour! Lord *preserve* me in *every moment* of *temptation*, and make me more entirely thine! Grant me more confidence in the immediate action of thy Spirit in the ministry of the word, that my communications of this nature

may be deep and clear, and under the unction of thy Holy
Spirit. *Amen!*

6 *mo.* 23.—This morning I have been favored, more than
usual, in my endeavor to pour out my soul before God in
prayer, in desiring more purity of heart, more faith; and that
it might please my compassionate Lord to sustain and console
me in my solitary lot, and preserve me faithful to the end of
the race. Many relatives and near friends were brought to
my remembrance, whom I endeavored to present to the
mercy of a merciful God.

In the same diary is an appropriate notice of Dr.
Steinkopf, and a tender tribute to the memory of Martha
Yeardley.

The other evening was spent at J. and M. C. S.'s with Dr.
Steinkopf. "The hoary head" of this aged and experienced
Christian is as "a crown of glory," for "it is found in the way
of righteousness." He is full of love, speaking constantly
out of a grateful heart of the mercies of his God. Before
parting he read a few verses, exhorted us, and supplicated
for us.

A little more than three years have fled away since my
precious and dearly-beloved M. Y. entered on a blissful
eternity. How do I feel the loss of her sweet, cheerful, and
edifying society! Ever since her blessed spirit fled from
earth to heaven, she has never by night or day been long
absent from my thoughts. How often does my soul pant and
pray for a preparation of heart for that blissful state where
she now is, near to her precious Saviour, who redeemed her
with his own blood. He enabled her to serve him when on
earth, and now she sings his praises in heaven. What a
charm did she impart to my daily life! Our pursuits were
always one and the same; and now what a desert I still have
before me,—but it may be very short.

In the Eighth Month, John Yeardley went to Minden
on a visit to Ernst Peitsmeyer, whose daughter Sophie

had been for some time his kind and cheerful companion, and who now, with her parents and other
friends, welcomed him again to Germany. Whilst at
Minden he derived benefit from the sulphur baths of
the Klause, not far from the town.

The bath, he says, is one hour's gentle exercise on the
saddle. The farm where the spring is stands quite alone in
the midst of a wood, and the way to it is delightful,—much
suited to my taste. Sophie rides sometimes with me; it
cheers me to have her trotting by my side.

The handful of inquiring persons at Obernkirchen,
whom J. Y. visited on his return from Norway, continued to claim his sympathy, and one First-day he
joined them at their usual place of worship.

It was, he writes, a refreshing time in this little meeting.
When the little company first met together they were dragged
into the street by the police; but they persevered, and, on
making an appeal to the magistrate at Rinteln, stated their
case with so much simplicity that the government has granted
them liberty to meet together undisturbed. How marvellous,
the Friends are protected; and the Baptists, under the same
government, are persecuted with increasing rigor! No interference on their behalf has been of the least use.—(*Diary and
Letter.*)

In the Fourth Month of 1855 John Yeardley received
a certificate "to visit his friends in Yorkshire, and to
hold meetings with persons not in church-fellowship"
with Friends.

I arrived at Halifax, he says, in a letter of the 28th of
the Fourth Month, on Fifth-day evening, and attended the
Monthly Meeting of Brighouse on the 20th. It looked formidable to me in prospect on the first entering into harness;

but I hope the meeting proved a good introduction, and I saw a good specimen of a large, harmonious, and well-conducted Monthly Meeting. There might be near 250 members present.

When he had completed the service, he took a week of repose at Harrowgate, where he briefly reviews his journey.

5 *mo.* 29.—In passing along through my native county, I found many countenances missing which were very familiar to me years ago, and who are now gone to their rest. But I was comforted to find in many places a race of young people springing up who bore the marks of being plants of my Heavenly Father's right-hand planting, and who gave hopes of becoming useful in his Church. It is with a grateful heart that I record the mercy of my Lord, in that he has granted me strength in a remarkable manner to do what he put in my heart to do, from place to place. Blessed be his name!

After having finished the service in Yorkshire, I have had a week's tarriance at Harrowgate. The rest and quiet have proved beneficial to my health, and very precious have been the seasons of sweet communion I have been permitted to hold with my God in this retirement.

This summer he repeated his visit to Minden, and hired a lodging at the Klause. A reflection in one of the letters which he wrote from this retreat affords a pleasing glimpse of his mind:—

I sometimes think that a large portion of comfort and joy are allowed to those who really love the Lord; and how chastened are the pleasures of the humble Christian! They abide with us long after the causes of them are passed away; and the more our permitted pleasures are enjoyed under a grateful sense of the goodness of the bountiful Giver, the longer they may be permitted to us.

In the Ninth Month, he attended the Two-months'

Meeting at Pyrmont. It was not without emotion that
he visited once more the place which had been so familiar to him in earlier days. The hopes he had then
conceived, and which, as we have seen, he had so fondly
cherished, with regard to the Society of Friends in that
part, had been disappointed; the little company had
dwindled in numbers and declined in religious influence;
and when he took leave of Pyrmont for the last time,
it was with a sorrowful heart.

From Minden, accompanied by Sophie Peitsmeyer,
he went southwards, and took up his abode at the little
town of Neuveville, on the Lake of Bienne, in Switzerland.

I spent, he says, two or three days at Neufchâtel, and
visited many of my old friends in the place and neighbor-.
hood; but it was affecting to find how many of those I had
known years ago were no longer on this earth. Madame
Pétavel was as warm-hearted as ever; the professor, her
husband, is ripening for heaven.

John Yeardley had gone to Neuveville with the
intention of passing the winter in Switzerland. After
remaining a month, however, he returned to England;
and this change of mind was the result of a remarkable
circumstance. He became silent and reserved, with the
air and manners of one who is not at peace with himself; until one night, when he was heard to cry out in
a loud tone, as though speaking to some one. The next
morning at breakfast he appeared subdued and full of
tenderness; and on his young friend inquiring what had
made him cry out in the night, he told her that he must
return home, for there was more work for him to do.
He said that a prospect of service in the gospel had
latterly opened before him, and that as he had greatly

desired to remain in Switzerland, he had striven against
the sense of duty and refused to yield; but that during
the night he had had a vision, in which he heard the
command repeated to return home and enter again
upon his labor, and that he felt, as he thought, the
touch of the heavenly messenger's hand. This caused
him to call out; and when he awoke, he found that
willingness of spirit had taken the place of his former
obstinacy. Thus turned from his own purpose, he set
about to accomplish the will of his gracious Master with
his usual resolution, and they made the best of their
way back to England. The nature of the service which
he saw before him is touched upon in the following
passage from a letter, dated Neuveville, the 14th of the
Tenth Month.

My home duties press heavily upon me. . . . . Very
long have I thought about the young men, and the younger
part of our Society; and I have a hope the way will be made
for my finding access to them, in a religious and social point
of view. Should it be permitted, the Lord grant that it may
tend to mutual comfort.

John Yeardley returned through Paris. He spent a
day or two in that great city, which he never saw "so
quiet and free from soldiers." We extract from his
Diary a short note of a conversation which took place
at the *table d'hôte* of the hotel where he lodged, and
which appears to us to be of an instructive character.
Two men contended respecting the motive by which
mankind are influenced to good actions. One attributed it to *reason;* the other held that it was *virtue*
which restrains from evil and impels to good, and
maintained that we must do good actions from the love

of justice and virtue, and not from the fear of punishment or the hope of reward. The latter had the
advantage over his antagonist in the argument:—

I had not, says J. Y., taken part in the conversation; but
at the close I felt constrained to tell the *Christian* that I
confessed myself on his side, because he had defended the
truth; only that what he called *virtue*, I called the *action of
the Spirit of God in the heart of man*. With much animation,
he clasped my hands in his, and cried, "That is the very
thing,—that is just what I mean!"

In the year 1856, he engaged in two religious visits
at home, both of them in accordance with the kind of
service which had been unfolded to him in the retirement of Neuveville, viz., mingled religious and social
intercourse with his younger fellow-members.

In reading the expression of his feelings in the
prospect of the former of these engagements, it is instructive to remark, that the same sense of entire
dependence which had bowed his spirit when required
in early life to make the first offering of this kind, was
present with him when now called upon to go forth in
his Master's name for the twentieth time, and when age
and experience had given him reverence among men.

1 *mo.* 8.—To-morrow is our Monthly Meeting, when I
expect to propose to my Friends a visit to the meetings com-
posing the Quarterly Meetings of Bristol and Somerset, and
Gloucester and Wilts. Every time any fresh exercise turns
up for me, it always feels as if it was the *first* time of entering
into the holy harness. If my friends permit me to proceed,
I hope I shall be helped through it; but it looks formidable.

21*st*.—Bristol is like a great mountain looking me in the
face, and weighing heavily upon my heart.

The following short memoranda of the way in which

he was engaged at Bristol are taken from his letters; the Diary, during his later years, supplies few notes, either of his labors or his experience:—

3 *mo.*—I met at Richard Fry's house a large number of young men and women teachers of the First-day School; forty-eight were present. An opportunity was offered for my receiving and also communicating information respecting schools and education. What makes the subject more interesting in Bristol, is the attendance of more than one hundred of the school children at meeting on First-day mornings, which, I think, has been the practice for about ten years, and their behavior is orderly and good.

31*st.*—I am somewhat busily employed in this busy city in visiting the young men. I find very ready access to them, and my engagement has the hearty concurrence of all my friends. I am abundantly convinced that it would have been a great mistake to have run away from the place without making the attempt at the performance of the present service. The usual meetings for worship have been seasons of divine favor, some of them, I think, extraordinarily so, which I consider a great mercy in my Heavenly Father, when I consider the weakness of the poor instrument. It has been announced for me to give a lecture this evening in the large meeting-house, on my travels in Europe, a *sound* which almost frightens me. Friends really do not know what a poor thing I am.

By the kindness of a friend, we have been supplied with a pleasing personal reminiscence of John Yeardley's visit to Bristol, which will help to represent him as he was in later years.

Bristol, 6 mo. 6, 1859.

Since thou informed me of thy intention to compile a memoir of our late dear friend John Yeardley, I have endeavored to recall the circumstances of his visit to this city in the spring of the year 1856.

My impression is, that the most striking feature in his character was his childlike simplicity, both in word and conduct.  This very characteristic, whilst it really increased his influence for good, especially with the young, rendered it perhaps more difficult to trace, and now to describe, the precise manner in which it was exercised.  I believe that his Christian labors here were very seasonable and very important, and that he was enabled to perform a service which scarcely any one else would have been equally qualified to render.

There was in him, so far as my observation went, no approach towards an assumption of spiritual dignity; nor was there, on the other hand, that which is perhaps a more frequent defect, anything of *feigned* humility.  His whole character seemed to me perfectly unaffected.  To whatever extent, therefore, his natural disposition may have fitted him for profitable intercourse with the young, I think that the qualities which I have attempted to describe rendered him peculiarly acceptable to them.  Many times, whilst he was amongst us, he alluded—I believe even in his public ministry—to his delight in their society, somewhat in this manner: " I love the company of those who tread the earth with an elastic step."  This prominent trait in his character was a striking illustration of what may be termed *the corrective tendency* of true religion, by which in advanced life he was enabled to place himself, under the precious influence of the love of Christ, in thorough sympathy with those whose circumstances, in many respects, were so different from his own.

But my object was to describe John Yeardley's meetings in Bristol.  The truth is, however, that in describing the man, one seems most truly to describe his service.  In addition to his family visits, he met a large company of our members in our meeting-house, and gave an interesting narrative of his journeys in Southern Russia and Greece.  He afterwards invited many of our young friends, especially those who were engaged as teachers in our First-day Schools, to spend an evening with him.  Meeting at the house of a kind friend, we had an opportunity of hearing from his own lips some interesting details of his labors, chiefly, I think, in reference to the schools in Greece. With characteristic simplicity, he made various inquiries respecting our own First-day Schools, in which he felt a deep interest. The occasion was of a very sociable and easy character, and well calculated to promote in his young friends the *healthy tone* of religious feeling which seemed so peculiarly to belong to himself.

After Martha Yeardley's decease, and as years rolled on, his mind dwelt still more habitually and more confidingly than ever on the approaching end of the race.

4 *mo.* 24.—I cannot say my spirits are always high. There is an individuality in the allotment of each of us which we must seek for grace and aid to endure to the end. The road may be now and then a little rough, but it cannot be very long, at least to some of us; and when the eye closes under the last gleam of earthly light, and then opens in the full brightness of eternal glory, to enjoy the fulness of a Saviour's love, it will be bliss indeed.

Thinking his state of health unequal to the attendance of the Yearly Meeting, he left London and again resorted for a while to the baths near Minden, where he passed two months in tranquil retirement. He had in former visits been deeply interested in the sufferings of a Prussian soldier who refused conscientiously to bear arms. The late Samuel Gurney wrote to the King of Prussia, on behalf of the young man, who was in consequence liberated from military service, but was sentenced to two years' imprisonment. The term was not nearly expired; but John Yeardley, whilst at Minden, heard that he had been released from prison by immediate command of the King. J. Y. had " spent a First-day with him within the gloomy walls in Duisburg," and was consequently the more ready to rejoice in his liberation.

On his return to England, John Yeardley proceeded to Birmingham. His service in this and the neighboring towns was similar to that which he had had to perform at Bristol. He says:

By day I called on the sick and such as were confined at home. In the evenings I met companies of young men and women. They were invited to the Friends' houses where tea was first served, and then a religious occasion of silence and exhortation, with supplication when felt to be under right pointing. The remainder of the evening was spent in social converse. I am very favorable to the mixing of social intercourse with gospel labor. All seemed pleased, and I trust we were mutually edified. I was often requested to give some account of my late journey and the state of religion in the various countries where I had travelled; and the conversation often turned on points connected with our religious principles.

Joseph Sturge, he continues, was from home. At the request of his wife I dined at their house with twenty-five young culprits, whom J. S. has in his Reformatory at Stoke, near Bromsgrove. They came in a van with horses to spend the day. They are all such as have been once or twice in prison, mostly for theft. I addressed them after dinner, and at tea-time I questioned them as to Jesus Christ our Redeemer, on God, Heaven and Hell, how to gain Heaven and avoid misery. I left them with a more favorable impression than I otherwise should have had. Severe measures had failed to improve them, but they seemed susceptible of kind treatment, and some of them gave hopes of amendment.

9 mo. 21.—Visited the Boys' and Girls' First-day Schools. Breakfasted with thirty teachers (young men) at the schools. About 370 boys present in two rooms. None are taken under fourteen years of age. Also a large class of adults. I addressed the two companies: then went to the girls; heard

them read, and addressed them.   There are about twenty
young women teachers, and perhaps 270 to 300 girls.

The morning meeting was large.   I was much pressed in
spirit to speak on the nature of the fall of man, and on the
necessity of having clear views of gospel truth.   I was told
afterwards that there was a Unitarian present.

He attended the Quarterly Meeting at Leicester on
the 24th, and the two following days met companies of
young persons, who were, he says, "much tendered in
spirit."   After some similar service at Stourbridge and
Coventry, he returned on the 27th to Stamford Hill.
He remarks in his Diary: "I believe the service of the
young Friends in the First-day Schools has been a blessing to themselves as well as to their pupils."

The next month John Yeardley made a religious visit
to Hertfordshire, and had two social-religious meetings
with the younger Friends at Hitchin; after which he
remained at home until the beginning of the Twelfth
Month, when he left England for Nismes.

One object in this journey was to revisit the school
which had been established by himself and Martha
Yeardley in 1842: another was the renewal of his
declining health.   Susan Howland and Lydia Congdon,
from the United States, who were then on a visit to
Europe, were bound for the same destination, and John
Yeardley gave them his company.

12 mo. 6.—On entering France, he says, we found a
sprinkling of snow and frost, but on leaving Lyons we left
all the wintry weather behind, and travelled on under a hot
sun, and bright, cloudless sky, which seemed to impart to us
all fresh vigor and spirits.   S. Howland remarked, In such
an atmosphere she felt another being.

At Nismes, the party found Eliza P. Gurney, and
Robert and Christine Alsop, on their way home from
the valleys of Piedmont. John Yeardley lodged at the
school, spent much of his time with the children, and
with the other English and the American Friends gave
his aid in some plans for their recreation.

12 *mo.* 25.—The evening of this day was a lively and
pleasant scene. The girls' countenances were brightened and
their hearts cheered by the presents made to them by the
English Friends present. The "tree" was new to them; it
was beautifully lighted with tapers, and bore a variety of fruit
both for mind and body.

1857. 3 *mo.* 2.—My dear friend —— proposed my giving
the school girls a treat before I left Nismes. We contrived a
visit to the sea, distant from Nismes about twenty miles. We
procured two omnibuses with six horses, and started at 5
o'clock in the morning. Long before the time appointed, the
little maidens were in the entrance-hall with their satchels in
their hand, containing each her dinner; twenty-seven in all.
The pleasure on the road was novel and great; but when they
arrived at the sea-shore their delight was complete; with light
hearts and quick heels, running and picking up shells, meeting
the waves as they advanced and receded. On our return we
visited the ancient town of Aigues-Mortes, near the sea,
famous for having been the place where the Protestant
women were confined and punished even to death. We
entered most of the strong and gloomy cells, and saw the
instrument of torture. The tower and fortress are a perfect
model of a feudal castle.

On his return to England, John Yeardley was taken
ill with bronchitis, which produced great bodily weakness, and caused him "many wearisome" nights and
days; but, he says, "my Saviour was near to console
and sustain me." He went for change to Bath, and
afterwards to Brighton with Margaret Pope:—

We made, he says, speaking of this visit many calls, and my hospitable hostess had many of the Friends to tea and dinner visits. Our social readings in the evening were often instructive in the conversation upon what we read, particularly over Hippolytus, who lived and wrote in the first half of the second century. The Chevalier Bunsen did good service to the Christian Church in bringing the life and some of the writings of this good man to light.

On his return home we find him still solicitous, as he had been in former years, for the intellectual improvement of his young friends.

11 *mo.*—During my stay at home I have renewed my German class for a few of my young friends. We have also commenced a soirée for German and French conversation. I love the society of my young friends, and am always anxious to promote their learning to speak German and French.

The Diary for 1858, the last year of his life, commences with a New Year's dedication of himself afresh to the service of his faithful Creator, and a prayer for a fresh anointing in the exercise of his ministry.

1858. 1 *mo.* 4.—How many and various are the thoughts which crowd on the mind on the commencement of a new year; perhaps none more important than to think I am one year nearer to eternity. A desire does live in my heart (cherish it, O, my God) to live more to thy glory on earth. How I long· to be favored with strength to do something for the cause of truth and righteousness, so long as I may be permitted to remain on the Lord's earth. I think with gratitude that he has blessed me with a little more faith of late in my ministry, and my very soul prays that in these requirings he may be pleased to put the unction of his Spirit into my heart, and his words into my mouth, and that under a right pointing, they may go forth with power.

Grant me, Lord, more devotedness of life, and a right and sure preparation for a peaceful death and a blissful eternity.

For some years before his decease, John Yeardley's thoughts were frequently occupied with the subject of the Millennium. Like some other good men, he thought he saw in the events which were taking place, the impending accomplishment of those predictions, whose fulfilment was to precede the "great and terrible day of the Lord." On one occasion, after mentioning a number of these "signs of the times," he winds up the enumeration and the thoughts to which it gave rise, with the following reflection:— '

Happy is the Christian who, in this time of conflict, can look beyond the passing events of time to the Great First Cause, and behold, as with the eye of faith, the providence of his God watching over all things, waiting to bring good out of evil, and causing all things to work to the one great point, when he will cause the wrath of man to praise him, and the remainder of wrath will he restrain. "Come, my people, enter thou into thy chambers and shut thy doors about thee; hide thyself, as it were for a little moment, until the indignation be overpast. For behold the Lord cometh out of his place to punish the inhabitants of the earth for their iniquity." (Isaiah xxvi. 20, 21.)

In the Second Month he spent a week at Chelmsford with Susanna Corder. His visit was prefaced by the following letter:—

Stamford Hill, 1 mo. 13, 1858.

MY DEAR FRIEND,

It would seem to me as if there were only left here and there a link of the chain of my original connexion on this earth. The best end of this chain is attached to those loved ones in heaven who are drawing me every day nearer to their happy and blissful abode, through the love of our glorified Redeemer. It is now many years since thou received her

29

once so dear to me as a bosom friend, to partake of thy wise counsels, and in her troubles especially to enjoy the sympathy of thy warm and affectionate heart.

I am now left alone for a short time: my young companion is at Norwich. If thou wert at home, pretty well in health, and withal not so much occupied as sometimes, it would be a great pleasure and gratification to me to pay thee a short visit; but, as an absolute condition, I must request thee to say, in perfect freedom, if it would be quite convenient. I want to ask thee *many*, *many* things.

> Thy friend, affectionately and very sincerely,
>
> JOHN YEARDLEY.

After his return home, having also visited Saffron Walden, he writes:—

1 *mo.* 25.—Just returned from a visit to Essex. I lodged a week at my dear friend S. C.'s, and was edified and comforted in her company. It has been a promised pleasure of some years' standing. The morning meeting on First-day, as well as the one on Fourth-day, was a season of spiritual refreshment, for which I was truly thankful. The Friends testified their unity and comfort: I called on most of them.

On the Seventh-day, C. M. conveyed me across the country to Saffron Walden. On the way we paid a sweet visit to the afflicted family of ———. At Walden I was affectionately cared for, and was much interested in the Friends there, whom I had not seen for eighteen years.

# CHAPTER XXI.

WE are now arrived at the closing scene of John Yeardley's labors. The impression which he had received, during his visit to Turkey in 1853, of the opening for the work of the Gospel in the Eastern countries, had never been obliterated; it had rather grown deeper with time, although his ability to accomplish such an undertaking had proportionately diminished. This consideration, however, could not satisfy his awakened sympathies, and, according to his apprehension, no other course remained for him but to prepare for a visit to the missionary stations in Asia Minor and the countries beyond, in order to deliver to the inquiring inhabitants amongst whom those stations are planted, the message of Christ's love to their souls with which he believed himself to be charged. And when he communicated to his friends the apprehension that this journey was required of him as the last offering of thanksgiving before his day closed, they were satisfied to "lay their hands upon him" for the work, thinking, perhaps, that the veteran soldier could not better end his campaign than with his arms in his hands, actively contending for the faith. That such might not improbably be the issue of the enterprise, John Yeardley himself believed; but it is doubtful if he correctly estimated the arduous nature of the journey. It would have been a bold undertaking in the vigor of his days:

(443)

at his time of life, and with his declining strength, it
was, humanly speaking, impossible that he should accomplish nearly all he had in view.

His Diary unfolds his spiritual exercises and his
natural feelings in the prospect before him.

3 *mo.* 17.—The last two months have been to me an awful
time of deep conflict of spirit, arising out of a prospect of
a religious visit to some places in Asiatic Turkey, and parts
adjacent. I do not know when I have had more conflict to
arrive at a clear pointing. I prayed earnestly and waited
long for that clear pointing of Divine Wisdom, without which
I can never move in concerns of this importance. In the end,
I am thankful to say, the cloud was removed and the sun
shone with brightness, and no longer was my poor tried mind
left in doubt as to the line of religious duty; and before mentioning it to any one, I communicated it to the Monthly
Meeting in the Second Month. Much unity and sympathy
were expressed, and the certificate ordered. It is now signed,
and is a sweet document, short and explicit.

I see and deeply feel the perils and sufferings which await
me, in venturing on untrodden ground, as it regards any
minister of our Society, and to such a distance, and among,
for the most part, an unbelieving people. But I can and do
look forward in calm confidence, trusting, as I have ever done,
in the aid and protecting care of my Heavenly Father, whose
cause I desire to serve, and whose will I wish above all other
things to do. My earthly career can never end better than
in the work of my Divine Master; and should it be his will to
terminate my life in the Arab tent, I shall have more consolation there than in an English home under the stinging sense
of a dereliction of my religious duty.

I am giving all my leisure hours to learn something of the
Turkish language, for travelling purposes, and for a little
social intercourse. Ever since this concern fastened on my
mind, it has been connected with having the company of my
young friend from the South of France, Jules Paradon.

May the Lord grant me resignation, faith, grace, and strength to do his holy will; and then, whether it end in life or death, his great name shall be praised. This testimony I record in gratitude and love to the mercy of my God. Amen.

Before leaving England, he paid a visit to Staines.

4 *mo.* 20.—I went down to Staines, and spent two weeks with Margaret Pope, which sojourn proved a strength and comfort to me. This dear friend is a succorer of many, and, I can truly say, of me in particular. We had several pleasant drives, and made friendly visits to the neighboring meetings and Friends. I also applied pretty diligently to the Turkish language.

Amply provided, by the kindness of many friends, with whatever could administer to his wants or ease the roughness of Eastern travel, John Yeardley left his home on the 15th of the Sixth Month. He arrived at Nismes on the 17th, and was joined there by Jules Paradon. His Diary supplies some notes of the voyage to Constantinople.

23rd.—Malta. Here we arrived at 4 o'clock this morning, after a favorable passage; thanks to the Preserver of our lives; great is his mercy and his love. My heart is filled with deep thoughtfulness, and I am very anxious to procure an interpreter, either at Smyrna or Constantinople. My faith is weak, but I trust the Lord will provide.

On descending the lower deck adjoining the large saloon, I found my faithful companion in calm but very earnest conversation with the commissary of the ship and a passenger of respectability, the Spanish consul of Smyrna. They had sifted from Jules the object of our journey, and when they found it connected with a religious mission, they both attacked him earnestly and showed themselves really opposed to the truth. But my young friend stood his ground well, and maintained the Christian religion. The opponents were both Romanists. They quieted down before the close, and treated us respectfully the remainder of the journey; we parted with them at Smyrna. I am thankful to have in my companion such a defender of the faith.

27th.—We arrived at Smyrna this morning, and in order to meet some of our Christian friends to whom we had letters of recommendation, we met them after their worship. Edward Van Lennep, the Dutch consul, and his brother Charles, the Swedish consul, received us with great kindness and cordiality through the letters from one of our Members of Parliament. It was very sweet to find these two brothers so imbued with religious feeling; they gave their hearts to help us in our prospect.

On the 30th John Yeardley and his companion landed at Constantinople; they found the heat and noise of the city very oppressive.

The people in the streets, says John Yeardley, are numerous beyond all description; thousands, and tens of thousands, standing, sitting, running, following, or pushing one against the other, talking and shouting in the ceaseless noise of the Armenian, Turkish, Greek, Syriac, Italian, French and English languages. The services of my dear Jules are most valuable; he makes his way with every one through his earnest kindness to serve the good cause.

When passing through the islands, he adds, the prospect was extremely beautiful; but my mind was always anxious in the prospect of the long journey before us; but the mercy of my God is great, and deeply humbles me in thankfulness for his goodness.—(*Letter of* 7 *mo.* 4.)

Very soon after their arrival, walking several hours in the heat of the day, John Yeardley had a slight attack of sun-stroke. The effect appeared quickly to pass off, and he was able to perform such religious duty as opened before him in the city and its immediate neighborhood.

*Diary.* 7 *mo.* 4.—We made a call at Bebek: Dr. Hamlin had gone to the city, but Dr. Dwight received us kindly. These two dear Christian friends called on us yesterday. This morning we attended the meeting in the Armenian chapel, and at half-past 1 we had a full company in the same meeting-house. They received in a free and brotherly disposition what I was favored to express in gospel freedom; I concluded in supplication. A kind and Christian man interpreted with simplicity into the Turkish language. The morning service was in the Armenian. We have already had many calls from these loving Christian friends in our hotel. What a mercy, and how encouraging, to be thus received in gospel love by strangers!

Respecting this meeting Jules Paradon says:—

About thirty-five or forty were present. Our dear friend's communication was short and simple; it breathed love to all. In fact, what he seemed to have most on his mind in all his public communications was, to show his hearers how much God loved them in even giving his own Son for them, and the high privilege we can enjoy in loving him.

They went also to Has-Keuï, where J. Y. desired to have a meeting with the girls of the school; but many had left for the vacation, and he was obliged to give up his intention.

On the 10th they went to Brusa, in Asia Minor, six hours by steam-vessel across the Sea of Marmora to Moudania, and six on horseback from Moudania to Brusa. The land journey was oppressive. A narrow path winds through a very rugged country; and there is only one halting-place, a guard hut, where they took

a cup of coffee, the only refreshment the inmates had
to offer. John Yeardley suffered much in this day's
journey.

He had two meetings in the Protestant meeting-
house at Brusa:—

Both, says Jules Paradon, took place after the usual service, which was expressly made short. The hearers, to the
number of about 120, were impressed and interested to hear
and see our dear friend come from so far to visit them in the
love of the gospel. Twelve or fourteen men came two evenings to see us at our lodgings; and on both occasions our
dear friend addressed them very sweetly. The heat tried him
very much, but he felt pleased and happy to be helped to
sympathize with so many simple, kind-hearted people.

At Demirdash (six miles from Brusa), he had a short
religious opportunity with a few persons.

On their return to Constantinople, finding that a box
of luggage he expected from London, containing a tent
and other equipments, had not arrived, without which
he could not pursue his journey into the interior, he
employed the interval in visiting Isnik, (the ancient Nico-
media,) and Bargheghik, two places in Asia Minor, not
far from the coast. Accordingly they started early the
next day, and reached Isnik late in the evening, weary
and exhausted, having been able to procure very little refreshment on the way. They proceeded to Bargheghik
the day following; John Yeardley walking about four
miles in the middle of the day, with which he was
extremely fatigued.

He had a meeting, continues Jules Paradon, late in the
evening, which proved highly interesting. About thirty men
and one woman attended. Our dear friend encouraged and
consoled the weak and the afflicted. The next day we returned

to Isnik, having to bear the heat of the sun from half-past eight till three in the afternoon. We had a meeting the same afternoon at half-past four, towards the close of which he felt weak, and seemed to end his address rather abruptly.

The fact was, that paralysis had supervened; and on his return the next day to Constantinople, his bodily and mental strength were seen to be rapidly diminishing. He still clung, however, to the desire of accomplishing the object which lay so near his heart, and could not be satisfied without going to Bebek to consult his missionary friends about his journey into the interior. Probably they perceived that he was totally unequal to the effort, and advised him to relinquish it; for on his return to the city he was induced to abandon the thought of proceeding farther, and to turn his mind towards home. On the 23rd he said, If after what had been done he was permitted to go home, it would be a satisfaction.*

On the 26th they embarked for Marseilles. John Yeardley bore the voyage well, walking on deck every day, but becoming continually weaker. They arrived at Marseilles on the 4th of the Eighth Month, and passed through France as rapidly as his state would allow. On the evening of Second-day, the 9th, he was favored to reach Stamford Hill; and though unable to speak, he recognized several of his near relatives, and signified his pleasure in being once more at home.

---

* After his return, a letter was received from one of the missionaries at Constantinople, expressive of the pleasure which his visit had given there, the regret of the writer that age and fatigue prevented him from pursuing his journey to the more remote stations, and the cordial welcome which "such Christian friends of any denomination" might always reckon upon from the missionary brethren.

He continued to sink until Fifth-day, the 11th, when he quietly breathed his last, an expression of peace resting on his venerable face. We may say, with one of his most intimate friends on the Continent, when he heard of his decease:—" So our beloved friend has been called to enter into his Lord's joy. Now he will see God, to whom he often used to pray. ' With thee is the fountain of life ; in thy light shall we see light.' "

His remains were interred at Stoke Newington, on the 18th of the Eighth Month.

---

OF the fruits which John Yeardley has bequeathed to us in the history of his life and Christian experience, none perhaps are of higher value than his diligent improvement of the talents he possessed and his steady and persevering pursuit of what he had in view. It is not so much what abilities a man has that determines his place in society, and the amount of his influence, as the use which he makes of them. Of this truth John Yeardley was a striking example. We have heard him say, in one of his early diaries: "I have clearly seen for what service I am designed in the church militant here on earth; therefore, through the assistance of divine grace, I hope to pursue nothing but in subordination to this main design." The service to which he was called was the Christian ministry; and, laying aside every meaner ambition, and indeed every other object, he addressed himself to preparation for this service as the labor of his life. He cultivated those habits of mind and body, and confined himself to the acquisition of those branches of knowledge, which, while they left his heavenly gift free and unsullied, would best subserve the exercise of it.

His industry and perseverance were remarkable. In none of his pursuits were these qualities more conspicuous than in his study of languages. It cost him, especially, an almost incredible amount of labor to master French. The slight elementary knowledge of this language which he acquired at Bentham cannot have given him so much as an insight into it; his acquaintance with it may be said to date from his visit to Congenies, when he had reached his fortieth year. Yet, by indefatigable exertion, maintained during many years, he became able to write and speak it fluently, though not correctly, and even to preach without an interpreter. The difficulty which he encountered in the acquisition of languages, from the late period of life at which he commenced, was enhanced by his ignorance of Latin, that best trainer of the youthful faculties, and by a natural inaptitude for the memory of words. A proof of the latter occurred when, with his quick-witted wife, he was occupied in conning over the Italian and Modern Greek Grammars, in preparation for their journey to the Ionian Islands. The difference in their natural capacities in this respect is shown in her playful expression; "I got my lesson in half an hour; while John has been three or four hours over his, and does not know it yet."

But although slow in study, he was quick and shrewd in the observation of actual life. This was apparent in his daily converse; and it may also be continually traced in his Diary, where, describing those with whom he became acquainted in his numerous travels, he seizes, on the prominent feature of their mind or manners, and with a word affixes to each his own particular mark. Of the hundreds of individuals who rise into view one after another in the course of these journeys, scarcely two are alike; a result which is, perhaps, due as much to the pen of the writer, as to the inherent diversities of the human character.

To this shrewdness of observation, he added a racy humor which those who knew him in his hours of relaxation and familiarity will not easily forget. His mind was stored with quaint and pithy phrases, and apt illustrations, which he not unfrequently seasoned with his native idiom, the broad Barnsley dialect. His north-country pronunciation, indeed, never entirely forsook him; and the singular graft of German which he made upon it during his residence abroad, caused it to be commonly supposed, by those who were strangers to his history, that he was a native of Germany.

The same moral constitution that enabled John Yeardley to pursue his objects with indomitable perseverance, sometimes betrayed him, as may easily be imagined, into a tenacity of purpose, bordering upon obstinacy. To the same strength of will also, acting on the defects incident to a neglected education in early life, must be attributed those strong prejudices which were at times to be remarked in him, and of which he found it extremely difficult to divest himself. But it was the triumph of grace, that whilst these faults of character and disposition remained for the most part only as a hidden thorn, the messenger of Satan to buffet him, the virtues to which they were allied, and all the faculties of his mind, were consecrated to the service of God and of his fellow-man, and his whole nature was enlarged, refined and elevated, by the all-powerful energy of the gospel.

" Very sweet and instructive are our recollections of the humility of his walk amongst us, and of the liveliness of his ministry, marked as it was by much simplicity, love and earnestness." To this testimony of his Monthly Meeting, all who were accustomed to hear him will readily subscribe.

We are able to append some notes of a few of his public testimonies, which we give as likely to be at once gratifying and instructive to the reader. The friend to whom we are indebted for them informs us that " the notes were written immediately after meeting, and are as nearly the words used as his memory would furnish." He adds, " They bring before the mind's eye and ear the face and voice of a dear departed friend, and, I believe, a true and enlightened servant of the Lord."

(8 *mo.* 1850.)

*Keep thy heart with all diligence, for out of it are the issues of life.*—(Proverbs iv. 23.)

We often are made to feel the force of this truth, when we have been unwatchful, and some cross occurrence has tried our tempers. How often we are made to see, and to show before others, what manner of spirit is in us. . . . .

Sometimes we are favored with such clear convictions of the worthlessness of mere worldly possessions and pursuits, and such delightful realizations of the happiness of seeking to do the Lord's work, that we are ready to express our astonishment that any human beings can be found so foolish as to devote their energies to the pursuit of things which never can give satisfaction, and which must needs perish. And then, perhaps, we are brought into a state of darkness and despondency, to show us our utter helplessness and un-worthiness, and the need there is for every one of us to "keep the heart with all diligence, for out of it are the issues of life." . . . .

Every individual, no doubt, has his own particular path of duty, which is designed to promote his own best happiness and the well-being of all mankind. How important for each to follow that path in watchfulness and obedience, that the work may not be marred! How important to keep the heart with all diligence, that the issues of life may be in accordance with the divine will!

---

( 9 *mo.* 1, 1850.)

*Since the people began to bring the offerings into the house of the Lord, we have had enough to eat, and have left plenty.*—(2 Chronicles xxxi. 10.)

These words have been impressed upon my mind this morning, and I have thought they were instructive, in a spiritual sense. I believe, if we were more earnest in bringing offerings into the house of the Lord—if each one of us was more diligent in contributing his share, and doing his part of the Lord's business,—we should have less anxiety about worldly things; we should have faith in the Lord's provi-dence, and, not only spiritually, but naturally also, we should have "enough to eat and plenty left."

---

( 11 *mo.* 24, 1850.)

In looking at the world around, we may be apt to think that the day is very far off when the Lord's kingdom shall be established in peace : but to those who, through the regener-ating power of Christ, have become subjects of the Prince of Peace, that day has commenced already ; and whatever storms may rage without, they will experience peace within. For "he will keep them in perfect peace whose minds are staid on him, because they trust in him."

---

(9 *mo.* 19, 1852.)

John Yeardley addressed the children with much feeling, telling them to rely on the Lord Jesus Christ in all their ways—to let him carry them in his bosom, and to run to him in danger or trouble, as they would to their tender mothers.

---

You sometimes are restless in these meetings, not knowing how to keep your thoughts fixed on heavenly things, and perplexed for want of some visible means of instruction. I believe your tender Saviour may often feed you, even while in this state, with food convenient for you. But remember, dear children, that he is always calling to every one of you, Come unto Me. Suffer little children to come unto Me, and forbid them not. O! come to him, my precious lambs, and he will feed you, and "lead you beside the still waters, and make you lie down in green pastures."

---

(12 *mo.* 8, 1854. At a Funeral.)

*And the ransomed of the Lord shall return, and come to Zion with songs and everlasting joy upon their heads: they shall obtain joy and gladness, and sorrow and sighing shall flee away.*—(Isa. xxxv. 10.)

In the pain of parting with the beloved object of our heart's affection, we forget the rejoicing which welcomes the ransomed spirit to its everlasting rest. But when the time is come for the Lord to pour in the healing balm into the sorrowing soul, then we find a little comfort. . . . .

"Watchman! what of the night? Watchman! what of the night? The watchman said, The morning cometh, and also the night: if ye will inquire, inquire ye: return; come." There are many in this company in the morning of life, enjoying the prospect of many days, and forming many plans for the future, with all the ardor of their youthful minds. May the present occasion prove the morning of their spiritual day ; and may they remember that the *night cometh as well as the morning.*

How thin is the partition which separates the present state from that of eternity! We mourn over those who are taken away from us, and we fancy we are left alone. But we are called to be *one in Christ.* I have great faith in the communion of saints, in the union of saints on earth with saints in heaven. And we are all called to be saints by walking in faith, by leading a life of holiness in the fear of the Lord. We say our beloved friends who have gone before us are dead. *They are not dead : they have but just entered into life.* Let us not mourn, then, as those who have no hope. Let us rather rejoice with them and for them, and so live that we may be among the ransomed of the Lord, who shall return and come to Zion with songs and everlasting joy upon their heads, and sorrow and sighing shall flee away.

THE END.

www.ingramcontent.com/pod-product-compliance
Lightning Source LLC
Chambersburg PA
CBHW022013110726
47901CB00006B/1507